The
Outcast Dove

The
Outcast Dove

SHARAN NEWMAN

A TOM DOHERTY ASSOCIATES BOOK
NEW YORK

THE OUTCAST DOVE

The quotation from Judah Halevi on page 15 is from *The Gazelle* by Raymond P. Scheindlin, Jewish Publication Society, 1991, used by permission.

This book is printed on acid-free paper.

A Forge Book
Published by Tom Doherty Associates, LLC
175 Fifth Avenue
New York, NY 10010

www.tor.com

Forge® is a registered trademark of Tom Doherty Associates, LLC.

Library of Congress Cataloging-in-Publication Data

Newman, Sharan.
    The outcast dove / Sharan Newman.—1st. ed.
        p.   cm.
    "A Forge book"—T.p. verso.
    ISBN 0-765-30377-9
    1. LeVendeur, Catherine (Fictitious character)—Fiction. 2. Christian converts from Judaism—Fiction. 3. Women detectives—France—Fiction. 4. Jewish families—Fiction. 5. Jews—Spain—Fiction. 6. Middle Ages—Fiction. I. Title.

PS3564.E92O95 2003
813'.54—dc21

                                                                2003047023

First Edition: December 2003

Printed in the United States of America

0   9   8   7   6   5   4   3   2   1

For Ann Cecile Bergman,
1959–2003
A gift of love and joy

Acknowledgments

This book would not have started and could not have been finished without the help of the following people. I can't thank them enough for their generosity in sharing their expertise. As always, any errors in this book are due to my own perversity or lack of comprehension, not their advice.

Fr. Chrysogonus Waddell, O.C.S.O., Gethsemani Abbey, Kentucky, for finding the evidence for the fate of Mayah and Zaida. I never would have believed it of the Cistercians if he hadn't found the proof.

Prof. Fredric Cheyette, Amherst College, for giving me an introduction to the wonderful people at FRAMESPA in Toulouse. Anyone wanting to know more about the south of France in the twelfth century should get his recent book, *Ermengard of Narbonne and the World of the Troubadours* (Cornell University Press). You don't need a degree to enjoy it.

Prof. Bernard Cursente, Centre National de la Recherche Scientifique, FRAMESPA (France Méridionale et Espagne), for welcoming me to Toulouse and allowing me to use the library at the Institute.

Dr. Laurent Macé, University of Toulouse-le-Mirail, for advising me on my research. His book on the entourage of the counts of Toulouse, *Les comtes de Toulouse et leur entourage* (Editions Privat), was invaluable to me, as was his help.

Mme. Claire Vernon, *Ingénieur* FRAMESPA, Toulouse, for her patience, friendship, and especially for trusting me with the keys to the library during the lunch hour.

Prof. John Hine Mundy, Columbia University, emeritus, who has done the most comprehensive work on medieval Toulouse in English (and possibly any language) for instant answers to my rather bizarre questions.

Prof. Lynn Nelson, University of Kansas, emeritus, for giving me the background on Fitero and the monastery there.

Prof. Olivia Remy Constable, University of Notre Dame, for telling me who would have bought Moslem slave women and sold them to the monks.

The hardest part of this book was finding Provençal Jewish customs in the twelfth century. There is little documentation remaining and so opinions varied. The following scholars very kindly gave me the benefit of their work:

Prof. Judith Baskin, University of Oregon, who not only helped with information on women, but also copied and sent articles that I needed.

Prof. Elka Klein, University of Cincinnati, for advice on women and ritual.

Prof. Susan Einbinder, Hebrew Union University, Cincinnati, for always being available to answer questions and for finding me a Hebrew translator. Her new book *Beautiful Death* (Princeton University Press) sounds like a mystery but is a fascinating study of Jewish poetry and martyrdom in medieval France.

Oran Hayden, Hebrew Union University, Cincinnati, for searching through difficult articles and medieval commentaries to find information and quotes and sending them to me in Hebrew with translations.

Prof. Sholmo Pick, Bar Ilan University, Israel, who answered an Internet query on the Jews of Provence, not knowing what he was getting into. I hope that his dissertation on the subject will soon be available in more than photocopies.

Dr. Gillian Pollack, independent scholar and author, Australia. Since all our correspondence was by e-mail, I never did find out exactly where she is. But her advice on burial practices was invaluable.

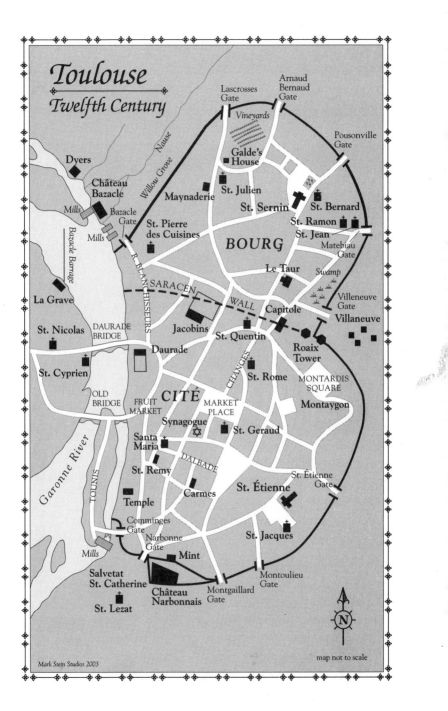

Toulouse
Twelfth Century

Dyers

Château Bazacle

Mills

Bazacle Gate

Mills

Bazacle Barrage

La Grave

St. Nicolas

DAURADE BRIDGE

St. Cyprien

OLD BRIDGE

Garonne River

TOUNIS

Mills

Lascrosses Gate

Arnaud Bernaud Gate

Vineyards

Pousonville Gate

Galde's House

Maynaderie

St. Julien

St. Sernin

St. Bernard

St. Pierre des Cuisines

St. Ramon

St. Jean

BOURG

Matebiau Gate

Le Taur

Swamp

Villeneuve Gate

SARACEN WALL

Capitole

Villaneuve

Jacobins

Daurade

St. Quentin

Roaix Tower

MONTARDIS SQUARE

R. BLANCHISSEURS

CHANGES

St. Rome

Montaygon

CITÉ

FRUIT MARKET

MARKET PLACE

Synagogue

St. Geraud

Santa Maria

DALBADE

St. Remy

St. Étienne Gate

Temple

Carmes

St. Étienne

Comminges Gate

Narbonne Gate

St. Jacques

Mills

Mint

Salvetat St. Catherine

Château Narbonnais

Montgaillard Gate

Montoulieu Gate

St. Lezat

N

Willow Grove

Nause

Mark Stein Studios 2003

map not to scale

The
Outcast Dove

One

A trade road, somewhere south of Limoges, France. Thursday, 15 kalends April (March 18) 1148, Feast of King Edward the Confessor. 24 Adar 4908.

יונת הרחוקים נדדה יערה / כשלה ולא יכלה להתנערה.
התעופפה התגופפה חופפה / סביב להודה סוחרה סוערה,
ותחשוב אלה לקץ מועדה / אך חפרה מכל אשר שערה.
דודה-אשר ענה בארך נדוד / שנים, ונפשה אל שאול הערה
הן אמרה "לא אזכרה עוד שמו" / ויהי בתוך לבה כאש בוערה.

Far-flung dove wandered to a wood.
Stumbled there and lay lame . . .
A thousand years she thought would bring her time,
But all her calculations failed.
Her lover hurt her heart by leaving her
For years; she might have died.
She swore she'd never say his name again,
But in her heart it burned like fire.

—Judah Halevi

*S*olomon nudged the corpse with the toe of his boot.

"Still warm," he said. "Hasn't been here more than a few moments, I'd say."

"I don't see a wound." Solomon's friend, Bonysach, knelt for a closer examination, then leaned back suddenly. "Think he had some kind of disease?"

"Looks healthy enough." Solomon knelt, too. "Apart from being dead, that is."

He ran his gloved hands over the limp body. "Wait! See here, an arrow went straight through his neck! It must have come out the other side. Amazing! I'd have thought only a crossbow would have that much force. Poor fellow must have run on until he choked on his own blood. Whoever shot him probably thought he'd missed."

Bonysach looked up. "Then it's likely that no one will be looking for him, right?"

Solomon considered. "Probably not," he admitted. "Although they might be tracking him by the blood stains. But I don't hear any dogs."

Bonysach drew his knife. "Then he's ours to claim. Let's get him gutted and cut up before he spoils. There's enough meat here to feed us all for a week."

Solomon paused. "I don't know, Bonysach. You know how lords are about deer poachers."

"That's why we have to hurry." Bonysach started to cut into the animal.

"Stop! Stop this at once! How can you do such a thing? That animal is unclean!" The third man in the group cried out in horror. He had refused to approach the body and had stayed on the path, holding the horses.

"It won't be when I'm done, Yusef," Bonysach told him. "I'm cutting out the sinews and taking only the parts the law allows."

"But it hasn't been ritually slaughtered!" Yusef pleaded.

"Yusef!" Solomon answered. "The damn thing bled to death; isn't that good enough for you?"

Yusef shook his head. He could see that the other two wouldn't be swayed by any argument of his but he intended to take the matter up with the elders of the *bet midrash* when they reached Toulouse. If they ever did. He looked into the dark forest, expecting it to erupt at any moment with knights or monsters. His neck prickled, anticipating the slice of steel at his throat.

Solomon continued with the work of getting the best meat from the deer before the hunters showed up. Of course, if he'd been a holy man, like Yusef, he would have cut up the venison and given it to the peasants in the next village they came to. Or he would have passed it by with eyes averted. But they had been living on dried fish and stale bread for too many days after a winter of famine. His body craved real meat.

His friend, Bonysach must have felt the same way. He was a respected Jewish merchant of Toulouse but the lure of fresh venison was too strong. His stomach overruled his conscience.

The path they were on was a main thoroughfare south through Burgundy to Provence. One could tell its importance by the beaten earth, devoid of plants. But it was still only wide enough to ride single file and the forest was encroaching on either side. This was one reason Solomon had dared take the time to cut up the deer. It was clear that the local lord wasn't fulfilling his duty to maintain the roads through his land. That meant it was unlikely there would be anyone patrolling it to challenge them.

"Hurry!" Yusef snapped, looking over his shoulder. "We shouldn't have let ourselves get so far behind the others. I don't want to camp alone in this forest. Who knows what's lurking in there?"

The other two made no objection. As the day ebbed and shadows lengthened, the tangle of vines around the trees seemed to have faces hidden in the brush. A branch hanging over the path shook as if someone were preparing to leap onto them. Yusef's packhorse shied as they passed under it, causing the man to drop the lead line.

"Our troubles are starting already. Impiety is always punished," he muttered as he dismounted to retrieve the line. "What if that animal wasn't really a deer?"

"What else could it have been?" Bonysach asked sharply. "Anyway, we weren't the ones who shot it."

"I think it was something evil," Yusef shuddered. "Put there on purpose to tempt you. You'll open that pack and find it writhing with snakes, mark my word."

He mounted again and they all set off at a quicker pace.

"What if the deer was divinely sent?" Solomon suggested after a moment of thought. "The Holy One may have taken pity on us. He may have decided that we'd mortified our flesh on salt cod soaked in beer for long enough."

Yusef grunted his doubt that Solomon was worth a heavenly gift.

Solomon glanced at Bonysach, trying to smile, but the dark

silent woods were pressing on his spirit. Despite his attempts at lightness, he couldn't prevent a shiver from running down his back.

Bonysach only gave a tired sigh. He was older than the other two, nearly sixty, and long days in the saddle wearied him more than he would admit.

They rode on in silence.

"Praise the Holy One!" Yusef suddenly cried. "We've found them!"

The path had widened to a clearing where a scattering of tents had been pitched and cooking fires started.

"Solomon! Bonysach! Yusef! Over here!"

Solomon turned to find the speaker. He grinned when he spotted his old friend, Aaron, from Toulouse.

"What are you doing on the road so early in the season?" he asked when he had reached Aaron's camp. "The best fairs aren't until after Pesach."

"I'm not going much farther," Aaron answered, pulling his cloak more tightly across his chest. "This far north and I'm already freezing. I just have to deliver a pair of horses to the archbishop of Bordeaux. He promised to pay on delivery and I need the money now."

"You might have to wait, then," Solomon commented. "He's probably already left for Reims. The Edomites are having another of their councils and the pope has summoned all the high clerics to attend."

"Perhaps," Aaron said. "I'm not privy to the archbishop's itineraries. As long as he left someone who can pay me, I'm not waiting on his return. As soon as I make the delivery and get the rest of my payment, I'm heading back to Toulouse and I won't go north again until the last of the storks have flown over. If the weather isn't warm enough for them, I know I won't be able to bear it, either."

"Poor thin-blooded Aaron!" Solomon laughed. "I'm going to be in Toulouse a while before I head farther south. I hope you return before I leave."

Aaron's expression turned serious.

"How far south were you planning on going?" he asked.

"All the way to Almeria," Solomon told him. "My uncle Eliazar has an investment in a ship due there next month. He wanted me to pick up his package to save the cost of a middleman. Why?"

Aaron shook his head. "You haven't heard? Almeria was taken by the Christians last autumn. The Spanish and the Genoese."

He seemed about to say more, but instead pressed his lips together as if biting back a sudden pain.

"Things are getting more dangerous south of the mountains," he went on. "The Christians are pushing farther into Saracen territory and the new rulers in Al-Andalus are pushing back. Between them, Israel is being squeezed out."

"The Edomites and Ishmaelites have been at each other for centuries," Solomon said. "We've always managed. Uncle Eliazar's goods were on a Christian ship from Alexandria. So I'll have to pay import fees to the Genoese instead of the Muslim lords. They'll probably be higher but we'll survive."

"Perhaps this time we won't," Aaron insisted. "Hundreds of our people have fled north to Narbonne. More have taken passage for Cairo. Face it, Solomon, whoever wins, we lose."

"Aaron!" Solomon was exasperated. "I've just spent the past week enduring Yusef's constant preaching on how each time we ignore one of the commandments we bring disaster on the Jewish people. I don't need to hear more tales of calamity. Has Toulouse become dangerous for us, too?"

"No." Aaron seemed almost sorry to admit it. "We get along well enough with the people there. Of course, our count has gone off with King Louis on this insane expedition, leaving his young son in charge. That could be a problem."

"Only if the boy decides to close the taverns," Solomon said. "Look, Bonysach and I have come by some fresh venison, not ritually slaughtered but properly butchered. Do you want to dine with us?"

"Well." Aaron looked at the ground. "I might just come by and give it a sniff. I have a skin of good wine from my sister's vineyard that I could share."

"It would be much appreciated," Solomon told him. "Come early. When the scent of the roast starts rising, you may not be able to get through the crowd."

Solomon poked at the meat as it turned on a makeshift spit. There was a satisfying sizzle as grease dripped into the fire. For the end of winter, the animal was well supplied with fat.

The aroma rose on the evening breeze. As Solomon had predicted, there was soon a ring of men around them, many with trenchers of hard bread to hold their slice and catch every drop of the juice. Despite his warning that the deer hadn't been properly slaughtered, Solomon noted several other Jews waiting among the Christian traders.

It should have comforted him to know that he wasn't the only one who wasn't observant. Instead he felt uneasy, as though he were personally responsible for leading others into sin. Well, he told himself, it wouldn't be the first time.

He lifted the meat from the fire and let it slide onto a brass platter one of the traders had loaned them. The juice ran in rivulets through the carvings. One of the men held out his bowl to catch any drop that might spill over the edge.

Solomon felt the change in the air before he saw what had caused it. A silence began at the edge of the group and rolled to the front where the first man had just speared a slice of venison

on the point of his knife. He looked up at the massive horse and
the massive man in chain mail riding him. Very carefully, he set
the meat back on the platter and backed away. The other men
were already moving toward their own tents.

Solomon didn't even glance at them, although he could feel
the warm moistness of the horse's breath on his neck. He took a
piece of the meat and set it on his trencher bread. He then picked
up the bread, took it over to the camp chair next to his tent, and
calmly began to eat it, tearing off bites with his teeth and letting
the juice run down his chin and onto the bread.

"I don't mind an unexpected guest," he said, finally acknowl-
edging the horseman in front of him. "But it is customary to leave
your mount and your sword outside the dining hall."

The warrior's foot left the stirrup with amazing speed as he
kicked the bread and meat from Solomon's hand.

"You stole my *sancnos* deer!" he roared. "Prepare to die!"

He dismounted and drew his sword.

Solomon stood, still holding the long meat knife. He saw a
man about his own height, but built solidly, with bowed legs that
bespoke more time in the saddle than on foot.

"So." Solomon shook his head sadly. "You are the idiot who
used a yearling for target practice and then didn't bother to follow
him to find out what damage you'd done. What kind of knight
are you? Who is your liege lord?"

The question was barked out like a battle command.

"The count of Anjou," the man said before he'd thought.
"Not that it's any of your affair."

"No," Solomon agreed pleasantly. "But it is strange that you'd
be so far from home and alone."

By now the man realized that he hadn't wandered into a small
camp of peasants that he could intimidate. There were ten or
fifteen men around him and several of them were clearly guards
hired to protect these traders. His wasn't the only sword out now.

"Th . . . that's not your concern, either," he stammered as he remounted his horse. "Since I am on an important errand for my lord, I don't have time to punish you as I would like. Be sure that I won't forget this insult."

The man rode off down the path, pretending not to hear the laughter that followed him.

"It's like you try to face down a man in chain mail," Bonysach said to Solomon. "But you never think of the consequences. What if he returns with friends?"

"I doubt he has any nearby," Solomon answered. "He may not even have a lord. Did you note his gear? The leather is worn and his cloak is threadbare. He was probably poaching, himself."

"His horse is old, too," Aaron volunteered. "Probably can't go above a trot."

"I almost pity him," Yusef added. "What's he going to eat tonight, now that you've taken his meat?"

"*Avoi!*" someone shouted. "The venison!"

The dripping grease had caused the fire to flare up, enveloping the remaining hunks of meat. Solomon wrapped his cloak around his hand and grabbed the spit, pulling it out. The venison burned like a torch for a moment and then died down.

"Barely seared," one of the traders pronounced. "Slice it up!"

Solomon looked at Bonysach, who nodded.

"Might as well get rid of the evidence," he said. "Just in case our friend there has friends of his own after all."

The men descended upon the meat. Solomon looked over at Yusef who was gnawing on the last of the fish, having first washed his hands and said the blessing. A few other men were sitting with him. They radiated pious disapproval. Solomon watched them a few seconds, then shrugged and returned to his venison, washing it down with a cup of Aaron's wine.

"Have more." Aaron filled the cup from his wineskin. He sat down next to Solomon.

"Do you want some meat?" Solomon asked.

Aaron sniffed the venison wistfully but shook his head.

"I need all the blessings I can get right now," he said. "I can't risk even a minor transgression."

Solomon knew Aaron wanted him to ask what the trouble was. He sighed. Why did people think he cared about their problems? But Aaron was an old friend, like Solomon still unmarried in his early thirties. And his sister made very good wine.

"So, what trouble are you in that you can't risk a mouthful of venison?" Solomon forced himself to ask.

But Aaron didn't immediately unburden himself.

"You've been to Córdoba, haven't you?" he asked instead.

"Many times," Solomon answered, confused by the sudden question. "We do business there with Yishmael, the pearl merchant."

"So you know his daughter, Mayah?" Aaron continued.

"Aha!" Solomon thought.

He nodded. "A lovely girl, if somewhat sharp of tongue."

"Really?" Aaron asked sharply. "She spoke most civilly to me. And she is well-educated both in Arabic and Hebrew, they say."

"They are right," Solomon answered. "Her French is also quite good. Am I to understand that you have an interest in Mayah?"

"I have discussed an alliance with Yishmael," Aaron said.

Solomon almost started to say that Yishmael liked his boys younger, but he took pity on his friend.

"I thought a mere Cohen wouldn't be good enough for Yishmael," he contented himself with commenting. "He would prefer a *nasi* for Mayah with proof of direct descent from King David."

Aaron smiled. "She is beautiful enough to be a queen," he said. "But her father still seemed to look kindly on me."

"Well, congratulations then!" Solomon finished his wine and stood.

"Well, there is a—" Aaron began, but Yusef chose that moment to interrupt, dragging Aaron off to help decide a debate on the age of a horse one of the traders had just bought.

Solomon wished he'd thought to refill his cup. He finished his slice of meat, savoring the flavor. A moment later, Bonysach joined him.

"After this meal, I'll sleep well for a change," he pronounced. "Two more days to Moissac, another day or so going upriver and then I can eat Josta's cooking again. This may just hold me until then."

Solomon winced at the name of the town. Bonysach noticed and apologized at once.

"I forgot what you went through in Moissac," he said. "But that was all a misunderstanding and at least your partner talked the abbot out of having you hanged. A pity he decided to return home instead of making this trip with us. What is his name again? Something foreign."

"His name is Edgar and it's just as well he decided to turn back. He was too worried about his family to be of any use," Solomon said. "He said he'd try to join us later. Anyway, he can't help with this. You know it's not a brush with the gallows that makes me dread going to Moissac."

"Yes." Bonysach was one of the few who did. "But you aren't likely to run into that monk. Don't look so ashamed. Many of us have family who have turned Christian. At least your Uncle Hubert came back to us, even if his brother didn't."

"All the same," Solomon growled. "Even the chance that I might see him makes my stomach as tense as a bow strung on green wood."

"Then I suggest you stay away from the monastery and spend your time in places a monk wouldn't be likely to go."

Solomon felt his muscles relax a bit. "That, Bonysach, is an excellent suggestion."

∞

So, two nights later, Solomon found himself soaking up to his waist in a large wooden tub. He ducked his head under the warm water. The first thing he had done upon their arrival in Moissac was go to the bathhouse. After almost three weeks of sleeping in a tent or fleabag inns and washing in cold streams, a real bath felt like the first garden of Heaven. And definitely not a place to find monks. He soaped his hair and beard and ducked again.

Fingers slipped through his matted curls and tugged him to the surface. Solomon grabbed at them.

"Ow!" The woman twisted her hand away. "You didn't have to be so rough . . . at least not without paying."

Solomon wiped the water from his eyes. The woman standing beside the wooden tub was wearing only a yellow *bliaut* with no shift underneath. He was sure of this because she had laced up the sides so loosely that he could see her skin from thigh to neck. Her long brown hair was also loose and her eyes were rimmed with dark kohl to make them seem larger and more appealing.

"I'm sorry, Englesia," Solomon said. "But you should know better than to catch me unawares."

She shook her head. "Always expecting an attack, aren't you?"

"That's right," he answered. "It keeps me alive. So, what are you doing here? You usually wait for me to come to your room. Anyway, I heard you had married."

Englesia smiled. "I did, a blacksmith. But he's gone off to make horseshoes for the count's army."

"Didn't he provide for you?" Solomon climbed out of the tub and reached for a linen *mantele* to dry himself.

The woman knelt to help him, working her way up from his feet.

"He left a bit," she said. "But, well, you wouldn't believe it, but all Miro's muscles turned out to be in his arms. I hadn't counted on giving up that much. So I decided to return to my old trade for a while. Just my special clients, of course."

She ran a soft hand up his thigh.

"That's too bad, but I can't help you." He looked down at her. "Englesia, get up," he insisted. "I'm not looking for company tonight."

"Really?"

Solomon was aware that his body was giving his words the lie. He pushed Englesia away.

"I came with a group of more than twenty men," he told her. "I'm sure you'll find many eager to purchase your favors. I have other plans."

A flash of anger passed across her face. Then she laughed.

"Whoever she is, Solomon, I'll wager she won't give you as good a game as I can."

Solomon pulled on his tunic and hunted around for his hose. "Perhaps not, Englesia," he said as he put them on. Last he buckled the sheath for his knife to his left arm. "Or perhaps I've just grown tired of playing by your rules."

He lifted the curtain and stepped into the passageway, letting the drape fall behind him. He was almost to the door before she stepped out. For a moment, she seemed about to come after him but then she shrugged and entered another cubicle from which the sound of splashing could be heard.

Solomon cursed himself all the way back to the inn. What had made him turn her down? Englesia had always given good value, even a bit extra. Could he have suddenly become squeamish about bedding married women, even whores?

He shivered, although the night was mild. It was this town, he decided. Moissac was the place where a few years before, he had been accused of murder. The true culprit had been found eventually, but Solomon wasn't about to forgive those who had assumed his guilt, nor the man who had encouraged them.

He walked faster. Maybe he should have taken Englesia's offer. It would have kept his mind from the memories. All he could
see now was the face of that hateful monk.

He reached the inn.

"Wine!" he shouted to the woman just entering from the door
to the cellar. "A pitcher full to the brim and no water."

He flung himself onto the bench in the corner. If he couldn't
allow himself to ease his body with a woman tonight, then wine
would have to do.

Yusef came for him the next morning. He found Solomon still
rolled up in his blankets, the wine cup overturned on the floor
beside him.

"What a *mamzer!*" he exclaimed in disgust as he pulled the
covers from Solomon's face. "This is what happens when you
refuse to stay with your own people. Get up at once. The boat is
loaded and we're leaving whether you're sober or not."

"Yusef." Solomon's voice was icily calm. "If you don't lower
your voice I shall cut your tongue out."

He sat up unsteadily, wincing as he opened his eyes. There
must have been wormwood in that wine. He couldn't have drunk
enough to feel this bad unless he'd been poisoned.

He looked down at himself.

"At least I'm dressed," he commented. "Help me with the
bedding and we can go."

Yusef just looked at him with revulsion.

"You can't even make it down the ladder," he said. "I don't
know how you got up to bed."

"Neither do I." Solomon stuffed the blankets in a leather bag
and picked up his pack. He let out a mighty groan.

"Just don't speak to me," he warned Yusef. "And if I stop
suddenly and bend over, get out of range."

"No fear about that." Yusef grunted. "You'll be lucky if I don't leave you sprawled in the street. If it weren't that your disgrace would reflect on the rest of us, I would."

"Good Yusef." Solomon put a hand up to block the sunlight as they left the inn. "I know I can rely on you. *Maine de esvertin!* I can't stand this town!"

Yusef suppressed a retort and sighed instead. Solomon was right in believing that he was dependable. No matter what Yusef thought of Solomon's behavior, he believed that the man was still a member of the community and deserved protection. Also, even though Solomon thought it was a secret, Yusef knew why he loathed Moissac so much. Bonysach had told him about the monk. It was this that made Yusef sympathetic, despite his own inclinations.

In Solomon's place, he would have felt the same.

The river Garonne joined the Tarn at Moissac. From there one could go all the way upriver to Toulouse. It was slower but safer and somewhat cheaper than the road, although every town seemed to have a toll to get past it and the bargeman had to keep a constant watch for floating mills in the middle of the river, attached to the banks by ropes that could knock a man or a barrel over the side.

Solomon was in no danger of going in. He lay flat on his back, his face covered by his felt hat.

He felt someone kneel next to him. A moment later his hat was lifted and a round, good-natured faced stared down at him.

"Are you able to take food, yet?" he asked Solomon. "We have some egg broth that would do you good."

Solomon stared up at him blearily. "Who are you?"

The man grinned. "Arnald of la Dalbade," he told Solomon. "Some call me Arnald Barleysilk." He indicated his frizzy light brown hair. "My father, Vidian, is a salt merchant in the Cité of

Toulouse. I was in Moissac to see my friend, Victor, who's a monk at the abbey. Do you need any salt?"

This was more information than Solomon could handle in his present state. He tried to focus on the man's first question.

"Egg broth," he repeated. "Yes, I think I'd like some."

He pushed himself up onto his elbows. The man helped him to sit.

"If you give me your bowl, I'll bring it to you," he offered.

Solomon felt for his pack.

"Thank you . . . Arnald," he said, handing him the bowl.

Solomon looked around. The river was wide here, with mostly forest on either side. He spotted a fish weir and a well-worn path, but no sign of a village. He wondered how long he had slept. His mouth felt like a freshly tanned hide but his head was clearer and his stomach not so rebellious.

Arnald brought back the bowl and gave it to Solomon.

"It's not very warm," he said. "The coals we brought on board this morning are almost spent."

Solomon took a sip. Tepid and bland, just what he needed.

"Thank you," he said.

He took a longer drink. It felt wonderful on his parched tongue. Over the edge of the bowl, Solomon realized that Arnald had sat down next to him and was watching with interest.

"Umm," Solomon began. "I'm grateful for your care, but really not up to conversation at the moment."

Arnald smiled. "Of course not. The innkeeper told me that you emptied three pitchers last night without even a crust to sop it. And that was the raw red from last fall. You must have a great grief to drown!"

Solomon put down the bowl to see this man better. Was he simple or just very young? Was he impressed by Solomon's capacity for drink or the depth of his assumed sorrow? Arnald was looking at him with an expectant smile. Did he think Solomon would confide in him on the strength of a kind gesture?

"If I had troubles," he told Arnald. "Then I must have drowned them. Apart from anger at my overindulgence, I feel fine. How far are we from Toulouse?"

"Oh, I don't know," Arnald apologized. "I could ask the boatman or one of your friends."

"No." Solomon finished the broth. "It's not important."

He forced himself upright and squinted around the boat. Yes, the other Jewish traders were standing in a cluster next to the pile of bundles they had brought. He could see his bags among them. Good old Yusef!

He managed the three steps to the group.

"I'm in your debt, Yusef," he said.

Yusef shrugged. "I'll consider it a *mitzvah*," he said.

"Very well," Solomon accepted that. "I shall repay the community in your name."

"I'd rather see you praying with us tomorrow morning," Yusef answered.

His eyes dared Solomon to refuse.

Solomon noticed that the other four men were waiting for his reply. He gave in.

"I will be there," he said. "But you'll have to help me with the words."

"Do you also need tallit and tefillin?" Bonysach asked.

Solomon heard the doubt in his voice.

"Actually, no," he answered. "Unless they've been stolen from my pack."

The men looked at him in surprised approval. Solomon smiled at them. No need to mention that he was bringing them as a gift for his Uncle Hubert from Abraham of Paris. Hubert wouldn't mind his using them. Now he just hoped he could remember how.

Solomon looked around the barge. As planned, the group had hired it just for themselves and their goods. The horses had been left in Moissac until their return. Fresh ones would be found in Toulouse. The only Christians on board were the boatmen, and Arnald.

Seeing that Arnald was now busy asking questions of the bargeman, Solomon leaned closer to Bonysach.

"What is the Edomite doing with us?" he asked.

Bonysach looked surprised. "The salt merchant's son? He told us you were friends," he said. "He said you had asked him to join us."

Solomon shook his head. "Never saw him before. He says he was at the inn with me last night."

Bonysach nodded. "The state you were in, you may have become sworn brothers. What possessed you to try to drain a vat by yourself?"

"I don't know," Solomon admitted sadly. "I've been to Moissac several times since my encounter with my . . . with that monk, but somehow, this time, the shame of it hit me like an anvil on my back."

The older man's face softened and he patted Solomon on the shoulder.

"The shame is not yours, my friend," he said. "But his."

He paused.

"You know we aren't angry with you for your behavior," he continued. "Not really. It's only that we fear that you spend too much time with the Edomites. We all have to live in a world of idolaters and unbelievers. It's the Law alone that keeps us safe. I think you enjoy flouting it."

"No," Solomon answered earnestly. "I respect the Law; I just don't see the need to observe it rigorously. But, Bonysach, I have never denied my faith. Nor have I doubted it. No matter what happens, I will die rather than be 'blessed' in their filthy water. I promise you."

Both men were silent a moment, remembering those they had known who had been martyred or forced to convert in the past two years. When King Louis had decided to raise an army to fight the Saracens, it was the Jews who were the first victims.

Bonysach shook himself. "Enough of misery. It's a beautiful spring day. We are safe and I, at least, am going home to my family. You'll stay with us again, won't you? Belide asks after you often. She's seventeen now, you know."

"Belide seventeen!" Solomon feigned shock. "The little girl with the skinned elbows and dirty face? I do feel old."

Bonysach looked him up and down. "Despite your current condition, you aren't decrepit, yet."

Solomon started to back away. He suspected what was coming.

"My friend, Abraham the vintner, says you need a wife," Bonysach went on.

"Oh, no," Solomon interrupted. "It's Rebecca, Abraham's wife, who feels I should be married. She has tried to match me to most of the eligible girls from Paris to Rouen."

"Those are French women." Bonysach dismissed them with a wave. "You know the women of Provence are more beautiful, more educated, more able to manage your business while you are gone and passionate enough to provide you with many children to carry on in your name."

"Bonysach!" Solomon was honestly shocked. "You can't be talking about your own daughter!"

"Believe me, I know Belide," Bonysach said. "She's ripe for marriage. But dutiful and pious," he added quickly.

Solomon was horrified and said so.

"Bonysach, you'd sacrifice your own child to see to it that I don't turn Christian? How can you even consider such a thing?"

Bonysach held up his hands in protest. "She doesn't feel it would be a sacrifice," he said. "Anyway, we both know that marriage won't stop a man who wishes to leave the faith."

Solomon shuddered.

"Old friend," he answered. "My head aches still from my excess last night. This is far too much for me to wade through now. But I know you can do better for your child than a man who eats and drinks with infidels and is never home more than a few days in a year."

Bonysach shrugged. "Actually, I do have a few other possibilities. It's Belide herself who wants the chance to reform you."

Solomon rolled his eyes. "Will someone save me, please, from infatuated young women who think I can be redeemed!"

The other men turned to stare at him. Solomon lowered his voice.

"I know you're a doting father, Bonysach," he said. "And I'm sure Belide is all you say and more. You must make her believe that I am a lost cause. She would weary of me within a year."

His friend gave a relieved grin. "I agree, Solomon. My wife has tried to tell her the same thing. Josta's fond of you, of course, but doubts you'll ever be domesticated and doesn't want Belide to waste her youth trying."

Solomon grinned back. "Give Josta a kiss for me with my thanks. And tell Belide that I have a pair of amber earrings that will be perfect for her bridal gift."

Bonysach moved onto speak to one of the other traders. Solomon collapsed against the pile of bundles in relief.

Arnald had been listening with interest. He came over and plopped down next to Solomon.

"You don't know what you're giving up," he said. "Bonysach is very rich and Belide is even more beautiful than he said. It's a pity she's Jewish."

Solomon tensed.

"How do you know Belide?" he asked suspiciously. "Is she why you wanted to travel with us?"

Arnald fidgeted with a rope end, unraveling the twine.

"Oh, I see her in the market," he said. "We sell little cones of salt there. I help my mother at the stall sometimes. Belide and I have been friends since we were children."

Solomon turned to him. "Look, if you took advantage of my state last night to wriggle your way onto this boat and ingratiate yourself with Belide's father, then you're not only mad, you're in serious danger of having to swim the rest of the way to Toulouse."

"No! I . . ." Arnald looked over Solomon's shoulder. Bonysach was deep in conversation at the other end of the barge. "I do like her. But nothing more than that. My father would kill me if I took up with her."

"So would hers," Solomon pointed out.

"Yes, I know." Arnald was sweating now. "It was you I wanted to meet," he explained. "Belide said you were used to Christians, that you understood our ways. She thought you might be willing to help us."

Solomon's eyes narrowed. "Who is 'us'? And what sort of help for you to do what?"

"Didn't Aaron talk to you?" Arnald asked.

"Aaron? The horse trader? We talked a bit, but he only spoke of his marriage plans."

"Yes, yes, oh good!" Arnald relaxed visibly. "Then he must mean to tell you the rest when he returns."

He got up. "That's all right, then." He brushed the back of his tunic. "I know you'll be willing to help, now that we've met. You're not afraid of anything. Say, captain!" He stopped the boatman as he passed. "Will we be home by sundown tomorrow? My mother worries, you know, if I walk home in the dark."

He sauntered off to the other side of the barge.

Solomon was too stunned to reply.

Two

Somewhere on the river Garonne, Monday, 28 Adar 4908, 4 kalends April (March 29) 1148.

"A scholar apostatized voluntarily. . . . He persisted in his apostasy . . . until he had learned their book of errors, made a bald place on his head, shaved off his beard, and barked from their altars. . . . He became a priest of Christianity."

—R. Eliezer the Great
Responsa
(*Responsa of the Tosafists*)

*T*hey tied up under a bridge for the night and left again at dawn. Feeling somewhat foolish, Solomon joined the other men for prayers, as promised. After the *Shema*, he did not give a good account of himself. What made him feel worse was that the men seemed more sad than annoyed that he had forgotten so much.

By late morning the forest on either side of the river was thinning. Fields and vineyards grew more frequent. Solomon noticed that villages had risen in new clearings made since his last trip south. The buildings and fences were of fresh wood, the tree stumps still raw between the riverbank and the huts. Now there were people everywhere, hoeing, fishing, sawing down more trees to expand the town. Children waved at them as they passed.

"Everywhere you look, the forest is being pushed back," Bonysach commented to Solomon. "Trade is getting better all the time. Even the peasants are becoming more prosperous. We hear it's not as good in the North."

"No." Solomon thought of the wasted bodies of the beggars in Paris. "There are new towns enough, but the famine of the past few years has caused some to be abandoned."

"Thank the Holy One, blessed be he, that we have escaped that," Bonysach said. "They say there's much resentment in France that the king has gone on this expedition to Israel."

"Yes, and it gets louder every time he sends back for more money without any victories," Solomon said. "What right has a king to starve his own land in order to wage war in another? I'd rejoice at his defeats if they weren't so bad for all of us in France."

Bonysach nodded. "Our count, Alphonse, left recently to join the expedition. While I would wish to see Jerusalem free of the Christians, the count has been a good friend to us and so I'd also like him to win all his battles and come home loaded with wealth."

"That's our existence in a nutshell," said Solomon. "We live in two worlds, feeling safe in neither."

"Perhaps you think we should raise our own army and retake the Temple for ourselves," Bonysach suggested.

Solomon gave a laugh.

"Has the Meshiach arisen to lead us? And where would the soldiers come from?" he asked. "All our great men are scholars. What would we do, argue the enemy to death?"

Bonysach laughed with him. "I know some men who could do it! If only walls could be brought down by words."

They didn't see Yusef come up next to them until he spoke.

"That is not a subject for jest," he told them. "Words built the world. How do you know the learned ones among us may not find the word that could end it?"

Solomon laughed again, but with less conviction.

"I don't want the world to end, Yusef," he teased. "Just for the Edomites and the Ishmaelites to give us back the land their ancestors stole."

"And I want my daughter to marry a prince and my sons to be great teachers," Bonysach said. "And all my goods to sell at ten times what I paid for them. If you find magic words that will do that, Yusef, I'll turn scholar, too."

Yusef regarded them with pity.

"You mock because you don't understand," he told them.

"Only those who give their lives to study can approach the divine knowledge."

Bonysach patted Yusef consolingly. "And that's why we support such scholars. But I don't expect any revelations in my lifetime, so allow me my dreams."

Yusef gave them both a superior smile. "Of course, my friend," he said. "But don't be surprised if someday soon you find yourself suddenly and sharply awakened."

As they came closer to Toulouse, the river grew more crowded. The passengers sat close to the center of the barge to stay out of the way as the boatmen steered through the maze of rafts, mills and other boats. They docked above the city, at the Bazacle port, where the merchants kept a shed to store their goods. Here, where the river picked up speed as it turned, there were several mills, a dyer's, and many storehouses.

Solomon paid the final toll and gathered up his packs.

"Don't forget," Arnald said, as they parted. "Aaron will tell you what we propose doing. With you I know we'll succeed!"

He hurried off before Solomon could protest that he had agreed to nothing.

"Come by for Sabbath dinner," Bonysach told him. "One of the prospects for Belide will be joining us. You can help judge his worth. Josta will be happy to see you."

Solomon promised he would.

Yusef caught up with him as he was heading for the city walls.

"Are you going to evening prayers?" he asked.

Solomon stopped with a sigh and set down his bag. "No, Yusef. I'm going to see if Gavi will take me in while I'm in Toulouse."

"Gavi!" Yusef said in shock. "But he's a tanner! Why would you want to stay there?"

Solomon put his hand on Yusef's shoulder. "Because Gavi has

no daughters. He doesn't try to make me a better Jew or even a better man. His wife makes good beer and they have an empty bed they're always happy to rent."

"But the smell!" Yusef made a face.

"They've never complained about mine," Solomon said. "So I can tolerate theirs."

He picked up the bag and continued on his way, leaving Yusef standing in the road, shaking his head in stupefaction.

The bells of Saint Sernin, Le Taur, Sainte Marie la Daurade, and Saint Pierre des Cuisines were tolling the start of Vespers in the Bourg of Toulouse when another barge docked slightly farther up the river. The men aboard were all clean-shaven and tonsured. They wore sandals and the dark robes of monks of the Cluniac order. They came ashore and headed directly to the priory of Saint Pierre des Cuisines, chanting the office as they walked. Before them people stepped aside, moving hand carts, piles of refuse and small children out of their path. The prior gave the citizens his blessing as he went by.

In the midst of the group was a monk whose cowl was pulled forward so that his face was partly hidden. He looked at the ground as he processed through the town. His demeanor was of a man whose whole mind was occupied with the contemplation of heaven.

Yusef and Bonysach stopped to let the monks pass. As he watched them, Bonysach gave a start. He blinked and looked again. Once the street was clear, he grabbed Yusef by the arm.

"Do you know who that was?" he asked. "The older man with the stoop walking in the center?"

"No, I wasn't looking at them," Yusef answered. Then he realized. "You don't mean him? Why would he be here? Do you think it means a new persecution? Could he have convinced those monks of his to follow us from Moissac and force us to convert?"

"I don't see how." Bonysach bit his lip. "Or why a whole troop of them would need to leave the monastery just to thwart us. It's probably just a coincidence."

"Perhaps, but I don't like it," Yusef said. "We should tell this to the elders."

"I think you're right," Bonysach said slowly. "They can decide what to do about it and whether Solomon should be told."

"One thing I am certain of," Yusef said with feeling. "I don't want to be anywhere nearby when he finds out."

The next morning, as Solomon shared bread and sausage with Gavi and his wife, Nazara, there was a knock at the door.

"Who could that be?" Gavi said as he rose to answer it. "I know it's too early for the tax collectors to show up and all my customers meet me at the market."

He opened the door. In front of him stood a thin old man, his full white beard tinged with remnants of the dark hair of his youth. He wore a wool cap and clothes of good linen stained with food and candle drippings.

"Welcome, Rav Chaim!" Gavi said in surprise. "You honor my home. Please come in."

Solomon stood, wondering why a respected teacher would visit a lowly tanner, especially so early. The sunlight was behind the visitor so Solomon could only see his form. Somehow, the man seemed familiar. He looked closer as the visitor entered and the light fell on his face.

"*Enondu!*" he exclaimed. "Uncle Hubert, is that you? I thought you wouldn't be in Toulouse for another week."

The man grinned as he hugged Solomon. "I couldn't wait for news of my daughter," he said. "Where is Edgar?"

"He went back to check on that same daughter," Solomon answered. "I've never seen such a uxorious man in my life."

"Catherine is well, though?" Hubert asked worriedly. "James and Edana aren't ill?"

"They were fine when we left," Solomon assured him. "Although you should have a new grandchild by the summer."

Hubert's grin widened. "Say what you like about the English, Edgar does give my daughter fine children. Is he coming back?"

"I don't know," Solomon answered. "If he thinks Catherine needs him, he may decide to stay until the baby arrives. I told him I'd be in Toulouse until after Easter but I'll wait no longer than that for him."

"Ah, well," Hubert began. "I might have a commission for you before then if you don't mind a short trip."

"Anything you like, Uncle," Solomon said.

Gavi's wife had been standing politely while they spoke, but she felt that she must show their guest some hospitality.

"Would you like some beer and sausage, Rav Chaim?" she asked. "We would be honored for you to join us."

Solomon remembered that Hubert had returned to his Hebrew birth name and this was what the people of Toulouse would know him by. Chaim, a fitting name for one who had been born into a new life.

He was amazed at the change in his uncle. As a young boy in Rouen, Hubert's mother and sister had been killed by soldiers on their way to join the first expedition to the Holy Land. The other men of the family had been away. Hubert had been taken in by a Christian of Rouen, baptized, raised and married as a Christian. His father and brothers thought he was dead and it was many years before they found him again. By then he was part of the Christian community.

Yet, in the autumn of his life, Hubert had returned to Judaism. It had meant leaving his children and grandchildren behind, knowing that he might never see them again. Leaving most of his wealth with Edgar and Catherine, Hubert turned his back on the life he had led for over fifty years. He had started in Hebrew school with boys of seven or eight, trying to pick up what he had barely started learning before his life had been torn in half.

But that was only two years ago! How had he attained such respect in so short a time? Solomon was mystified.

"Uncle," he said as they sat at the table and Gavi poured the beer. "When I last saw you, you had scarcely begun your *aleph-bet*. What miracle has led you to the rank of teacher?"

Hubert smiled sheepishly. "I'm rather embarrassed by that. It's not my learning they seem to respect."

"Rav Chaim has become a *parush*," Gavi explained. "An ascetic who spends every hour of the day in study and prayer."

"Most days," Hubert added. "Most hours."

"You are devoting your life to the study of the Torah," Gavi's wife, Nazara, said. "Such dedication to the words of the Creator is always to be honored."

"You forget that I have a lifetime of study to make up for." Hubert was clearly ill at ease.

"We're all proud of you," Solomon told him. "I even have a gift for you from your old friend, Abraham the vintner. 'For the lost sheep,' he said. 'Who found his way home.'"

Hubert smiled but seemed preoccupied.

"Abraham was always a good friend," he said.

He finished his beer and, when Gavi started to pour more, put his hand over the bowl.

"I am grateful for your hospitality, *Mar* Gavi." He inclined his head to Gavi and his wife. "But I mustn't stay. Solomon, would you walk back to the synagogue with me? I've been given a bed there while I am in Toulouse."

"Of course, Uncle," Solomon answered. "Just let me put on my boots."

The two men walked in silence along the river before turning into the Cité, the part of town under the protection of the count.

Just before they entered the gates of the Cité, Solomon rounded on Hubert.

"Now that you have my guts twisted like a bloom of iron hot from the kiln, tell me what's wrong," he demanded.

Hubert grimaced. "Clearly, I've lost the skill to hide my true emotions. The talents a trader needs most are a hindrance to the kind of study I've been doing."

"Uncle!" Solomon warned.

"I came this morning because I was eager to see you, of course." Hubert fiddled with his beard nervously. "But I also am the unwilling bearer of some upsetting news."

He took a deep breath.

"Solomon, your father has been seen in Toulouse."

Solomon's face shut. His gray eyes were like stone.

"My father is dead," he said evenly.

Hubert bowed his head. "Solomon, you can't ignore the truth. I know the pain he has caused you. Even when I was a Christian in name I was appalled at what he did to you and your mother."

"He killed her." Solomon's voice remained flat.

Hubert sighed. "Yes, he did, as surely as if he'd put a knife in her heart."

Suddenly, Solomon exploded. "That's exactly what he did, Uncle, and in my heart, too! And, if Edgar hadn't defended me in Moissac six years ago, he'd have put a rope around my neck as well. In thirty years he has become more evil than when he left us. If you've come to warn me to avoid the thing he has become, you needn't worry. I wouldn't let myself be soiled by the touch of his shadow!"

He turned away, staring at the currents in the river.

Hubert gave him a moment to control his anger.

"Solomon," he said softly. "Remember that Jacob was also my brother. He still is."

Solomon turned his head sharply.

"How can you say that after what he has done? Especially now that you have become such a 'holy man' and scholar?"

He was shocked to see tears on Hubert's cheeks.

Hubert wiped them away with the back of his hand.

"You and I know how far I am from being either," he said miserably. "All I can do is strive. But in my study I have learned one thing. 'Even though a man be a sinner, he is still Israel.' Jacob will remain my brother no matter what."

"That's nonsense, Uncle," Solomon said. "Do you think you can redeem him? He is a black monk who spits on Israel. *Kaddish* was said for my father. Let him stay in his grave."

Hubert rubbed his forehead. "I would like to, believe me. I have no desire to debate him. Only the Holy One, blessed be he, can change Jacob's heart. But, if that should happen, I am prepared to forgive him. Are you?"

Solomon snorted. "No, Uncle, I'm not."

He started up the path to the Cité. "If that's what you wanted of me," he continued over his shoulder. "Then you've wasted your time. I'm grateful for the warning and will be sure to stay away from any taverns where monks are likely to congregate."

"Solomon." Hubert's voice followed him. "It may not be that simple."

Solomon continued up the path. Hubert hurried after him.

"Jacob is here for a reason," he insisted. "Easter is coming. The monks of Moissac have priories throughout Toulouse. I think they're planning something."

Solomon covered his ears with his hands.

Hubert tugged at his arm. "You can't ignore this. All of Provence is in turmoil. There have been rumors for weeks that something dreadful is going to happen."

Solomon slowly lowered one hand. "Like a forced baptism?" he asked. "Accept Jesus or die?"

"No one knows," Hubert said. "But Jacob may be in Toulouse to try to confound our community in one way or another. Certainly, it would elevate him in the eyes of the other monks if he brought more of us to his faith. Jacob is a skillful speaker. He was the scholar of the family. He knows the Law as well as any of our teachers."

"So, the Edomites want to have another debate. That isn't a reason for panic," Solomon tried to reassure him. "They talk; we talk. They say they've won and everyone goes home. Along with throwing stones at us in the street, it's just another part of their Easter rituals. Forgive me if I don't attend. Although," he added sadly. "As I recall, we usually aren't give the chance to decline."

Hubert puffed as he followed Solomon up the path.

"There's more! Things are different this year," he gasped. "Slow up a bit, Nephew!"

Solomon turned and saw that Hubert was indeed pale and breathless. Too late he remembered the fainting spell his uncle had suffered in Paris a few years before. He wasn't used to thinking of Hubert as old; he wasn't sixty yet. But now that he looked closer he realized that beneath the flowing beard Hubert's skin was lined and that his clothes hung loosely.

Solomon leaped back to give his uncle an arm for support.

"You've been fasting, haven't you?" he accused. "I've heard there were scholars practicing foolish asceticism, aping the Christian hermits. As if starving ever made a man holy."

"Just because the Christians do it, doesn't mean there isn't some virtue in it," Hubert snapped. "Fasting cleanses the body and allows the spirit to break free. And a man who is looking inward for enlightenment often finds that earthly needs are meaningless."

"Clearly you haven't reached that level, yet," Solomon

snapped back. "Or you wouldn't be here now. Perhaps you should go back to your cell and leave me to deal with the world."

Hubert sagged and lowered himself to sit on a stone block.

"I would like nothing better." He sighed. "I'm sorry for my harsh tone. You haven't been in Provence recently. There's something in the air, I think. The usual rumblings against the Jews are only a background to some other change that's coming. But we will be caught up in it and we must prepare."

Solomon put his hand on Hubert's forehead.

"I repeat," he said, "you're sickening for something. Have you been to a doctor? When were you last bled?"

Hubert shook him off. "I tell you, the signs are there. Danger, upheaval, strange weather, a host of falling stars. It all portends a new order. At first I tried to ignore them but then the count left for the Holy Land and now the bishop has gone to the Pope's council in Reims. We are left without our guardians. Something evil is coming. It may well devour Christian and Jew alike."

Solomon squatted to look his uncle in the eye. "Hubert, you're giving me chills. What are you talking about? What signs? Are you involved in divination sorcery?"

"Lower your voice!" Hubert leaned toward him. "Of course not. I only seek such knowledge as the Holy One deigns to reveal to the least of His servants."

"What does that mean?" Solomon asked wearily.

Hubert leaned so close that his whiskers were brushing Solomon's ear. "I believe I have been sent a revelation," he whispered. "While meditating on the Holy Name."

Solomon rocked back on his heels. "God's blood! I'm surrounded by saints and lunatics! Eat more than bread and bitter herbs. Have some good wine. Then, if you still have visions, I'll pay attention."

His uncle looked up at him with such misery that Solomon forbore making any more comments. He helped Hubert up and led him to the synagogue, giving him over to the care of the other scholars.

"Rest now," he ordered. "Eat something. I'll return this evening and we can talk then."

Hubert looked as if he would protest, but then nodded.

"Just be careful," he begged.

"I promise." Solomon laughed. "I'm only going to talk with Bonysach about the spices Edgar and I want. The worst danger I shall face is his lovesick daughter."

In the dortor of Saint Pierre des Cuisines, Brother James changed his travel stained robe for a fresh one. He had waited until his fellow monks of Moissac had left the room before removing his clothes. They all knew what he had been born but still he was ashamed to have them see the circumcision. He considered it the mark of a pact his father had made with Satan in his name, but without his permission. After thirty years, James had managed to destroy almost every part of the man who had been Jacob ben Solomon of Rouen. Only the scar of his mutilation remained to remind him every day. Once he had attempted to cut his member off entirely but he had fainted at the first touch of the knife. His abbot had forbidden him to try any such thing again. James had listened patiently to the sermon. It was better, the abbot insisted, to fight temptations, even if they were only those of memory, than to make oneself a eunuch.

The abbot didn't have James's memories.

"Brother James, aren't you dining with us?" The voice had a laugh in it that roused James from his gloom.

"Just finished lacing my sandal," he said as he rose with a smile. "Thank you for coming back for me Brother Victor."

The young monk brushed away the thanks. "I wouldn't have you miss another fine Lenten supper with a reading from Saint Ambrose all because you were lost in your private devotions."

"You are always thoughtful." James forced himself to smile. "I look forward to both Ambrose and the supper."

Brother Victor took his arm. "And then a good night's rest," he said. "You'll need all your strength for the task ahead."

James gave the young monk a tired smile.

"I don't know how I would survive without your help," he said. "Certainly I could never have faced leaving the cloister if you hadn't volunteered to come with me."

Victor laughed. "This is a treat for me, Brother James! I haven't been back to Toulouse since I entered the monastery. And then there's the adventure of travel as well as the knowledge that we are on a mission of great importance. I'm grateful you were willing to let me join you."

James looked at the young man. Victor's bright brown eyes showed no trace of deceit. Or fear. James's heart warmed to him. He had a boy's hopeful, trusting view of the world. If only the world were as he saw it!

James sighed and allowed Victor to take him in to dinner.

In his small room, Hubert ate a meal more simple even than that of the monks. A bit of bread was enough, and a cup of water to keep the crumbs from sticking in his throat. Too much food clogged the mind and promoted drowsiness and he had so much more to learn, to understand, to seek. He knew he would never be a great scholar or judge. The fine points of the Law were too complicated for him. But the Torah, the words that made the world, yes, that was something he could study. Over and over he read them aloud, gently pointing to each letter with the silver *yad* that had once belonged to his brother Jacob.

Perhaps the learning that Jacob had abandoned when he con-verted was somehow contained in the slim pointer. It seemed to Hubert that meanings became clearer when he used it. The letters were reflected in the silver as it caught the light of his lamp and

illuminated the page. Sometimes the words seemed to grow until
they filled his vision and then he could see into the space beyond
them, as if they were windows into the palace of the Lord. At
these times he felt no hunger, thirst, or bodily pain. It was as if
he were surrounded by joy and wonder.

But not tonight.

The letters lay still and lifeless on the page. He read the same
passage a dozen times before realizing that he hadn't taken in the
meaning. The ghost of his brother had come between him and
the words. He wanted to curse Jacob. But all he could feel was
grief and his own self-doubt.

Jacob had abandoned his family to follow a false god. But
Hubert had been raised to believe in that god. Lately he had come
to believe that, like Moses, he had found his way home to his
own people at last. But hadn't he also abandoned a family? His
daughter, Agnes, despised him. His other daughter, Catherine,
grieved for him although she loved him still. His poor son, Guillaume, had no idea what he had done or even that Hubert had
been born a Jew. Guillaume thought that his father had gone on
a long and dangerous pilgrimage, from which he was not expected
to return.

The only difference between the brothers was that Hubert
still loved his family. He had left Paris to protect them. Jacob
had done everything he could to eradicate any connection to his
old life. Six years ago he had proved that when he allowed his
own son, Solomon, to be arrested for murder. His vicious denunciation of the Jews at that time had left deep scars in Hubert as
well as in Solomon.

Hubert suddenly sat up straight on his stool. He hadn't been
seeking a revelation tonight, but one had just come to him anyway. He wondered how he could have ignored this truth for so
long.

He really didn't like his brother, Jacob. He hadn't liked him when he was an observant Jew. It was just possible that, even if Jacob hadn't converted to Christianity, he would still be unlikeable.

Jacob was an unpleasant person, no matter what his faith.

"If he wasn't my brother, I'd have done my best to avoid him," Hubert said aloud.

Hubert arose from the stool, wincing at the creak of his knees. He needed to walk and think. He had told Solomon that Jacob was still part of Israel, no matter how far he had strayed. The lost lamb must be sought, even if in this case it was more of an old and ornery ram. Hubert believed this in his mind but not his heart. It astonished him how much he still resented Jacob for what he had done. Despite all his fine talk, Hubert could not bring himself to forgive.

No wonder he had not been allowed to make the ascent even to the first of the halls of the palace of the Lord! He was unworthy.

What could he do?

For now, Hubert knew only that the room was too small for his anguish. He put on his cloak and stepped out through the dark meeting room into the chill evening air.

Three

Toulouse, that same evening. The house of Bonysach.

S'elha no m vol, volgra moris
lo dìa que m pres a coman:
ai, las! Tan suaver m'aucis
quan de s'amor me fetz emblan
que tornat m'an tal deves
que nuill 'autre no vuelh vezer

If she doesn't want me, then that day
I would die at her command.
Alas! Suicide seems sweeter
than this love that has twisted me so
that no other woman would have me.

—Cercamón

*W*elcome, Solomon!" Bonysach's wife, Josta, greeted him with a warm hug. "It's been too long since we've seen you. Sit down, have some wine and tell us the news from the North."

Solomon took the cup gratefully. "A blessing on you, Josta!" he cried. "I have missed your smile and, even more, your cooking."

He settled himself into a chair in the courtyard, next to a table laden with a platter of olives, cheese and dried fruit. As he reached for a plump prune, he spied a small hand come out from under the table, snatch a handful of olives and vanish.

Solomon bent down and lifted the tablecloth. Two pairs of identical mischievous brown eyes gazed back at him.

"Peace to you, little ones," Solomon said. "And who are you?"

"My brothers," a female voice said in disgust. "And they give us no peace, so they deserve none from you. Muppim! Huppim! Get out from under there! Go wash your hands!"

The two boys grinned at Solomon, not at all fazed by the wrath of their sister.

"Go on," Solomon told them. "Has no one told you what I do to those who would steal the food from my plate?"

"No, tell us now!" They spoke at the same time.

Solomon seemed to consider. "No, it's too terrible. You would both have nightmares."

"You'll never get them to move that way." The girl came over and pulled the boys out by their ankles. "Now go!" she ordered.

They scrambled up and, laughing, finally obeyed.

The girl smoothed her skirts and adjusted the silver band holding her dark hair in place. She then faced Solomon and held out her hand. His eyes widened as the light from the setting sun fell on her face. He dropped the prune, stood, and bent over her hand.

"Belide?" he asked. "Can it be? What has happened to the little girl who used to go for rides on my back?"

Belide sighed, shaking her head. "Oh, her childhood ended sadly." Her voice rose again. "When her twin brothers arrived creating too much work for her poor mother to do alone!"

From just inside the house there was the sound of giggling.

"Fortunately," Belide continued. "My mother and father are even now looking for a good man to take me away and give me a nice, quiet home of my own."

She gave a short laugh at Solomon's expression. "You needn't fear, my former donkey. Father has explained that you think I'm far too ugly and useless to attract your attention."

"Belide! That's not what I said!" Solomon sputtered.

"Never mind." She patted the hand she was still holding. "I've decided that you don't wish to marry me because your heart has been broken and you are pining away for the love of a high-born woman who can never be yours."

Solomon started and dropped her hand.

"Daughter, stop teasing our guest." To Solomon's relief, Bonysach came out to the courtyard. "She listens to those troubadours in the streets and gets such idiotic ideas. What ever happened to the great stories of battles and honor? All the songs today are full of innuendo and adultery."

"Papa, you are hopelessly antiquated." Belide gave him a kiss.

"Now that you are here to entertain our guest, I'll see if Mother needs help with the dinner."

Bonysach seated himself on the other side of the table and refilled Solomon's wine cup before filling his own.

"I apologize for not being here to meet you," he said. "We had some trouble dividing the goods we brought back. Yusef insisted that there was a parcel of Flemish wool missing. We finally convinced him that his tally must have been wrong. Japhet's and mine agreed. But that's nothing to bore you with. Have you seen your uncle?"

Solomon nodded. "He's much more frail than I remember. I would think that after all he's given to the community in Arles, they could at least feed him."

"Oh, didn't he tell you?" Bonysach offered him some olives. "He left Arles and is now living in Lunel. There are some great scholars there who have allowed him to study with them."

"But he can't possibly have learned enough in two years to understand the subtleties of *halakhah*." This had been troubling Solomon since the discussion that morning.

Bonysach shrugged. "I don't know about that. Our scholars certainly respect him. Perhaps someone taught him the secret word of memory."

Solomon grimaced. "That's as much a fireside tale as the ones the *jongleurs* sing. But it is his health that worries me. He must be made to rest more."

"That, my old friend, is more than I can do." Bonysach offered him some cheese. "Or you, I would guess. He is attempting to touch the mind of the Creator. That's a noble and terrifying task. Of course it's wearing to his body. One can't approach the Throne on a full stomach, which is why I have no ambition to be more than I am."

"A good thing, too," Josta said, as she entered from the house.

"If all the men were scholars then we women would have even more work to do and we'd have you underfoot all day while we did it. Come in now, my dears. Your dinner is ready and the poor young man has arrived, bearing sugared almonds for Belide. The twins have already finished them and he looks as though he fears that they'll start nibbling on him next."

"Come, then!" Bonysach laughed. "We'll see if this man has wit enough to survive marriage to Belide."

As soon as Vespers ended Brother Victor and Brother James went to meet with the men who had been hired to protect them during their journey. One, Berengar, was a native of Toulouse and an old friend of Victor's. He was the younger son of a local nobleman and had been asked to find other trained knights willing to undertake the assignment.

"It will certainly be dangerous going into Saracen territory," Berengar said. He was a burly young man, who had aspirations of an heiress and a castellany of his own. "But the purpose is a noble one. Saint Maurice and Saint Nicolas will certainly watch over us. Don't you agree, Jehan?"

"What you propose is a task that God must approve," the other knight agreed. "But even so, my good monks, there's no reason for you to put yourselves in danger. The road will be full of hazards even if we are not betrayed in the end. We could be your emissaries and fulfill the mission guided from afar by your prayers."

Brother James studied the man carefully. Jehan was older than Berengar, perhaps forty, with a face that had seen too many campaigns. He had the air of one who did not expect life to improve but endured it anyway. James regarded him with suspicion.

"I'm afraid that will be impossible. You'll need us for the negotiations," he explained to the knights. "I can speak their language. Can you? You wouldn't want to rely on their interpreters. Most of them are Jewish, after all. And the abbot made it clear that Brother Victor is to be in charge of the funds. He is very proud to be so trusted."

Berengar stiffened at the presumed insult, but Jehan just smiled. "A wise precaution," he said. "Large sums can tempt even the most honest man."

Brother Victor laughed. "I believe that the abbot simply thought thieves wouldn't guess that I was carrying anything of value."

Jehan looked at Victor's fresh, naïve face and agreed with the abbot.

"Yes, that's wise," he considered. "Perhaps you should let people think you are with us by chance, on your way to visit another monastery."

"That is an excellent suggestion." Brother James was relieved that there would be no more argument. "It will draw attention away from us entirely. Who would notice a couple of poor monks in the wake of stalwart warriors? You're sure that all the arrangements have been made?"

"Of course," Berengar answered. "My father and the others have been planning this all winter. And Jehan, here, just returned from Spain with the latest information on the progress of the fight to reconquer the Saracen lands."

"So you know the route?" James asked. "Very good. I've heard that God has given the armies of Spain great victories."

"The war is going well," Jehan agreed. "Far better than the one King Louis has undertaken. Almeria is in Christian hands now and Tortosa will be soon."

"Yes." Brother Victor nodded. "We've heard about the call for armies to lay siege to Tortosa. They say that even the Vicountess Ermengard of Narbonne will lead her men into battle."

"She's a formidable woman," Berengar said. "I wouldn't doubt it. All the more reason for us to succeed in our mission so that more men will be able to fight, don't you agree, Jehan?"

The knight shrugged, causing the mail shirt he wore under his cloak to clink. Brother James looked at him in surprise.

"Why are you wearing armor?" he asked. "This is a town, not a battlefield. And we are in a house of God."

Jehan looked the monk up and down before he spoke.

"You have the appearance of a man on the far side of your prime, Brother James," he said consideringly. "Thin, from fasting no doubt, and wrestling with Satan. But the greatest earthly danger you are likely to face is from a fish gone bad. I was born the year King Philippe died. For a monk, my age would be of no great merit. But I can tell you that among men who live by fighting there are few gray hairs. I have survived this long by assuming that evil can enter even the house of God and that it often carries a sharp knife."

Brother Victor leaned over to whisper something in Brother James's ear. James nodded.

"Very well," he said. "Berengar, we agree that you have chosen the right man for this task. I'll rely on you to choose two more men to accompany us."

He reached into a small leather bag at his belt and drew out a few coins.

"Only *ramondins*, I'm afraid," he said, handing them to Berengar. "But they should buy the two of you a bed for the night and food. Come back tomorrow and we'll give you twenty *moneta decena* of Count Alphonse. That should be enough for supplies and to show our good faith."

"Twenty deniers of Toulouse." Jehan pursed his lips. "Your faith will have to be stronger than that. If I return alive from this, I expect no less than twenty gold *marbottins*."

"But this is an act of charity!" Brother Victor protested. "Wouldn't you want us to do the same for you?"

Jehan rubbed at a flea crawling up his arm. "Yes, I would. If not, I would have insisted on a hundred."

James laughed. "A man who knows his own worth! But just in case you don't succeed, where should we send your wages?"

"In that case"—Jehan's hard face grew almost wistful; but it was only a momentary change—"give the money to the Knights of the Temple, to keep the road to Jerusalem safe. And send to the canons of Paris enough for ten masses to be said for my soul. Come, young Berengar. Let's see what kind of bed these few sous will get us."

After they had left, Victor turned to James. "I'm sure you're right that this Jehan will be an asset to our party. He's rough but battle hardened. He'll not shrink from a foe. It saddens me, though, that he is so alone in the world. Everyone needs a family to care if they live or die."

"No they don't," James said sharply. "All anyone needs is Our Lord Christ and his Virgin Mother. Beside them all other relations are meaningless."

Victor rested his hand on James's shoulder, waiting until he grew calm. He smiled gently at his friend.

"You are right to chide me," he said. "I am blessed with all my brothers here and the love of Our Lord, especially since my parents in the flesh have died. But I suspect that this Jehan of Blois hasn't found such a happy replacement. He seems a very sad and lonely man. I shall pray for him."

James shook his head. "Victor, you shame me. Sometimes I think you are almost with the angels already. Of course, when you explain it like that, I shall certainly pray for him, too."

It was a good evening. Solomon's stomach was full; his wine cup was as well. Muppim and Huppim had provided uproarious entertainment, often at the expense of Samuel, Belide's befuddled suitor. But once the sweets had been served, Josta took pity on the young man and sent the twins off to bed in the care of a stern nursemaid.

"The nights are growing milder," Josta said. "Soon we'll be able to take all of our meals in the courtyard again."

"I'm amazed to see fresh greens on the table," Solomon said. "In Paris the first shoots have barely appeared."

"Why you live in that cold, damp place, I'll never understand." Bonysach shivered at the thought. "I dread making the trip to the fair at Troyes each year. I always return with the grippe."

"You need a son-in-law to take over the traveling for you, as I did for my uncles," Solomon said, with a glance at Samuel. "Do you enjoy travel, Samuel?"

"I? Well, Toulouse is the farthest I've ever been from home." A bright blush started up the young man's neck. "But I would like to see more of the world."

"Samuel is a fine scholar," Bonysach said. "His teacher is the great Rabbi Abraham, head of the *Bet Din* of Narbonne. It would be a waste of his talent to send him on errands."

"Oh, no, *Mar* Bonysach," Samuel began. "That is . . . however, I fear I don't have the skill to be a successful trader."

"Nor need you," Solomon said, taking pity on him. "I have more than enough competition. And the way we all argue about our contracts we need more wise judges well versed in the Law to keep us from doing each other violence."

"Oh, yes!" Samuel nodded. "I mean, I'm sure you wouldn't . . ."

Josta intervened. "Stop teasing him, both of you. Belide, why don't you and Samuel take a stroll around the courtyard? There's just a tiny slice of the old moon left. It's lovely, set up against the stars."

"Of course, Mother." Belide looked down modestly. "Samuel, would you care to examine the moon with me?"

Solomon suppressed a laugh.

"Leave the door open to light your way," Josta said mildly.

Samuel rose and bowed to the elders, then offered Belide his arm.

"You weren't kind to the boy," Josta said when they had left.

"If he's to endure life with this family, he'll need the leaven of humor," Bonysach replied. "Now, Solomon, about the goods you wanted."

Josta went out to the kitchen to oversee the cleaning up.

It was some time later when she returned.

"Hasn't Belide come back in?" she asked. "They've been out there far too long."

"Our daughter is more than a match for that one," Bonysach answered, his mind still on the negotiations.

"He may be more than he seems," Solomon suggested. "Perhaps we should go and see."

But they had no sooner stepped into the dark courtyard than Samuel came running toward them.

"Is Belide with you?" he asked, panting.

"Of course not!" Bonysach answered. "She was with you. What did you do with her?"

"Nothing!" The scholar took a step back. "She told me to wait for her. I thought she had to go . . . you know. So I waited. It seemed she was taking a long time. I thought she might have become tired of me and gone back inside."

"She didn't." Bonysach was starting to be alarmed. "Which way did she go when she left you?"

"That way." Samuel pointed toward the other side of the house.

"The garden gate," Bonysach said. "What is that girl playing at? Come, Solomon. We have to find her. I swear, if she is whole and unharmed, I'm going to thrash her!"

Compline had ended and the monks had all retired for the night. Brother Victor had been especially thoughtful to Brother James, making sure he had a thicker mattress and a hot herb drink to ease the pains in his joints. James fell asleep quickly, grateful once again for the kindness of the young man.

The moon was only a fading sliver when Victor rose from his cot and tiptoed carefully through the straw on the floor of the refectory. He paused before he left, listening for a change in breathing that would mean he had wakened one of the others. After a moment, he decided that it was safe to continue. He slipped through the half-open door and down the stone stairs. If he remembered right, there was a space in the cloister wall where the rock had crumbled and only a tangle of vines separated the monks from the outside world.

He knew what he was doing was strictly forbidden and what he planned to do even more so. He tried to imagine what the penance would be. How could he even confess such a thing? Disobedience, lying, pride, even theft were all sins he could tell. But he wasn't sure that even his confessor could understand why he had to do this. All he could do was pray that God, who knew his heart, would forgive.

The street was dark but Victor knew the way. He hurried to the meeting place, his heart thumping with excitement and fear.

"Wait!" Josta stopped Bonysach from running out into the dark. "Think first. Why would she leave so suddenly? Is she playing a joke on poor Samuel? If so, it's gone on far too long."

"It's not like her," Bonysach said. "And to go out alone in the middle of the night! That's madness!"

"Bonysach." Solomon lowered his voice and moved closer to his friend. "Is it possible that she isn't alone?"

Bonysach's head turned sharply toward his wife. "Josta?" He glared at her. "Has she been seeing those gentiles again?"

Josta turned her hands up in exasperation. "We can't keep her from the Edomites, *m'anhel*. She knows that she mustn't go to their gatherings. But she can't understand that it was permitted when she was a child and not any more."

Bonysach snorted. "She's just like your father. I remember when he . . ."

Solomon didn't want to find himself in the middle of a family argument. He interrupted Bonysach.

"Can you think of a reason why she might want to run out for a few moments?" he asked. "Belide must have known she'd be missed if she stayed out longer. Is there a festival tonight?"

"No, I'm sure not," Josta said. "It's still Lent. The Christians wouldn't let their children have a public celebration."

"Something private, then." Solomon tried again. "At a house nearby. Perhaps another Jewish friend."

Bonysach shook his head, but more doubtfully.

"I can't think why, but it's a place to start," he said. "I don't like our friends knowing that we have a wanton for a daughter but I'd rather she lost her reputation than her life. If she's not with a neighbor, they'll help us search."

Josta handed him a lantern. Her hand shook but her voice was steady. "Wear your cloak; the night is growing chill. Hurry back."

Despite his guilt at being out after Compline and without permission, Brother Victor was enjoying his adventure. He had left Toulouse for Moissac and the monastery when he was ten. Since then his life had been ordered, confined, and predictable. He loved it. He loved his fellow monks, even prickly Brother James. But he had longed for a more dramatic way to prove his faith than the daily round of prayer. This trip into Spain, with the possibility of martyrdom, was just what he had dreamed of. And then he had learned of something that brought him to a true test of faith.

Was obedience more important than conscience? Was it pride that made him think he was doing something noble? Or was his mission just, even if the abbot would have been horrified? Victor wasn't sure; he only felt that he had to do what he could to redress the wrong done by his brothers.

The stars shimmered in the black sky. It seemed to Victor that he could almost hear them singing. The young monk felt they were telling him that he had done well. He had been given the chance to prove that charity to all was integral to the Faith. And the girl had been so sweetly grateful. Now he had only to return to Saint Pierre, slip back into the dortor and catch what sleep he could before the call to Matins.

He had just entered a narrow street not far from the priory of Sancta Maria when someone tapped him on the shoulder.

"I'm sorry," he said as he turned. "I have no money, only a blessing to give you. Oh," he added in relief. "It's you! What are you . . . ?"

The blow hit him square on the chin and threw him against the corner of the building behind him. His head smashed into the sharp edge of stone and he slumped to the ground.

Down by the river, on the other side of the priory, Hubert was surprised to find himself sitting in the dark. Lost in his internal wrangling, he hadn't noticed the last of the daylight slipping away. He had gone to sit under the new half-built bridge where the sound of the mill wheels endlessly turning had soothed his weary spirit. Solomon's confusion at his altered appearance had wounded him. He wished Gavi hadn't treated him with such honor. He had never pretended to be a great scholar. He had definitely not announced that he was a holy man.

In truth, he felt a fool for trying at his age to attain a level other men had spent their lives reaching for. It was the height of arrogance to believe he would ever learn enough or be able to cast away the passions of the body long enough to be admitted into the divine presence.

But if he didn't make the attempt, he would never know.

He had sat on the bank, with his head bowed, pondering these things. Perhaps he had also dozed a little. How else could the night have crept across the town without his notice?

The starlight was so intense that all the world around him seemed unreal. He couldn't tell shape from shadow as he stumbled up the path from the river. At last he reached the top and was able to see pale light seeping through shuttered windows. It only confused his vision and made the way between the buildings harder to tread. He cursed himself for not having brought a lantern.

It was only when he came out into an open space that he realized he had gone too far north. He was in the market square of Saint Geraud. At least here there were torches lighting the doorway to a tavern. For a moment, Hubert was tempted to enter. A bowl of beer, did it really matter who brewed it? Was one drink going to keep him from attaining the garden of paradise?

Yes, he told himself sternly. I will not listen to the voices of the demons of doubt. It's time I stopped this foolishness and went to my bed.

He turned decisively to the right, in the direction of the synagogue. As he did, someone burst from a narrow side street and nearly knocked him over. The person didn't bother to stop, but ran across the square and vanished into the night.

Hubert peered into the dark alleyway but neither saw nor

heard anyone else. There was a light flickering at the other end. He made his way down cautiously. Suddenly, the light vanished. He walked more quickly. As he did, he stumbled against something in the path and only barely escaped falling.

He leaned over to see what had nearly tripped him and touched rough wool over flesh. A man! Hubert knelt down, feeling to find out if the person were hurt or simply overcome with wine. His fingers ran over a smooth face up to a head with a bald spot at the crown.

"A cleric," he said. "Your superior will have something to say about your being in this state, my man."

Then he felt the warm sticky liquid just behind the tonsure.

"Oh dear," Hubert said.

That was when the woman screamed.

Four

A crossroads near the synagogue, some time after Compline, the same night.

"Manifestum sit omnibus hominibus . . . hanc cartam audientibus, quod ego Idelfonsus. Comes Tolose, dico . . . quod nullo modo habeo questam neque toltam in civitate Tolosa neque in in surburbio sancti Saturnini, nec in hominbus et feminis qui vel que ibi sunt vel ibi erunt."

Let it be known to all people . . . who hear this charter, that I, Alphonse, count of Toulouse, say . . . that I have no part of the levies and tolls in the city of Toulouse nor in the suburb of St. Sernin, nor of men or women who are or will be here . . .

Charter of Toulouse, July, 1147

$\mathcal{N}$ow there was light all around him. Doors burst open and dogs started barking. Men with torches appeared from nowhere.

"You! Old man!" a deep voice shouted. "Don't move!"

Hubert looked around. Old man? They couldn't mean him. He stood up.

"There's a monk here whose been injured," he called to them. "His head is cut open and he's unconscious, but still alive. He needs help."

The watchmen gathered around Hubert. One bent to examine the body.

"He's not one of ours," he announced. "Anyone here know who he is?"

They all shook their heads, then looked at Hubert.

"I'm only a visitor here," he explained. "I wouldn't know your clerics."

"And what were you doing out so late?" The head watchman asked in suspicion.

"Going back to my bed," Hubert said. "Are you going to send for someone to see to him?"

The watchman signaled to one of the men. "Wake the porter at Saint Étienne and tell him to send some lay brothers and the infirmarian."

The man nodded curtly and left.

"Now, what do you know about this?" The guard was a big man, who knew the value of looming when questioning a suspicious character.

"Nothing." Hubert tried to back away from him, but there was a wall behind. "As I entered the street at that end." He pointed. "Someone rushed by, nearly knocking me down. He may be the one who attacked the monk."

"What did this man look like?"

"I didn't see his face," Hubert said. "If I hadn't heard him coming toward me, we would have collided. He was cloaked, but I don't think he was much bigger than I. That's all I can tell you."

By now the small crossroads was crowded with people, all wanting to know what had happened or giving out their speculations as fact. From windows, others leaned out and added their opinions of this interruption of their sleep.

The watchman cursed as someone ducked under his arm to get a better view of the man lying in the street.

"Ot! Rufus!" he shouted to his campanions. "Move these people back. They'll trample the monk."

Another man was pushing to get through. The watchman started to bar passage but then saw his face.

"*Senhor* Bonysach!" he exclaimed. "I'm glad you're here. I've got an injured monk not of this town and this witness, or perhaps attacker, also a stranger. I don't know who to report to."

Bonysach bent to examine the monk, still bleeding quietly into the hard earth of the street.

"I don't know this cleric, either, Malet," he said. "Although his face is familiar. He must be a visitor at one of the priories. What on earth was he doing out after compline?

"Now, this man"—he nodded in Hubert's direction—"is one of my people, a scholar visiting from Lunel. I can vouch for his character."

"Thank you, *Senhor*. I'm glad to know that, at least. But his story will need investigation just the same. You'll see that he stays in town until the matter is resolved?" Malet asked.

"Of course," Bonysach told him. "I'm sure it will be soon. When the monk regains consciousness, he can tell us what happened."

"Of course." Malet was doubtful. He had seen the wound in the torchlight and it was deep. He turned to Hubert. "You may go, *Senhor*, but be prepared to answer the vicar's summons for questioning."

"I will be. Thank you," Hubert said. "I am staying at the synagogue, if you need me."

He started to leave, but Bonysach caught his arm, leading him away from the center of the crowd, but also in the opposite direction of the synagogue.

"Belide is missing," he told Hubert in a low voice. "We thought she was in the garden with Samuel, but she slipped out instead. We have to find her at once!"

"Of course." Hubert had daughters. He didn't stop to ask who Samuel was or what a girl of that age was doing out at night, hopefully alone. "What can I do?"

Solomon had ignored the furor at the marketplace. Whatever was going on was well attended. If Belide were there, she would be found.

He wasn't sure what to do next. For all he knew, Bonysach had found his daughter among those who had responded to the cry of the watchmen. She may even have been the one who screamed. But something told him that if she were unharmed, she wouldn't have stayed when the crowd started forming. It was better to start from the house. There must be some sign indicating which way she had gone.

As he hesitated, he felt someone coming up behind him.

Solomon pulled his knife from the sheath and spun around.

"No!" There stood Samuel, his hands up in supplication. Solomon relaxed.

"I'm sorry," he told the young man. "I didn't realize that you had followed me. Do you remember anything Belide said or did before she left that might help us find her?"

Samuel shook his head. His face crunched in concentration.

"I was so nervous," he explained. "She was laughing at me, I know. I was relieved to be alone for a few minutes."

"Girls of that age can be unthinkingly cruel," Solomon told him. "Actually all women can. It doesn't mean she doesn't like you. Now, please, think! Anything. Did you hear or see anything odd before she left?"

"An owl hooted," Samuel said. "It had the strangest cry. I looked to see what kind it was but, of course, saw nothing. For some reason, that made her laugh, too."

"Of course!" Solomon put his knife back in the sheath. "Idiot child! Someone signaled to her and she went. Well, if he's still with her when Bonysach finds her, I just pray he's Jewish or he may find out what forced conversion feels like."

Samuel's jaw dropped. "You mean she used me to find a way to go meet a lover? I can't believe it!"

"Actually." Solomon paused. "I can't either. She couldn't have thought there would be time for *joliveté*. I know that in the heat of lust one does insane things, but still . . ."

He thought a moment.

"Samuel, let's go back to the garden and see if we can find some trace of your owl."

At first, Hubert was too stunned by his easy escape from the crowd to focus on what Bonysach was saying.

"I thought surely the guards would accuse me of attacking the monk," he said as they left the square. "A stranger and a Jew. What else did they need?"

"Proof, I would think," Bonysach said shortly. "And I spoke for you. I'm considered one of the leaders of the town, after all."

"Really?" Hubert was impressed. "It would never happen in Paris."

"Another reason not to live there," Bonysach answered, quickening his pace. "I just hope I don't have to raise the cry to find Belide. It would ruin my standing among the other leaders of the Cité if it got about that my daughter had turned whore."

"You don't know that." Hubert was panting as he tried to keep up.

"Why else would she rush out alone into the night?" Bonysach didn't notice that Hubert was falling behind.

To Hubert his friend's voice was distorted, as if under water. He felt as if he were under water, as well, his lungs gasping for air.

"Help!" he managed to force out as he fell.

"Hubert!" Bonysach reached him in time to keep him from collapsing. "Here, lean on me."

"No," Hubert managed to gasp. He leaned forward, letting his head drop until the dizziness passed and he could breath again. "It's nothing, truly. Give me a moment. We must find Belide."

"I must find my daughter," Bonysach said firmly. "You are going back to your room and rest."

Hubert nodded. "Yes. I'm afraid I'll be no use to you. I can find my way back. Don't waste your time on me. She could be in grave danger."

"I know," Bonysach said quietly. "But I can't leave you in this state."

Hubert took a deep breath and stood up straight.

"There," he said. "I told you it was a passing attack. The night air, I suppose. I was down at the river's edge. Stupid of me. Now go, find Belide. And, when you do, don't punish her too severely. I don't think she ran out just for a moment's pleasure."

"It's not like her," Bonysach agreed worriedly. "But her mother says she's been odd lately. I should have listened to her, but Belide seemed no different to me."

"Bonysach," Hubert said. "Stop trying to understand. Just go."

The street was empty, the noise from the crowd fading. Bonysach thought of thieves and cutthroats prowling in the darkness. Hubert was in danger from them but his only daughter much more so.

"I'll come by the *bet midrash* and look in on you as soon as she is safe at home," he promised.

When he had gone, Hubert made his way slowly back to the synagogue. He saw no one on the way.

"Josta, is she back?"

Josta didn't need to answer. Solomon knew from the woman's face that Belide was still missing.

"Forgive me, *Na* Josta," Samuel said. "I should never have let your daughter out of my sight."

"I think someone signaled to her to come out," Solomon told her. "She may have only intended to be gone a few moments."

"Yes," Josta said. "I had figured that out. But something happened."

She clenched her teeth to keep her mouth from trembling. Solomon wanted to say or do something to comfort her but feared that any such gesture would make her break down entirely. So he waited.

With an effort, Josta regained her composure.

"Belide is a good girl," she said. "But she listens too much to all these new songs and stories the wandering *jongleurs* tell. Her head is full of blighted passion and noble sacrifice. As if life didn't give us enough opportunity for that."

"Is there any friend she might be trying to help?" Solomon asked. "Someone she would risk your anger to meet?"

"That's what I've been trying to think!" Josta rubbed her forehead. "Belide has many friends. She sees them at the market or walking by the river. I try to know who they are, but the Christian ones don't often visit."

"What about a boy named Arnald Barleysilk?" Solomon asked. "His father is a salt merchant, I think."

"Yes, I know him," Josta said. "He lives close by. He and Belide played together when they were children but I don't think she's seen him outside of the market since then."

Solomon told her of his meeting with Arnald on the barge. As he did, the worry in Josta's face turned to anger.

"He said that he and Belide were helping Aaron ha-Cohen?" she asked. "That's nonsense! How could they help him? What could Belide and Arnald be plotting?"

"I don't believe they're lovers," Solomon said, trying to reassure her.

"Oh, no." Josta gave a humorless smile. "Belide wouldn't do anything that simple. From what you say, they're still playing some sort of game and Aaron is involved. I thought he, at least had more sense. My servant, Jermana, says that an injured monk has just been found in the street. Is he part of it, too?"

"I don't know; I didn't see him," Solomon said. "I only heard the commotion. Perhaps he was attacked by a robber."

"Monks have no money," Samuel spoke up. "Who would try to steal from one?"

"Maybe it was too dark to tell what he was," Solomon said. "Or perhaps he was set upon by one of these preachers who want to do away with clerics. The point is that I don't think it concerns Belide."

Josta went to fetch her head scarf and shawl.

"Solomon," she said when she returned. "Will you come with me to the salt merchant's house? If Arnald isn't with Belide, he may still know where she has gone."

"And if he is?"

"Then we had better find him before her father does." Josta set a small oil lamp inside a closed lantern and handed it to Solomon. Then she turned to her other guest.

"Samuel," she said. "I apologize profoundly for the behavior of my daughter and, I assure you, she will also do so as soon as she is found. We would be honored if you would return to dine with us on the second night of Pesach."

Samuel seemed taken aback.

"You want me to go now?" he asked. "Shouldn't I stay to help you."

Josta put a hand on his arm. "You have been put out far too much already. We meant only to give you a pleasant break from your studies and look what happened. We'll let you know in the morning if Belide is home."

With a hurt look, Samuel acquiesced, bowed, and left.

"Now." Josta took a deep breath. "Let's go find my daughter."

Brother James was deeply asleep. The rigors of the journey had reminded him that he was no longer young. So it was several minutes before he realized that the man shaking him wasn't part of some troubled nightmare.

"*Adonai!*" he cried, raising one arm to protect himself.

"Brother James! Please wake up!"

James finally became aware of where he was. He opened his eyes. There was a man standing over the bed, not a monk. He carried a small tallow candle that gave off more smoke than light.

"Who are you?" James demanded. "What do you want from me?"

His voice held a quaver of terror.

"It's Marfan, Brother James," the man told him. "I'm the bailiff for the monks here at Saint Pierre. There's been an accident. Your friend, Brother Victor, has been hurt. The prior sent me to take you to him."

James was now fully awake. "Victor! What happened?"

He looked over at the bed next to his. It was empty.

"I don't know exactly," Marfan told him. "A watchman from the Cité arrived a few moments ago. He said that a monk had been attacked in the street. They took him to Saint Étienne, but he wasn't from there. The watchman has been going from one priory to the next to find who had strangers staying with them. Brother Victor is the only one missing."

"Attacked? I don't understand." James fumbled with the laces on his sandals. "What was he doing out of the priory?"

He stopped. "*Senhor* Marfan," he said. "Could you wait for me in the porter's alcove? I'll only be a moment."

As soon as the bailiff had left, James went to the pack Victor had brought with him. During the day, Victor always carried the gold in bags tied to a belt under his robes. He had taken the belt off and put it in the pack before going to bed. James felt for it in the darkness. When he reached inside, his hand touched one of the bags, the coins solid under his fingers. He exhaled in relief. Whatever Brother Victor had been doing, it wasn't because he had succumbed to cupidity. He hurried to where Marfan was waiting.

"I'm sorry to keep you," he said when he rejoined the bailiff. "I was still stupefied by sleep. Now, can you tell me more about what happened? How seriously was Victor hurt?"

"The watchman said he took a blow to the head," Marfan told him. "Knocked him out cold, but the watchman said he'd seen worse. He'll probably be awake by the time we get there."

"*Gratia Deo!*" James made the sign of the cross. Marfan did likewise.

The streets were now completely deserted. Even the taverns were quiet, the last customer having been thrown out or rolled under a table to await the dawn. A cat leapt silently from a wall, intent on chasing a rat. The motion startled James and he quickened his pace. It was less than a mile to the church of Saint Étienne but it seemed to the monk as if they were trapped in an unnatural shadow from which they would never escape.

Marfan was unaware of the fancies of his companion. He assumed the monk was praying for the welfare of his friend. So he was surprised at the joy with which James greeted the sight of the lantern at the gate to the church of Saint Jacques, at the back of Saint Étienne.

"Ah, the porter is waiting for us, no doubt," he said. "I'll leave you then. I'm sure they'll give you a place to rest the remainder of the night. I hope Brother Victor is recovered by now. Good night to you."

James rang at the gate and a moment later it was opened, not by the porter but by a fellow monk.

"You must be here about the injured man," he said.

James nodded. "Brother Victor, of Moissac," he said. "We only arrived today. How is he?"

"I'll take you to him," the monk said.

Solomon had some qualms about waking a respectable salt merchant and his family in the middle of the night but Josta didn't hesitate. She pounded loudly on the thick door, waited a moment, then pounded again.

"Give them time to put on a robe," Solomon told her.

But the door opened at once. The man facing them was wide awake and fully, if hastily, dressed.

"Josta," Vidian said. "You've come for Belide. It's all right; she's here."

He led them up the stairs to the family chamber.

"I've been trying to get some sense out of them," he said as they climbed. "But neither one is talking. They've had a fright, I'm sure, but aren't hurt."

"Belide will be soon," Josta promised, "for the fright she's given me."

"I don't blame you," Vidian said. "But wait a bit. She seems to be punishing herself quite effectively."

He opened the door.

Belide sat by a coal brazier, a blanket around her shoulders and a bowl in her hands. On the other side sat Arnald, devouring a leg of chicken. When they saw Josta and Solomon, both of them stood.

"It's all my fault, *Na* Josta," Arnald began.

"No, Mother, I was the one who talked him into it," Belide insisted.

Josta glared at her daughter from the doorway but Solomon noticed that her hands weren't clenched, but open, as if she desired nothing more than to hold Belide in her arms.

However, her words were not of comfort.

"You have shamed yourself and your family by your actions tonight," Josta said. "You will now apologize to *Senhor* Vidian for disturbing his rest. Then we shall go home."

"*Na* Josta." Arnald put an arm around Belide, forgetting the drumstick he still held. "I swear to you by all the saints that your daughter is blameless in this."

Josta sighed. "Arnald, don't perjure yourself. Belide, come. We shall discuss this at home."

Arnald was about to protest but Belide gave him a warning look. She handed him the blanket and bowl, then bowed to Arnald's father.

"*Senhor* Vidian," she said. "I humbly beg your forgiveness for the trouble I've caused. Thank you for taking me in at this hour and for the warm broth. Please don't be angry with Arnald. He has done nothing wrong."

Vidian shook his head. "If that is so, then I want to know what the pair of you did do."

Belide and Arnald looked at each other and then at the floor.

"You see?" Vidian turned to Josta and Solomon. "And they expect us to trust them. Take your girl home, Josta. Maybe you and Bonysach can get the story from her."

As they were leaving, Arnald spoke up.

"Solomon, is Brother Victor all right?"

"Arnald!" Belide cried.

Solomon raised his eyebrows. "If you mean the man who was attacked, I don't know. And I'm sure your father will want you to tell us how you know his name when no one else seems to."

But Arnald was taking his orders from Belide.

"I can't tell you," he said. "I swore an oath."

Vidian snorted his disgust. "What do you think you are, boy, some knight on a mission?"

"No, Father," Arnald said miserably. "But I still can't tell."

"Then I believe we should take our leave," Solomon bowed.

Vidian said nothing as he took them back to the door to the street. Just before he let them out, he stopped and looked at Belide. She seemed more pitiful than defiant, her large brown eyes glittering with tears.

"If my son has dishonored you in any way, girl, say so," he told her.

"Oh, no!" Belide clasped her hands. "He is the most noble, self-sacrificing man I know. Please don't punish him!"

Vidian threw up his hands.

"*Forssenat*, the both of them!" he said. "Good luck in getting any sense out of her."

He shut the door.

Solomon saw them back to the house. Josta walked in front, her back stiff with anger and mortification. Belide followed, occasionally sniffing back tears. He felt acutely uncomfortable. This was a private matter. As soon as he had seen them through the gate, he thanked Josta for the dinner and turned to go.

"At this hour?" she asked. "All the way back to the street of the *blanchisseurs*? Nonsense. We can make a bed for you here for what's left of the night."

"I'm sure you don't need me in your house now," he said.

At this moment the door opened.

Bonysach didn't say a word. He just took Belide in his arms and held her tightly, tears streaming down his face.

"I'm sorry, Papa." Belide wept. "I'm so very, very sorry."

"Was she harmed?" Bonysach mouthed to Josta.

His wife shook her head. Bonysach lifted his face.

"May the Holy One be praised and thanked for the safe return of my child," he said.

"Amen," Josta agreed. Then she gave them a push into the hallway.

"Now, everyone to bed," she continued. "I do not want to hear another sound until the first cock crows."

Brother James sat by the still figure in the infirmary bed.

"I don't understand," he said for the tenth time. "What was he doing out there?"

"Perhaps some errand for the prior?" the infirmarian suggested. "The porter at Saint Pierre thought Prior Stephen shouldn't be disturbed so late but we can ask him in the morning."

"But Victor will be awake by then, surely," James said. "He can tell us himself. Isn't that true?"

He looked up at the infirmarian, who bit his lip in worry.

"I've done all I can," he said. "It's little enough, a compress of herbs to reduce the swelling and draw out any poison from the wound. There is blood in the white of his eyes. I fear that it indicates an excess of malevolent humors pressing against the inside of his skull."

"Can't you stop it?" James asked. He had an image of Brother Victor's head expanding like a pig bladder until it exploded.

The monk rubbed his hands. "I've heard that trepanning might release the noxious fumes building up and reduce the pressure, but I've never done it, nor am I allowed to take a knife to another human being. You know that."

"But there must be a doctor in Toulouse who isn't a cleric!" James persisted.

"Yes," the infirmarian said slowly. "The best one is Master Mosse. His home isn't far from here.

"Mosse," James repeated. "A Jew."

"He's a very good physician," the infirmarian said. "Last year he cauterized our sacristan's hemorrhoids with hardly any pain, he said. Brother Ugo can't praise him enough."

James clenched his teeth. "Are you certain that cutting a hole in Brother Victor's skull will save him?"

"No, I'm only certain that, if it isn't done, he'll die," the monk answered simply. "Barring a miracle, of course," he added.

Brother James bent over Victor. His breathing was so faint that James could barely hear it. His face was calm and empty, as if his soul had already departed.

"There must be another way," James muttered. "God would not deliver me to my enemies now."

"What was that?" The infirmarian came closer. "Do you want me to send for Mosse?"

"No," James answered. "Not yet. I will sit with Victor, to watch and pray. When the prior comes, he must decide."

The infirmarian looked doubtful but Brother James seemed adamant. And perhaps, the monk considered, it was better to pray for a miracle than to seek the help of an infidel. Although, he reflected, Brother Ugo had been glad that, when prayers failed, Master Mosse had been there to relieve his suffering.

James knelt by the bed, his eyes riveted on the cross hanging above it.

"Please, Lord, if this is a test of my resolve, don't let Victor be the price," he begged. "He's all I have!"

God mustn't let Victor die. Not when James needed him so much. Victor's faith was clear and pure. He was beyond being a good Christian. He was simply a good man. James had spent the first half of his life trying to decipher the word of the Lord, to find the hidden message that would make sense of this world. He had spent the second half in rejection of that search, trying instead to open his heart to God's will and accept it without question.

He feared this would end in failure, as well.

There were preachers in Provence these days, illegal of course and undoubtedly heretical, who said that all flesh was created by Satan and the greatest blessing one could ask would be to be freed from it and allow the spirit to return to the Creator. That was wrong; it had to be. And yet . . .

James pressed his fingers hard against his forehead and cheeks, trying to force out the momentary doubt. Over and over, he repeated the Credo. "I believe in God the Father and in his only son, Jesus Christ, I believe in . . . Dear Lord, please save Brother Victor. If You do not, I shall still believe but, if You do, then I can be sure."

He prayed unceasingly through the night but to no avail. Sometime between Matins and Lauds, well before dawn, Brother Victor's spirit slipped away.

Solomon woke to the shouts of the twins as they came into the hall and found him curled up on a makeshift bed.

"What are you here for?" Muppim asked. "Did you drink too much to find your way home?"

Solomon pulled the blanket over his head. "Go away," he grunted.

Huppim tugged at the blanket. "Does that mean you're going to marry our sister?"

"No!"

Solomon swatted at the child, but Huppim avoided the blow easily. Both boys retreated, however, lured on toward the kitchen by the smell of fresh bread.

Solomon rolled over, his face to the wall and tried to return to sleep. His head ached as though he had drunk a vat. If only he had stayed with Gavi. The tanner was an uncomplicated host, glad of anyone who would brave the stench of his work to enjoy his company.

The household was rousing now. There was clatter from the kitchen and thumps from the upper floors as people prepared for the day. There was nothing else for it. Solomon swung his legs off the bed and hunted for his tunic and boots.

Josta entered just as he was folding the bed against the wall. She was dressed carefully but her drawn face showed that she had slept little, if at all.

"Belide has been forbidden to come down," she told him. "Until she explains her actions last night. She's up there like a martyr with the knife at her throat, insisting that she swore to tell no one."

"Well, it doesn't sound like a lover's tryst." Solomon yawned. "Pardon me."

"No, I beg your pardon, for keeping you up so late and for bringing you into this," Josta said. "I don't know what is the matter with the girl."

A thought crossed Solomon's mind. Should he even suggest

it? Josta was worried enough, but she should be warned, just in case.

"Is it possible that Belide is planning to convert?"

He regretted his words when he saw the horror on Josta's face.

"Oh, no!" she said. "Belide would never . . . never . . . oh no!"

But they both knew it was a convincing explanation. Why else would a monk agree to meet with a Jewish girl in the middle of the night? What else could be such a horrible secret that she had to hide it from her parents?

"Josta!" Solomon reached out to steady her. "Here, sit down. I may be completely wrong. I'm sure Belide is a good, pious young woman."

"Of course." Josta tried to calm the fear in her stomach. "There must be another reason. But I am going to ask her, all the same. I'll know by her face, even if she denies it."

"It seems that I've disrupted your life far more than you have mine," Solomon said sadly. "Let me know if I can help you in any way. I'll take my leave now. No, don't worry, I'll get a *gastel* from the baker to break my fast. Tell Bonysach that I'll see him later. I'll be at the house of study to visit my uncle this afternoon. If you'll permit it, I'll come by afterwards."

"Of course." Josta gave him her hand. "Thank you, Solomon." She gave him a wan smile. "If you continue acting in such a kind and responsible matter, I may reconsider your suitability as a son-in-law."

Solomon was glad to see she could still tease him.

"I promise you, *Na* Josta," he said. "This is only a temporary improvement. Tomorrow I shall be as dissolute as ever."

Brother James was too numbed by the shock of Victor's death to understand what the men around him were saying. Expressions of sorrow, platitudes on the release from earthly pain, promises of prayers, the words skimmed over him like gulls chasing a wave.

Finally, someone took him by the shoulders and led him to another room where he was given a hot drink, after which he slept.

Later the prior and his fellow monks from Moissac came for James and took him back to Saint Pierre des Cuisines. He was sent to his bed in the dortor. A few moments later, Prior Stephen came in.

"You needn't worry about anything," his superior told him. "Brother Victor's body is being taken back to Moissac. You may go with him, if you like. We'll find someone else to make your journey."

This brought James briefly to awareness.

"No, of course not," he said. "Victor believed in it; I must complete the mission. Those men may die if we don't reach them soon."

"True," the prior admitted. "And your ability to converse with the Saracens would be a great help. But it's not worth risking your health. We can make a final decision later. Now you must rest."

Rest? That wasn't right. "Oh, no," James insisted. "I mustn't ever rest. Constant vigilance is required. I can't relax my guard a moment."

The bells began to ring. James looked about in panic.

"What is the hour?" he asked.

"Sext," the prior answered. "You didn't sleep long."

"I did!" James cried. "I missed two of the Offices. I must join the others."

The prior put a hand on his shoulder, keeping James from rising from the cot.

"You are excused for the day." He made it a command. "If you wish, you may repeat the psalms from your bed. I'll send someone later with a calming *tisane*. Drink it all."

James did his best to obey. He lay still, reciting the Office of Sext. The hardest thing he had had to learn was to use the Latin version of the psalms. When he was anxious or tired, the Hebrew kept coming into his mind. He concentrated harder.

Just as the bells tolled the end of the Office, James remembered something. Looking around to be sure no one was watching from the doorway, he got up and went over to where Brother Victor's pack lay, just as it had the night before.

James took out the belt with the bags of money. Even here he felt better keeping it in his own care. He shook it out, preparing to wrap it around his waist. He stopped.

Brother Victor had been carrying six bags, each holding ten gold coins.

Now there were only four.

Five

The home of Bonysach, Sunday, (March 28) 1148, 29 Adar II 4908. Passion Sunday, Feast of Saint Ambrose, who tried to convince the pope not to rebuild a synagogue in Rome burnt by zealous Christians. The pope did it anyway.

> "'Bella,' fich m'ieu, 'pois jois reviu
> ben nos devem apareillar.'
> 'Non devem, don, 'que d'als pensiu
> ai mon coratage e mon affar.'"

> "'Lovely girl,' I said. "Since joy awakens
> [in the spring] we ought to become a pair.'
> 'No, we shouldn't sir, for there are other things
> that fill my heart and thoughts.'"

> —Marcabru,
> *L'autrier, a l'issuda d'abriu*

*S*he's been up there two days now," Josta fretted. "I don't think this punishment is going to work."

"Has Arnald's family had any better luck?" Solomon asked.

"I spoke to his mother, Maria, Friday before the Sabbath started," Josta said. "He hadn't confessed to anything yet. He won't say where he met Belide or why they were out. Maria thinks he's trying to act 'noble,' like the heroes in those stupid *gestes*. She told him he's better off as a salt merchant who doesn't keep things from his mother. She's as close to wit's end as I am."

"Do Arnald and Belide know that the poor monk has died?" Hubert asked.

"They do." Bonysach looked out into the courtyard, where rain was pooling in the hollows of the flagstones. "It seems to make them even more determined to keep silent."

He drummed his fingers on the arm of his chair.

"They can't have had anything to do with the attack," Solomon said. "Whatever they're hiding, it's not criminal."

"How can I be sure?" Bonysach said. His drumming grew more staccato. "They shouldn't even have known the monk's name! No one else in town recognized him. The man entered the monastery as a child and his parents are long dead."

He sighed. "I have to meet with the other good men of the town and Bourg tomorrow to discuss how we can make the streets

safer for clergy out after dark. The monks at Cuisines have demanded that we find the perpetrator but even they know that's
nearly impossible. He could be anyone, most likely some cut-
throat pretending to be a pilgrim."

"So you see about getting more watchmen," Solomon said.
"Suggest to the monks that they keep a closer eye on their visi-
tors. And that will be an end to the matter."

Bonysach wasn't assured. "But what if Belide was nearby
when the man was attacked and someone saw her?"

"They would have spoken up by now," Josta said. "Wouldn't
they?"

"Perhaps," Bonysach said.

"What if she or this Arnald saw someone else?" Hubert asked
suddenly.

They all looked at him.

"I'm sorry," he said. "But they might have seen the man who
hit the monk. They knew he was hurt, you said. I only caught a
glimpse of a figure in the dark but they might have been where
they could see him. What if he was someone they could identify?"

"You think their silence is from fear?" Josta eyes grew wide
at the idea.

"It's possible," Solomon considered. "For themselves or for
someone else."

Josta threw up her hands.

"I can't endure this any longer," she stated. "I'm bringing her
down and beating the truth out of her, if I must."

Bonysach reached out and caught her arm as she stood.

"My dear, you know very well that you would stop at the first
cry she made," he said.

"But we must do something!" She was at the edge of tears.

Solomon sighed.

"Would you like me to try?" he asked. "Both Belide and Arnald told me that they wanted my help. I didn't speak of it before

because I promised them my silence until Aaron returns from Bordeaux. He seems to be a part of it, too."

"Aaron?" Bonysach looked at him. "But he's a respectable trader. What would he be doing plotting with these children?"

"Perhaps that's one thing I could ask her," Solomon said.

Stephen, prior of Saint Pierre des Cuisines, and, Rodger, prior of Saint Pierre of Moissac were old friends. They had been novices together and so it was a relief to both of them to be able to consult about the unfortunate tragedy.

"James is taking the death of Brother Victor very hard," Stephen said. "Do you think he's capable of concentrating on the task ahead?"

"Brother James does not make friends easily," Rodger explained. "Of course we are all brothers in Christ, but James is very severe with himself and others. We try to overlook it. All the same, I think that Victor was the first person in years who really got close to James. It's no wonder he grieves for the boy."

"They weren't 'special' friends?" Stephen asked worriedly.

"Oh, no! Not at all!" Rodger said. "More as if Victor were the son James never had. He was proud of the boy and saw a great future for him. Now, that's shattered. But it makes him all the more determined to fulfill Victor's goal."

"And the missing gold?" Stephen asked. "What shall we do about that?"

Rodger shook his head. "It does credit to Brother James that he told us at once about its loss. I think that either Victor took it with him when he went out and his attacker stole it or that someone here at Saint Pierre took the bags from his belongings. If it involves a venal monk then we must deal with the matter privately."

"And if not?"

"That," Rodger said, "is much more troubling. We still don't know what made Victor leave his bed without permission. Could he have planned to steal the gold himself? What if he delivered it to a confederate, who then disposed of him? And why arrange a meeting so late, when a lone monk would be remarked upon and questioned? It makes no sense."

"I know," Stephen agreed. "In any case, it's up to the abbot to decide if Brother James should be allowed to complete the mission. The messenger should return from Moissac within the next day or two. Until then, we shall continue with preparations for the journey. Do we have any volunteers to go in Brother Victor's place?"

They discussed the details for some time. However, when Stephen got up to leave, Prior Rodger had one more matter to discuss.

"Whoever we pick will have to be aware of the temptation that Brother James will be exposed to on this journey."

Stephen nodded. "I understand that James has always shown himself to be a most devout Christian and your abbot is confident that he is safe even among those who were once his people, but there's always the possibility . . ."

" 'Like a dog to it's own vomit,' " Rodger quoted. "I know. It were better that he lose his life than his soul. You might impress that upon the man assigned to go with him."

After his summons to the priory, where he learned of the change in plans, the soldier, Jehan, returned to the cheap inn where he and Berengar were staying. He ordered bread, beer, and soup and sat down to wait.

It didn't take long. He'd barely finished the soup when the first man came in. He was lean and watchful. He spotted Jehan at once but didn't approach him until the innkeeper had pointed him out.

Jehan invited him to share the beer.

"I hear you're looking for men who can fight," the new arrival said. "Where and who for?"

"First, I need to know a few things about you," Jehan said. "Do you owe service to any lord hereabouts?"

"Nah." The man took the offered bowl and drank deeply. "I fought for the Count of Foix last year but finished my time with nothing much to show for it. A man told me to go south. Count Ramón is gathering an army to lay siege to Tortosa, they say. But I don't know that I want to be in an army again."

"It wasn't to my taste, either," Jehan agreed. "You have your own horse and weapons?"

"I do." The man grimaced. "That horse is worth twice as much as I am. The one thing I brought out of the Count's war. So, what's the job?"

"Simple." Jehan smiled. "Get a pair of monks through Spain to Valencia and back."

"What!" The man rocked back on the bench. "That's Saracen land. What reason could there be for monks to go there? If they plan to preach to the infidels, I'll have no part of it. The Saracens don't just kill people who try to convert them; they cut off bits beforehand and feed them to their dogs. Then they burn you as a sacrifice to their gods."

Jehan looked at him in disgust. "You know nothing but rumors and stories from the bottom of a mug. I've spent the past two years down there and I know what they're like. I've fought against them and with them, under King Alfonso Enríquez. They're a strange people, it's true. Almost as bad as Jews in their commandments about food. Worse, if you count the ones who don't drink wine. But they have no idols that I've seen. Instead they think we do, with all our statues of the Virgin and the saints."

The man looked at him in suspicion. "What are you?" he asked.

"A soldier," Jehan answered shortly. "And I've killed enough men to know that all blood is red. I also have lived long enough not to trust any one on either side. Have you?"

The man stood.

"I don't know what you're paying for this folly," he said. "And I don't want to. I don't travel with madmen."

The few others in the tavern glanced at them briefly and then returned to their own business. The first applicant stalked out.

Jehan started on his bread, now softened by the last of the soup.

Two more men came by, but one wanted too much for the job and the other looked as though he'd cut their throats the first night out. Jehan ordered more beer and glanced at the man sitting in the corner.

Jehan had noticed the man some time before. He had ordered one pitcher of beer and was drinking it slowly. The purse he had shaken the sliver of coin from looked empty. He fidgeted with the bowl, tapping it on the table in an annoying cadence. Occasionally, he would look quickly in Jehan's direction, then away. Jehan wondered when he'd find the courage to come over.

Finally the constant tapping got on his nerves. Jehan rose and went to him. As he approached, he noted that the man's clothes were worn, but of good quality, especially the boots. His tunic was closed with a tarnished silver brooch that had lost its stones. Under the tunic, there was the glint of mail, well oiled and polished.

"You've been watching me," he said without preamble. "I'm going to Valencia to ransom knights taken in battle with the Saracen. Will you come with me?"

The man gave a surly look, as though he would refuse. Then the look turned to shame.

"I can't," he said into his cup. "I don't have a horse anymore."

Jehan studied him. "Lose him in a tournament?"

The man gave a short laugh. "Me? I don't go to those things. If you have to know, I lost him at dice. All or nothing."

"But you kept your sword and mail," Jehan noted.

"I'd wager my mother before my sword," the man replied.

Jehan sat down across from him.

"If a horse were provided," he asked. "Would you take the commission? Payment in gold to you or your family by the abbey of Cluny at Saint Pierre of Moissac."

The man tried not to show his eagerness, but it was evident in the way his shoulders relaxed as if a burden had been lifted from them. Jehan had been right in gauging the contents of his purse.

"When do we leave?" he asked.

"Shortly after Easter." Jehan held out his hand. "Now, what is the name of my new sergeant?"

"Guy of Anjou." Guy took the offered hand. "A free man of decent birth and no prospects."

"Jehan of Blois." Jehan smiled. "The same."

Solomon was having a much more difficult confrontation. Belide had been brought downstairs and now sat facing him. Her expression was a mixture of fear and defiance. How was he to get her to confide in him?

He took a straight back chair from by the empty hearth, spun it around and straddled it so that he could rest his arms on the top. He looked over them at the quivering girl.

"What's wrong?" he asked. "Do you think your cowardly parents have delegated me to whip you until you tell all?"

To his surprise, she nodded.

Solomon laughed. "Well, they probably should have. You're acting like a child too young to understand reason. Now, you and Arnald both say that this adventure you have undertaken was concocted by Aaron, the horse trader, right? Well, I don't believe you. I've known Aaron since you were in swaddling and he's not one for mysterious plots and sneaking about by night. Nor would he ask you to do anything that might endanger your life."

"I wasn't in danger!" she blurted out.

"Oh?" Solomon leaned forward, tipping the chair precariously toward her. "A man died. It could have been you. Did you see who hit him?"

"No, I had already gone by then . . ." Belide clapped her hand over her mouth.

Solomon let the chair fall back with a satisfied thud.

"So." He smiled. "You left a guest in your garden to run out into the night in order to meet a black monk. Or was it both Arnald and the monk? And you wonder why your parents are angry with you? What would you think if a child of yours behaved like that?"

Slowly, realization swept through Belide. Her mouth dropped open and a deep blush rose from her neck to her forehead.

"Oh, Solomon! They can't think that I was going to convert and marry Arnald?" she said. "That's ridiculous! I would never do such a thing!"

"I'm glad to hear it," Solomon told her. "And your parents will be, as well. But that still leaves the problem. What were you up to with two Christian men in the middle of the night?"

Gloom settled on her again as she slumped on her stool. She sat for a moment, biting her upper lip. Finally, she came to a decision.

"I can't tell you everything, because I don't know it," she muttered at the floor.

Solomon got up and came to kneel beside her. He felt like a priest waiting for a confession. The thought made him queasy.

"How did you know Brother Victor?" he asked quietly.

"I didn't," Belide said. "I only met him briefly in the square.

He seemed a good man, for a monk. He comes from near here. Arnald and Aaron were both friends of his. When he went to Moissac, Arnald asked him for advice. He offered to help. At least that's what Arnald said. I think his sympathy was genuine. Look at the risk he took, leaving his cloister so late at night."

"Belide." Solomon's voice held a warning. "Help you do what?"

Belide sank even lower.

"Rescue a woman from the white monks in Spain."

"What?" Of all the possibilities Solomon had considered, this wasn't even on the list.

"Aaron told us. He knows her. She was taken by the Genoese last fall, when they raided Almeria," Belide said. "She was then sold as a slave and brought to Catalonia and now some white monks have her, but Aaron doesn't yet know where."

"Belide, you can't have this right." Solomon took her shoulders and pulled her up to face him. "I don't much care for monks of any sort, but I'm fairly certain that they don't buy female slaves to slake their lust, as least not officially."

"I only know what Aaron said," Belide insisted. "Brother Victor was going on a mission to Spain to ransom Christian knights from the Ishmaelites. Arnald told him about this woman and he said he would help."

"But what have you to do with it?" Solomon was completely baffled.

"Well." The blush started again. "Brother Victor could only get away after the other monks had gone to sleep. Arnald was worried about the watch stopping him on the way to the meeting."

"He's had trouble with the watch?" Solomon asked.

"A couple of times," she admitted. "They caught him taking stones out of the Saracen wall to block the creek that goes past the Senoris tower. But Raimon Senoris deserved to be flooded!

He's an arrogant pig! And there was something about climbing up the tower of the Roaix and pissing off the top last Saint Martin's day. His aim was very good."

"I see." Solomon coughed explosively. "Sorry. So Arnald doesn't get on with the nobles in town. No wonder he didn't want to be caught out alone. You came along to protect him?"

"Well," she said earnestly. "If a watchman came by, he could say he was just making sure I got home safely, you see."

"Of course." Solomon stared at her, trying to remember if he had been this foolish at seventeen. A quick rummage through his memory told him he had been much worse.

"I wanted to help," she insisted. "It was my idea. Arnald's father had told him that if he got into any more trouble, he wouldn't buy the *casal* Arnald wants next to the one Aaron's sister owns. He's going to start growing his own vines and sell wine to the monks. But he can only do it if his father permits him to use the money."

This was getting too complicated for Solomon.

"So," he interrupted, "you and Arnald were both acting in a spirit of pure goodness and charity. Therefore, you feel your punishment is totally undeserved."

"That's right." Belide smiled at him. "Can't you just tell my parents that, without going into the details?"

Solomon stood, glad of the chance to stretch. He looked down at Belide.

"I'll tell them that you have done nothing that will shame your family," he told her. "But my recommendation will be that you not be allowed out alone until you are either well past thirty or safely wed."

Ignoring her indignant protests, Solomon went to reassure Bonysach and Josta. Then he set out to find Arnald. He might not be allowed to speak with the boy, but he had to try. If his help was being asked for this bizarre quest, he needed to know more than Belide could tell him.

"You sent for me, Father?" Brother James stood at the doorway to the chapter of Saint Pierre des Cuisines. Prior Rodger beckoned him to enter.

"Sit down, please," he said. "I know you haven't slept well the past few nights. You must be tired. Prior Stephen and I are concerned that this tragedy will affect your ability to complete this mission. Perhaps we should consider letting you return to Moissac and finding someone in Spain to interpret for us."

James had sat as requested but the prior's words caused him to leap up again.

"No! You mustn't replace me!" he begged. "I'm perfectly able to do this. It's not only my duty to those poor captives, but also what I owe Brother Victor's memory. If I don't go, I will have failed him."

"Calm yourself, my brother," Rodger said. "You know that Victor would not want you to ruin your health out of a sense of obligation to him. We were concerned about how well you could endure the journey even before this sad event. Forgive me, but you are not a young man, you know."

James tried to stop the shaking in his hands. Of course he knew. By his reckoning, he was sixty-two this summer. But he wasn't infirm or feeble. Perhaps he was more tired after a day in the saddle than he had been in his youth. That was all. He told the prior as much.

Rodger looked at the man before him. James was of middle height, lean from fasting and work. The fringe of his tonsure had more black than gray in it. His eyes were alert and he could still read a page without squinting. Rodger suspected that James was more able to stand a journey than he, at least physically.

"Very well," he conceded. "There's no doubt that your skills will be needed. Prior Stephen and I need to nominate another monk to accompany you. Is there anyone you would prefer?"

James exhaled in relief. He could not have endured the shame of being left behind. As for someone to take Brother Victor's place . . .

"I can think of no one," he said. "I shall abide by your wisdom."

"Good. You may leave then. May our Lord bless you." Prior Rodger dismissed him.

James stayed where he was.

"Yes?" Rodger asked.

"Have you heard anything?" James blurted. "About the man who killed Victor? What is being done to capture him?"

"The bailiff of Saint Pierre has met with the count's guards and the Good Men of Toulouse," Rodger told him. "As I understand it, they are at a loss. None of the inns or shelters for pilgrims reported anyone returning after hours that night. Nor was anyone missing the next morning that they know of. All strangers in town have been accounted for."

"What about the man found with him?" James asked.

"He was vouched for by both one of the citizens of the town and the leader of the synagogue," Rodger said. "Apparently quite a harmless old scholar. The watchman didn't think him capable of striking a blow hard enough to break a man's skull."

"He was a Jew?" James jaw tightened. "Why did no one tell me this?"

Rodger knew he had to tread carefully here.

"There was no need to mention it," he said lightly. "All agreed that he had nothing to do with the incident."

"Then why was he out so late?" James countered.

"A desire to walk out a philosophical quandary," Rodger said. "I understand that it's not an unusual habit among scholars."

James was forced to admit that it was the case. He had often done the same thing, himself, in the days when he had wrestled with the inconsistencies of the Law. But a plausible excuse was still just that, nothing more.

"He may have had a partner to strike the blow," James continued. "Perhaps his apparent weakness was intended to lure Victor to the spot where his murderer waited. Have his goods been searched for the missing gold?"

Rodger paused. He didn't know. "I'll ask the bailiff to find out," he said.

James took a step forward.

"Why don't you let me question him?" he asked. "I know these people. I know their tricks. I'd soon find out if he was lying."

The prior was at a loss as to how to answer. He remembered the incident a few years before, when James had tried to convict a Jew of murdering one of their monks. That had ended in embarrassment for the abbey and a scandal regarding the dead man's past. And yet, James's questions were valid.

The bell over their head began to toll, causing both men to start.

"None already!" Prior Rodger exclaimed. "We must be on our way to the chapel."

"But the Jew," James said. "Will you let me speak with him?"

"I must consult with Prior Stephen and the bailiff," Rodger said. "This isn't our town. We must abide by their customs. I shall give you the decision as soon as possible."

With that, James had to be content.

Solomon found Arnald in the marketplace sitting glumly in front of an assortment of salt cones. He brightened when he saw Solomon.

"How is Belide?" he asked.

"Languishing in her cell," Solomon answered. "But otherwise unharmed. Whatever possessed you to bring her into this insane rescue plot of yours?"

"Hush!" Arnald looked around to see if anyone was listening. "What did she tell you? Do her parents know?"

"Everything and not yet," Solomon answered. "Although why they shouldn't is inexplicable to me. As is your part in it."

"Aaron is my best friend," Arnald said simply. "He would have gone alone to Spain and stormed the place where this woman is being held. I persuaded him that he'd only be killed. Victor is . . . was . . . another friend. Both Aaron and I knew him before he decided to turn religious. I thought he might have a better plan."

"And did he?" Solomon could feel himself being pulled in but his curiosity was too strong to resist.

"He thought we should try to buy her back," Arnald said. His disappointment was obvious.

Solomon relaxed. "A much more sensible idea. So that's why Aaron is in Bordeaux selling horses so early in the year? I thought it was for his wedding to Mayah. Why is a man about to be wed concerning himself with the fate of another woman?"

Arnald began to fuss with the cones, rearranging them on their trays.

"I think she may be a relative," he told Solomon, his eyes on his work. "He didn't tell you?"

"No," Solomon snapped.

He could tell that Arnald wasn't giving him the whole truth but couldn't think of the right question to make him spill it.

"I'm surprised that your father has allowed you out," he said instead.

"He has other ways of keeping me on a short tether," Arnald answered, his shoulders drooping.

"Ah, yes, your vineyard," Solomon said. "Belide told me. Why don't you earn the money for it, yourself?"

"I have," Arnald said. "But until I'm twenty-five, my father has the last word on what I do with it. Isn't that the custom where you come from?"

"Not that I know of," Solomon answered. "So you risked your future when you agreed to help Aaron."

"I told you," Arnald said. "He would do the same for me."

"But why didn't Aaron go to the community?" The secrecy of it was what puzzled Solomon. "You know we ransom our own."

"Aaron said that he couldn't," Arnald answered.

Solomon knew that he would get no more from him. He wished Aaron in the darkest level of *sheol* for setting this nonsense in motion, but not until he had returned to explain everything.

"Solomon!" Arnald called as he turned to go. "Will you take a message to Belide for me? Tell her I'm proud of her and that I'm sorry. Please?"

"Very well," Solomon said. "But I won't see her until tomorrow. I'm going to have a word with my uncle and then spend a peaceful evening with my friend, Gavi."

"Berengar, I want you to meet the third member of our party, Guy of Anjou." Jehan had found the new man a place at the inn where they were staying. "He says he can fight and I've just tested his skill with a bow. All he needs is a horse. Will your monks provide one?"

Berengar looked Guy up and down. If he was intimidated by being in the company of two such battle-hardened men, he didn't show it.

"If they don't, I'll find him one, myself," he promised. "I've not had such luck as you. All the knights of the town have either left with Count Alphonse for the Holy Land or they are preparing to join the army of Count Ramón and lay siege to Tortosa."

"No one will help in freeing their brothers in arms?" Guy asked. "Have they no honor?"

"They tell me we're on a fool's errand," Berengar said. "They would rather liberate them through battle than with money."

Jehan snorted. "They try that and the first missiles sent over the city walls will be the heads of the hostages. I know."

Guy nodded agreement. "I saw much the same in Normandy, and we were fighting other Christians. Who knows what Saracens will do to their prisoners?"

"Don't worry," Jehan told the boy. "We'll be able to find more men to act as guards before we cross into Spain. Not everyone wants to be at the mercy of some nobleman who doesn't want to fight if it's wet out."

"That's right," Guy said. "And, if it's anything like the north, there's many a man who won't follow this Ramon because of something his father did to their grandmother."

Berengar grinned. "That's true enough."

"What about the death of Brother Victor?" Jehan asked. "Will that change matters? I've not heard that anyone has been arrested for the crime."

"The word is that it was some drunken pilgrim," Berengar said. "There isn't much chance of finding him. I spoke with Prior Rodger this morning after Mass and he said we owed it to Brother Victor's memory to complete his task."

"I'm sure his soul will guide us." Jehan crossed himself, as did the other two.

"He was a saintly man," Berengar said. "I never met anyone so willing to believe the best of people."

"That's a good way to get oneself killed," Guy remarked. "I'm glad I'm a suspicious bastard."

"Amen," Jehan said.

"Come in, Solomon." Gavi was delighted to see him. "We were beginning to wonder if you had found a more pleasant place to stay."

"Thank you, Gavi." Solomon entered the house. "A blessing upon you for taking me in again. Your home is a haven to me in an insane world."

"It sounds as though you need beer and a nice roast chicken." Nazara laughed.

"Chicken this early in the year?" Solomon asked. "I hope you didn't kill a hen just for me."

"She stopped laying over the winter," Gavi explained. "We gave her time to make up her mind to start again but when she didn't, well, we were going to wait for Pesach but . . ."

"I'm honored," Solomon told him.

He was careful to eat enough to seem appreciative but still leave some for Gavi and his wife for the next day and the next. It made him angry to see how Gavi was ostracized by the rest of the Jewish community for being a tanner and then by the other tanners and leatherworkers for being a Jew. No one could say a word against him as a man. He did his work well, paid his tithes and taxes, was always ready to help. But when the tables were laid for Passover and friends invited, Gavi was never on the list.

"Did Yusef find you?" Gavi broke into his thoughts.

"Yusef? No. Did he say what he wanted?"

"No, only that it was important." Gavi tried to refill Solomon's bowl.

"Everything is important to Yusef," Solomon said. "No more, thank you. I've eaten enough to last a week. Yusef probably wants me to join him at prayers. He won't get me that way. They have more than enough for a *minyan* in Toulouse."

But he was fated to have his evening interrupted anyway. They had scarcely finished the meal when someone knocked timidly at the door. Gavi went to open it and returned with Josta, looking flustered.

"A blessing on the house," she greeted them. "I beg your pardon for intruding. Solomon, I searched Belide's room this afternoon and found something. I don't know what to do. I haven't even told Bonysach."

Solomon sighed. Gavi and Nazara withdrew without any fuss to let them talk privately. Gavi worried that he should have offered his guest something to drink, but Josta was clearly too agitated for social niceties.

When they were alone, Josta took something from the purse at her belt. She held it out to Solomon.

"I'm a coward," she told him. "I'm afraid to ask my own daughter how she came by these."

In her hand was a small bag. Solomon took it, surprised at its weight. He opened it and gold coins spilled out. The slanting rays of the sunset fell on them like a breath that made the metal glow with life.

"Saracen gold," Josta said dully. "No one has that much gold unless they've done something unspeakable."

Solomon was forced to agree.

Six

The same evening, on the path between the home of Gavi, the tanner, and Bonysach, the merchant.

ראובן בא לבית הכנסת וצעק ואמר: "אי קהל הקדוש, גויה אחת עומדת בביתו של שמעון ובאה אמש בביתי וחרפני וגרפני! ואתם יודעים שהיא מועדת ורגילה לעשות כן לכלכם!" וענו כל הקהל, "כן הוא כדבריך--אף לנו הרעה אותה גויה!" זה אומר, "אותי הכה במקל," וזה אומר, "אשתי קראה זונה," וזה אומר, "אותי קראה קרנן."

"Ruben came to the synagogue, shouting: "In this holy community there is a gentile girl, who works in Simon's house who came to my home last night to aggravate and insult me! And you know that she does this all the time to all of you!" And the entire community responded: "It is just as you have said; she has been wicked to us as well!" One said, "She beat me with a stick," and one said, "She called my wife a whore," and one said, "She called me a cuckold!"

—Sefer HaKolbo

*I*t had taken Solomon almost the entire walk back to her home to calm Josta and convince her to let him handle the matter of the gold.

"She's always been a good girl," Josta wept. "Naughty at times, but never devious, never defiant. I don't understand."

"I think I do." Solomon stooped and wet his sleeve in the rivulet running alongside the path going past the Daurade. He used it to wipe Josta's face.

"There," he said. "That's better. You don't want the neighbors to see you like this."

The mere thought made Josta straighten her back and dry her eyes.

"They would love to have a chance to pity me!" she muttered. "As if it were my fault their husbands are such . . . well, never mind. You say you know how Belide came by this?"

She opened the hand containing the bag of coins.

Solomon covered it with his.

"Not here," he said. "I have a guess. Can you get these back where you found them without her knowing?"

"I am her mother!" Josta said.

Solomon took that for a yes. "Then please do and don't tax her about it for now. I think it would be better if you let her tell you, herself. She will. I promise."

Josta looked at the bag. The worn cotton and frayed silk tie gave no indication of the wealth inside. She tucked it into her sleeve and tied it tightly.

"Very well," she said. "No one but you and I will know of this until Belide comes to her senses. But it had better be soon! Now, since you have already eaten, I won't ask you to come in."

She didn't even let him go with her to the gate but left him at the corner.

"*Leila tov*, Solomon." She smiled an apology. "Thank you for being our friend."

The spring evening was soft and full of music, from the chanting of the monks countered by the songs from the tavern, to the performance of the *jongleurs* in the street hoping for a few more pennies to feed themselves that night. Solomon stood for a while listening to a tale of love spurned and love lost and wondered why anyone would pay to be so disheartened. He threw the singers a coin out of pity and went back to Gavi's to sleep alone.

Tomorrow he would deal with Belide.

Arriving early the next morning, Bonysach found the square next to Saint Pierre des Cuisines already crowded with citizens. The sun had barely risen but the council and Good Men of Toulouse wanted to get this business done early so that they could get on with their own work.

A temporary platform had been set up at one side of the square for the town leaders to stand and address the crowd. At the moment, only Peire Caraborda and Stephan de Pertici were there. Adalbert of Villeneuve, who lived in the suburb just outside the eastern wall of the Bourg, arrived next. The rest of the citizens weren't ready to wait for the last two. From a neighboring yard a goat bleated painfully, waiting to be milked. A fugitive chicken flapped its way among people's legs, pecking at them in panic as it sought an escape.

At the edge of the square Bonysach found one of the Good Men from the year before, Mancip Mauranni. Both his name and face confirmed Mancip's Saracen father. The father had come to Toulouse in the wake of some Berber conflict and converted to marry a well-dowered woman of the town. Mancip had become a powerful landowner who had also married well.

Bonysach never felt comfortable around Mancip. The man was always friendly toward him but underneath the manner, Bonysach felt a reproach. If Mancip's father could become a Christian, then anyone could, and should. It was a constant reminder to Bonysach that he would never be completely accepted in the town of his birth, no matter how much he seemed to be a part of it.

"Bonysach!" Mancip grinned. "It seems our taxes are about to be raised. Do you agree that we need to hire more watchmen? Why doesn't the count's vicar take on the expense? After all, this man was killed in the Cité, not the Bourg."

"Is Lord Poncius here?" Bonysach looked around for the vicar.

"I haven't seen him, yet, but he'll show up," Mancip answered. "He won't dare let them make a new regulation without at least pretending to give his approval."

Mancip moved on, greeting one of the tower lords with the same hearty familiarity that he had shown Bonysach.

With a sigh, Bonysach turned to scan the crowd for other friends. Across the square, he spotted Arnald's father, Vidian. He wasn't sure that he wanted to talk with him at the moment, but Vidian saw him and beckoned him over.

"Look, I'm sorry about my son," Vidian began when they were close enough to speak without being overheard. "He acted stupidly but he swears he meant no dishonor to your daughter."

"I believe you." Bonysach nodded wearily. "Belide is being punished for her part in whatever it was. She won't be seen out alone for many months."

"If we decide to increase the watch, Arnald may not dare leave the house, either." Vidian sighed. "That boy has been a trial to me ever since he sprouted his first whisker. When I think of how proud I was the day he was born!"

He paused, looking at something over Bonysach's shoulder. "Say, what are your twins doing here?"

Bonysach turned around.

"Papa! Papa!" Muppim and Huppim shrieked in unison as they darted around people and pushcarts to reach him. "You have to come home right now!"

Huppim reached him first. "Babylonia came to our kitchen and started spitting in the dishes!" He was hopping from one foot to the other in his eagerness to tell. "She was calling us awful names!"

"Mama tried to stop her but Babylonia hit her with the milk pitcher!" Muppim, the more timid, was near tears.

"What!" Bonysach grabbed Muppim's hand and started back through the crowd. "Huppim, has anyone sent for Yusef? If not, you go tell him. This has gone too far! Muppim, is Mama badly hurt? Where were the servants?"

"They hadn't come yet." Muppim sniffed. "Not when we left. Belide came running in to save Mama and knocked Babylonia down."

"Belide was sitting on her when we left, trying to make her be quiet," Huppim added. "She sent us for you. Mama's face is bleeding and her voice sounds funny."

"Huppim, go!" Bonysach ordered.

"Do you want me to come back with you?" Vidian offered. "I can act as witness to the actions of this woman."

Bonysach paused. "Yes, thank you," he said in relief.

They set off for the house.

Solomon had broken his fast with Gavi and was ambling in the direction of the synagogue. He wanted to get there too late for prayers but in time to see his uncle before Hubert began his study for the day. It was delicate timing. As he passed Bonysach's home, he was grateful that it was too early for a visit. The problem of how to make Belide confide in her parents was a knotty one and he had come up with no good argument yet.

He had gone only a few steps more when he heard women shrieking from the house. As he raced toward the noise, he drew the knife he kept hidden in the sheath strapped to his arm. Running to the back, he found that the gate had been left open.

The sight that greeted him when he entered the kitchen caused him to stop, arm raised and jaw dropped.

The room was a mess of spilled flour, broken crockery, and a slime of milk and broken eggs flowing from the table to the floor. In the midst of this, Belide was sitting firmly on another woman who was screeching vile curses at the top of her lungs.

"Devil's spawn! Murderers! Filthy infidels *Jusiue maldizidor!*" She didn't seem to take a breath between the words. "You pollute the world with your presence!"

"Don't answer her, Solomon," Belide said. "She only wants attention. See to my mother, I daren't let this *mostelonne* get away."

Solomon hadn't noticed Josta sitting on a stool in the corner, a cloth to her face. He sheathed his knife, went over, and squatted next to her. When he lifted the cloth, he saw a large red swelling on the cheek and jaw. A cut next to her lip had left a smear across her face.

"Josta, you need a poultice for that," he said. He felt along her cheek with his fingers. "I don't think the bone is crushed but you'll have bruises and a black eye for sure. What is going on here?"

"Yusef," Belide said in disgust. She twisted on her prisoner to face Solomon. "Babylonia here works for him. She came over to borrow some salt, she says. But she couldn't leave without trying to pollute our food. How he trusts her to work in his house, I don't know. She probably polishes the silver with pork fat."

Solomon gaped at the struggling woman. Her thin face was sallow, her hair greasy. The hands that Belide had tied together were rough, the nails long and dirt encrusted. "This works for Yusef?"

"We don't understand it, either," Josta said from the corner. "It's the scandal of the community. This isn't the first time she's done something like this. She hates Jews."

"Yusef." Solomon couldn't make this fact enter his mind. "The terribly pious Yusef who berates me every time we meet for the way I consort with Edomites and ignore the law? *That* Yusef?"

Belide sighed and bounced a bit on the woman in an effort to stop her constant flow of invective.

"Yes," she said. "He refuses to send her away. But this time he won't get off with a fine. She could have killed Mother! Be quiet, you idolatrous whore!"

She bounced again, harder. The servant was cut off in midshriek. She gagged and began coughing.

"Josta!" Bonysach's voice came from the hall. "Josta, are you all right?"

The woman tried to rise but sank back on the stool. Muppim ran into the room, followed by his father and Vidian.

"Mama," he cried. "She didn't kill you, did she?"

Josta put her arms around the boy. "No, no, of course not," she said.

"Not for want of trying," Belide said grimly.

Bonysach was kneeling by his wife, examining the wounds to her face.

"Vidian," he said. "Will you swear to what you found here? That my wife has been struck and that this woman has been restrained but not harmed?"

"Of course," Vidian said. "Everyone knows Babylonia. I wouldn't have her in my house."

"Jew-lover!" Babylonia croaked.

Vidian looked down at her with contempt.

"Another sound out of you and I'll have you up before the council," he warned. "They're meeting at this moment, so there'll be no delay in presenting the case."

The woman gave him a venomous look but held her tongue.

Solomon was completely baffled by the situation.

"Will someone please tell me why Yusef, of all people, protects this woman?"

Belide glared at Babylonia. "No one knows," she said. "Some think she provides him with some service beyond the usual duties, but that's more than my imagination will credit. Others say she holds a dark secret about him."

"That's nonsense," Vidian interrupted. "Yusef was born in Toulouse and spent his whole life here. If he had done something scandalous, someone else would know."

At that moment Yusef entered, Huppim at his heels. Bonysach left Josta's side to confront him.

"Look what that *jael* of yours did to my wife!" he shouted. "You'll pay for this, Yusef! I'll have you up before the congregation!"

To Solomon's astonishment Yusef seemed neither surprised nor angry. He took in the destruction of the kitchen and the darkening bruises on Josta's face.

"I am so sorry for what she did to you, *Na* Josta," he said. "I should have kept a closer watch on her. I will pay any fine the *tubei ha-ir* set me."

He sighed and motioned Belide off Babylonia. He bent over his servant.

"Come home now, Babylonia," was all he said.

He held out a hand to help her up.

Meekly and silently, the woman got to her knees, holding out her bound hands. Yusef untied the cords. She got to her feet and stood, her gaze fixed on the stone floor.

"I promise to deal with her, Bonysach," Yusef said. "This will not happen again."

"You know it will," Bonysach told him angrily. "None of us will be secure until you send that woman from your home. I'm going to recommend that until you do a *herem* should be placed on you."

Yusef blanched. "Exile? You can't mean that!"

"To protect my family? Of course I can!" Bonysach said. "Now, take her and go!"

Yusef bowed to them all and left, a transformed Babylonia trotting docilely behind him.

"Is that all that's going to be done with her?" Solomon asked. "A Christian master would have beaten her soundly and then tossed her into the streets."

"That's up to Yusef to decide," Bonysach said. "Belide, help your mother up to her bed. And call Rahel to see to her injuries."

"Yes, Papa." Belide went to free her mother from the overwhelming attentions of the twins.

It was a sign of how badly Josta was hurt that she made no protest. She only sighed as she left the chaos in her kitchen.

"At least it's almost Pesach." The unswollen side of her face tried to smile. "We were going to scrub and purify the house in any case. Solomon, thank you again."

He leaned over her while Belide was busy with the little boys.

"Do you think this has anything to do with last night?" he whispered.

"No," Josta answered. "I'm sure not. Ohhh, my poor face, how it hurts. Later, Solomon, please come back later."

He promised and, after being assured that there was nothing he could do to help, he left.

As he continued on his way to the synagogue, Solomon reflected that the relationship between Yusef and his servant was as much of an enigma as the divine mysteries Hubert was trying to unravel. But he wasn't as certain as Josta that the attack was unrelated to the death of Brother Victor or Belide's bag of coins. Hadn't Yusef also been in Moissac when Arnald had asked Victor for help? And hadn't he also been in the camp days before when Aaron had spoken to Solomon? Yusef could well have reasons of his own for wanting Brother Victor dead and for creating trouble in Bonysach's home.

No, he had no intention of leaving Yusef out of his suspicions. Although it might be too much to hope that he could ever have the joy of seeing the man's pious haughtiness broken if the vicious behavior of his Christian servant couldn't crack him.

Brother James had also gone to the meeting in the square. He had hoped to be asked to speak on behalf of his murdered friend but the leaders of the Cité and Bourg had ignored him. After only a few moments of debate, the decision was made to increase the number of times the watch went out each night. James did not expect them to adjourn immediately. He stood puzzled as the men began to disperse.

"What about the villain still at large?" he demanded. "Is it the custom in Toulouse to give cutthroats the run of the town?"

Stephan de Pertici was about to give a short answer to the

voice from the crowd. He had vineyards to tend. Then he saw that the speaker was a monk.

"Every effort is being made to discover the culprit," he answered politely. "No one in Toulouse would condone violence against the clergy. If you like, Brother, perhaps your prior could arrange for a guard to accompany the monks when they must go out at night."

His tone made it clear that he felt any monk out alone after Compline deserved his fate.

From the mutterings among those remaining in the square, James realized that the citizens of Toulouse agreed. No one here was going to help him. Sadly, he returned to Saint Pierre des Cuisines.

But no one at the priory seemed eager to track down Brother Victor's killer, either.

"He's probably long since removed himself from the area," Prior Stephen told him. "Certainly no one has reported a man trying to spend gold coins. With no description it would be impossible to find him. Leave vengeance to Our Lord and pray for the soul of Brother Victor."

"But what about the man found with him?" James persisted. "This Jew. Did no one question him?"

"From what I understand, the man is a respected scholar, well known to them," the prior answered. "The watchman says he made no attempt to escape but rather tried to help. He was simply a bystander who could provide no useful information."

"I would like to talk with him myself," Brother James insisted.

"Ah, well." The prior was clearly uncomfortable. "Your feelings about your former coreligionists, while laudable, might make it difficult for you."

"I can overcome my antipathy for a time if it helps find Victor's murderer," James said.

"Yes, of course. However"—Stephen sighed—"it's also possible that they won't permit you to see this man."

"Can't you order them to admit me?" James asked.

"I'd rather not," the prior admitted. "The Jews are favored by Count Alphonse and many others of the town. They were active in defending it against the French invasion a few years ago. You don't understand the politics of Toulouse. There's a fine balance among the Burghers, the Count, Saint-Sernin and those of us who are affiliated with Moissac and Cluny."

"What has that to do with this Jew?"

The prior felt James was being deliberately obtuse.

"If the Jews complain that you are persecuting one of their people," he said. "They can bring a charge before the town leaders. People will take sides. Old grievances will be remembered that have nothing to do with this."

He put a hand on James's shoulder. "If I thought that anything useful would come of your talking with this man, I would permit it. But I believe that you are simply unwilling to accept Victor's unfortunate death. Attend instead to your devotions. It's only in them that you will find the answers you seek."

Brother James nearly blurted an angry response. He stopped himself in time. That's what the prior expected. He knew they all thought he could never achieve the true submission to authority required of every monk. After all, he came from a stiff-necked, proud, and stubborn people.

He bowed his head. "As you wish."

However, in the time he had between Sext and None, James fully intended to seek out this so-called scholar and make him confess the truth. Of course, he couldn't be seen near the synagogue. He had to find a way to make this man come to him.

He left the priory bustling with plans. In the crowded streets and the bright sun, it never occurred to him to worry that someone might be following him.

∞

"Uncle, you said you had a commission for me." Solomon caught at Hubert's sleeve as he passed from the meeting room to his cell. "Uncle? It's Solomon, remember? Where are you?"

Hubert squinted in the dim passage. The small round windows of the synagogue building let in only enough light to find one's way from room to room. The thick unripe-olive-colored glass created a perpetual twilight even at noon. Still, Solomon thought, that was no reason for Hubert to pass nearly under his nose without noticing him.

Hubert gave his head a shake to clear it.

"I'm sorry." He smiled. "I was trying to keep something in my mind, but it seems to have flown. Never mind. If the Holy One means me to know it, He'll send it to me again. What was it you wanted?"

"Could we sit a moment?" Solomon guided him to the open court where a few scholars were arguing happily. At a table to one side was a pitcher and next to it several cups. The day was growing warm and the air was saturated with the perfume of jasmine. For the space of two heartbeats Solomon had an intense image of a woman he had loved once in Córdoba. Then the voices of the men pulled him back to the present.

He sat Hubert down and fetched him a drink from the pitcher, cold well water flavored with mint and honey. He waited until Hubert had finished the cup.

"Now, Uncle," he said. "I have promised not to leave for Spain until after Pesach. Or at least until Aaron returns to explain this mysterious rescue he has plotted with Belide and her friend. But that doesn't mean I must stay all that time in Toulouse. Knowing that man is here in town torments me. I'm afraid to raise my eyes from the ground for fear of seeing him."

"What would you do if you did?" Hubert asked softly. "If you turned a corner and came face to face with your father?"

Solomon looked away. He seemed not to notice that his right hand was moving toward his knife.

He looked back at Hubert. His hand fell to his side.

"I would run," he said. "As far as I could, as if the devil and all his hounds were at my heels."

Hubert gave a deep sigh and covered his face with his hands. When he lowered them, Solomon saw in surprise that he was smiling.

"My greatest fear has passed," he told Solomon. "Your anger is so strong, I thought you might . . ."

"What? Confront him? Tell him what I think of him?" Solomon raised his voice to be heard over the men debating on the other side of the courtyard. "Or, maybe you think I would kill the bastard?"

The courtyard was suddenly quiet. A dove in the rainspout was startled to hear his own coo. Everyone looked at Solomon.

"Anagogically speaking," he said to the scholars.

"Aah . . ." The men went back to their topic.

"Well, Hubert, do you have an errand that will get me out of town for a while?"

Hubert glanced nervously at his fellow scholars.

"Yes, I do," he said. "Something else that I should have seen to before I left my former life. I need you to find someone for me in Carcassonne. Will you do that?"

"I'll leave tomorrow." Solomon got up as if preparing to set off at once. "Tell me who, where to find them, and what the message is."

"I'll have all you need ready in the morning," Hubert said.

"Good," Solomon answered. "I'll be on the road as soon as the city gates open."

Josta lay in her bed swathed in bandages that had been dipped in something both sticky and foul-smelling. Her face ached and she was sure she felt a loose tooth at the point where the pitcher had hit her jaw. She wished her family would stop hovering over her and go make sure the work was being done properly. She could heal just fine by herself but someone needed to make sure the new maid didn't put the cheese in the same bowl with the sausage.

"Beride, where are your brovvers?" she mumbled through her wrappings.

"Jermana took them to the market." Belide's face floated in the space above her. "We wanted it quiet for you."

"Bedder I cn hear 'em."

"What?" Belide sponged more of the balm onto the bandages. "Don't try to talk, Mama. Rahel says it will strain your jaw."

"Hmmmph!" Josta closed her eyes and submitted to her daughter.

Belide tried to be gentle but every touch of the sponge made her mother wince.

"I'm sorry, Mama." She tried not to cry.

Josta wanted to tell her that it was the pain in her heart that was wracking her, not the bruise on her face. Who was this child? It seemed like her own loving Belide, but what if she were like the serpent in the heart of the fruit? Could this child she had borne, nursed, scolded, and cherished have been replaced by another being, one who could lie with a sweet face? One who would deceive the ones who loved her best?

What was a lost tooth compared to the empty cavern left in her heart that had once held her faith in Belide?

When Hubert entered his small room and shut the door, he could still hear the shouting of the students as they argued the reading of the day. Somewhere farther away a donkey was protesting his load. The woman next door was singing to her child. Life was everywhere around him.

Then he began to read. As he shaped the letters on his lips and in his mind the world ebbed away until he was left on an empty silent shore. The ground seemed to slide from him like sand pulled back into the ocean, but he felt no fear. The words became solid under the pointing finger of the *yad*. Words of gold with hearts of fire. They lit the path for him ever higher, a spiral that climbed so high the end of it was hidden in the clouds.

Hubert began to climb and the words led him on. He hungered and it seemed that the hand of the pointer became a spoon, sustaining him with the wisdom of the Torah, sweet as honey. He was no longer a man seated before a book but part of the book, the essence of it, not the ink on the page. Higher and higher he ascended. The clouds were thinner now, almost ready to part. Hubert strained to see beyond them.

From nowhere there came a huge crash of thunder. It shook the pathway and sent him rolling down, down deep into the abyss.

Hubert cried out. He couldn't get his breath. He tried to stand but fell back into his chair. And the thunder became ever louder.

"*Mar* Chaim!"

The door opened. The student Samuel gasped in horror at the form of the man slumped over, about to fall from the chair.

"*Mar* Chaim," he repeated as he leapt forward and pushed Hubert back upright. "Are you ill? What can I do?"

Slowly Hubert returned to life. He seemed confused; a man wakened from a deep dream. Samuel was frightened by how gray his face was and how cold his hand. It was several moments before Hubert knew him.

"Samuel?" he asked. "What are you doing here?"

"I came to deliver a message for you," the young man told him. "But perhaps I should return when you are better. I can see you are ill. Should I fetch Mosse, the physician?"

Hubert drew in a great breath. The living letters had abandoned him. Once again he needed air to survive. His flesh settled upon him again and he felt the pounding of blood rushing through his body. It was enough to make him weep.

"No, Samuel," he said. "I have seen Mosse many times. He never tells me anything new. Now, what was your message?"

"There is a knight of the town asking for you," Samuel said. "His name is Berengar and he wants you to go with him. He says one of the friends of the monk who was killed would like to speak to you."

A shudder passed across Hubert's shoulders. "Did he ask for me by name?"

"No, only for the man who had found Brother Victor." Samuel looked around for a blanket to throw over Hubert's shoulders. "Shall I tell him you are not well enough to go out this morning?"

"No." Hubert leaned against the desk as he stood. "It was meant to be. There's no point in delay."

"I don't understand. Should I came with you?"

Hubert smiled at him gently. "You are a good, kind man, Samuel. But don't worry. Someday you will understand that there are demons that a man must face alone."

Samuel was too respectful to disagree with him, but he resolved to tell the leader of the synagogue about this at once. Demons of the soul were a man's private business; one needed friends to battle demons in the street.

Seven

An enclosed garden near the priory of Saint Pierre des Cuisines, Monday, 3 kalends April (March 29) 1148, 29 Adar II 4908. Feast of St. Rieul, bishop of Arles in 130, who saw the names of martyrs written in blood on the breasts of doves.

Ben es mos mals de ben semblan,
Que mais val mos mals qu'autre bes;
E pois mon mals aitan bos me's
Bos er los bes apres l'afan.

My pain truly seems beautiful,
For my pain is worth more than others;
And since my pain seems somewhat good to me
The joy that comes after it will be better.

—Bernart de Ventadorn
Non es meravelha s'ue chan *ll. 29–33*

*B*erengar stopped Hubert at the gate.

"I'll announce you," he said. "Brother James may be at his prayers. If so then you must wait until he finishes."

"Yes, of course." In a calmer state Hubert might have been amused at the young man's dim respect for the duties of clerics. Now it was just another moment of torture.

Hubert rubbed the sweat from his palms as he waited while Berengar approached the monk seated on a stone bench beneath a towering elm tree. The man seemed old, his shoulders hunched, hands shaking even in repose.

Berengar returned.

"He'll see you now," he said and added with a warning glance, "I'll be here to escort you back."

"You needn't worry. I have no plans to harm him." Hubert opened the gate and went in.

At first the man only watched as Hubert walked across the grass. The leaves of the elm cast dappled shadows that obscured the features of the person coming toward him. As he came closer, James's look of polite suspicion slowly changed to one of confusion. His eyes narrowed as he tried to make out the shape of Hubert's face.

"You are the man who found Brother Victor?" he asked, standing to meet him.

Hubert nodded.

"But I know you!" James brought his face close to Hubert's. He bent his head to one side. His mouth fell open.

"It can't be!" James recoiled in horror. "Oh, Christ protect me! Oh, Hubert! Oh, sweet Jesus! What have you done?"

"I've come home, Jacob," Hubert said softly. "To the true faith. At last our mother's ghost no longer weeps in my dreams. How well do you sleep, my brother?"

"No!" James backed away. "This is a test, a diabolical vision. You have a wife, children. You can't have dragged them into this . . . this depravity with you."

He covered his eyes and began reciting a *Pater Noster*.

"Jacob, I won't vanish at the sight of a cross," Hubert spoke over the Latin. "If it's any comfort to you, among my children, only Catherine knows that I have returned to the faith and she has shown no interest in converting."

". . . *libera nos ad malo*." James peered from between his fingers. Hubert was still there.

"Did you kill Brother Victor in order to punish me?" he asked, his voice quavering.

"Jacob! Of course not!" Hubert stepped toward him, arms open. "The poor man! I would have saved him if I could but I came too late. It was only chance that brought me to where he lay. I knew nothing of who he was or where he came from. Certainly I never imagined that he was a friend to you."

He stepped closer.

"Don't touch me!" Brother James backed into the tree. He raised his hands in command.

"Jacob." Hubert spoke as to a wounded animal. "I mean no harm to you or any of your brother monks. I only want you to remember that I was your brother first. Jacob, please."

"Stop calling me that!" James lunged sideways, putting the bench between him and Hubert.

"Is anything wrong?" Berengar called from the gate.

"No! Stay where you are!" James ordered him.

Berengar frowned, but came no closer.

Hubert sighed. "Very well . . . James. You see, I can say it. I don't mind the name, you know. Catherine named her first son James, for the saint of Compostella."

There was no sign of interest from the monk. Hubert sighed again.

"I can tell you nothing about the one who attacked your friend," he said. "Someone bumped into me as I entered the passageway, but I had no sense of his size or appearance. I've already explained this to the watch and to your prior. So, unless you wish to torment me with false accusations as you did your son, I shall return to my studies."

He thought the jab about Solomon would provoke a reaction, but Brother James seemed not to have heard. He continued to stare at Hubert.

"What you have done is worse than murder." His voice held more wonder than rage. "To deny your Savior. You will spend eternity in Hell."

"There are those, my brother," Hubert answered. "Who would say the same of you. I didn't seek you out, knowing what you have become. I would have been content to leave you as you are. But now that I see you . . . oh, my brother . . . I'll pray that if you don't find the truth, you may at least find peace."

He expected another outburst, but Brother James was silent, one arm stretched out as if to ward off attack. To his dismay, Hubert saw James's fingers moving in the old signs to ward off evil. His eyes were closed and he may not have even known that he was using the gestures his mother had taught him a lifetime ago.

There was no point in trying. Hubert shook his head in sorrow.

"Good-bye, Jacob," he said softly. "May the Holy One, blessed be He, protect you and show you the way home."

There was no response. With a sigh, Hubert turned and left the garden. He nodded to Berengar at the gateway.

"Perhaps you should see to Brother James," he said. "I believe he has overtired himself."

The walk back from Saint Pierre des Cuisines seemed endless to Hubert. What had he been hoping for? Jacob had left them thirty years ago. This monk was not his older brother. Brother James was a stranger who wanted desperately to destroy any vestige of Jacob of Rouen.

Would that include denouncing his own brother as an apostate Christian?

Hubert understood then that the millstone weighing down his spirit, making each step, each breath a burden wasn't caused by age or illness, but dread.

"Berengar!" Jehan greeted the knight from across the tavern. "We have a cup here engraved with your name. It's dying of thirst. What took you so long?"

Berengar made his way to the table where Jehan and Guy sat. By the look of it, they had been there for some time. Cheese rinds were scattered on the floor around them. The men were using some of them in an attempt to build a fortress perched on a mound of olive pits.

"Maybe we should get some honey to stick them together," Guy suggested. "What do you think, Berengar?"

"I think you're both drunk," he said. He reached for the ewer and turned it upside down but only a dribble of wine ran out.

"We are that," Jehan admitted. "But don't worry, you can join us."

He got up and poked at a child of about ten, dozing next to

the wine cask. "You! Ganton! Get your spigot and draw us another *sestier* of wine."

The boy opened his eyes and yawned. Then he smiled at Jehan and unfolded himself slowly.

"*Algramen, Senhor,*" he said. "As soon as I have your money."

Jehan made as if to cuff the child. The boy didn't flinch, but stood smiling, his hand out. Jehan fumbled in his purse.

"Here." He dropped a quartered *raimondin*. The boy caught it, tested it with his teeth and then went off to get the wine spigot.

"Now, Berengar." Jehan sat down again. "Don't look so sour. We have nothing better to do while waiting for this expedition to set out. Why not become better friends with the local wine?"

"And cheese," Guy added, still trying to get the fourth wall of the tower to stand.

Berengar tapped his cup on the table impatiently.

"I live here," he reminded them. "This is the food I was weaned on. But don't let me keep you from wallowing in it. I suppose you'll want to try the local whores next?"

"Did that last night," Guy said. "Maybe later. Oh, *merdas!* There it goes again. There must be something we can use to keep these stones from sliding."

"Berengar." Jehan wasn't showing the effect of the wine as much as Guy. "Why are you so upset? Has something happened?"

The boy arrived with the brimming pitcher and another dish of olives. Berengar filled his cup and took a long swallow before answering.

"I think I just saw Brother James confront the devil."

The other two looked at him and then each refilled his cup.

"Tell us all about it," Jehan said.

Before he left for Carcassone, Solomon felt obligated to visit Bonysach. He hoped that Josta had suffered no permanent harm from her attack. But he also hoped that the incident would relieve him of his promise to speak to Belide about the gold.

The servant had barely let him in when Muppim and Huppim were upon him, dragging him into the courtyard.

"Papa has gone to see the elders," Huppim explained. "He's going to make Yusef pay for what his maid did to Mama. We'll entertain you until he gets back."

"I can stand on my head," Muppim offered.

"Thank you," Solomon told them. "But I would really like to see your mother, if she's well enough. Or your sister."

"Mama needs to sleep." Muppim sighed. "That's why we can't stay inside. I'll get Belide."

Huppim remembered his manners and got a basin and jar of soap for Solomon to wash his hands.

"Oh, I forgot the towel," he said.

"Never mind." Solomon wiped his hands on his tunic. "Why aren't you and your brother at *cheder*? Don't you have lessons?"

"Not yet; we'll start this Shavuot." The boy didn't seem eager for education. "Do you want me to do a somersault for you?"

He was energetically rolling across the court when Belide appeared.

"Huppim!" She grabbed him by the neck and pulled him up. "That's a silk tunic! Look, it's all over mud and grass stain. What were you thinking?"

Her glare included Solomon.

"He was trying to be a good host," Solomon told her. "Thank you, Huppim. I was extremely entertained."

Huppim wrenched himself from her grasp, tearing the collar off the tunic. Before she could scold him further, he ran back into the house.

Belide turned back to Solomon.

"I came to see how your mother was doing," he said.

"The doctor gave her a draught for the pain," Belide answered. "She's sleeping now. He face is swelling and the bruises are darkening, but Rahel says she's suffered no serious harm."

"I'm very glad to hear it." Solomon waited.

"Oh, forgive me!" Belide suddenly realized that he hadn't even been asked to sit. "Would you like some water? Lombarda!" she called the servant. "Would you bring a plate of prunes and cheese for *Senhor* Solomon."

"I won't stay long," Solomon said as they sat by a small table in the courtyard. "I'm leaving for Carcassonne tomorrow and just wanted to be sure everything was taken care of here first."

"I thought you'd be with us for Pesach," Belide said.

"I'll be back by then," Solomon said. "I hope your mother will be well enough to participate in the Seder. What a terrible thing to happen! I still don't understand about this woman of Yusef's. Where did she come from? Why does he keep her?"

Belide shook her head. "No one knows the answer to either of those questions. She seems to have been part of a group of pilgrims that stopped at the hostel of St. Raimon about five years ago. Why she stayed in Toulouse and how she came to work for Yusef are complete mysteries."

"If her hatred for Jews is so great, why does she work for one?" Solomon wondered. "And why did she go with him so docilely?"

"I don't care," Belide said angrily. "She attacked my mother in our own home. If the elders won't drive her out, then I hope my father goes to the vicar or the Good Men of the town for justice. Are they waiting for that *cecha* to kill someone?"

"Belide." Solomon paused while the servant set the plate of food on the table along with a cloth and bowl of water. "There's something else I have to ask you about."

Belide jumped up. "She didn't bring you anything to drink. I'll fetch the pitcher."

If she hoped Solomon would forget his question, she was

disappointed. After he thanked her for the water, he started again. He was tired of her evasions. This time the question was blunt.

"Did you and Arnald steal a bag of coins from the monk who was murdered?"

"No!" Belide's eyes were wide with indignation. "Where did you hear that? Brother Victor *gave* it to me, to help free the poor woman."

"He gave you money for a Jewish ransom?" Solomon found that unlikely.

"Yes." Her head bobbed in emphasis. "Arnald told him all about it and he said that it was his duty to undo the misdeeds of his fellow Christians, even if it meant that not all the knights the Ishmaelites are holding could be freed."

"Belide, did you hear him say this?"

"Yes." She leaned closer to him so that he couldn't avoid her eyes. "I swear that's what he told me when he gave me the coins."

Solomon pushed his chair back and stood. He dipped his sticky fingers in the bowl and wiped them on the towel.

"I believe you're telling me only as much of the truth as you think you can get away with," he told her. "But not all of it. You should know that your mother found the bag and is greatly worried. She would probably heal much more quickly if you confided everything to her. You have no idea of the disaster your actions could bring. I hope your parents can make you realize this."

There. He had done as Josta had requested. His conscience was satisfied.

But like a rat left alone with the cheese, his mind couldn't help from nibbling at the problem.

What if Belide were lying to protect Arnald? What sort of monk would choose to save a Jewish girl from slavery rather than a Christian knight from death? But why would Brother Victor be carrying gold at all? What if Victor hadn't been assaulted by chance?

Who else knew that he had the ransom money?

Solomon was brought up short by the face of his father as he had last seen him. If 'Brother James' knew Victor meant to help the Jews, would he kill him to prevent it?

Solomon felt a spasm deep in his gut. He clenched his teeth, fighting back nausea. He was furious that even the thought of this man could make him feel so sick. His anger flowed to Aaron, Belide, Arnald, even to Edgar for leaving him to finish the journey alone. What right had they to make him a part of their problems? He wanted no more of it.

Right now all he really wanted was to take care of Hubert's business in Carcassonne and continue on far into Spain, leaving the whole mess behind.

"Reb Chaim! What did they want with you? You look worn out. I knew I shouldn't have let you go off with that Edomite alone!"

Hubert was surprised to see Samuel waiting for him in the street outside the synagogue.

"Nonsense," he said, though he accepted the arm the young man offered. "I'm just a bit winded from the walk back. Fasting is good for releasing the spirit to travel but it slows the body considerably."

He let the young scholar fuss over him for a few moments more, then extricated himself.

"Are any of the elders within?" he asked.

"I don't think so," Samuel answered. "Most have returned home before evening prayers. Is there something you need?"

"No, no," Hubert answered. "I only wanted to ask a question, but I think I'll lie down a while in my room."

"Very good." Samuel almost pushed Hubert in the direction

of his bed. "Do you have water?" He peered into the pitcher. "Enough blankets?"

"Yes, Samuel, I'm fine." The young man's energy was becoming more wearing than the exertion of his walk.

"Then I'll just let you rest."

"That would be good." Hubert smiled and nodded until Samuel finally went away.

Then he let his head sink to his chest. The weight of his sorrow was pulling his body down.

He had been stupid, stupid and arrogant. He shouldn't have tried to reconcile with his brother. Now that he had lost so much weight and let his beard flow he might have been able to fool Jacob into thinking he was a stranger. And what of this supposedly missing gold? What was that about? Would Jacob now accuse him of stealing from a dying man?

At least Solomon would be leaving in the morning. He had been right when he chose to avoid any chance of encountering his father. Hubert wished he had done the same.

He lay back on the narrow bed, pulling the blanket around his shoulders. The plaster walls were chill. He closed his eyes and tried to remember his vision of ascending through the Torah to the garden of paradise. Instead he saw the faces of the grandchildren he had left behind in Paris. They looked at him so reproachfully.

Hubert tossed on the bed, unable to find a place of ease. Not for the first time, he wondered if he were really trying to find truth or only to hide from all the mistakes in his life.

When Samuel came in to light his oil lamp, Hubert didn't wake.

Brother James was having an even more uncomfortable afternoon.

"I believe I requested that you not seek out the man who

found Brother Victor." The prior lifted his right eyebrow.

"I only wanted to . . ." James caught himself. "You did, my lord prior."

The eyebrow returned to its normal level.

"I can see that this encounter has disturbed you." The prior's voice softened. "I fear that this man's stubborn adherence to his superstition was more upsetting than anything he could tell you about poor Victor."

James looked at the floor.

"It's true that I am easily angered by their unwillingness to accept the truth of Our Lord's sacrifice," he said. "I hoped I could contain my feelings while speaking with the man."

"Did he tell you anything we didn't already know?"

James kept his eyes down. The prior's attitude grated on his already raw temper.

"No, my lord prior," he said.

"We shall have to decide on a penance for your sin of diso-bedience," the prior continued. "It shall be assigned on Friday in Chapter, as usual. Until then, perhaps you should pray assiduously for the soul of Brother Victor. And, of course, for the success of your mission."

James finally looked up. "The abbot has sent word that I may continue?"

"He has." The prior pursed his lips. "We still need to find an acceptable companion for you. Someone young enough to help you on the journey but mature enough to resist the many traps and snares you will run into along the way."

Mentally James translated this as a man able to carry him if he collapsed who would also watch him like an eagle for any sign of backsliding.

"I shall be satisfied with whomever you choose," he said aloud.

"Of course you will, Brother James." The prior dismissed him with a wave. "Of course you will."

A few days later, Belide was hanging bed linen out to dry on the laurel bush in the garden when the bush spoke.

"Belide!"

She nearly dropped the pillowcases in surprise. She stepped away quickly, in case the bush showed signs of bursting into flame.

"Belide, can you hear me?"

There wasn't even a wisp of smoke so Belide moved closer. The voice seemed familiar and far from divine.

"Arnald, what's wrong?" she whispered. "What are you doing? My father will kill you if he finds you here."

"I know, but I had to talk to you." Arnald sounded as if he was trying not to sneeze. "Can I come out? There are thorns in here."

"No!" Belide looked over her shoulder. "Papa is gone, but my annoying little brothers could be anywhere and they love to tattle. Now, what is it?"

"You won't believe it," Arnald said from the greenery. "My father wants me to go on Victor's mission."

"What?" Belide peered into the leaves to see his face. He must be joking.

"Father thinks I should leave for a while," Arnald went on. "He's tired of having to ransom me from the Watch. He gave a very long lecture about how I should take life seriously and do something for the good of my soul and on and on. But he heard that they need guards for the monks and asked Prior Stephen at Saint Pierre if I would do."

"Oh Arnald!" This time Belide did drop the damp linen.

Fear of discovery forgotten, she reached into the bramble and pulled him out. His face was scratched and there was a spider web hanging from one ear. "I thought you told me they were going all the way to Valencia! You could be killed!"

Arnald raked his hands through his hair, dislodging twigs, leaves, and the spider.

"Would you care if I died?" Arnald asked in surprise.

"Of course," Belide said. "You're my best friend."

"Oh," Arnald answered. "Well, don't worry. My father isn't that angry with me. He wouldn't risk my getting killed. I'm his only son. But how can I go with Aaron if I have to make this journey instead? He needs me."

"Oh," Belide said. "Yes, I see the problem. Aaron has to have a Christian with him. But you can't defy your father now, not without telling him everything."

"Maybe I should." Arnald shivered. "There's something down the back of my *chainse*. Can you shake it out?"

He turned around so Belide could put her hand up the back of his under garment.

"You know you can't," she told him as she tried to get at the bit that was scratching him. "You father would tell mine and then all Aaron's plans would be for nothing."

"BELIDE!!"

Arnald leapt back into the laurel, leaving Belide sitting on the grass surrounded by crumpled laundry.

"Just what were you doing!" Bonysach roared. "Arnald, you show yourself at once!"

"Papa, I can explain!" Belide got up quickly. "Really, it was nothing. Arnald came to tell me that he's going into Andalusia with the monks."

"Soon?" Bonysach glared at Arnald who now had a new assortment of scratches.

"Immediately after Easter, *Senhor* Bonysach," Arnald said. "I wanted to let Belide know but didn't want to bother anyone, so I . . ."

"Climbed the wall," Bonysach finished. "Thoughtful of you. Leave by the gate."

"Yes. Of course." Arnald edged around the garden, keeping his face to Bonysach. "Please tell *Na* Josta that I hope she is recovering quickly."

"Arnald," Bonysach warned.

Arnald reached the gate but the latch stuck. After a couple of tries, it popped open and he escaped.

Bonysach turned to his daughter.

"Papa, I swear," she began when they were interrupted by the sound of snickering from the house.

Belide looked up. Muppim and Huppim were hanging from the window.

"How long have you been there?" she called.

"We saw Arnald hide." Muppim laughed. "Did he scare you?"

Belide turned back to Bonysach. "You see?" she said indignantly. "I couldn't misbehave if I wanted to with those two little *malvatz* brothers of mine."

She was trying not to cry. Tears were an unfair weapon against her father, to be used only in desperation. "He just came to tell me he was going. He knew you had forbidden me to see him but he wanted to say good-bye. That's all."

Bonysach believed her as far as it went. But he was sure that Belide wasn't giving him the whole truth and what bothered him more was that Josta seemed to be keeping something from him as well, something that worried her. He was certain that it involved Belide.

He clenched his teeth to keep from swearing. It was an evil day when his wife kept secrets and his daughter cringed from him as if he were a tyrant.

Vaguely, he felt that in some way the dead monk was to blame.

"Take the linen back to the laundress, Belide," he said at last. "I'll have to pay extra to get those stains out."

"Yes, Papa." Belide would have preferred a beating. Wrath radiated from him like flame.

She scurried away, bitterly regretting that she had ever let Arnald talk her into this. So far, her mother had kept silent about the gold, but what would happen if her father learned of it?

Belide prayed that Aaron would return soon, to bear the brunt of the explanations. Even for the sake of true love, this was becoming more than she could handle.

Solomon suspected that his uncle's need for a messenger had been invented. All he had been asked to do was report to the Templar consistory at Carcassonne that Hubert LeVendeur had turned his trade over to his son-in-law Edgar and his partner, Solomon. A note with Hubert's mark and seal were enough, along with a promise of the same price for pepper as always. The commander seemed perfectly happy to continue the connection. It was all taken care of in a moment.

But Solomon lingered in Carcassonne. He knew no one in the fortress town. He felt no obligation to stay with one of the Jewish families. He spent his time wandering along the wall that ringed the hilltop, sometimes stopping to look out over the greening forest blotched with new villages and vineyards. Once he passed an entire afternoon just watching the birds; storks heading north for their summer nests, hawks that would circle and then dive upon some hapless creature like lightning bolts. To the south the mountains rose, one moment seeming close enough to reach in a day's walk, the next obscured by fog as if they had never been.

He spoke only to get what he needed to live. When he wanted company for an hour, he bought it. The women seemed grateful that he didn't require conversation.

His thoughts stayed in the present, if he had them at all. He didn't wonder about anything, but marveled at the heat of the sun on his face and how the same warmth could make a rose unfold. The days crept toward Passover and his promise to return to Toulouse.

Finally, he knew he could put it off no longer. Solomon paid his bill at the inn, retrieved his horse, and set out.

Hubert had been wise to give him a reason to leave. The time alone had healed his raw spirit. He could now contemplate the possibility of an encounter with his father without panic. What could Brother James do to him that he hadn't done already?

Two days later he spied the towers of Toulouse, visible for miles before one reached the city. When trees hid the view, he followed the Hers river north until the towers reappeared. The roads were well maintained, with tolls every few miles and no sign of robbers.

Solomon rode through the Narbonne Gate feeling calm and at peace with the world and his place in it. He even edged his horse aside without resentment to allow a pair of armed soldiers to pass.

One of the soldiers nodded thanks. Solomon looked at him, then looked again. The soldier stopped abruptly and did the same.

"It can't be!" Solomon cried. "You were sent to Jerusalem! You should be dead!"

The other man's cry was even more aghast. "*Filz de porcel!* Am I cursed? Can I never be free of this torture? How long have you lain in wait to trap me? Did you bring that witch with you, Solomon of Paris?"

Solomon was too stunned to reply. He had girded himself to face Brother James. It had never occurred to him to prepare to meet his old enemy, Jehan of Blois.

Eight

Wednesday, 7 Ides April (April 7) 1148, 9 Nissan 4908. Feast
of St. Hegesipius, Jewish convert and travel writer.

ושנים עשר עומדין במלחמה:
שלשה אהובים,
שלשה שונאים,
שלשה מחיים,
ושלשה ממיתים.

Twelve stand in war:
Three love,
Three hate,
Three give life,
And three kill.

—Sefer Yetzirah, 6:5

*T*he two men faced each other in mutual horror, blocking the street. When neither moved, Berengar reached over to touch Jehan's arm.

"Jehan?" he said uncertainly. "We need to hurry. My father and the other lords are waiting for us."

Jehan turned to him jerkily, as if startled from a nightmare. Berengar gestured that they should move on. After a moment, the knight recovered enough to shake the reins. His horse obligingly stepped forward. As the two men continued toward the gate Jehan turned around every few steps to look behind. Solomon was still watching him.

"What is it?" Berengar asked, twisting to see. "Who is that man?"

"You see him, then?" Jehan exhaled in relief. He had feared it was a vision, a remnant of the madness that had once claimed him.

"Of course. Black beard, dun horse, right?" Berengar answered. "An acquaintance of yours?"

"Yes." They were out of the city now, in the *salvetat* of Saint Catherine. Jehan set his horse to a quick trot, forestalling any more questions.

Berengar scratched his head, then followed, urging his own mount to pass. Soon both were at a full gallop. Jehan leaned low in the saddle oblivious to both the woman whose basket of turnips spilled as she jumped from his path and the chickens squawking their terror as they fluttered out of reach of the pounding hooves. The wind shrieked through his chain mail helm, drowning out his howling memories.

By the time they reached the villa of Berengar's father, Jehan had managed to recover from the shock and appear once again the imperturbable warrior, ready for anything. Inside he was still shaking. Solomon wasn't merely an old enemy, but one who knew too many of the secrets Jehan had thought buried forever. How could he keep the man from telling them?

Solomon sat stone-still until Jehan rode out of his sight. He was too stunned to move. It was impossible. The last time he had seen the man was a year before. At that time Jehan had been weighted down with penitential chains, on his way to Jerusalem. How had he escaped? What was he doing in Toulouse?

Even stranger, why had he not attacked him?

Over the past ten years, every time Jehan had crossed his path, the man had tried to kill him, either by denunciation to those in power or more directly, with a sword. Perhaps, like Solomon, he had been too shocked to act. But what would he do if they met again?

Just what he needed, one more enemy in Toulouse.

Once he had returned the horse to the ostler, Solomon made his way to the synagogue quickly. The tranquility he had gained during his stay in Carcassonne evaporated like spit on a hot stone.

The first thing he had to do was warn Hubert.

The courtyard of the *bet midrash* was full of scholars, each one shouting to make his argument heard above the raucous debate. A quick glance told Solomon that Hubert wasn't among them.

"Samuel." He grabbed the young man's arm to get his attention. "Have you seen my uncle, Rav Chaim?"

"I think he went to his room after morning prayers," Samuel told him. "To study." He sighed. "I wish I had my own private Torah to read each day."

"He earned it," Solomon said. "Be grateful that you didn't have to endure his life."

He went back in and knocked on Hubert's door. He waited, knocked again, and then entered.

Hubert was sitting on a stool before a high lectern on which a book lay open. He was slowly pointing to one word after another with a long silver rod that ended in a tiny hand, the index finger gently resting on the letters.

"*Vihi she'amdah la'avoteinu velanu. Shelo* . . ."

Solomon leaned over his shoulder. "Preparing for *Pesach*, Uncle?" he asked. "I think I remember this part."

Hubert dropped the *yad*. "Solomon? What are you doing here?"

Solomon stooped to pick up the pointer. "I promised I'd be back by now. Remember? But I need to warn you of something."

Hubert sighed. He understood now why Christians became hermits.

"Was there a problem with my message?" he asked. "The Temple knights of Carcassonne don't want to work with you?"

"No, that's fine, but we have another problem," Solomon said.

He told him about seeing Jehan.

Hubert's shoulders sagged. "This is too much! I had hoped he was dead. Why do the Saracens kill everyone except the man who most deserves it?"

"You understand that you can't let him see you?" Solomon wasn't sure how far Hubert had ascended into philosophy. He didn't seem to be as practical as in the old days.

"Of course." Hubert looked up at him, his eyes sharp. "The damned *rabaschier* suspected me of apostasy long before I really renounced Christianity. If he sees me now, word will get back to Paris within the month."

"Uncle, there's a lot more at stake than your old friends in Paris finding out." Solomon wanted to shake him. "Have you looked outside your own window? Don't you know what time of year it is?"

"Oh, that." Hubert smiled. "Easter in Toulouse isn't so bad, I understand. They don't strike a Jew on the Cathedral steps anymore in vengeance for Jesus death. The community just pays a fine instead."

Solomon rolled his eyes. "Oh, so that makes us all one happy family. Don't be so complacent. You said it yourself. The bishop is still in the North. The count has gone off to Jerusalem. Who is supposed to protect us if the Edomites decide to murder us all for the death of their god?"

Hubert looked up at him, eyes bright with joy.

"Our Creator, of course," he said. "Who else?"

"Right, fine job He's done the last thousand years or so," Solomon muttered.

"Solomon!" Hubert was shocked. "That's blasphemy!"

"Yes, yes, I know," Solomon spoke quickly to avoid a lecture. "The greater the suffering we are sent, the greater our reward when the Messiah comes. I have no doubt that it will be any day now. But I would like you to be alive to see it. So don't go out any more than is necessary and, when you do, wear a hood or a floppy felt hat or something to keep your face hidden."

"Perhaps I should dye my beard red as well?" Hubert suggested. "But no, Jehan has never seen me bearded so this is disguise enough."

He seemed disappointed.

Solomon gave up. If Hubert wouldn't take the threat seriously, there was nothing more he could do.

"Very well. I've warned you. How you behave is your affair. Now, what else has been happening while I was gone? What about that dead monk? Did they find who killed him? Has . . . the . . . the other one been bothering you any more?"

Hubert shook his head. "I've heard nothing more from Jacob. I doubt he will try to accuse me. The general belief is that the unfortunate Brother Victor was attacked by a common cutpurse."

"Good." Solomon opened the door to leave. "It's likely that's the truth. I suppose I should report to Bonysach now. Have you seen him since I left?"

"Only here," Hubert said. "Josta's face is still badly bruised. They came last Thursday to lay charges against Yusef. He was fined and told to keep his servant under control or be banned from the community."

"I'm glad they were firm with him," Solomon said. "*Herem* would destroy Yusef. I can't believe he would risk it just to keep that woman in his house. She must know some dark secret about him, whatever Bonysach says."

"Perhaps." Hubert was losing interest. "If that was all you wanted, Solomon, I need to finish this passage before the light goes. My window faces east, you see. I'm glad you're back, and I'm grateful for your concern but I really must. . . ."

His eyes strayed back to the page, the letters clear in the morning light.

Shaking his head, Solomon shut the door.

Jehan of Blois was not making a good impression on the lords of Toulouse. Berengar was wishing he had brought Brother James, instead. He could have convinced them to give more toward the release of the captive knights. But Berengar had felt that these men had had enough of preaching. It seemed better to show them how well their money would be guarded on the route.

But Jehan wasn't acting like a fearless warrior. His eyes moved from side to side, as if trying to see what was behind his back. His right hand gripped and released his sword hilt, leaving it shiny with sweat. In short, he was giving an excellent likeness of a man who was terrified.

Finally Berengar found an excuse to pull Jehan aside.

"What is wrong with you?" he demanded. "My father was going to give you reasons to assure you I wouldn't be a burden on this journey. Now he's wondering if you're the one who needs protecting. And he's not alone."

He nodded toward the men seated around the table, conversing in low tones, their gaze directed anywhere but at Jehan.

The two knights were on one side of a long table set up near the vineyard owned by Berengar's father, Lord Falquet. Their villa was nearby, fenced but not fortified. Beyond it, Jehan could see the spire of the church of Saint Lezat. A cool breeze set the leaves fluttering in the sun, making piebald patterns across the company. Servants brought them dried apricots and Lenten concoctions made from eggs, cheese, olives, garlic, and spices. The wine they poured was clear and cool from the stream.

Jehan snorted. The men even had thick cushions to protect their tender backsides from the wooden seats. What did these people know of warfare? Occasionally they might be raided by an angry neighbor or an ill-armed band of *ribaux* from the forest. They hadn't passed weeks on end sleeping with one eye open and a knife always to hand. Nor had they spent their lives taking on tasks too dangerous or dirty for the flabby burghers and haughty nobles to attempt. He'd lay oath to that.

Who were they to doubt his competence?

He stood, knocking over a bowl of pickled quince. He thumped the table, shaking the cups.

"If you want to know what I can do, then ask me!" he said.

The conversation around the table stopped. Everyone looked at him.

Jehan stared back at the men, all dressed in long parti-colored *bliaux* embroidered with silk flowers and gold thread. "Or why don't you challenge me and see who survives?" he continued. "I fought with fat old King Louis in the Auvergne and against the young king when he invaded Champagne. I've seen to it that the Countess Mahaut and her children traveled safely in the midst of famine and rebellion. And I've saved more than one overly ambitious trader from death when he misjudged the greed of his enemies. The scars I bear are nothing next to the ones I've carved."

He paused for breath, his hatchet glance daring them to interrupt.

"Where did you celebrate the Nativity of Our Lord last year?" He pointed at Berengar's father. "I heard Mass amidst the ruins of Lisbon. I thanked God that I had been chosen to be one of the first to breach the city walls and free it from the infidel. But, looking at you, I wonder if the Saracens have taken Toulouse while I was fighting in Portugal. In those long robes you look just like the painted *femmelets* who offered themselves to us at the city gates, hoping to save their lives by giving us their asses."

"How dare you!" The man across the table from him was so angry that he didn't bother to stand as he drew his knife and lunged.

Jehan stepped back, avoiding his attacker easily.

"Careful," he told the man. "You might tear your skirt."

Two more men rose and advanced on him, knives out.

Jehan laughed. This was something he understood.

He drew his sword and his *coutelet*, the short knife meant for slashing at anyone who attacked from his left. His muscles tensed, ready to move in any direction.

"Is this why you told Guy to stay behind?" he called to Berengar. "To see if I could defeat your friends on my own? What sort of treachery are you expecting on our journey?"

"No! Of course not!" Berengar tried to trip the man advancing on them. "All of you, stop! Are you barbarians?"

The men ignored him. Jehan moved without looking to a position where his back was protected. He smiled at the men coming toward him and they suddenly remembered that he was wearing mail. It wasn't as fashionable as silk but it would effectively blunt a sword while their elegant clothes wouldn't even soak up blood.

They hesitated. In the moment of uncertainty, Berengar's father stepped in.

"Peire! Vital! Drop your weapons," Lord Falquet ordered. "You, too, Willel. And someone help Orso. He's stuck himself to the table."

Jehan's eager grin was more of a reason to retreat than Falquet's command. The men backed off at once.

Lord Falquet came over to where Jehan stood, his back to a wine cask, his sword and knife still raised.

"The remark about our dress was unwise," he told the knight. "But you've made your point. I believe you will guard both my son and my money well. We agree to make up the rest of the funds needed for the ransom. I can have it collected for you by the feast of Saint Ambrose."

Slowly, Jehan sheathed the sword. He'd made new enemies today. Good. It helped him push the faces of old ones farther back in his mind.

"That's more than a week after we intended to leave," he told Falquet. "Brother James wanted to set out Easter Monday."

"It's the best I can do," Berengar's father told him. "Gold coins aren't that easy to come by. I'll explain the problem to Prior Stephen. If he can find the money elsewhere, I won't delay you."

Jehan stuck the knife in his belt.

"As long as my men and I are housed and fed, you may take all summer," he said. "It's the men in chains in Valencia who will suffer. When you have everything ready, you'll find me at the Plucked Crow. *Mes seignors*." He managed to give the words a slur of scorn.

Berengar looked from Jehan to his father and the other men, then back to Jehan. Falquet and his friends were now treating the knight with nervous respect. This removed the last of Berengar's doubt. This was the hero he had expected. He made a quick rearrangement of his loyalties.

"You'll find me with Jehan," he said.

Solomon found Bonysach's house in chaos. All the furniture was piled in the courtyard and half the pantry was being emptied into the midden. Servants were busy everywhere, carrying, scrubbing, polishing.

Solomon finally spotted Belide in the center of the commotion.

"Not the best time for a visit, I see," he observed. "May I help?"

The girl was thumping dust out of a thick wall hanging, now dangling on a line between two trees. She handed him the woven beater at once.

"Mother just uses Passover as an excuse," she grumbled as she rubbed her sore arm. "There aren't likely to be crumbs in the tapestry."

Solomon had the feeling he was being watched. He took the beater.

"The search for *chametz* must be thorough, Belide," he said as he prepared to strike. "If there's even a speck of leaven in the house the Angel of Death might mistake us for a gentile family and not pass over."

He heard a gasp from knee level and looked down. He thought so. Two faces looked up at him from between the legs of stacked chairs.

"Are you boys helping prepare for Pesach?" he asked the twins.

Muppim and Huppim both nodded vigorously.

"We've found every scrap of bread," Huppim said. "And put it in the pit to burn."

He pointed to a hole in the earth lined with stones and partly filled with bits of leavened bread along with a few wooden bowls that had cracked or chipped during the year.

"And we've been scouring pans all day," Muppim added.

"We put a wash tub over in the corner for them," Belide explained. "That way they can help, get wet, and stay out of the way."

"Excellent." Solomon smiled at the dripping children. "You'd better return to it before I strike again, or you'll both be covered in unkosher dust and have to be scrubbed yourselves!"

His blow to the tapestry justified his warning. The twins scurried out of the way and Belide started coughing.

"A . . . much . . . better . . . achah . . . job than I could do," she choked. "Thank you."

Solomon patted her back. "There. You should have moved back, too."

He raised his arm again, then lowered it. He checked to see that the boys and the servants were all out of earshot.

"How is your mother?" he asked. "Did you speak to her?"

He whacked the cloth again, giving Belide a moment to answer.

"Mama's much better," she told him. "And I told her everything I knew. You were right. She didn't betray us, not even to my father. She's agreed not to say anything to him until after

Pesach. Also, she means to have a long talk with Aaron when he returns."

"As do I. Did she tell you that you acted like an idiot?" he asked.

Belide hung her head. "In a lot more words."

"Good," he said. "That's all I came to find out. Give your parents my regards."

He handed the beater back. Belide took it with reluctance.

"You will be at the Seder?" she asked.

Solomon paused. "I don't know."

"Why? What's wrong?"

"I've been thinking about it," he said. "All Jews are equal at Pesach, right? No matter what, we are all still Israel, even me?"

"Of course." Belide was confused. "Has someone said you weren't? Who? Not Yusef?"

"No." Solomon took her hand. "I was thinking of someone else. Please tell your parents that I thank them for their invitation. However, I have decided that I would prefer to be at the home where Gavi and his wife celebrate the Seder."

"Oh, Solomon! A tanner at the Seder table!" Belide tried not to show her distaste. "And you want me to tell my parents. You *have* found a way to punish me for the trouble I caused."

"You know, Belide," Solomon answered. "I didn't even think of that."

During Holy Week the monks were kept busy with special prayers and processions added to the hours of the Office. It was a time that Brother James usually treasured. As a young man he had been one of the despised people ordered into the church and forced to listen to hours of sermons exhorting them to convert. Now he was one of the elect, a participant in the divine Mystery. He gloried in the transformation. Now Easter was his holy time, too.

But this year his devotions were disrupted by far more mundane mysteries.

Despite the counsel of the prior, James couldn't put the murder of Brother Victor aside. It seemed to him that his friend had been completely erased by the other monks. Of course his name would go onto the scroll taken to all the daughter houses of Cluny and his soul would be prayed for. But here in Toulouse, where he had died, no one even said his name. Another monk, Brother Martin, had arrived from Moissac. He took Victor's place in the chanting and slept in his bed.

Victor's death was a tragedy, they said, but there was nothing more to be done. Clearly it had been a random act of violence. Perhaps one day a miracle would reveal the villain.

James refused to believe that. His heart was open to miracles, but God must certainly expect him to do his part.

That was why he had insisted on interviewing the man who found Victor.

But seeing Hubert like that had shaken him as much as losing his friend. Hubert had been his only brother in the flesh who had also been Christian! Even though they hadn't been friends, at least James had been comforted knowing that one of his family was also part of the church. How could Hubert have turned his back on the light that he had been raised in? Didn't he know how fortunate he was? Had he no fear of damnation?

Now James was left with a worse dilemma than before. A word from him would send his brother to his death. As Easter drew near, with the image of the crucified Christ always before them, even the tolerant citizens of Toulouse would call for the blood of an apostate. It was James's duty to denounce him.

Was this the ultimate test of his faith?

James had already abandoned his family to follow Christ, just as the Gospel commanded. He knew that if his eye offended, he should pluck it out. But what of his brother's eye? Would condemning Hubert save his soul? If a man converted in fear of the flames, was that enough? Logic told James that it couldn't be. God couldn't want an impure sacrifice.

James paused in his deliberation. Was he thinking like a Talmudic scholar instead of an obedient monk?

Or was he unable to face the thought of sending his little brother to his death?

He didn't know. All he was sure of was that he wasn't strong enough to decide. This fear, added to his inability to resolve the death of Brother Victor, consumed James. He tried to appear tranquil. What if the prior should decide he was too unstable to make the journey to Valencia? He could let that happen. Then he would have failed Victor as well as himself.

The strain affected his digestion. It made him grateful for fast days and long hours of prayer. When it came time for bed, he was almost too exhausted to unlace his sandals. He fell at once into oblivion.

But the other monks complained that he disturbed their sleep with his cries.

The day was still young when Solomon escaped from the Passover cleaning. The bright sunshine and lilac-scented air made it hard for him to remain on guard. He tried to recall the peace he had gained in his sojourn in Carcassonne. He heard the rhythmic calls of vendors and followed them to the square of Saint Pierre where he realized that it was market day. For a time he wandered among the stalls, stopping now and then to admire a brightly colored length of cloth or a set of silver earrings.

"Your lady would look beautiful in these." The woman held them up for him to examine.

"No, thank you," he told her. "They are skillfully made but gold suits her better."

He passed on. Now, why had he said that? The first image

that had come to him was that of Edgar's sister, Margaret, and how her gold and pearl earrings glimmered against the radiance of her red hair. Of course, he told himself. He had promised a present for the girl. It must have been in the back of his mind. He would have to get something for Catherine and the children, too, on his way back to Paris.

The square was becoming crowded with people intent on getting provisions for Easter, when the long fast would finally be over. Solomon went on up the street, past the remains of the Saracen wall and into the Bourg, dominated by the cathedral of Saint Sernin. He had no particular place to go but he felt the need to keep moving.

On one corner he bought a few hard-boiled eggs and some fresh parsley from a peasant woman who had come in for the day to sell her surplus. He continued north, leaving a trail of eggshell behind.

He was almost at the parvis of the cathedral when the smell hit him. As he came out of the street he realized that he had made a wrong turn.

In the square the butchers had set up their stalls. At this time of year, fresh meat was almost unheard of. But Solomon was assailed with the odor of pork—smoked, dried, salted; pig in all its forms, ready for the Christians to break their Lenten fast. He put his arm over his nose and backed out, trying to breathe through his sleeve.

Once upwind of the smell, Solomon leaned against a venerable elm and inhaled deeply. He couldn't understand how the Edomites could gobble the unclean meat so eagerly. Even thinking about it made him gag.

Once he had regained his composure, Solomon decided to head outside the town walls into the villages clustered outside the Bourg, between the wall and the Hers river. Perhaps he could find someone selling wine in the open air. It would be nice to spend the afternoon under the trees watching other people work.

If he went as far as Matabiau, he could relax for a time with-out fearing that he would be confronted by either the father who wished he were dead, or the knight who would be happy to do the job.

The village was just as he had hoped. There was no tavern but a cask of wine lay in a wooden cradle and there was a charm-ing young woman happy to draw a pitcher for him. He took it and his cup across the road to a spot in the shade. The grass was soft and new. He settled on it and leaned back against a smooth tree trunk to observe the world.

He was wakened by the tolling of church bells. By the angle of the sun, he realized that it must be Vespers. He checked the pitcher; it was still half full. Ah well, he thought as he stretched, there are worse ways of passing a day.

And better ones, he added. He sat up in alert amusement as a woman slithered out the half opened door of a cottage on the other side of the road. She was heavily veiled and tried to keep to the shadows as she headed back to the city.

Solomon shook his head in disapproval. Clearly the woman was new at this. She might as well shout to the world, "Adulteress passing!" She hadn't even brought a basket to fill with herbs or roots as an excuse for being gone so long. He hoped she had a very stupid husband and neighbors who all were blind.

A few moments later, the man came out. He was either more practiced or so besotted that he didn't care who saw him. He went over to the wine seller and gave her a coin to fill his cup. As his head tilted back to drink, Solomon saw his face.

Oh *merdus!* The man was Arnald.

Solomon tried to move back out of sight but Arnald chose that moment to look up. He dropped his clay cup and it broke on a stone.

Arnald waved at him and tried to smile.

"Solomon!" he said. "I didn't expect to see you here."

That was evident.

Solomon smiled back. "I came out for a quiet afternoon and fell asleep," he said. "I'd best be getting back to town. Gavi will be expecting me."

"I'll walk back with you," Arnald offered.

Solomon could think of no reason to refuse. They set off in silence but Solomon could sense the volcano building in the young man.

"*Please, oh Lord of the Universe,*" he prayed. "*Don't let him confide in me!*"

But why should God answer the prayers of one who only calls upon Him in adversity?

"Solomon," Arnald began. "I know I can trust you."

Solomon's heart sank.

By the time they reached the Matabiau gate Solomon knew everything about Arnald's magnificent lady. She was pure and fair and unhappily yoked to a boor of a lord who didn't appreciate her fragile nature.

"This wouldn't be the lord you baptized from the tower, would it?" Solomon asked.

"That was before I knew Philippa well," Arnald said. "I acted childishly. She has taught me to express my feelings with more refinement."

"I'm sure she's been an excellent teacher," Solomon agreed.

This comment passed well over Arnald's head. He smiled with rapture and spent several more moments detailing how perfect his beloved was.

Despite himself, Solomon felt sympathy for the boy. At least his own youthful passions had been conducted far from home. And none of them had been deep enough to risk the threat of either disembowelment or marriage. He wondered how far Arnald had fallen.

"If, by some mischance, this woman's husband should fall ill and die," he asked by way of a test. "Would she then be able to marry you?"

Arnald chewed on that a while.

"Well," he said at last. "I will have my own vineyards, when I'm of age. And I'll inherit the salt marshes, of course. But it wouldn't be enough to give her all she deserves."

A bell of relief rang in Solomon's heart.

"Too true." He shook his head. "A precious jewel like that, can you imagine her having to care for a home and children as your mother does?"

Arnald didn't answer. His face showed that the vision of his love didn't fit with the mundane running of a household. Solomon relaxed. There was a shred of sense left in the boy. He wondered if Vidian knew about his son's indiscretion. If so, it would explain his insistence that Arnald go on this expedition with the monks. A few weeks out of town might save Arnald's life.

Arnald left Solomon at the *rue des Blanchisseurs* where Gavi lived.

"You won't tell anyone of this, will you?" Arnald was already regretting his confidences.

"I haven't heard a word," Solomon told him almost truthfully.

Arnald headed off home and Solomon gratefully approached the door to Gavi's house.

He had only raised his hand to the knocker when the door flew open.

The man who faced him wasn't the tanner. He was taller and more beaten by weather than leather. Solomon blinked. The man grinned.

"They told me I could find you here," he said.

Solomon didn't know whether to hug him or knock him down.

"Aaron Ha-Cohen," he said. "Do you have any idea of the trouble you've started?"

Nine

The home of Gavi the Tanner, that afternoon.

<u>תלמוד בבלי: מסכת כתובות, דף כג, עמוד א</u>

ת"ר: אמרה "נשביתי וטהורה אני, ויש לי עדים שטהורה
אני," אין אומרים נמתין עד שיבאו עדים," אלא מתירין
אותה מיד; התירוה לינשא ... ואם באו עדי טומאה, אפי' יש
לה כמה בנים--תצא.

Our rabbis taught: If a woman says, "I was kidnapped, but I
remained sexually undefiled, and I have witnesses to my
purity," the judges do not tell her, "We will wait until the
witnesses arrive." Rather, they permit her to marry
immediately. If, however, witnesses arrive later and testify
that she had been defiled, she must leave her husband, even
if she has children.

—Babylonia Talmud,
Ketubot *23a*

$\mathcal{A}$aron's grin faded.

"Perhaps we should talk outside," he suggested. "So that Gavi can get on with his work."

Solomon followed him up the road.

Aaron said nothing until they reached the willow grove outside the Bazacle gate. The mills nearby creaked steadily, covering the sound of their conversation.

"Now will you explain why you didn't tell me what a mess you were sending me into?" Solomon demanded. "I walked into this like a goat to the knife."

Aaron sighed.

"If I had known what was happening, I wouldn't have stayed away so long," he told Solomon. "I went to the synagogue and then Bonysach's looking for you. They told me what happened to Brother Victor. I can't believe it. Victor was a good man, for a Christian. He and I played together when we were boys. But I never suggested that Arnald contact him about this and certainly not to ask his help. Who would go to the *Edomites* to ransom a Jewish woman? I wasted time in Bordeaux selling my best horses rather than receive aid from anyone."

"But why *not* ask?" Solomon insisted. "Not the Christians, of course, but the community here. Why such secrecy in buying the freedom of a captive? Haven't we always redeemed our own at any price. And why are you spending so much time on this woman when you should be preparing for your marriage to Mayah?"

Aaron couldn't look in Solomon's eyes. He stooped, picking up a handful of pebbles and turned to toss them, one by one, into the stream flowing between the willows.

"Did Belide and Arnald tell you what has happened to this captive?" he asked.

"They said that a Jewish woman has been taken along with some Moslem ones in Almeria and then sold into slavery," Solomon said. "There was something about monks, too, but that didn't make any sense."

The next pebble hit the water with a hard splash.

Aaron voice was tight as he explained.

"When the Genoese conquered the town, part of it was given to them as booty," he said. "They took some captives to sell elsewhere. Others they traded at once to Catalonian merchants. I thought for a while she'd been taken to Genoa, or even Africa. Then a message came. How she managed to send it, I don't know. She was still in Spain. The men who had bought her were taking her north, but she didn't know where."

His fist clenched the remaining stones. He drew his arm back and hurled them all as far as he could.

"I went three times into Spain trying to find her, but it was hopeless," he went on. "Then I learned that the white monks of Fitero had started a new grange in Navarre and that they had brought in Saracen captives to work on it. Among them were women taken in Almeria."

"But the workers would have been men," Solomon broke in. "To clear the land and build the grange."

"Certainly," Aaron said. "But the good brothers didn't feel it safe to deprive these savage infidels of the natural release of sex and so . . ."

"They set up a brothel at the monastery?" Solomon still found this hard to believe, especially of the Cistercians.

"They permitted one to be established near the building site just for the Saracens." Aaron's hands hung limp at his sides. "Of course one couldn't expect Christian whores to pollute themselves with infidel seed."

"Of course not," Solomon said. "Although I imagine a number of the local Christian men have no such fear of pollution. It's a terrible thing to have happened and I'm sorry for the poor women, even the Saracen ones. But I still don't understand why you are the one to free them or why you can't ask your neighbors to help."

"They can't know." Aaron finally turned to face his friend. "Especially not here. Solomon, the woman we have to free *is* Mayah."

"Mayah!"

Solomon felt as if a mule had just kicked him in the stomach.

"But . . . but how?" he stammered. "That can't be! She doesn't live in Almeria. Her home is in Córdoba."

"I know," Aaron said. "But her father sent her away last summer to stay with a cousin. Both the Christians and the Berbers were threatening Córdoba. Yishmael thought she'd be safer in Almeria."

Solomon's vague pity turned to deep horror as he imagined the beautiful, spoiled, brilliant girl he had known in Córdoba in the hands of slavers. It would have been easier to learn of her death.

Aaron answered his expression.

"Now do you understand?" he asked. "Now will you help us?"

Solomon drew in a deep breath. He felt dizzy with shock.

"I had already promised to help not knowing who she was," he told his friend. "And now that I do, I will give anything necessary to free her, including my life."

Aaron bent his head to hide tears.

"Thank you," he said. "So you see why I couldn't go to the community."

"No, not really," Solomon answered. "You wasted a lot of time trying to do this alone. They could have sent out messengers to find what had happened to her and . . . oh, of course."

He couldn't believe his stupidity. Aaron's face said it all.

"If you went to the community then everyone would know she had been violated," he finished. "You still want to marry her, don't you?"

Aaron nodded. His eyes pleaded with Solomon to understand.

At last, Solomon did. It wasn't just the shame of rape but the fact that it had been done by men who weren't Jewish. A woman taken by the gentiles was forbidden in some cases even to return to her own husband. The harsh law was ancient, going back to the time of the Romans at least.

"But that can't be true now," he protested. "I'm sure there were women taken by the Edomite soldiers in Germany who married after they were returned to their families."

"How sure?" Aaron asked. "Do you know any? Even more, do you know one who was permitted to wed a Cohen?"

Now it was Solomon who looked away. This was one of the times when he was glad not to be asked to defend his faith. Cohens were the descendents of priests. When the Temple was rebuilt, they would serve in it as before and, like Caesar's wife, a Cohen's had to be above reproach or even suspicion.

"I'm not a scholar," he said at last. "There may be precedents."

"I haven't found any," Aaron said grimly.

"Wait a minute." Solomon realized what Aaron was planning. "You're saying you mean to save her and marry her anyway, don't you? No matter what?"

"Yes," Aaron answered. "And I can't believe anyone as lax about the Law as you are would try to stop me."

"Of course not," Solomon assured him. "I'm just wondering if Mayah will agree."

He shouldn't have said that. He could tell from Aaron's re-action that he hadn't considered the possibility that Mayah might not allow him to enter a sinful marriage.

"But all that matters now," Solomon added hastily, "is to free her at once. I can be ready to leave at dawn."

"I wish it were that easy." The sun was low in the sky now, bathing the Bourg behind them in rose and gold. Aaron explained as the two men started back.

"Arnald's eagerness to help has made my original plan im-possible," he said. "From what Belide told me, the two of them have made such a point of having a secret that now everyone wants to know what it is."

"Did Belide mention that she still has the bag of gold from Brother Victor?" Solomon asked. "No, I can see that she didn't."

He related the entire story as he knew it.

Before he had finished, Aaron was pounding his palms against his forehead in consternation.

"I'm a complete fool!" he growled. "Why did I ever trust those children?"

Solomon had been wondering that himself.

"I say take the coins and use them," he advised Aaron. "There's no way we can return them to the monks without being accused of murder."

"I won't buy Mayah back with unclean money," Aaron said.

"Right," Solomon answered. "Very noble of you. Although I've always found that coins wash easily. But why don't we discuss it later. This is hardly the place."

They were back in the *rue des Blanchisseurs*. The inhabitants were bustling about, preparing for Easter the next Sunday. They paid no attention to Solomon and Aaron but both men felt it would take little more than a comment to make them the center of a mob.

"I'll be at my sister's home, if you want me," Aaron told Solomon as they parted at Gavi's gate. "Can you come by to-morrow?"

Solomon promised.

"Thank you." Aaron shook his hand. "Thank you! I knew you wouldn't let me down. This is the first moment of hope I've felt in weeks."

As he watched Aaron leave, Solomon had one of his rare forebodings. This journey would bring disaster, most likely for him. Angrily, he shook off the sensation. It was probably the result of too many dried prunes. Even if it were a true sending, it didn't matter. He had meant what he said. To rescue Mayah, he would pay any price.

He recalled the last time he had seen her. Slight, dark and with an iron will, she had told him that she intended to devote her life to study. Her doting father had indulged her desire for books in Arabic and Hebrew. Solomon wondered how Aaron had convinced Yishmael to let the jewel of his household marry a horse trader, for all that he was a Cohen. Perhaps something about Aaron had touched Mayah's heart.

He tried very hard not to imagine what was happening to her now.

When he returned to the house, Gavi's wife answered his knock at once and astonished him by throwing her arms around his neck, kissing him on both cheeks.

"Nazara, what is this?" he cried, half in earnest. "I thought you were a faithful wife!"

She released him at once and laughed.

"That was gratitude, not lust," she chided.

"Oh, and what have I done to deserve such a reward?"

"This afternoon, just after you left," she said as she sat him at the table and poured mint water for him to wash his hands. "Who should come to our door but *Na* Josta! Her poor face! I tried not to show I noticed but it does look dreadful. I hope there will be no scars. Anyway, I told her you weren't here and, do you know what? She said she'd come to see me! Me! I couldn't believe it."

Solomon tried to insert a comment but her words flowed on.

"She told me that you had reminded her that she had been neglectful. She was ashamed of herself for not visiting us more. Can you imagine? With the smell of piss everywhere, who would? Well, apart from you, of course," Nazara added.

Solomon wasn't sure how he should respond to that. Luckily, he didn't have to.

"*Na* Josta told me that this was a time of year when it was especially important to remember that we are all Israel and in the eyes of the Holy One, blessed be He, equal."

She stopped and smiled at the memory.

"And then she asked us to join them at their Seder," she ended triumphantly.

Solomon dried his hands. He was pleased that Josta had acted so quickly. But now that the invitation had been issued, he wasn't so sure that he should have meddled. What if his friends felt that Josta had acted out of condescension?

Nazara took the bowl and emptied it out the window. Then she returned to Solomon.

"And?" he asked nervously. "What did you tell her?"

"That we would be honored, of course," she said. "Don't worry, Solomon. I know she wouldn't have offered if you hadn't said something, but she was so kind and embarrassed about asking so near the holiday that I knew she really wanted us to accept. Don't you agree?"

Solomon heard the tinge of doubt.

"I do," he said. "Josta is a good woman. You and Gavi will be a welcome addition to the company. Of course, you might want to prepare yourselves for the twins."

Brother James was not pleased when Prior Stephen told him that his trip would be delayed another week.

"But Brother Martin and I are ready to leave," he said. "We have guards and provisions for the journey. The thief only got part of the ransom money. There's still enough to free at least ten men."

"But the donation from Lord Falquet would allow us to liberate five more," Stephen said patiently. "Five who might die of starvation or torture before another party could reach them."

Reluctantly, James admitted the logic of this.

"Also," the prior added. "After Easter there will be several trading parties setting out. It's always better to travel in as large a group as possible, to fend off marauders."

James stopped himself from saying that he knew it well, having spent his early life in a family of merchants. Prior Stephen was continually testing him. James was determined that the man would never win. He wasn't sure if it was Jewish stubbornness or Christian obedience; but, in, either case, Stephen was not going to find cause to send him back to Moissac.

But he didn't know how he could endure another week in Toulouse. Since he had seen Hubert, James had felt like a man tied between wild horses. One pulled him to reveal what he knew and prove for all time that he was completely Christian. The other jerked him back with the thought that it would be more for his own pride than Hubert's soul. And running in and out of his constant internal disputation was the memory of the little boy at the window in Rouen, waving good-bye to his big brother, Jacob, as he left to study in Champagne.

He tried so hard. He prayed and prayed for guidance. Why was there no answer?

That evening, Berengar told Guy about Jehan's defiance of the lords.

"I've never seen my father so impressed," he said wistfully. "And old Orso pinned to the table by his own knife stuck through his sleeve! What a glorious sight! He won't live that down soon."

"It sounds as though Jehan will need us to watch his back until we leave," Guy commented.

"Do you think so?" Berengar eyes lit. "Maybe we shouldn't have let him go out alone tonight."

Guy snorted and reached for the pitcher. "That one doesn't need a wet nurse. He said he was going to do a bit more sinning before being shriven on Friday. I'd do the same if I had the coin."

He gave Berengar a hopeful look.

"Sorry," the young man answered. "Food, wine, and a bed. That's all they'll pay for. Company you have to arrange yourself."

Guy sighed. Berengar tried to think of something to cheer him.

"I hear there's a *jongleur* staying here tonight," he said, refilling their cups. "He has a couple of other people with him who act out his songs in a dumb show."

"Either of them female?" Guy asked.

"Don't know," Berengar said. "But those women charge more than the town whores. You have to pay for imagination. Now, if you can be really charming, Adelina there might give you a tumble out back behind the stable."

Guy squinted to see through the smoke from the oil lamps. The woman cutting cheese for the guests was not particularly attractive. Her skin was bad and the light brown hair escaping from her head scarf was wispy. But, from what he could tell, all the parts were in the right places.

"What's wrong with her?" he asked Berengar.

"Do you mean, is she diseased?" Berengar answered. "Not that I know. Her father's a cripple who keeps her home to care for him. She works here now and then and picks up a bit extra when she can. She'll let you do what you like for a few ribbons or a length of wool, if you don't take too long."

"Don't think I've got that much." Guy returned to his wine. "Can't you give me a loan? Your father's rich."

Berengar grimaced. "That doesn't mean he ever lets me near his purse. He thinks the best way to keep his sons from rebellion is to make sure they have nothing of their own."

"Where I come from that's the best way to guarantee they'll rise against him," Guy noted. He was still staring at Adelina. Was Berengar playing him for a fool? He didn't relish being rejected by a tavern drab.

"Well, I figure I can wait a couple years more," Berengar said. "Why don't you at least talk to her? She'll let you know if she's interested. I'm going out for a piss."

Guy waited a few moments for him to return. When it seemed that Berengar had abandoned him, too, he decided that he had nothing to lose and got up to try his luck.

Solomon knew that it wasn't wise for him to go to a tavern that evening. But the delirious preparations for Pesach at Gavi's made him feel very much in the way. It would be worse at Bonysach's. He thought of going to see Aaron but his sister was no doubt also in a frenzy of cleaning. He didn't even consider visiting his uncle. So that left the choice of a solitary drink someplace not too far from the synagogue. If he'd been a local Jew, the other men would have overlooked his existence as an infidel, remembering he was also a neighbor, but strangers were always fair game. Solomon hoped that everyone was too involved with their own business to pay heed to him.

He got a bowl of sour *pinot* with a pot of lavender water to blunt the taste. Then he looked around for a quiet, dim corner to enjoy them in.

That was when his luck ran out.

There was a rustle as a man on one side of the room nudged the one next to him. Solomon heard the muttering. The words weren't clear but the meaning was. He moved away from the men, hoping that he could put down the wine before one of them jumped him.

The tavern was just a narrow room that might once have been a corridor between streets, now roofed over, with straw spread on the earth. Both ends were covered only with burlap curtains. Solomon gauged the distance to the nearest and what he'd have to leap over to get out quickly.

A sensible man would have left then. But Solomon had paid for his drink and he wasn't going to let some half-wit Edomites keep him from drinking it.

He put the bowls down on a bench and was about to sit when someone spat on his boot.

He rubbed it off on the leg of the bench, thankful that he wasn't wearing sandals.

On the other side of the room someone snickered.

He told himself that he had asked for this. He should have stayed with his own people.

The bravest of the men got up and faced him.

"I know you," he said. "Saw you with Bonysach. He should have told you that we don't drink with filthy Jews." He belched in Solomon's face. The reek of garlic and rotten teeth was choking. "Go back to your sty, pig."

"Dirty Jew kills our Lord and Savior and then wants to drink our wine," another man growled.

Solomon revised his opinion of their sobriety. He hoped the

ones still seated were too drunk to stand. It would give him infinite joy to knock the man flat. In his state it wouldn't take more
than a push. But he knew that any action he took would be
brought back to the community. Homes had been burnt and Jews
beaten to death from smaller sparks.

He edged toward the doorway.

The man advanced. Solomon noted the broad shoulders and
muscled forearms. Wonderful. He was probably a smith, used to
knowing he was stronger than most of the men around. He could
smash Solomon's face open, if he didn't pass out first.

"There's no need to cause trouble, Friend," he said softly.

The man's fist crashed into him.

Solomon was quick enough that the blow only glanced his
shoulder and sent his tormentor tottering forward. Before Solomon could reach the exit, the man made a leap for him, catching
him by the belt.

Solomon grabbed a low beam and managed to stay upright,
but his weight plus that of the smith threatened to bring down
the flimsy roof.

By now the man's friends had staggered up to join the fun.

"Got him by the tail, you do!"

"Let's have those boots. Who'll bet he has goat hooves?" The
speaker grabbed Solomon's foot.

He kicked out, trying to control himself enough to keep from
doing them any damage. His belt was about to snap along with
his temper.

Hell, he thought. *They'll tell the bishop I caused any mark they
have. Why not give them a few?*

His right hand reached into his sleeve for his knife.

A shadow blocked the lantern light. Solomon felt his leg
yanked and then released as the drunk was picked up and tossed
against the far wall. Next, the smith gave a howl and let go
Solomon's belt to clutch his own groin.

◆

For an instant Solomon thought that perhaps the angel Gabriel had descended from heaven to destroy the foes of Israel. Hadn't he just told his uncle that it was about time for the Messiah to arrive?

Then the light struck the face of his rescuer.

Solomon gaped in disbelief. He squeezed his eyes closed and then quickly opened them. What he saw was no less astonishing than a divine savior.

Jehan of Blois stood in front of him, grinning.

"It fills my heart with joy to see you looking so foolish," he said. "I can't believe you've lived this long, the way you invite trouble. But if anyone ends your life, it will be me, not some miserable wine-soaked scum."

He took Solomon's bowl from the bench and drained it, ignoring the curses and groans of pain from the floor.

"I'd get out of here now," he told Solomon. "Unless you want to wind up hanged as an Easter offering."

His words broke Solomon's paralysis.

"I would thank you but I know you'd throw it back in my teeth," he said. "It should give you much more satisfaction to know that I'm in your debt."

Jehan grinned once more. It was an expression of pure gloating.

"Oh, it does," he said.

As Solomon reached the street, he was disgusted to realize that he was shaking as if he had the palsy. He tried to tell himself that it was from anger. But deep down he knew that what he was feeling was pure terror.

Had any of the past hour really happened or had he been caught up in some demonic vision? Had he really been in a dank tavern or on the edge of the grave? The damp, mud-drugged straw, the narrow room, the smell of rancid animal fat as it burned, the faces blurred by smoke, made it a charnel house in his memory.

It couldn't have been Jehan of Blois who had just saved him. Jehan would have slit his throat as he hung from the rafter. It must have been an incubus in his form. Only that made no sense. Why would Satan protect him from the Christians? But then why would a messenger of the Holy One come in the shape of his worst enemy?

Come to think of it, why would an angel come to him at all?

It was full dark now, the waxing moon just rising. The bells of Toulouse were ringing Compline. Good Christians were saying their prayers and preparing for bed. The watch would be making their rounds soon. Solomon should be on his way to Gavi's and his own bed. But he needed time to sort out his thoughts. He needed to convince his limbs to be still.

The street of the tanners and bleachers of cloth wasn't far from the Garonne. Instead of going directly to Gavi's, Solomon went down to the river's edge. He pulled off his boots, tunic, hose, and leather *brais*. Clad only in his shift, he plunged into the icy water.

He surfaced a few feet downstream, gasping but clear headed. As he waded, dripping, back to shore he heard a howl of terror from someone standing above him on the bank. He peered through the darkness, but saw no sign of anything dangerous. All the same, he retrieved his clothes in haste and hurried back to the warmth of the tanner's home.

A few moments later a harness maker stumbled into his house. When his wife could get any sense from him, she learned that he had seen John the Baptist rising from the Garonne, shaking his head in reproach.

"Never again, I swear," the man vowed. "I promise you, Tilna, I'll sin no more."

The next day his wife bought a candle to light at the church of Saint John. He was a saint that she had greatly underappreciated.

It was full dark when the monks finished Compline and proceeded in silence to their dormitory. Brother James was near the end of the line. His steps faltered with fatigue; it was an effort not to stumble into the man in front.

He was at the bottom of the stairs when the commotion began. Someone gave a cry and a moment later one of the younger men came running down, bumping against the others in his haste.

"What is it?" James asked the man ahead.

He feared he might be chided for breaking silence but now all the monks were trying to get into the room. Finally, James reached the top of the stairs. What greeted him was pandemonium. Some of the beds had been overturned and all the bedding torn off and thrown about the room. Straw mattresses had been slashed open and the innards scattered. The thin pillows were in shreds, feathers drifting though the air and landing on the monks as they tried to salvage what they could from the mess.

James crossed to what was left of his own bed. It was in the same state as the others. What could have done this and why? Around him the monks were speculating.

"Some evil spirits must have flown in the windows to create havoc while we were at our prayers," one suggested.

"Did no one hear anything?" another asked.

James noticed something near him on the floor. He took a candle from the sconce on the wall and bent down to examine it.

Some feathers were stuck to the wood in a clump. James blew on them and a few fluttered loose. Gingerly, he touched the sticky substance holding the others in place. He sniffed his fingers.

"Mud," he said. "And the print of a boot heel."

His new partner, Brother Martin, came over to see.

"Fairly solid evil spirits," he commented. "But how did they get in here?"

The loud voice of the priory doorkeeper rose from the stairwell.

"I told you, my lord," he insisted. "No one entered the priory after Vespers. I let the cook's helpers and the waste collector out. No strangers at all."

The prior entered the room, followed by the porter who whistled in amazement.

"Aren't you lads a bit old for pillow fights?" he asked.

Brother Martin spoke for them all.

"Several of us were up here just before Compline," he told the prior. "This had to have been done while we were in the chapel."

"Well it wasn't by an outsider," the doorkeeper stated. "Nor no sane man, to my mind. Could have been squirrels."

Prior Stephen raised his eyebrows.

It might also have been a troop of monkeys or lions," he said. "But I find the theory of demons more believable."

He addressed the monks.

"Did any of you see anyone, stranger or not, enter the dormitory?"

They all shook their heads.

"Ghosts, perhaps?" one suggested. "Damned souls who wish to keep us from our rest."

"We've had no previous visitations," the prior said. "Any other possibilities?"

"Whoever it was," Brother Martin said, "he was well shod."

He showed the prior the boot print.

"There's another here." James had been continuing his search. "And one more at the window."

He looked out. There was an old chestnut tree whose branches scraped against the wall. It would be no trick for an agile man to climb in and out again.

The other monks came to see. A few feathers clinging to the bark just outside convinced them.

"So, Brother Olivier, you are exonerated," the prior said.

"No one gets past me," the doorkeeper muttered. "Thank you, my lord," he added.

"Brother Martin, Brother James." Prior Stephen beckoned to them. "Come with me. Bring torches. I want you to see if you can find which way our vandal went. The rest of you, salvage what you can to sleep on tonight."

James followed Brother Martin reluctantly. He tried to stifle a yawn. The odds were that the street would be so scuffed that they would have no way of tracing the intruders. How many feathers could have stayed on their clothing? Perhaps they would find a scrap torn from a pair of hose or a shift, but that would be no use unless they also found the man who wore them.

But, although the two monks searched on hands and knees, they found nothing but a few dents in the soft earth where the intruders had landed.

They reported this to the prior in his quarters. James tried not to look longingly at his pristine bed.

"I didn't expect there to be much more evidence," the prior admitted. "At least there was enough to prove this a deed of human wickedness."

He laced his fingers as if praying for guidance.

"It is unlikely that the name of the one who did this will be discovered until we know why it was done," he said, staring straight at James. "And I believe that you hold the answer. Do you agree, Brother James?"

James nodded wearily. The bags of gold tied on the belt beneath his robe clinked in response.

Ten

*Toulouse, Holy Saturday, 4 Ides April (April 10) 1148, 12
Nissan 4908, Shabbat Ha Gadol, the Sabbath before Passover.*

A porta inferi erue, Domine, animam meam.

From the gate of hell, Lord, deliver my soul.

—*Antiphon for Holy Saturday*

*L*ike the rest of the Jews in Toulouse, Solomon spent the days before Easter trying to be inconspicuous. His near disaster in the tavern had disturbed him deeply. The greatest shock was knowing that it was his old enemy Jehan who had kept him from setting off a brawl that could easily have become a riot. He shuddered every time he thought of it.

"Are you sickening for something?" Aaron asked him. "Galde here has a poultice that will cure almost anything if you can survive the smell."

"But it needs to be freshly compounded to work," his sister reminded him. "And it's the Sabbath."

They were in the courtyard of Aaron's sister's house in the Bourg, near the church of Saint Julien. Galde and her husband, Vital, had five arpents of vines just north of the town wall from which they made wine for both Jews and gentiles. Galde also grew herbs and mixed medicines that she sold in the market. Aaron had traded jars of her salve to cure creaking joints as far away as London and Toledo.

Vital, Galde, and Aaron had just returned from services. Solomon had declined, fearing whom he might meet on the way. Instead he waited for them in the courtyard, his thoughts on Mayah.

Galde went to get the tray of cheese, greens, and the last of the bread that she had prepared Friday afternoon. Vital excused himself, yawning, for a Sabbath nap, leaving Aaron and Solomon alone.

"Does your sister know of your plans for this rescue?" Solomon asked as soon as she had left the room.

"No," Aaron answered. "And not even Belide and Arnald know Mayah's name. I've told Galde that I'm going to fetch my bride from Córdoba. Mayah's father and I have been discussing the arrangements for over a year now. He was to have the *ketubah* drawn up last autumn. No one will be surprised when we return. Galde and Vital are eager to welcome her."

"Aaron, why didn't you get the ransom money from Yishmael?" Solomon asked. "He would have given you money, men, and weapons. You can't be trying to save him the anguish of knowing about this."

"Solomon, where have you been this past year?" Aaron answered. "Yishmael collapsed when he learned the news. He died a week later."

"Oh, my poor friend!" Solomon exclaimed. "May his soul be at peace and his memory honored. But is there no other family?"

"Mayah's cousins have taken her property," Aaron went on. "They have assumed she's dead, or will be soon. As long as we don't press them for her inheritance, they won't make trouble about the marriage."

"Well, at least with the excuse of going to get your bride, you have a reason for your impatience to be off," Solomon said. "And especially to be heading south when everyone else is going north to the fairs. But, if you must continue this pretense, you need to show more cheer. I've observed the phenomenon often and your behavior falls short of the rapture of a man about to wed."

"Galde puts my gloom down to lovesickness," Aaron explained. "She keeps trying to slip herbs in the soup to cool my inflamed heart. Mostly they just irritate my bowels."

He sighed. "The time of year has been a problem, too. With most people going north to the fairs, I've been hard put to gather a party of travelers strong enough to risk the Navarrese bandits. However, that may have resolved itself. Yesterday, Arnald told me that his father is insisting he join this group going to ransom captured knights in Al-Andalus. He didn't know what to answer. I told him to agree to go. The one thing I hadn't worked out was how to get Arnald to come with me. I need a Christian to treat with those who own the brothel. Now I can arrange for all of us to leave Toulouse in the company of the monks and, when we get to Navarre, you, Arnald, and I will make a detour to this monastery."

Solomon had been listening to this with growing dread. It was clear to him just which monk would be a part of the delegation. His father spoke good Arabic, as well as Hebrew. His uncles had often lamented not having Jacob to speak for them in Spain. It made sense now. That was why he had left the safety of his monastery. And if the two groups traveled together, there would be no way for him to avoid the monk James.

It was too much to ask.

"Aaron! No!" Solomon thumped both hands on the table, causing a vase to rock. Aaron steadied it, giving Solomon a quizzical look.

"I can't do it," Solomon insisted. "Not those monks. I'd rather we take our chances alone."

At this moment, Galde returned with the tray and set it on the table in front of them. Solomon stared down at the plate.

The smell of cheese and pickled onions was overpowering on top of the news he had just had to stomach.

"Excuse me." He clamped his hand over his mouth as he rose. He knocked the chair over in his haste to reach the outhouse.

"Poor Solomon!" Galde exclaimed. "Perhaps, in an emergency, I could mix a poultice. The Creator, blessed be He, never meant the sick to go untreated on the Sabbath."

"I think he'll be all right as soon as he empties his stomach," Aaron answered. "I seem to have upset him but I can't understand why. He does business with monks all the time. Why should it bother him to spend a few days on the road in their company? Even Yusef endures it without complaint."

Solomon returned a few moments later, wiping his mouth.

"I apologize, Galde," he said. "I must have eaten a bad olive."

Galde gave him a cup of water with instructions to sip slowly. As he did, Solomon reflected that he should have had someone read his stars before he set out from Paris. Then he might have been forewarned that Fate was going to send him a particularly nasty future.

At Saint Pierre des Cuisines, the monks' dormitory was almost back to normal. The mattress and pillow stuffing had been swept out and new rushes laid on the floor. There wasn't enough spare bedding to replace all that had been destroyed but several of the brothers volunteered to sleep on the hard floor with only a blanket. As soon as they spoke up, the rest insisted on doing the same.

"As our life is in common," a young monk said. "So should we live and sleep in an equal state."

There was no way to avoid the floor after that.

Saturday afternoon, the monks retired for a rest before the all night Easter vigil. As he tried to find a comfortable position on the hard boards, Brother James prayed that God would be merciful and spare his back. Even the usual monastic mattress made his first steps in the morning agony. He bunched his robe on one side to cushion his thigh and was just dozing off when he sensed someone standing at his side. He opened his eyes.

Brother Martin loomed above him, a blanket draped over his arm.

"Here, Brother James," he said. "Take my cover. I don't need it in this warm weather."

James thought quickly. Should he accept the offer in a spirit of grateful humility? But that would be admitting he was in need of extra care. Yet to refuse would seem churlish. He couldn't deny that the extra thickness under his hip bones would be very welcome. A voice inside reproved him at once for yielding to physical weakness. Every twinge should be an offering.

He made up his mind.

"A kind gesture, Brother Martin." He smiled. "But there may be many nights on our journey when we'll have only the bare earth for a bed. I should prepare myself now."

Martin squatted next to him.

"Brother James, there's no need to deny yourself a bit of comfort," he said. "I've seen how, even at Moissac, you are hard on your body. You accept the most irksome tasks. You could spend all your days in the scriptorium or teaching. Prior Rodger says you are a brilliant scholar, adept at rhetoric in many languages."

"He is over fulsome in his praise," James answered. "But even if it were true, there are no words, even the most holy, that are more pleasing to Our Lord than honest work done in His name with love."

Martin crossed himself. "I understand. I'll not try to force comfort upon you. But at least allow me to share your burden."

James eyes narrowed. "In what way?"

Brother Martin leaned closer so that the other monks couldn't overhear.

"When the abbot selected me to take up Brother Victor's unfinished work, I understood that I was to smooth the path for you," he said. "You no longer need bear the weight of the ransom yourself."

Instinctively James's arm went over the money belt. Brother Martin laughed.

"Do you fear me?" He rocked back in amusement. "For shame, my brother. Why do you think the abbot chose me? When this was first planned, Victor was picked for his good heart and his gift for making friends. You, because you can speak for us and negotiate with the Saracens. But after what happened to poor Victor, the abbot decided a good heart was not enough and that you should have a protector."

He stood again. From his viewpoint on the floor, James felt as if he were in the shade of a towering cliff. Martin laughed again.

"When I was in the world, my friends called me 'the ox,'" he said. "And not just for my strength. After eight years at Moissac, I still don't know the Office. I spend half my time bowing."

James had noticed that. Each time a monk erred in the prayers, he bowed to the altar to ask forgiveness. Martin spent a lot of time bent over.

"But," the monk continued, "I can walk all day and not tire, stand against any wind and carry your load, and you too, to the end of the road. The abbot said that you were too stubborn to make use of me. I hope he misjudged you."

Martin didn't wait for an answer but returned to his own place on the floor. As he tried once again to settle into a position conducive to sleep, James saw the monk's blanket, neatly folded, lying next to him. It made a most welcome cushion.

Jehan came into the main hall of the Plucked Crow, carrying a pack. He set it down by the table where Guy and Berengar were idly casting dice.

"What's that for?" Berengar asked.

"It is my custom to pass the night of Holy Saturday in a vigil of prayer and penance," Jehan answered. "I'll return after Mass tomorrow."

"Do you know something about this mission that we don't?" Guy asked. "I've been shriven, of course, just in case, but I figured I had plenty of time to do my penance."

"A vigil is a good idea; I'll go with you," Berengar announced. "We can do it over at the church where Saint Sarni fought the bull. It's more fitting for men like us and won't be as crowded as the cathedral."

"You have a local saint who was a bullfighter?" Guy asked doubtfully.

"Don't you know him?" Berengar was astonished. "He was a bishop or something, back when the Romans ruled us. Saturnus is the Latin name. You French call him Sernin. He was to be martyred by being tied to a maddened bull. It dragged him the length of the street from the cathedral to the Capitole."

"What happened then? Did he tame it?" Guy asked. "Or did a bolt from heaven strike it dead?"

Berengar thought. "I don't remember. Maybe Sarni just died. The priest will know the whole story."

Jehan wasn't interested in local history. "That church will do as well as any. The place isn't important. I have performed this expiation on mountainsides and by the side of the road."

He faltered as a memory of shame stabbed him.

"And," he added, "it's something I must do alone."

Guy shrugged. "Fair enough. I've said the prayers the priest set me and given a candle to the Knights of the Temple. My sleep will come easily. I'll see you tomorrow at Mass."

But Berengar wasn't so easily put off.

"I have much to repent of," he said. "I should also fast and pray. We can encourage each other if our will should falter."

"My atonement requires solitary meditation," Jehan explained, wondering if the boy would ever take the hint.

"Oh." Berengar scratched his head. "Then we should probably go somewhere outside the walls. Maybe across the river."

"I'm sure I can find a place." Jehan bent to pick up his pack again.

Berengar reached it first. "Here, I'll help you."

He started to hoist the pack, grunted, and dropped it again with a clank.

"What do you have in here?" he asked, trying again. "Bars of gold?"

Guy sat up straighter.

"You sure you're not leaving town?" he asked.

Jehan moved Berengar off the pack and opened the flap.

Inside were coils of iron chain.

"What are you doing with that?" Berengar asked. "Are you planning on taking prisoners tonight?"

Jehan didn't answer. He closed the pack, lifted it with ease and left the inn.

Guy shook his head.

"You simpleton!" he said to Berengar. "What form a man's atonement takes is none of your concern. Leave him to it."

Berengar sat back down slowly.

"Did you see how the weight of those chains was nothing to him? He must have been carrying them a long time. I wonder what he did to deserve such a penance."

"Take my advice," Guy said. "Don't ask him."

Solomon judged that it was safe to go out again on Easter morning. The bells were ringing all over town. The cathedral was packed and Christians were busy celebrating the return of their god. It had always been a mystery to Solomon why his people were reviled in the streets as those who had killed Jesus when, without that death, no resurrection could have occurred. However, most of the things Christians believed baffled him, despite the best efforts of numerous priests and his cousin, Catherine, to make them sound logical and appealing.

At least the laws God gave to the Jews weren't intended to make sense. The teachers in Troyes had explained that to him when he was a boy. It was enough that the Creator understood the rules. His only duty was to trust and obey.

Solomon had wasted too many years in fighting that dictum. Perhaps he had absorbed some of Peter Abelard's teaching through Catherine and Edgar, who had been students of the philosopher. Laws should make sense, divine ones especially. Why should men have been given minds if not better to understand the Mind that created them?

Finally he realized that his intelligence wasn't up to the task. Nor was his piety. What remained was a simmering resentment of those to whom faith was clear and unshakeable.

This Easter morning he was surrounded by them.

His route took him past the cathedral of Saint Sernin and along the road to the Saracen Wall, which separated the Bourg of Toulouse from the Cité. He realized at once that it had been a stupid choice for it was the main street for Easter processions. He was forced against the buildings with the rest of the populace as priests and monks paraded by, carrying crosses and relics of the saints.

The progress of the clerics was slow as many of the devout crowded forward to touch the reliquaries. Many of them held up sick or crippled children, hoping that the saints in the shrines would notice and take pity on them.

Amidst the crowd wandered peddlers, their backs loaded with tin crosses or emblems of the saints. There were also sellers of sweets, to break the Lenten fast and, as always, beggars.

Solomon looked for a passage that would take him away from the throng. He kept his back against the wall, edging along it to find an opening.

Finally he felt air on his neck. Behind him there was a narrow alleyway that seemed to go through. He stepped back into it and bumped against someone sitting in the shadows.

He fell over with a curse and the clanking of metal.

There was a grunt of pain and then a familiar voice.

"I thought you might do that," Jehan said. "When I saw you enter."

Solomon sat up, rubbing a scraped knee.

"You might have warned me," he said. "This was a new stocking. Now it's ripped clear through and I'm bleeding on it."

He stopped as his eyes adjusted to the dim light of the passage.

"Why are you sitting here wrapped in a chain?" he asked. "Not that I don't approve but I assumed that you had escaped the jailer who had charge of you when you left Paris."

Jehan made no answer. He stretched out his arms and stood up amidst a cacophony of iron. Then he held out his hand to help Solomon rise.

Solomon looked at the hand in suspicion and got up on his own.

"I have no jailer outside my own soul," Jehan said as he unwound the chain. "I began to understand that the farther I went from Paris and Catherine LeVendeur. Once I was free of the torments of that witch and her sister, I expiated my sin in battle against the infidels."

"You killed a man in Paris," Solomon reminded him. "And before that, your madness nearly got Catherine's sister killed. And so you feel you've atoned for death by taking more life?"

"No." Jehan finished freeing himself from the chain. "Only sincere contrition will redeem me. I work at it every day. Seeing you makes me aware that I have not completely renounced old enmities. And so I must continue to force my body to submit to restraint. If not, I can never learn to govern my spirit."

He let the iron fall in a long spiral into a leather pack at his feet. Solomon saw that he was barefoot and wearing only a linen shift. He had seen many such pilgrims and penitents in his life. Even the highest nobles had humbled themselves for the good of their souls. But he could not believe it of this man.

He must be planning something.

"Well, I should be going." Solomon checked the passage for further obstacles. "Enjoy your suffering. Yours is a laudable goal. I wish you success."

He half expected Jehan to answer with a threat or try to stop him, but the man simply watched as Solomon walked through the long, dark alley.

When he emerged into the sunlight, Solomon felt as if he'd been released from the belly of the whale. Nothing found inside Leviathan could possibly be stranger or more unsettling than a seemingly penitent Jehan.

He was beginning to feel that no corner of Toulouse was safe from surprises.

Normally the person he would have gone to first was his uncle Hubert. But Hubert was becoming more distant with every conversation. Solomon couldn't decide if the change was a result of increased piety or creeping senility. He only knew that his own heart was deeply troubled and there was no one to share it with.

He wished he hadn't let Edgar go home.

Belide was washing the Passover meat platters. Her mother sat nearby polishing silver.

"Do you need another pillow, Mama?" she asked. "A hat to shade you from the sun? I'll go get it."

Josta put down the shining spoon and picked up another.

"The sun isn't too bright, dear," she said. "I'm quite comfortable."

Belide worked quietly a little longer. Josta could see that her daughter wanted to tell her something. She hoped it wouldn't be any more revelations about Arnald or Christian gold. She finished the last spoon and started on the salt cellar.

"Your brothers should be back soon," she commented. "I do love them but the quiet is restful."

Belide took a deep breath. "Mother," she said.

Josta steeled herself.

"Yes, dear?"

"Is Samuel still coming to the Seder tomorrow?" Belide asked.

"Why, I suppose so," Josta answered. "He hasn't told your father that he won't be. Is that a problem? Are you worried that he won't want to eat with Gavi?"

"No, of course not," Belide said. "At least, I hadn't thought of it. It's just that, when we go to services, he never looks at me. I'm sure he doesn't want to speak to me after what I did."

"Perhaps he's just behaving properly until he speaks to your father," Josta suggested. "Does his indifference bother you?"

"Not in the slightest." Belide gave the platter her complete attention, not looking up. "I simply thought that he might find another visit to us uncomfortable."

"I suppose, my dear, that depends on what you do to him the next time he visits."

Josta gathered up the silver and took it back into the house, leaving her daughter to think that one out for herself.

Solomon sat at one of the long tables set up in the square, cradling a bowl of beer and watching a woman in a short *chainse* and multicolored hose do flips over a brazier of glowing coals. Once she had the attention of the crowd, two men got up and lit tapers from the brazier. They proceeded to light streams of fire from their mouths, shooting them at each other until Solomon was sure one of them would ignite.

Instead, the woman returned with a dragon's head, as large as that of a horse. It was made from cloth on a wooden frame, with evil black eyes and a cavernous mouth. A long red tongue like a whip dangled from it. The woman danced around the men as they tried to catch the head in their flames.

"Your mortal fires can't hurt me!" the woman cried. "I am the pet of Satan and bathe each day in a molten inferno! I come to herd sinners like you into the depths for my master."

The men continued to try to set fire to the dragon but the woman nimbly avoided them all the while drawing them closer to a pile of boxes set up on one side of the square. There was a cloth draped over them but as she came close enough, the woman pulled it down to reveal a giant hell mouth, open and grinning.

The audience gave a cry of horror and delight.

"There is no hope for you!" the dragon taunted the men. "Down you go!"

She pushed them into the maw of the beast and, with hideous screams, the fire eaters vanished.

"That is the fate of sinners!" the woman sang, still dancing the dragon head about the square. "Who's next? You? Or you?"

She pointed to several of the spectators.

"Your neighbors don't know your sins," she leered at one well-dressed man. "But my master does. Your gold and silk are no protection from him."

"That's one who won't leave a coin on the plate," a voice said in Solomon's ear.

He turned around. Arnald grinned at him.

"Father let me out for the day," he explained. "Since I'm about to leave on a dangerous journey for the good of my soul. Want a sausage?"

He held out a hard greasy stick, well gnawed. Solomon leaned back to avoid the smell.

"Too much garlic?" Arnald asked. Then it hit him "Oh, damn. I didn't mean to . . . I forgot it was pork."

"Keep your voice down," Solomon hissed.

He glanced around. No one seemed to have heard.

They turned their attention back to the players. The woman had made the rounds of those closest to her, suggesting that they had committed everything from gluttony to lascivious behavior with their goats. The rest of the audience roared with laughter.

"Ah, you can't hide behind your wife!" she chided one man. "Even if she is a mighty warrior, who outlasts you in every battle! The sharpest spindle can't dent my scales! I tell you all." She swept the dragon head in a circle. "There is no protection from me! One by one, you shall all enter my master's kingdom!"

One of the fire eaters returned from behind the hell mouth. He was now garbed as a demon, with horns, a sooty face, and a huge false nose that hooked over his mouth. His tunic was hitched up in back to show another face tied to his buttocks, the forked tongue protruding obscenely. At the orders of the "dragon," he picked up a young woman from the crowd and prepared to toss her into the abyss.

The scream she gave sounded genuine. The man near her tried to intervene, but, as he rushed to save her, the dragon head was thrust in his way.

"What could a puny mortal do to rescue her from the consequence of her own sin?" The woman spoke softly but the words reached to the edge of the square.

"This isn't funny!" The man made as if to push the player over.

"Help!" the captive shouted from the arms of the demon. "My lord Jesus, save me!"

Arnald nudged Solomon. "I *thought* she was part of the act."

At that moment, the dragon woman looked up. She pointed to the top of the boxes where, over the entrance to Hell, stood a figure robed in white. He had a gold sheen to his face. Even his beard sparkled. He spread his arms. In one hand he held a thurible, used by priests to sprinkle holy water upon the faithful.

"Release her, in the name of Our Lord!" he commanded the demon, sending down a shower upon it.

With a cry, the demon put down his burden, who scampered back to the crowd.

"Who are you?" the demon whimpered, cringing. "Why have I no power to resist your will?"

"I am the messenger of the Son of God!" The player waited for the cheers to die down. "Death has no dominion over him. And those who believe shall live with him in everlasting joy. They need fear you no more!"

The dragon now approached. Next to Solomon, Arnald leaned forward in eager anticipation.

"I love this part," he said.

"My master is Lucifer!" the dragon said proudly. "He was once as you, a mere servant of a demanding Master, but now he rules his own domain! Your glory may daunt this feeble minion, but the true power of Satan cannot be defeated!"

The woman now held the dragon head up almost to the height of the man. A pole at the back let her stretch it out away from her body.

"Look at these pathetic creatures." She turned the head to encompass the circle of people. "Every one of them has listened to the sweet words of my Master and sinned. And will again. They have no chance of escaping his net."

The angel ignored the dragon head waving directly in front of him. He stretched out his hands to address the audience.

"Do you have faith?" he asked them. "Do you believe in our lord, Jesus, born of the Virgin, who performed the miracle of the fishes and the loaves, who healed the sick and called Lazarus forth from the tomb? Do you believe that he suffered and died for your sins and descended into Hell?"

He pointed to the crude monster beneath him.

"Yes!" the crowd responded.

"And," the man said with loud passion, "do you believe that on the third day, he rose from the grave and, forty days later, ascended into Heaven, from whence he shall come to judge the living and the dead?"

"Yes! Yes!" Even the wealthy man was on his feet, shouting with the others.

The man smiled.

"Then all the might of Satan shall not prevail." He raised his arm. "And all his servants shall be defeated. Begone, foul creature!"

The man sprinkled something from the thurible onto the dragon head.

At once it burst into flames.

The woman dropped it onto the brazier, where the painted face blackened and shriveled until there was nothing left but ashes.

The audience in the square cheered and tossed coins on to the large salver that the "demon," his nose and horns removed, was passing around.

Arnald settled back next to Solomon.

"I never figured out how they light the dragon," he said. "Do you think there's a live coal inside?"

"I don't know," Solomon answered.

He took a sip of the beer, trying to appear unaffected. He should have expected it. Easter was hardly a day for the usual ribald performances. He told himself that the features of the demon could easily have been meant to be a Saracen, not a Jew. More likely it could serve as both.

It seemed that he was doomed to endure an Easter sermon, no matter where he was.

Next to him Arnald chewed on his sausage, occasionally stopping for a garlic-laden belch and a swallow of beer.

"It wasn't as good as last year," he commented. "They had five players then, so the damned soul didn't have to be the angel, too. But I always like to see the dragon explode."

Solomon awoke from his dismal reverie long enough for Arnald's comment to penetrate.

"That's the most important part of it to you?" he asked. "You come to this performance every year just to see the dragon burst into flame?"

"Of course." Arnald wrapped the last third of his sausage in oilcloth. "I keep hoping that eventually the whole stage will catch, maybe even spread far enough to burn down the Roaix tower. What other reason could there be?"

Solomon took a deep breath. Suddenly the air seemed cleaner, even though pungent with garlic and pepper.

"I can't think of any," he said.

He stretched his legs out under the rickety table and called for more beer.

Eleven

The home of Bonysach, Monday, 14 Nissan 4908, Ta'anit Bechorot (Fast of the First Born) Erev Pesach. Pridie Ides April (April 12).

הא לחמא עניא די אכלו אבהתנא בארעא דמצרים.
כל-דכפין ייתי ויכל.   כל-דצריך ייתי ויפסח.

"This is the bread of poverty and suffering
Which our fathers ate in the land of Egypt.
Let all who are hungry come and eat.
All who are in need, let them come and celebrate
Passover."

—Maggid,
from the Passover Haggadah

*J*osta looked around the kitchen contentedly. Despite everything that had happened, the house was prepared for the holiday. Every room had been searched for *chametz*. The law was that any piece of bread larger than an olive had to be disposed of. But Josta was more particular than that, to the dismay of her servants and daughter. Every cupboard and box had to be emptied of even the sliver of a crust. That morning, to the delight of the twins, they had burnt it all. And, just in case any had been missed, the formula had been recited to deny ownership.

"Mother," Belide had said. "Why bother with that? There's no *chametz* anywhere. A mouse couldn't find a crumb after the cleaning we've done."

"We don't want to be charged with even that much," Josta told her.

Belide sighed. She didn't understand that Josta would have recited the prayer even if she had been certain they had destroyed every single piece of leaven in all of Toulouse. It was part of the law she followed, the rules for survival that she was trying to impress upon her daughter. Wasn't it said that even the least commandment must be honored? It might seem trivial to her but who knew its importance to Heaven? Josta took no chances.

But for once she was calm in her mind. Between the servants and an unusually dutiful Belide, the house was beautiful. Muppim and Huppim had gathered wildflowers that were now strewn among the rushes on the floor. The scent of spring intensified as they were crushed beneath her feet. The table was prepared, the silver wine cups and spoons released from the iron treasure box and polished until they shone.

Josta paused to caress the Seder platter that Bonysach had brought all the way from Alexandria in the first year of their marriage. Then, lest the Almighty One think her too proud, she said a quick prayer of thanks for all she had been given.

"Mama!" Huppim broke into her reverie, hopping from one foot to the other in impatience. "The *chametz* is all burnt up. May I have some matzoh now? I'm hungry."

"Me, too." Muppim was never far from his twin. "With honey?"

Josta smiled dotingly on her sons, born after ten barren years, when she had despaired of ever having another child. Then she frowned. It wasn't good to let the evil spirits know how special the boys were to her.

"Look at your hands!" she said. "Covered with soot! Go out and wash at once."

"Then matzoh?" Muppim asked.

"One piece," Josta said. "I'll tell Jermana that's all you may have."

"And honey." Muppim was not to be deterred.

"Very well," Josta conceded. "Only a spoonful."

She'd have braved the stings of a thousand bees to scrape it from the comb herself for them. She'd pierce her breast like the phoenix and sustain them with the blood of her heart. But she'd rather have her tongue ripped out than tell them so.

"And don't get your good clothes all wet!" she shouted after them.

If Solomon thought it odd to be burning *chametz* next to a large mound of dog dung, he made no comment. The courtyard of Gavi's home was small and entirely given to his craft. Fresh hides were nailed on one wall. Tubs crowded the rest of the space with the scraping tools neatly ranged on a table in the middle. Gavi had covered the dung heap with canvas but the odor couldn't be disguised.

Afterward all three of them went to the bathhouse. From his solitary tub, Solomon could hear the laughter as Gavi and Nazara scrubbed together. Their excitement over the coming Seder surprised him. Josta must have given her invitation with great delicacy.

Solomon put on his newly washed *chainse* and, in honor of the festival, a long *bliaut* rather than his usual leather *brais*. The movement of air between his legs was pleasant but disconcerting. It made him feel unprotected from sudden attack. Added to that he was wearing hose in blue and yellow stripes. His cloth hat matched the hose. From a dark recess in his pack, he brought out a silver chain from which hung a cluster of garnets. He pinned a similar cluster to the hat. Finally, he took out a pair of soft leather sandals dyed a bright blue. He put these aside to carry with him. He would wear wooden sabots through the muddy streets and at Bonysach's gate exchange them for the fine ones.

There was a wavery mirror at the tailor's next to the bathhouse and Solomon stopped to study the effect of his finery.

"Anyone would take you for a nobleman!" Nazara's face appeared in the mirror next to him. "Come away. You know it's bad luck to look in a mirror for more than an instant."

He turned around to admire her.

"Nazara, you look far too beautiful to be married to anyone less than a king!" he exclaimed.

She laughed and spun around. Her robes were all of different

shades of green and her silk veil was shot through with threads
of gold. She wore earrings of emerald and gold, her entire dowry.
Solomon's compliment was sincere. Nazara was as fine a lady as
he had ever seen.

His comment didn't please her, however. She threw her arms
around Gavi.

"I am the wife of a king," she said. "He rules my heart and
my life."

Gavi looked at the ground in embarrassment.

"My parents gave me a great treasure when they chose her
for me," he told Solomon.

He gently lifted Nazara's arms from around his neck.

"You don't want to crush your sleeves," he reminded her. "It
took hours to pleat them with the gauffering iron.

"Goodness no!" she said. Worriedly, she examined the folds
in the long sleeves of her *bliaut*, then sighed with relief.

"Shall we go now to the House of Prayer for the services?"
she asked the men.

"Why don't I meet you there?" Solomon suggested. "I need
to return my pack to your house. Shall I return your other clothes,
as well?"

Gavi laughed. "We can all do that on the way, Solomon. You
aren't getting out of it that easily. What will it hurt you to pray
with the community and listen to the cantor's song?"

Solomon had many answers for that but none that he could
give his friend.

"Very well," he answered in resignation.

"You may be glad you came," Nazara told him. "You are too
much in the company of Edomites. It's time you remembered how
to celebrate with your own people."

Guy and Berengar were tossing stones into the river. They were
finding it hard to occupy themselves while waiting for the monks

to be ready to leave for Spain. Guy wished he still had a horse of his own. Then he could go out hawking, if he had a hawk. The two men had spent the morning in mock combat and still had hours of daylight to fill.

"Mmmm . . . smell that lamb roasting!" Guy licked his lips. "Someone is giving a feast tonight!"

"Oh, that's the Jews," Berengar said. "They're having Passover. It's like the Last Supper, I think, without the foot washing. Anyway, it's always about the same time as Easter. I don't know what they do for it, but I have friends who have gone and they say the food is wonderful, but the bread too flat to hold much meat sauce."

"I wonder if I could pass for Jewish long enough to get a slice of that meat."

"I hear they have to feed anyone who comes to their door," Berengar told him. "I never thought to try it, but if you want to get out your begging bowl . . ."

"Me? Ask those people for charity?" Guy turned red at the idea. "Not if I were starving."

"All right, calm down," Berengar said. "I was only joking. Lots of Christians go to Jewish homes for Passover. The bishops preach against it, but they do anyway. Doesn't that happen in Anjou?"

Guy shrugged. "I don't know. There aren't any Jews in my town. I never saw them much until I came down here. At least I don't think so. They aren't what I expected. A man from England told me you could always tell them by their horns."

Berengar was puzzled by this. "There's a big horn they blow in their synagogue now and then, but I don't think many of them are very musical."

"No, idiot, on their heads." Guy gestured. "They're born with horns, the Englishman said. They saw them off when they're babies but you can still see the scars."

Berengar shook his head. "I think your friend was making a goat of you. That sounds ridiculous."

"I'll bet you just never looked," Guy muttered. "I bet that if you push back their hair, you'll see the stumps of those horns."

"How much?" Berengar asked. "What will you bet?"

Guy laughed. "You know I have nothing left to wager."

"Your sword?" Berengar said hopefully. He had admired it during their practice.

"I'd bet my soul first," Guy snorted.

Berengar thought. "All right. What about this? If you can find traces of horns on the head of a Jew, then I'll give you my bridle with the silver links. My uncle gave it to me when I brought down my first boar."

Guy knew the one he meant. It was useless for anything but display but he might be able to get enough for it to buy a decent mount.

"And what do you get if I lose?" he asked.

Berengar smiled wickedly. "I get to see you at the gate of Bonysach the Jew, begging for a cut of roast lamb."

Samuel ben Abraham adjusted the collar of the new *bliaut* his mother had sent him. She had designed and embroidered the intricate pattern herself. Wearing it was like having her there to hug him. He wished she were. He was reciting a poem of his own creation at the service today. It would have been nice to know there was one person in the room who would listen to it uncritically.

Once he had finished dressing, he went to check on Rav Chaim. The old man had become alarmingly vague of late and Samuel had taken it upon himself to see that he remembered to perform daily tasks like washing and eating.

As he feared, Hubert was sitting at his Torah wearing only his shift and nightcap. Even his feet were bare.

"Master?" He spoke softly so as not to startle him.

Hubert didn't look up. Samuel came closer, placing a hand on his shoulder.

"Master?" he asked again.

Hubert started and dropped the *yad* on the floor.

"Samuel!" he said. "What are you doing up so early?"

Samuel stooped and retrieved the pointer. "Master, it's past the sixth hour. Look."

They both stared up at the window. The sun had passed above the synagogue. The light entering the room was diffuse, making a rippled pattern on the pages.

"Didn't you notice?" Samuel asked.

Hubert shook his head. "They made their own light," he whispered, still staring at the page.

Samuel wasn't sure what to do next. It was possible that Reb Chaim was just an old man teetering on the rim of dotage. But it was equally possible that he was in the presence of a living saint. Should one tell a saint that he needed to wash his face and feet? Could he be trusted to get his clothes on in the right order?

Samuel tried to think of something in the Talmud that would guide him. There must be directions about saving a holy man from public shame. But how could he be sure it was shameful? Perhaps the Holy One, blessed be his name, was demonstrating that one who neglects himself in the study of the Torah rises beyond the normal laws.

Slowly Hubert straightened on his stool. With a groan, he attempted to stand.

Samuel was at his side at once.

"Do you wish to rest awhile, Rav Chaim?" he asked. "I can come back before sundown with water for washing and fresh clothes."

He helped Hubert to his bed and made him lie down.

"So peaceful." Hubert sighed. "So quiet. Rabbi Akiba is the only one in the garden."

He closed his eyes.

Samuel was so shaken by these words that he had to lean against the door and catch his breath. He knew the story well.

Four wise men entered the garden of the Lord. One saw inside it and died; another looked and went mad. The third began to chop the plants down like weeds. Only Rabbi Akiba entered the garden with peace in his heart and was unharmed.

Was the old man chastising him for his concern with mundane matters?

Or had Rav Chaim had a vision of Akiba?

Samuel knew he was not learned enough to judge.

The elders were all busy preparing for the service. Samuel tried to decide who would be most understanding of the situation.

Halfway across the court he realized that he would have to make a detour. He hurried out the back gate, to the latrine.

The time it took gave him a chance to consider what he would tell the elders. As he got up and adjusted his robes, he said the prayer of thanks for a successful bowel movement. It was true that emptying the body helped to clear the mind. Samuel felt much less agitated as he opened the door.

From behind it there came a grunt and, before he could take more than a step a bag was dropped over his head and his arms were pinioned.

"Help!" he cried. "Thieves! Murder!"

"Shut him up!" someone hissed. "Let's get a look at his head."

"How are we supposed to do that with a bag on it?"

"Like this!"

Samuel's shout was cut off abruptly as something sharp hit the side of his face and the world went black.

∞

The synagogue was crowded by the time Solomon arrived with Gavi and Nazara. He wondered if he could offer to wait outside. Before he had a chance, he saw Bonysach coming toward him, hands outstretched. Solomon created a smile.

"*Senhor* Gavi!" Bonysach exclaimed. "How good to see you! We are all delighted that you will be joining us at our Seder."

Gavi nodded nervously. "We are honored by your hospitality, *Mar* Bonysach."

"Solomon." Bonysach turned to him. "I haven't seen your uncle, yet. Perhaps you could see if he's ready. I believe the cantor is about to begin."

Solomon found Hubert sleeping soundly. The green tint of the light through the thick window made his skin almost translucent. Solomon wondered how the strong decisive man of his childhood could have become this frail so quickly. He stood a moment, watching the measured breath, then he quietly left the room.

When he got back to the meeting room, Solomon found that the service hadn't yet started. He told Bonysach that he was letting Hubert rest. Bonysach agreed.

"Rav Chaim has been pushing his body too hard lately," he said. "Sleep will do him good."

"He may even be able to stay awake for the whole of the Seder tonight," Solomon answered. "Better than I usually manage."

At that moment, the cantor stood and began the psalms for Passover. Behind him a man played softly on a viol while another tapped the beat on a tambor. The cantor sang in a deep rich tone that had many wiping their eyes. Then he smiled and the song changed to one of joy, a celebration of freedom. Solomon found his feet twitching. Not everyone resisted the urge to dance.

When he had finished, the cantor paused and looked about.

"Samuel?" he asked. "Are you ready?"

No one answered. The leader of the synagogue sent a boy out to find him.

"Perhaps he's stricken with terror at the thought of facing the congregation," he joked.

The boy came back a few moments later shaking his head.

The buzzing that had begun in the room grew louder.

"This isn't good," Bonysach said to Solomon. "I don't want my daughter to marry a man too spineless to speak in public."

Just then there was a shout from the court and two men burst in half-carrying a dazed and rumpled Samuel.

"We found him in the back, by the acacia trees," one said. "Looks as though he's been set upon by those cursed Edomites."

A woman began to wail. Her lament was taken up by the others.

Mosse, the physician, made his way to the bench where Samuel had been seated. He looked into the young man's eyes and examined the bruise on his temple.

"Do you know who did this?" he asked.

Samuel didn't answer. He stared at his hands and then felt his neck. His chin quivered.

"Those *mamzers* tore my mother's collar!"

It was some time before order was restored. Many people left at once to check on the safety of those who had been left at home. Others stayed to offer advice or aid.

"We ought to go to the count's vicar at once!" Yusef said. "It's his job to protect us."

"Why don't we wait until Samuel can tell us what happened?" Galde's husband, Vital, suggested.

"It would be better to have as much information as possible," Aaron agreed with his brother-in-law.

"While those ruffians get their friends to say they were somewhere else!" Yusef countered.

THE OUTCAST DOVE

"Or gather more *ribaux* to come back and attack us all!" a man shouted from the back.

"That's enough!"

Everyone stopped and stared at Solomon.

Had he spoken? He must have; the room was waiting for him to explain his outburst. What had got into him?

"If you go on in this way, you'll start a riot yourselves," he told them. "We need to know what happened. Look at Samuel. Was he robbed? He's still wearing a gold ring and pin. Did they steal your purse, Samuel?"

"Didn't have one," Samuel muttered from behind the physician's ministrations.

Mosse finished rubbing a salve on Samuel's chin.

"You'll be fine, young man," he said. "No teeth loose or bones cracked. You might have some trouble chewing your meat tonight, but that's all."

The elders decided that Solomon had said enough. After all, he wasn't even a member of the congregation. The leader resumed his authority.

"Now Samuel," he said with a smile. "Can you tell us why you were attacked?"

"No," the young man said plaintively, still fingering his torn collar. "There were two of them, at least. Maybe more. I never saw them. They wanted to examine my head, I think. I must not have understood."

"Did they call you names?" the leader asked. "Accuse you of anything? Try to pull out your beard."

"No." Samuel rubbed his head and then looked at his hand in revulsion. "My hair is all sticky! Do you think they rubbed a poison on me?"

The physician sniffed. "Smells like that hard candy with honey and violets. There was a woman selling some by the Capitole this morning."

Bonysach scratched his ear. "It doesn't sound like the usual harassment. More like some jest that only makes sense from the bottom of a wine barrel."

"There was a strong smell of wine," Samuel said. "And mushrooms. Now I remember. The bag they threw over me must have been used to carry them."

The teacher patted him on the shoulder. "A terrible thing!" he repeated. "It seems you happened across some *oms tafurs* looking for trouble. They deserve punishment and we shall take it up with the townsmen, but you mustn't let it spoil the festival."

For once, none of the scholars broached a dissenting opinion.

"This is a joyous time," the cantor declared. "The attack on Samuel is lamentable but it doesn't seem to be a harbinger of any disaster for the community. The sun is going down and I know we all wish to be home for the lighting of the candles. When the court meets on Thursday, we can decide how best to handle this insult."

"Is that acceptable to you, Samuel?" the leader asked.

"I don't wish to keep anyone from the Seder," Samuel said.

Bonysach helped Samuel to his feet. "Good man! Are you well enough to walk as far as my home? I know that my wife and daughter will take good care of you once we get there."

That brought a light to Samuel's face.

"I'm sure I can make it," he said. "But what about Rav Chaim?"

"Uncle!" Solomon exclaimed. "I had forgotten all about him!"

"Where is he?" Bonysach was alarmed. "Could he also have been set upon? Perhaps we were too quick to make light of this."

"He was in his room," Solomon said. "But I'd have thought all this commotion would have wakened him by now."

They rushed to Hubert's cell and tumbled in the door without knocking.

Hubert dropped the garter he was tying to the top of his hose.

"Is there a fire?" he asked.

Bonysach recovered first.

"Yes," he said. "It's in my kitchen court, under a slowly turn-ing lamb. And I need you to help me contain it."

"You've got to do it!" Berengar crowed. "And tonight! The deal was to beg for freshly roasted lamb! Oh, this will be good."

Jehan had returned to the inn in time to learn of Guy's loss.

"Stupid!" he shouted at the knight. "Twice stupid, first to bet on anything so ridiculous and second to believe anything told you by an Englishman! No wonder you're penniless."

Guy dug his boot heel into the soft wood of the floor of the inn. He kicked out a splinter. "It was just a joke," he muttered. "For something to do. And that damn Jew was asking for trouble, all got up fine like a nobleman."

"He did look an ass, didn't he?" Berengar chuckled. "Coming from the privy. Didn't even have time to pull up his hose."

Jehan shook his head. "You didn't kill him, did you?"

"Nah," Berengar said. "He was starting to come round before we left. Anyway, I was right, no horns. Not even scars where they'd been sawn off. So Guy has to fulfill his pledge. Right?"

Jehan didn't want to be the judge in this. The three of them were going to journey together for several weeks, through dan-gerous country. He, Guy, and Berengar would be responsible for the safety of unarmed clerics. They would have to trust and de-pend on each other. It was an evil omen to start with resentment already festering.

The other two were waiting. Jehan clenched his teeth to keep from telling them both to go to hell. Saint Morice save him! These were the best men he had been able to find.

"What kind of knight are you, Berengar?" he asked. "To set a man a dishonorable pledge? Not only is it demeaning to him, but to all Christians. Do you want the Jews to think they are the only resort for those of our people who are in need? Aren't they arrogant enough without that?"

Berengar bit his lip. "I hadn't thought of . . ."

Jehan turned his anger on Guy. "And you! What kind of example are you setting this boy? A soldier who has no control over himself is useless."

He paused, shoving down an uncalled for memory.

"I should make you do this." He pointed his finger just under Guy's nose. "Just so you'll never forget the humiliation."

Guy cringed. Berengar brightened with hope.

"But it wouldn't just be your shame." Jehan turned away in disgust. "It would be mine, too. And yours, Berengar. We are companions now and our deeds, both brave and stupid, are shared. You'll have to find another way to pay the debt, Guy."

"Maybe he could climb the wall and steal the lamb before they can eat it," Berengar suggested. "That would be good. Then they couldn't go on with their ritual. He would be helping to defeat the followers of Satan, right?"

Jehan shrugged. "That's between the two of you," he said. "But no begging."

They were still arguing about it as Jehan climbed to the sleeping loft. He lay down on his pallet and pulled the blanket over his head. Solomon had implied that his penance for killing the man in Paris hadn't been hard enough. Jehan was glad that his old enemy didn't know the truth. His real crime was that he had fallen in love with a woman he could never have.

For that, life was his penance.

Samuel had been fussed over and coddled beyond his imagination. His mother couldn't have been more sympathetic than Josta, and the admiration in Belide's eyes made him wonder if she had been told just how ignominious his assault had been.

"I didn't have a chance to fight back," he admitted to her.

"Against so many? How could you?" she responded. "They are the cowards. Filthy pig-eaters!"

"Belide," her mother cautioned. "I don't allow such language in my house. Come, it's time to light the candles."

The men stood respectfully as Josta, Belide, and Nazara recited the blessing and lit the candles for Passover. The glow on their faces made the three women almost angelic. Solomon blinked away tears. Even Muppim and Huppim were still for once.

They sat then, on chairs and benches piled high with cushions. The twins had to be lifted onto theirs.

"Papa, why are we . . . ?" Muppim asked.

"Not yet!" Belide stopped him. "I'll tell you when to ask."

Bonysach poured the first cup of wine, then filled those of his guests. Josta added water to the twins' cups. Bonysach returned to the head of table. He raised the cup, smiling at them all and began.

"Baruch ata Adonai, Eloheinu melech ha'olam, boreh pri hagafen."

As the blessing continued, Solomon had the sense of having returned to the shelter of his childhood. He was Israel, wrapped in divine love as in his mother's arms. If only he could stay there forever.

Everyone joined in the end of the blessing, the boys prompted by Belide.

". . . *shehecheyanu vekiyemanu vehigiyanu lazman hazeh.*" Blessed is the Lord, who let us be here now.

They drank the first cup of wine and the Seder began.

Muppim and Huppim took turns with the four questions, speaking in Provençal since they hadn't started Hebrew school yet. They both sprinkled more wine than necessary on the tablecloth as the plagues of Egypt were mentioned, thrilled at being permitted to do something that would normally be forbidden.

"Dayenu! Dayenu!" they shrieked, bouncing on the pillows.

"*Dayenu,* indeed," Bonysach told them. "That will be enough."

Nazara smiled. "It's good to have children at the Seder. Thank you *Na* Josta, for letting us share yours."

"You will have your own one day," Josta said. "If you pray and be patient."

"Have to do more than that." Bonysach laughed.

Josta hushed him but she was laughing, too.

By the time they started the meal, both boys were yawning. They were determined to stay awake until they could search for the *afikomen,* the piece of matzoh bread that Bonysach had broken from the loaf and hidden while they covered their eyes. The one who found it could have a present and in this their normal unity was suspended.

The servants brought in platters of lamb sliced into pieces that could be eaten with the fingers. There were also fresh greens and, as always, mounds of olives.

They continued telling stories over the meal, some for the benefit of the twins, some for their own edification. With some coaxing, Samuel stood and recited his poem. Everyone pronounced it brilliant.

"I tell you, nothing of our cantor's could touch it," Bonysach told him.

Samuel beamed at them all, his face as red as the roses his mother had sewn onto his collar.

Hubert was silent and ate little. Solomon watched him closely, worried that he was too weak for the late evening.

"Uncle?" he asked quietly. "Would you like to rest a while, before the final blessing?"

Hubert seemed surprised to have all eyes on him.

"Of course not," he answered. "I beg your pardon. I was not dozing, but remembering. Since I left Paris, this is the first time I've celebrated Pesach in a family."

He looked at the twins. "Perhaps I shouldn't speak of it before them."

Josta and Bonysach exchanged a glance; she nodded.

"They are the ones who most need to hear your story," he told Hubert.

The others murmured agreement.

Hubert smiled at the twins. "Don't worry, I won't take long," he said. "When I was younger than you are now, Christian soldiers came to my house. They took my mother and sisters. I hid in a cupboard and was found and raised by a merchant, Gervase of Rouen. He baptized me and raised me as his own."

"You, Rav Chaim?" Muppim's eyes were enormous with astonishment. "You were once a Christian? How could that be?"

"It happens all the time," Josta told him. "Not here, thank the Holy One, blessed be He. But in France and Germany."

Without another word, both boys got up and climbed onto their parents' laps.

"Tell them how you came home," Bonysach said to Hubert.

Hubert took a sip of wine. "For many years I thought I was the son of Gervase. I didn't remember my mother, except in dreams. But the Creator of all things guided me to Paris, where my brothers, Eliazar and Jacob, found me. Even though I had lived so many years among the Edomites, they welcomed me back. They taught me the Seder as your family is teaching you, even though I was already grown up and should have known it."

Muppim giggled.

"Since then I have slowly been finding my way home." Hubert's voice broke and he took a bit more wine. "Even though the Temple is still in ruins and we are still in exile, I feel as though I have been brought out of Egypt to freedom at last."

He sat down and fumbled for the handkerchief tied in his sleeve.

"Thank you, Rav Chaim," Bonysach said.

They were all washing their hands in preparation for the final cup of wine when they heard a great crash from the courtyard, followed by unearthly wailing.

"Demons!" Gavi cried.

"Soldiers!" Hubert started shaking. "They've found me!"

"It's Pharoh's men, come for Rav Chaim!" Muppim leapt from his father's lap. "We won't let him take you again!"

The boys threw themselves around Hubert. Solomon, Gavi, and Samuel ran out into the garden, picking up weapons as they went. Solomon cursed the vanity that had made him leave his long knife behind. The arm sheath hadn't fit under the tight sleeves. Bonysach followed with a lantern, although the full moon gave enough light for them to catch sight of a pair of bare legs and feet vanishing over the top of the garden wall.

The howling receded down the alleyway. Solomon tried to climb after them but was impeded by his long robes.

"*Damledu!*" he swore, as he fell back to the ground.

The others were surveying the damage.

The rose bushes were trampled and branches had been broken on the laurels.

"Someone came over the wall!" Gavi said.

"And back again." Samuel pointed to the roasting pit. The banked coals had been scattered and were glowing across the grass. "It looks as if they stepped right on top of the firepit."

"Barefoot?" Bonysach said. "That would account for the noise. But why? First Samuel and now this. What do these *vilans* want? Are they mad?"

Solomon shook his head. Neither this nor the attack on Samuel made sense to him, but he was certain that there was a reason. If he could have caught the man on the wall, he would have had it.

Never again, he vowed, would he be found outside home without his knife and his pants.

Twelve

The priory of Saint Pierre des Cuisines, Toulouse. Wednesday, 16 Nissan 4908, Pesach II, first day of the Omer. 18 kalends May, (April 14) 1148.

Ben es mortz qui al cor non sen
D'Amor qualque doussa sabor
E que val viare ses amor
Mas per enuey far a la gen?

Death is welcome when the heart does not feel
The sweet savor of love
And what use is it to savor one's love
If it causes jealousy in others?

—Bernart de Ventadorn

*B*rother James!" Martin took the steps to the dortor two at a time, causing the whole building to shake. "Lord Falquet has sent us his offering ahead of time. There is enough now to free all the captives. We can leave by Friday!"

James met him at the top of the stairs.

"Friday? *Domine gratia!* That's wonderful!" he exclaimed. "But how will everything be arranged so quickly?"

"Most of the supplies have already been prepared," Martin said. "I understand our guards are more than ready to depart. And I just spoke to Aaron, the horse trader. He told me his party was also eager to start out and they will share the cost of the guards. Your prayers must have been heeded, Brother James."

"Yes, I can't believe it," James said. Then he stopped. "Aaron is willing to set off early? But it's the middle of Pesach."

"It's what?" Martin only half heard. His mind was already on the final preparations.

"Nothing." James caught himself. But the news worried him. Why would a Jew be so willing to start a journey in the middle of Passover? Was it that he considered trade more important than faith? Or was it essential that he travel in this particular party? Had Hubert told the other Jews of Toulouse about their encounter? Could they think that, after so many years, he could be brought back to Israel? Or was this somehow connected to

Brother Victor's murder? Did Aaron know how much gold the monks were carrying? Could he be under orders to prevent the release of the knights?

James's conjectures raced to even greater extremes. What if this Aaron were in league with the Saracens? He might have promised them new monastic hostages. Or perhaps Aaron was planning to kill him. If the leaders of the Jewish community had given up on his reconversion, they might have decided it was better for him to die than risk the possibility of him convincing other Jews to follow his path.

The thought of martyrdom cheered the monk considerably.

His mind had wafted to selecting appropriate readings for his feast day when a loud cough from Brother Martin brought him back.

"Oh, yes," he said. "What task has been assigned to me, Brother?"

"Nothing, Brother James." Martin smiled proudly. "I have taken care of everything for you. I just need to inform *Senhor* Aaron of the time of departure on Friday."

"Friday, you said?" James had to share his suspicion. "A man named Aaron Ha-Cohen is willing to set out on a journey on a Friday in the middle of Passover? That doesn't seem strange to you?"

Martin shrugged. "I told him that we would travel on his Sabbath and he said that the urgency of his mission permitted it as long as he didn't ride."

"What could be that important?" James asked.

"He didn't say," Martin said. "But I overheard some friends of his talking. It seems he has contracted for a Spanish bride. I guess that the burning of his loins is more important to him than his superstitious rites."

He nudged James.

"Perhaps you could use the time on the road to help him

appreciate the joy of accepting Christ," he suggested. "And how much greater it is than satisfying the craving of the flesh."

James gave the massive monk a long look.

"How long have you been in the monastery?" he asked.

Martin seemed puzzled by the question.

"I was an oblate," he said. "My parents gave me to St. Peter and Cluny when I was eight."

"That makes many things clear to me," James told him with a pat on the arm. "I promise that I shan't miss an opportunity to preach the faith. But I don't think this is a time when *Senhor* Aaron is most likely to be receptive."

Aaron raced down the narrow streets of Toulouse, oblivious to what he stepped in. He leapt over barrels and swung around carts with the ease of a tumbler, never breaking his stride.

When he reached the house of the tanner he didn't so much knock at the door as collide with it. Nazara opened to find him panting and dripping, too out of breath to greet her.

She closed the door and returned a moment later to hand him a basin and towel.

"My thanks, *Na* Nazara," he gasped. "I apologize for my state. Is Solomon here?"

"At the *bet midrash* visiting his uncle, I think," she told him. "At least that's what he said when he left this morning."

Aaron finished wiping his face and returned the towel and basin.

"Thank you." He took a deep breath and set out again.

Solomon was seated in the court with Hubert when Aaron burst in.

"We leave Friday at dawn," he said without preamble. "I don't want to hear any rebukes."

"I've already said I can go at once," Solomon answered. "Now, Uncle, please have a bit more soup. I don't care how sustained you are by the Torah. You need real food, as well. You don't want me to tell Catherine that you're starving yourself."

Hubert picked up his spoon. His daughter had enough worries without that. Dutifully, he swallowed the soup.

Aaron let his wobbly legs fold onto the ground but didn't stop talking.

"Galde is furious with me," he said. "She can't understand the rush to fetch Mayah, since the marriage can't be held until after Shavuot."

Hubert looked up from his soup.

"Who's getting married?" he asked.

"Aaron," Solomon told him. "To the daughter of Yishmael of Córdoba."

"Little Mayah? But she's just a baby," Hubert said.

"That was the last time you saw her," Solomon answered. "Mayah is now well past the age of consent."

"Then congratulations, Aaron!" Hubert smiled at him. "Will my old friend, Yishmael, be coming for the event?"

Solomon gestured to Aaron not to tell Hubert that Yishmael was dead, but Aaron didn't need to be warned.

"Yishmael won't be able to make the journey," he answered. "Although I know how much he would like to be here."

"A shame." Hubert sighed. "I'd like to see him again. Well, I had planned to return to Lunel after Pesach but perhaps I should stay for the wedding."

"Aaron!" Samuel had joined them. "I just heard that you are finally going to get your bride. That's wonderful. But you need more than Solomon to accompany you. Let me come, too."

Aaron's head jerked up in alarm.

"Samuel, this isn't a ride to the next town," he explained. "Mayah lives in Spain. We may be gone a month or more."

"I know," Samuel said. "But I've been thinking lately that I've been looking for wisdom in the Talmud alone. I need to understand the world, as well."

"I'm sure you can do that in a less radical manner," Solomon said. "And with more planning. We leave the day after tomorrow, you see. Not only in the middle of Pesach but Sabbath eve."

Samuel regarded them thoughtfully.

"I'm surprised that you would do this, Aaron," he said. "I thought you were more observant. But that's all the more reason why I should come along. The three of us can make an *eruv* at our camp to observe the Sabbath."

Solomon bit his lip. "I don't think three men are enough, especially if I'm one of them. Samuel, we won't be in the company of Jews, but Christians. The only group Aaron could find to travel south now is that of the monks of Saint Pierre."

Instead of disturbing Samuel, this information made him even more avid to go.

"I've always wanted a chance to talk with monks," he said. "Outside of the churches, of course. I've been studying Latin in Narbonne and I believe that they really need a better translation of the psalms for their prayers."

Solomon threw up his hands.

"I think you're mad," he said. "But it's not my job to bring you to reason. I'll meet you Friday, Aaron. Where are we gathering?"

"Just outside the Narbonne Gate," Aaron said. "Samuel, why don't we speak with the elders about this. It's a noble offer, but I really can't let you make such a decision without counsel."

They went in search of authority.

Hubert finished his soup and then stood slowly, leaning on the table.

"Help me back to my room, please,"

He held out his arm to Solomon.

As they started back, Solomon had the odd sensation that Hubert wasn't so much leaning on him for support but tethering himself lest he float away.

Neither spoke until they entered the room and Hubert shut the door. He sat on his bed, looking up at Solomon. All at once, his eyes were sharp, without a trace of uncertainty.

"You know that Jacob will be in the party with you," he said. "And still you are going."

"Yes." Solomon spit the word out.

Hubert nodded. "In that case, you must make a promise to me, Nephew, by anything you consider holy. You can't get away with mouthing words to humor an old man. This is a vow I want you to keep, no matter what."

Solomon sat down next to him.

"Don't ask it," he begged. "I can't be tied to such a thing."

"You must be." Hubert's voice was firm. "Swear it. There has to be something you believe in enough to keep you from an act that will damn you forever."

Solomon tried to look away, but Hubert's gaze held him fast.

"There is nothing," he said. "Nothing at all. But you are wrong in your fear. I'm not plotting to kill Brother James. I'll avoid him as much as possible. I loathe the thought of having to see or speak to him.

"I am not a man who plots murder. Nevertheless, I can't promise that he won't come to harm."

"Solomon, please," Hubert insisted. "It's not for him, but for yourself."

"No." Solomon put his arm around Hubert's shoulders, trying to soften the harsh words. "If he threatens me as he did before or tries to hurt any of my friends, he shall be stopped. And I will do anything I must to see to it. Hubert, don't you understand? Now that he knows you are living again as a Jew, he has the power to have you put to death for apostasy. He can destroy the lives of your children and grandchildren. What is my soul compared to that?"

He tried to smile, perhaps to reassure his uncle that a soul wasn't that great a loss. Beneath his arm, he could feel Hubert sag in despair.

"I would not have you trade your soul for my life," Hubert said at last. "Or even Catherine's. I would gladly die for my children and theirs, despite the danger to them that my actions have caused. So it would dishonor you to imply that you would do less."

"Thank you, Uncle."

"All the same," Hubert added. "Just remember that if you harm Jacob, you may well lose everything, including the lives you would protect."

"How do you think I could forget?" Solomon snapped back.

At this point, he felt that he would rather face his own execution than the next three weeks on the road.

"*Na* Josta?"

Josta opened her eyes. She had been dozing over her embroidery.

What is it, Jermana?" she asked the servant.

"That man is here," Jermana answered. "That Yusef. Shall I tell him you are still too ill to see him?"

"No." Josta sighed. "He knows I've been up for days. He didn't bring that woman with him, did he?"

"If he had, I'd have turned him away without bothering you at all," Jermana huffed.

"Tell him I'll be down in a moment," Josta said. "And offer him some wine. I don't want to be remiss in my manners."

"If you insist," Jermana answered. "But it won't be from a new jug."

When Josta entered the hall, she found Yusef standing nervously. He held a cup of wine in one hand and a piece of matzoh, spread with oil and herbs, in the other. Jermana had served him and taken away the tray.

"A blessing upon this house and all in it," Yusef greeted her, looking for a place to put down his cup.

"And to you," Josta answered. "What brings you here? Bonysach is at the Bazacle, inspecting a shipment of silk."

"I have come to see you," he explained. "I have the money the elders set to recompense you for the hurt my servant caused."

Josta went to an alcove and brought back a small table. Yusef set the cup on it, balancing the matzoh on top. He took out a bag from around his neck and carefully counted out the coins.

"Two-thirds to you," he said. "And the rest to Bonysach."

"I'll let him know," Josta told him. She didn't touch the money. "Is there something else?"

Yusef nodded. "I wanted to tell you again how grieved I am by Babylonia's behavior. I thought she was getting better but this last outburst was one of her worst. The elders are right; I can't risk the safety of my friends by keeping her in my home."

Josta exhaled in relief. "May the Holy One, blessed be He, be thanked! You should have sent her away long ago! Let the Edomites take care of her."

"I can't do that, *Na* Josta," Yusef said sadly. "I'm not sending her away; I'm taking her."

"What! Where?" Josta couldn't believe it. "Yusef, this woman can't mean so much to you. You are a good man, who has always followed the Law. Why would you accept exile for her sake?"

"This is a burden I have taken up," Yusef answered. "I can't set it down until I know Babylonia has found peace. Samuel told me that Aaron is leaving for Spain. We shall go with him. Or, if they won't let us join the party, we'll follow behind like beggars."

He bowed to her. "Thank you for seeing me, *Na* Josta," he said. "Give my respects to Bonysach. I have told the elders that, if I do not return, my share of our goods is to be given to the poor of our community, since I have no family."

Josta was so stunned that she forgot to see him out. Jermana heard him fumbling with the catch on the door and hurried to open it for him. When she returned to the hall, she found her mistress still standing, shaking her head in confusion.

Jehan poked his head through the hole into the loft at the inn.

"No falling into a wine vat tonight!" he told Guy and Berengar. "We set off at dawn on Friday and I expect you to spend tomorrow checking every piece of gear you have. We've had our respite. From now on lives will depend on our being vigilant. What was that?"

"I didn't say anything." Berengar grinned.

Jehan frowned. "Just remember, *my Lord Berengar*, that all your father's wealth and position won't keep a Saracen sword from lodging in your gut. Nor can you call on him to defend us when we are attacked. The men we are going to ransom learned that."

"I know," Berengar answered, the smile gone. "I won't disappoint you."

"He's been working," Guy told Jehan. "He's getting better at aiming for vulnerable spots instead of just parrying blows. And he's not at all bad with a sling."

"My friends and I use them for hunting small game," Berengar explained. "But Guy pointed out that a well-shot stone could bring a man down from a horse."

Jehan nodded approval. "Never tried it myself, but I'd like to see what you can do. Get your gear. We'll find an open field and test it."

Berengar was down in an instant, dropping through the opening onto the floor below. Guy came more slowly down the ladder, trying not to cry out as his feet hit the rungs.

"What's wrong with your feet?" Jehan asked.

"Stepped in a nettle patch by the river," Guy answered shortly.

Berengar stifled a laugh.

"I hope you got all the thorns out," Jehan warned. "Those things can fester. You don't look like you'll be good for much for a while."

"Don't worry," Guy said. "I can still ride."

"Maybe," Jehan said. "But can you walk far enough to reach your horse?"

Berengar snorted. Guy glared at him.

Jehan regarded them both with suspicion. He guessed that they had been making wagers again. Idiots! All he could hope was that this new man, Arnald, would have more sense than these two.

Solomon had little to prepare. He had money enough, carefully secreted in various places in his packs and on his body. He had the tokens from his other uncle, Eleazar, in Troyes. These would identify him and release the goods from the ship in Almeria. He wondered if he would ever get there. The danger involved in freeing Mayah was only a small worry. What he doubted was his ability to survive days in the company of both Jehan and Brother James.

So when Aaron came to him with his troubles, Solomon found he had used up all sympathy.

"The elders have decided that Samuel may come with us!" Aaron moaned. "And that's not the worst of it."

"Josta told me about Yusef." Solomon forestalled a recitation of this new woe. "He has his own concerns. I doubt he'll try to follow us up to the monastery."

"But he'll know I didn't go to Córdoba!" Aaron complained.

"Perhaps," Solomon answered. "He may not notice. That servant of his will occupy most of his attention, I'd guess."

"But what can we do about Samuel?" Aaron persisted. "If he sees that we're leaving the group, he'll want to come with us. If he finds we've gone, he'll want to know where and why!"

He was sitting on a log across from the vineyard his sister and brother-in-law owned. The vines were covered with soft green leaves. Hidden among them were the buds of wine to come. From nearby came the hum of bees. Solomon thought wistfully that this would be a good time for a nap.

Instead he grabbed Aaron by the shoulder and shook him hard.

"What is wrong with you?" he shouted. "While you agonize over who might find out what happened to Mayah, she is still enduring it! What is more important, her honor or her life?"

"But if it's known, our marriage will be forbidden!" Aaron wailed.

"Aaron, even if it's not known, the marriage is forbidden," Solomon said. "Do you think you can keep a secret from the Almighty One? What you care about is the community and how they will treat you and Mayah?"

"No! I only care about Mayah!" Aaron said.

"Then let's go save her." Solomon released his hold. "And let the dice fall where they may."

Thanks to the skill of Brother Martin, Brother James also had little to do. But he did it with great energy. He went to the priory barber to have his face and tonsure shaved. After checking to see if the moon was in the proper phase, he also decided to be bled. He was worried that the presence of Jews among his traveling companions might cause an over production of choleric bile in his system. Better to drain some of it off as a precaution.

He also had realized that the bags of gold coins were chafing his skin. He accepted the discomfort gladly but decided that the strings tying the bags to his belt were too easily broken. After much thought, it came to him that he could fold over the edge of his cowl and sew the coins inside it. While living in the monastery he would normally not get the same clothing back from the laundry, but for this journey he would only have one change of his outer robe and the cowl would be the same all along.

When he put it on he was pleased with how much less noticeable it was than in the lumpy bags at his waist. He wished he'd thought of it sooner. Perhaps Brother Victor would still be alive if he had carried the money where a thief could not find it.

James crossed himself and said a prayer for his lost friend.

"I promise," he whispered. "Every man we free will know that you are the one he should thank."

The morning was crisp and pale as Solomon led his horse through the streets to the Narbonne Gate. People were already stirring. He could hear the squawking as chickens and ducks fought for the grain a little girl tossed to them. A woman passed him, buckets of new milk hung from a pole across her shoulders. He stopped her and bought a cup. The warm liquid helped calm his agitated stomach.

There was no point in asking himself why he was doing this. He was caught in a nightmare. Any way he turned would bring him to the same end. Each time he thought he was free, a new monster rose to attack. Like a fly caught in a web, he had ceased struggling and now awaited the spider with worn submission.

The juvenile exuberance of Arnald's greeting fell on him like a bucket of icy water.

"This is wonderful!" he cried, rising in his stirrups to wave as Solomon passed through the gate. "It's going to be a beautiful day. Perfect for a ride. The monks and their guards and servants are already here. Father wants me to stay close to them, but I don't see why I can't ride with you and Aaron."

Solomon looked around. Above him loomed the massive fortress of the Château Narbonnais, where the count stayed when he was in the Cité. A watchman gazed down on him. Solomon moved farther away from the wall, in case the man was thinking of relieving himself between the merlins.

"Where is Aaron?" he asked.

Arnald moved closer. "I think he and Yusef and Samuel are saying morning prayers."

Solomon rolled his eyes. Of course they were.

"You watch," he said. "The three of them will spend this whole trip dancing around and through the Law, trying to offend the Almighty as little as possible and still do what they want."

"Are you calling them hypocrites?" Arnald asked.

"No more than the rest of us." Solomon laughed at his expression. "I'm one, myself, for that matter, on some subjects, but when I break one of our laws, I don't pretend it's anything but a transgression."

Arnald chewed on that a moment. "*Senhor* Solomon," he said at last. "I like you, but I don't understand most of what you say."

Solomon was saved having to reply to that by the arrival of the others.

As the two groups moved closer to each other, Solomon tensed for the moment when his father would recognize him.

But it was Brother Martin who caused the first disruption.

"That's a woman!" he cried, pointing.

All eyes turned to Babylonia, sitting pillion behind Yusef on his horse.

"This is my servant," he told them.

"Ha!" Brother Martin replied. "Your concubine, I have no doubt. We won't share the road with fornicators."

Berengar gave a loud guffaw and even Aaron smiled.

"Then it will be a lonely road, Brother Martin," Jehan said.

Yusef didn't join in the humor.

"Babylonia is my servant," he repeated. "That is all. She has fallen ill and I'm taking her to a family in Spain who will care for her. I am willing to pay for the protection of your guards if we may travel with you. I already arranged this with Aaron."

"Then welcome!" Guy called. He paused and reconsidered. "Wait, it's not leprosy, is it?"

The word brought them all to attention.

"Of course not!" Yusef denied it at once, but fear echoed more loudly in their ears.

"Let's see her." Martin gestured to Jehan and the other guards. They didn't move.

"Jehan, bring her over so I can see if she shows signs of the disease," he ordered them.

Jehan crossed his arms. "My men and I took your coin to protect you from bandits, marauders, even bear and other savage beasts. Lepers weren't in the bargain."

Babylonia herself broke the impasse.

"Pig! Bastard!" she screamed as she slid from Yusef's horse. "How dare you call me unclean! I'm whole as you are. More. There's not a blemish on my body. I'll prove it."

She tore off her veil and started pulling her *bliaut* over her head.

"Babylonia!" Yusef dismounted hurriedly, landing on the ground with a thump.

He tried to keep her from removing anything more, but she was strong in her fury.

"Called me a whore, he did!" she shouted. "A Jew's whore! I spit on them all. Bad enough! Now he says I'm leprous. I'll show him. Let me go!"

"You see?" Yusef told them as he attempted to control his servant. "It's not her body but her mind that's ill. Will someone help me?"

No one moved. By now a small crowd had collected.

"Beat the demon out of her," someone suggested. Several others agreed.

"Where will it go, if he does?" someone else asked. "Anyone have a goat? They're born possessed."

Since no one had brought a goat, the spectators started backing away. No one wanted to be caught by a demon on the run.

"Idiots!" Brother Martin strode up to Yusef and Babylonia. "You can't bring a madwoman with us, either. She needs a good exorcism. Let me baptize her. That will drive the devil out."

"She's already one of yours; it seems the devil returned," Yusef panted. "I know of a convent that will take her in and keep her from hurting anyone else. But I have to get her there."

Martin hesitated. He had assumed that Babylonia was Jewish. That changed things.

"Why haven't you taken her to the local priest, then?" he asked.

Yusef had managed to get Babylonia calm enough to put the *bliaut* back on. His own hat had fallen on the ground and his cloak had been turned almost back to front in the struggle.

"I have," he said shortly. "To the parish priest, the hospice of Saint Jean. I even asked the bishop for help. No one wanted her. She's not of Toulouse."

Martin was silent. He watched the way that Yusef held the woman, firmly but not lustfully. She was still at last, head bowed. He couldn't imagine anyone taking on such a burden if he could have passed it to someone else.

"She'll have to be restrained day and night," he told Yusef. "And gagged if her outbursts continue. Do you agree to that?"

Yusef put one hand on Babylonia's shoulder. With the other he lifted her chin.

"Do you understand what Brother Martin said?" he asked.

Her eyes flicked to the monk with a look of undiluted hatred.

"Yes," she said. "I will be good."

Yusef turned back to Martin. "Thank you," he said.

Martin looked at the sky.

"We've wasted enough time," he said. "We need to be at L'Isle Jourdain by nightfall. Is everyone ready?"

"My friends and I are," Aaron said.

"We wait only for you," Jehan told him.

Brother James said nothing, only pulled his cowl farther over his face.

Yusef got back on his horse. He reached down to pull Babylonia up behind him. She couldn't make the leap and was about to try again when Brother Martin strode over and picked her up as easily as if she'd been a child, setting her on the horse.

"Now," he said. "May God grant that we have no more such disturbances and that our journey be swift and uneventful."

None of the travelers had trouble saying "Amen" to that.

As they set off, Solomon saw his father look around at the others in the party. When his gaze came to the Jews, it passed without interest.

It was almost worse than rejection. Brother James hadn't recognized his own son.

Thirteen

Saturday, 19 Nissan, Fifth day of Pesach, 4908, 15 kalends
May (April 17) 1148. Feast of Saint Fructius, bishop of Braga,
who, before he cleaned up, was mistaken for an escaped slave
and a wild beast.

Ad omnem quippe anime virtutem vera Dei et hominum
dilectio suficit . . . Sed sicut nos Domine ab infidelibus separe
voluit, ne per ipsos scilicet corrumperemur ita et operum
ritibus, ut dixi, faciendum esse decrevit.

*True love of God and men is sufficient for every virtue of the
spirit . . . but just as our Lord wished to separate us from
unbelievers that we not be corrupted by them, so he decreed that
this be accomplished by means of ritual acts. . . ."*

—Peter Abelard,
"Dialogue of a Philosopher with a Jew and a Christian"
(1079–1144)

*O*n the first day of the journey, Brother Martin discovered with surprise that the Jews both irritated and fascinated him. Having spent most of his life in the monastery, his vision of the Hebrew people was a tangle of revered Patriarchs and despicable slayers of Christ. These men fit neither image. They seemed much more like the Christian laymen he knew both in appearance and dress. Of course, they did have some customs that set them apart. The little boxes they tied to their heads and arms while praying were delightfully absurd. Martin wondered how a grown man could permit himself to look so foolish.

Other customs, however, were harder to mock; the way they observed their Sabbath for instance.

Saturday morning, the party left at sunrise from the village of L'Isle Jourdain following an ill-kept path through the woods.

When the road widened enough for a horse to pass, Berengar, in the lead with Jehan, fell back to see how everyone was doing. He noticed Brother Martin watching the Jewish men behind him.

"They make good time, don't they, considering," he commented.

Considering that the men were all walking, he meant. Brother Martin had been surprised that morning when the Jews had announced that they couldn't ride on the Sabbath. After an inner struggle, even Solomon had decided to observe the prohibition. His reason was not piety, but a determination to distance himself from anything Brother James might approve of.

But James paid them no attention. He rode near the front of the line of men, keeping close to Jehan and Berengar. It was Brother Martin who found the behavior of the Jews annoying, as if they were flaunting their devotion to their religion. This implied that, somehow, his was lacking.

Added to this was the obvious eagerness of the young man, Samuel, to engage him in theological discourse. Martin was acutely aware that although his faith was firm, he was no match for the wiles of a scholar.

It was these things that made the monk feel that Jews in the flesh were even more aggravating than those in monastic readings. It puzzled him that no one else seemed to be uncomfortable. Berengar and Arnald took their behavior for granted. Jehan just grunted total disinterest in anything Jewish and Guy followed his lead. That left only Brother James to ask. But here Martin's courage failed.

James had hardly spoken since they set out. He rode with head bowed, as if carrying a great weight. He ate little and, although they had been given a dispensation allowing them to forego their duties, he recited the hours as close to the proper times as he could manage. Martin had been warned that Brother James needed protection from the temptations of his former coreligionists. But Martin wasn't sure what form these would take. So far there had been no contact between them at all. He wondered if the abbot had meant that the Jews might try to abduct Brother James and drag him back to their synagogue. That would be easy for the burly monk to prevent, but if anything more subtle were attempted, he feared he would be useless.

As the days progressed, Martin had the feeling that James had no need for spiritual protection. He seemed to be building a wall of prayer around himself. The psalms mounted, solid as bricks, with not even a chink for the alluring sound of Hebrew to enter. But sadly, there wasn't any way for Martin to reach in, either. Inside his cell of words, James was alone.

They were following the great pilgrim route that ended at the shrine of Saint James at Compostella. In many ways it was a good choice. There were inns and shelters at regular intervals. The monks could be certain of a bed at a monastery or priory at each stop. But, especially as one came closer to the mountains, the hazards increased.

"I thought our job was to fight off bandits, not pay them," Guy grumbled on Monday as they were stopped by yet another toll taker blocking the road.

"Be grateful; our swords keep them from doubling the price," Jehan said. "Keep good watch at the rear. Tell that Arnald boy to do his best to look fierce. The ones who collect the tolls will signal their friends ahead if they think we're easy picking."

"Won't be anything left to pick at this rate," Guy grumbled.

"Wait until we get to Saint-Jean-de Sorde," Jehan told him. "The ferrymen there not only charge a fortune, they do their best to tip the raft over. That way they can scavenge what they like from the drowned pilgrims."

"I don't suppose they'd throw dice for the crossing fee?" Guy wondered.

"Then they could fleece you without getting wet!" Jehan couldn't believe it. "Guy, when are you going to face it that, in your case, Lady Fortune is a disease-riddled whore?"

Guy set his jaw in defiance. "My luck will change soon. I know it," he insisted.

"Yes," Jehan agreed. "It will get worse."

It was Tuesday afternoon when they reached the infamous ferry. The eyes of the ferryman lit as he saw the party approaching, a tic at one corner computing the number of coins he would get for each mule and packhorse on top of the price to take the men across the river.

By the time they reached the bank, his grin was ecstatic.

"Greetings, my lords." He bowed. "Good monks. On your way to the shrine of the blessed apostle, no doubt? I'll be pleased to assist you, unless you want to walk across."

He roared at his own joke. It tickled him every time he told it. Once a heretic had taken him up on the idea. He hadn't gone more than three steps before his faith failed him and the devil dragged him under. That tale had earned the ferryman free cider and wine in the taverns for many a year.

No one in the group laughed.

"How much?" Jehan asked. He casually took out his knife to clean his fingernails.

"Ten *pogesia* for each man, eight each for the monks." The man bowed to Martin and James. "Two *sous* for each horse and mule. Three if they are *sous* of Narbonne."

Jehan looked at Brother James.

"Three *pogesia* for each of the soldiers," James said. "We are clerics traveling in the service of Cluny. You have no right to charge us at all."

The ferryman laughed again. He was feeling very cheerful that day.

"The bishop doesn't feel that way," he explained. "Nor does my lord of Saint-Michel. When they come for their share of the toll, they expect each pilgrim and priest to have paid."

"We shall pay the normal fee," James said calmly. "Plus a *pagosi* as your cut. But you have more than doubled the amount they charge."

"I have my own saints to honor." The ferryman smirked.

"Saint Mammon and Saint Luxuria, I have no doubt," James answered.

The ferryman rubbed his forehead. "I never heard of those, but I'll light a candle to them if you think I should. Now, you can pay my fee or find your own place to ford. There may be one a day or two upriver. Or maybe not."

James beckoned to Jehan. Behind them, Solomon and Aaron were becoming restive.

"The monk can't think he can bargain with that old thief," Aaron said. "Doesn't he know that the man will have a score of friends waiting in the woods?"

"He should," Solomon answered. "Perhaps he's forgotten."

His friend looked questioningly at him and Solomon realized that Aaron hadn't heard the story of Jacob the convert. Perhaps only the older men knew, the ones who had met Jacob and his brother Eliazar when they were young merchants. The knowledge gave him a pang of sadness that he couldn't understand.

Jehan and Brother James had finished their consultation. Jehan seemed particularly pleased. The ferryman's smug expression faded to worry as the knight rode up to him. His hand moved in a series of gyrations.

"Does he have the palsy?" Brother Martin asked Brother James. "I don't want to risk my life on the skill of someone who shakes."

"I'd rather that than trust it to this man," James said sourly. "He's telling his friends to be ready to attack us if he doesn't like the taste of our money."

Jehan leaned down to speak to the ferryman. Their voices were too low for the others to hear. However, when they had finished, the man was grinning again so broadly that the black stumps of his upper molars were visible.

Jehan drew several small coins from his purse and gave them to the man.

"You get the rest when we are safely across," he reminded the man. "Berengar, you go first. Then the monks, then Guy."

Berengar had been at the rear, talking to Arnald. He had observed the haggling without much interest. That was something traders did. It wasn't until he reached the river bank that he saw what was to take him and his horse across the swift river.

"You must be mad!" he cried. "That's no more than a hollowed log!"

"It's carried better men than you!" the ferryman retorted. "Why a few years ago the abbot of Cluny was my passenger. He told me he had never felt so safe, just like in his mother's arms. There was even room for his little white mule."

"Where? On his lap?" Berengar turned to Jehan. "You can't mean us to pay money for the chance to drown?"

"It's this or turn back," Jehan told him. "Get in the boat. Put your horse on the lead and tie it to your wrist. He'll swim behind. Go on, do you want the others to think you hide a curling tail in your *brais*?"

"I'm not a coward!" Berengar said. But he made no move toward the ferry.

"Let me go first," Brother Martin said. "If it will hold me, then the rest of you should have no trouble."

"No, you need someone to guard you on the other side." Jehan shook his head at Berengar. "Who knows how many thieves are hiding there."

"Guy! Our young nobleman is afraid of the water," he called.

Guy sighed. "I'll go first if he won't," he said. "Anyone want to wager that Berengar ends up in the river?"

"I'll take that," the ferryman said.

"No, you won't," Jehan snapped. "Berengar, hurry. We've wasted too much time already."

Berengar was white with terror but, in the end, he preferred losing his life to his reputation.

With many grumblings, the other guards and the monks were taken across. Jehan went last.

"Wait!" Aaron called as the knight stepped into the ferry. "You're being paid to protect us, as well."

"From outlaws, not boatmen," Jehan called back. "Deal with him yourselves. We'll meet you at Hostavalla tonight."

"You . . . *vopils!*" Aaron shouted. "*Ganador!* Bastard! *Salier-issugua!*"

"Aaron!" Solomon exclaimed in admiration. "Very good. Although he's probably done even more disgusting things in his life. I was wondering when the old Jehan would appear."

"Why didn't you warn me?" Aaron asked.

"I didn't think of it," Solomon admitted. "It never occurred to me that you might trust a Christian."

"Excuse me?"

Solomon turned around. Arnald was still with them.

"Sorry," he said. "So shall we find out what kind of bargain that monk and Jehan made for their own passage?"

While they had been talking, Yusef had already approached the ferryman.

"Greetings, Fortus." He nodded.

The ferryman nodded back. "You brought a friend this time, *Senhor* Yusef." He smirked at Babylonia, who glared at him.

"So what did they agree to pay in exchange for giving you free rein to gouge us?" Yusef asked.

Fortus chuckled. "Seven *pogesia* for each man, including the monks, two sous for the battle horses and one each for the mules and pack animals."

"You did well," Yusef told him. "I'm inclined to give you a couple of sous extra just for the entertainment."

"I hate those monks." Fortus's cheerful mask fell and the anger showed through. "They all think they're Christ, Himself. But He cared for the poor. They just take from them."

Yusef nodded. "If I ever met a cleric who could heal the sick or raise the dead, I might convert, myself."

"Well, they say the apocalypse won't come until the Jews all accept Our Lord as their savior," Fortus said philosophically. "If that's what it will take for you to turn Christian, I figure we'll all be here a long time yet. So, five men, one woman, four horses, three mules. Not taking much to trade this time, are you?"

"Things are too unsettled in Spain," Yusef said. "No one's buying."

He gave the ferryman the money.

They made it across without incident, although Arnald prayed loudly to a saint Genesius, to whom he offered several candles before they reached the opposite bank.

"Don't know why you think he'll help you," Fortus said. "Saint Genesius knew how to swim."

"Exactly," Arnald said. "If I fall in, he's just the saint I want looking out for me."

Jehan expected to endure a tirade from the Jews for leaving them on the other side of the river, but no one said anything. Upon arriving at camp later that day, they checked their packs for damp and then took out cloths to dry the horses. Arnald made it clear to everyone that he was expending some of the travel money his father had given him on a candle at the first shrine they came to.

"How many times will we have to do this?" he asked the world in general. "I swear I saw demonic claws just below the surface of the water. I was sure they'd tip the boat over."

"It's just a little water," Berengar said. "Anyone would think you'd never been baptized."

This was such a turnabout from his behavior on the other side of the river that everyone forgot resentment to gape at him.

Berengar shrugged and laughed. "Well fooled, weren't you?" he said. "The ferries farther up the Garonne from Toulouse are far worse than that. I only wanted to see if that old *espoarit* would try anything, believing I was too busy reviewing my sins to notice."

"You had me convinced," Arnald said. "And I didn't blame you. I've never been in anything so rickety that still floated."

They continued on with no further conversation. The day was long, but twilight had still settled on them before they reached the town of Hostevalla. It had been built around hostels for the pilgrims, for several roads met there. The next morning they set out for the new town of Santa-Maria-Cabo-la-Puente established at the foot of the Pyrenees by the king of Narvarre for the comfort and taxation of pilgrims and traders.

"It's clouding over," Aaron said as they continued south. "I hope we don't have to camp out tonight."

"If we make it to Cabo-la-Puente, I'm fairly sure I can find us a place to stay," Solomon told him.

"Why? Do you have a deal with one of the innkeepers?" Aaron joked. "Wait a bit! I know that smirk. What's her name?"

"She's a widow named Cauzida," Solomon answered.

"A widow." Aaron nodded knowingly. "Fairly young, I would imagine."

"Well, the last time I saw her she still had all her teeth." Solomon laughed. "Of course, that was five or six years ago. I'm hoping she's held up and hasn't remarried."

"If it gets us a bed tonight, I hope so, too," Aaron said.

Cabo-la-Puente was a town that existed only to serve the needs of travelers. Berengar and Guy were happily surprised to find that not all the services were those that pilgrims would be expected to enjoy. One building, especially, drew their attention. It was clearly a tavern below but the shutters of the upper windows were wide open. Women leaned from them and called down to the men, offering unimaginable delights.

"Warm the bath for me, my Angels," Berengar called up to them. "I'll be with you soon."

"No you won't," Jehan told him. "Even when you see the monks safely to the priory, you still have to watch out for the Jews."

"We're in a town!" Berengar protested. "What could happen to them here?"

"Everything from having their purses cut to murder," Jehan answered. "I don't like Jews, either, but we took their coins and we owe them. So stay out of the brothels and water your wine. You can immerse yourselves in sin when the job's done."

"Can we follow the Jews if one of them goes to the brothel?" Berengar asked hopefully.

"No." Jehan smiled. "If he's that foolish, then no one can help him. You'll take shifts watching outside their inn. Arnald, you and Guy go first."

"Can't I sit inside with them?" Arnald asked, looking up. "It's going to rain."

Jehan grimaced. "I forgot you were a Jew-lover. As long as you stay sober, I don't care. But Guy will have to agree to it as well."

Guy wasn't pleased with the idea, but a glance at the sky, where dark clouds were gathering before a sharp northern wind, convinced him.

"As long as they don't try any of their sorcery on me," he decided.

"Good. Berengar and I will see to the monks," Jehan told them. "We'll meet at the monastery gate tomorrow just after Lauds."

Solomon smiled when he saw Arnald enter the inn.

"I wondered how long you'd last out in this weather," he said.

"You can bet that Jehan has found a warm corner to curl up in."

Then he noticed Guy.

For the first time, Guy noticed him, too. "Jehan told me that he knew you in Paris," he said. "I'm supposed to watch out for you. He says you're tougher than you look."

"That's right," Solomon agreed pleasantly. "Did he tell you anything else?"

Guy shook his head. He was about to say more but a welcome sound caught his attention, the rattle of dice in a cup.

"Who brought a *tric-trac* board?" he asked.

"It belongs to the innkeeper," Solomon said. "Samuel and Aaron are just throwing for amusement. There's no money on the table."

"Why not?" Guy went over to watch.

"We're forbidden to gamble," Samuel explained.

"So are Christians," Guy said. "But it's only a minor sin."

Samuel thought that over. "How do you know?"

"Guy," Arnald warned. "We're not to play games of chance with the people who hired us. And you have nothing to bet with."

"No," Guy said sadly. Then a thought struck him. "But we could play for my wages, double or nothing. What do you say?"

Behind him Arnald shook his head violently.

"Guy, Arnald," Solomon interrupted. "This is our hostess, *Na* Cauzida. Cauzida?"

He had hoped to be able to greet her privately. She had welcomed him warmly on his last visit, but who knew what had passed in her life since then?

"Solomon!" Her smile was casual, as if he was a neighbor who dropped in every week. "Good to see you again. You have a different party this time."

"Three of my fellow traders." Solomon waved to Aaron, and

Samuel, who stood and bowed. "Yusef will be with us in a moment. He has a servant woman with him. She'll need a bed to herself."

"Of course, and these men?" Cauzida gave Guy and Arnald a smile that made even Guy think about something besides games of chance.

"Our guards," Solomon told her. "There are four altogether. At least these two will need a place."

She thought. "That will be a crowd but, yes, I can do it. It happens that you are the only guests tonight unless the storm brings more. There's a place in the kitchen for Yusef's servant. The loft upstairs is divided by a curtain. Jews on one side, Christians on the other?"

"Thank you, Cauzida." Solomon's eyes asked another question.

"Perhaps you could come with me while I figure the price," she answered. "Helian!" she called into the kitchen. "See that the straw upstairs is clean and put another bone in the soup."

"It's mutton," she told Solomon. "Will your friends eat it?"

"I will," he said. "Now, shall we do the reckoning?"

They went into the next room.

Guy swore and spat on the flagstones. "Damn! She was ripe! I should have known he'd have her bagged already. You know what they say about Jews."

Arnald had gone back to the game. "No, what do they say?"

Samuel also seemed interested. "No one told me anything. Maybe I should know before I'm married."

Guy looked from one to the other. He suspected they were laughing at him.

The servant came in from the kitchen, carrying a plate of cheese and olives. He was followed by a small child of uncertain sex dressed in a long tunic. Its feet were bare. The sight of so many men didn't seem to bother it.

"Gossave!" It greeted them.

"What?" Guy asked staring at the child.

"She means 'God save you,' " the servant volunteered. "If you'll keep an eye on her, I'll go up and see about the straw. Just see she doesn't go near the coals."

The three men instinctively backed away from the child. She didn't seem worried by the reaction. Samuel smiled at her nervously. She smiled back and came over to the table. She tried to pull herself onto the bench but didn't seem to have the coordination.

"Up," she commanded, giving them a confident grin.

Samuel obliged. "Odd-looking thing," he said.

"Maybe she's part Saracen," Guy suggested.

"Of course not," Arnald said. "She's an idiot-child. Haven't you ever seen one before?"

The little girl was now seated on the table. She had straight dark hair, cut short and a curiously flat face with almond shaped eyes. Her tongue seemed too large for her mouth and from her flat nose thick mucus was flowing. Samuel looked around for a cloth to wipe it with.

"I've known only one," Samuel said. "A friend of my mother's had a son who had the same sort of features. It didn't live long."

Guy shuddered. "If she were mine, I wouldn't grieve."

"I don't know," Arnald said. "She has a certain appeal. Sort of like having your own pet monkey."

He patted her on the head. "Nice monkey,"

"Meow!" she said.

They all laughed. "She got you!" Samuel said. "You're not a monkey, but a nice kitty, aren't you?"

At that moment, the door to the inn banged open and Yusef blew in along with a burst of rain.

"Babylonia's missing," he gasped. "You've got to help me find her."

For a moment everyone just stared at him. Then Arnald said what they all were thinking.

"Why?"

"Because she could be in trouble," Yusef answered. "She might have fallen and broken her ankle, or been set upon by thieves. There are plenty of unrepentant rapists and murderers concealed among the pilgrims you know."

"It would be a desperate man who'd try to rape her," Guy said not softly enough.

Yusef glared at him.

The bang of the door brought Solomon and Cauzida running from the chamber. Solomon quickly finished buckling his belt.

"What is it?" he said.

"What are you doing with my child?" Cauzida demanded at the same time.

"Your what?" Solomon said.

Cauzida lifted the girl from the table. "Anna," she said. "My daughter."

"We were only looking out for her," Samuel explained. "We would never hurt her."

Yusef explained the situation to Solomon.

"If Babylonia's run off there's nothing we can do tonight," Guy spoke up. "It makes no sense to go out. In the dark and in this weather, we'd never find her. Those lunatics are sly. They can hide so's you could walk right by and not spot them."

"She'll die if we don't find her," Yusef pleaded.

Solomon sighed and reached for his cloak.

"I'll go with you, Yusef," he said. "Where did you last see her?"

"I'll come, too." Aaron stood up. "The poor thing may be wandering witless through the town, prey to evil of all sorts."

Arnald realized that his sojourn in the warmth was to be short lived. His feet were still soaked from a leak in his boot. He wiggled his toes, feeling the water squelch between them.

"Maybe she escaped you to join her own people," Guy suggested. "She's probably at one of the pilgrim hostels."

Arnald brightened at this. Even Samuel looked hopeful. But Yusef shook his head.

"She wouldn't go back to them," he said with certainty. "She'd been forced into making a pilgrimage when I found her."

"What for?" Solomon asked. "Attacking her mistress? Yusef, how could you take her into your home and then let her wander freely? She could have been doing penance for murdering her own children."

"What's this?" Cauzida said, clutching her daughter tightly. "Solomon, what have you brought into my home?"

"Babylonia did nothing wrong," Yusef said. "She's been wickedly mistreated. No." He forestalled Solomon's reproach. "I don't condone the offenses she committed against Josta or, even worse, how she tried to pollute the food. I only say that her unbalanced mind comes from great tragedy. The sin is mine, for thinking I could heal her. Please, help me. She mustn't suffer more because of my pride."

And there it was, Solomon thought. Yusef was a humorless man, rigid in his observance of the Law. He spread disapproval like fertilizer, believing that it would improve the lives of those it landed on. But at the end of the day, he was a good man in the true sense, not just a community leader, like the Good Men of Toulouse.

"I'll take a lantern and check the side streets," he said. "She may have taken shelter in one of them."

"Guy and I will ask at the monastery and the pilgrim hostels," Arnald offered.

Guy started to protest, then gave it up. The odds were against him.

"Will you come with me, Aaron?" Yusef asked. "There are

places by the river where women are sometimes taken."

"No!" Solomon interrupted. "That is, I should go instead. The two of you could get into serious trouble inquiring about a Christian woman. I know how to find out."

"They probably all know you by name there anyway," Arnald leered.

They soon worked this out and the men prepared to leave. Solomon agreed to search by the river. Cabo-le-Puente was a funnel for several mountain streams. Mills, waterfalls, conduits, there were too many places where one could be trapped by the water.

"What about me?" Samuel asked. "I want to help, too."

Even Yusef was alarmed at the thought of this innocent outside after dark.

"Someone should be here if she returns," Solomon told him. "And to relay messages when we come back and go out again."

"Please! Let's go at once," Yusef begged. "Babylonia may be lying in the muck, drenched and feverish. We can't delay any longer."

They were soon wrapped as well as possible against the weather. Yusef and Solomon carried closed lanterns, oil lamps enclosed in glass balls with a vent at the top and hung from leather straps.

"See that you don't break it," Cauzida told Solomon.

"I'm sorry," he whispered. "Will you wait up for me?"

"After putting Anna in danger from a madwoman?" she answered. "We'll sleep with the door barred."

Solomon didn't have to ask which side he'd be on.

Jehan and Berengar had taken Brothers James and Martin to the gate of a priory of their order. The porter greeted the monks with little enthusiasm but told them that, yes, there were spare beds. Jehan was relieved to hear that. He didn't relish spending another night in the draft from Brother Martin's snoring.

"You'll be ready to leave tomorrow right after Lauds?" he asked Martin.

"Oh, yes," the monk assured him. "It's not as though we have much to pack."

"Are you certain that you want to stay here?" Berengar asked. "It's not a very secure place. These walls would be easy to climb, if anyone wanted to enter."

"But why should they?" Brother James asked him. "What would monks have to steal?"

"Gold patens, silver candlesticks, reliquaries encrusted with precious stones," Jehan recited. "Good wax candles, silk and linen altar cloths, food, horses, leather shoes."

"You see?" Berengar said. "Not to mention the money you carry. You'd be safer with us guarding your door at the inn."

"We'll remain with our brothers and trust, as always, in God's protection," James said. Martin nodded his agreement.

Jehan shrugged. "It does seem as if Our Lord has sent weather that not even the most determined thief would risk. If it continues like this, we may have to wait before attempting the mountains. For now, Berengar and I will return to the inn."

The monks vanished into the shelter of the monastery. Berengar shivered inside his lambskin cloak. The rain was dribbling from his hat down his neck.

"Go on back," Jehan told him. "I want to check all around the monastery. You're right that it would be easily entered. The wall may be even worse in the back by the gardens."

"But you said yourself that no one would try to harm them on a night like this," Berengar said. "After all, no one knows they're carrying anything of value. And they're the ones who insisted on staying here."

"Perhaps," Jehan answered. "But I'm being paid to foresee even the most unlikely situation. Go ahead. I won't be long."

The last of the daylight was enough for him to follow the

wall around the priory. Like the rest of the town, it was new and mostly built of wood, or even withey reeds woven to make a fence. Enough to keep pigs and chickens in their places but not to stop an invader.

The land went down to a stream. At this time of year it was too fast to risk a boat on. The bank was steep and mostly mud but it appeared that cattle had been watered here recently.

He realized this when he slipped on a pile and landed flat on his ass. For a moment, he lay there, letting the rain wash him. Then he made himself get up, wincing at a pain in his right knee that seemed to get worse every year.

What was he doing here at this time of life? By now he had meant to have a castle of his own with a fine well-born wife and sons to leave his land to. *Merdus*, he thought. He knew men his age who had grandsons. But he was standing in a pasture in the rain, covered in cowshit and owning little more than his sword and his horse.

Solomon was part of the reason he didn't have the life he wanted. But even more it was Hubert LeVendeur and his daughters who had ruined every thing. Catherine was a witch who cast a curse on him so that her sister, Agnes, would never love him. Between them the two had driven him insane.

He didn't know what miracle had given him back his senses. Perhaps God had blessed him for fighting the Saracens. That had been awful enough to drive any man sane. But Jehan always feared a return of the madness. When he had first seen Solomon in the street, he had almost believed it was a fantasy. It was the hate on his old adversary's face that had reassured him.

And now, oddly, of all the people in the party, Solomon was the one person that Jehan was sure he could trust.

The insight was enough to shake him from his self-pity. That and the rain and the smell of the cowflop. He started to work his

way back to the road, suddenly aware that the last of the light
had vanished.

When Berengar got to the inn, he was surprised to find it empty.
He banged on the table until a woman came out, carrying a child.

"We're full up," she said.

Berengar looked around. "With what? I'm supposed to meet
my friends here. A couple of soldiers and a pack of Jews."

"Oh, yes," she said. "You have a place in the loft. Clean straw.
Your friends all went out hunting a madwoman. I'll leave a brazier
burning and some spiced wine for when they get back. And tell
then to be sure the door is barred unless they want to be murdered
in their beds. I'm not sitting up all night."

With that she went into her room.

With nothing better to do, Berengar poured himself some
wine and set about cleaning his boots.

Jehan had passed from introspection to anger. It was dark, windy,
cold, wet, and he hadn't had dinner. He was using the wall of
the priory, now stone where it backed on the chapel, to feel his
way. Loose strands of ivy whipped his face and he caught at them
to steady himself. At first he swore at the monks who had hired
him. Then at Berengar for already being someplace warm and
dry. Finally he settled into a rage that covered anything in his
way, from the ivy to the sharp stones on the ground that kept
sending him off balance.

It was one of these that sent him crashing against the wall.
At least that's what he had expected. But he felt only empty air.
He managed to save himself by grabbing wildly at the ivy but he
still landed hard on one hand, gashing his palm.

"Saint Stephen's broken stones!" he swore, shaking it to ease
the pain.

The next moment he felt his wrist seized by an iron cold claw, the nails digging in.

"Holy Virgin, Mother of God!" He screamed in blind terror. "Save me!"

He tried to pull away but the thing only dragged him down, into the dark mouth of Hell. As it did, Jehan caught a whiff of a smell he was all too familiar with. He had thought he had reached the pinnacle of terror, but now he knew how much worse it could get.

The smell was fresh blood.

Fourteen

In the midst of the storm.

התאבלי, נפשי, וסות, וסות אבל לבשי, ועל שקך תני חבל

מכרי משושך לצמיתות; גואל אל יהי לעד ולא יובל.

Oh mourn, my soul, and with a mourning cloak be clad and
put ropes upon thy sackcloth; . . . Sell thy joy forever; it
shall never be redeemed.

—Moses b. Jacob ibn Ezra
Dirge on the Death of His Brother

*G*et off me!" Jehan screamed. "Let go!"

A sudden light shone on his face.

"Thank you, oh Blessed Mother, thank you!" Jehan breathed, half thinking an angel had come to save him.

He looked down at what was holding him. He wished he hadn't. Babylonia's face was a handsbreadth from his. She looked worse than ever, her headscarf missing and her braids undone. Her face was smeared with blood as was the hand that gripped him like a claw. Jehan drew his knife. He'd make her let go if he had to slice off her hand. Then he saw what was across her lap.

"Sweet Jesus!" He gagged. "Woman, what have you done?"

The light behind him came closer and became an oil lantern. Solomon held it higher to see what Jehan was leaning over.

"You bastard!" he cried when he saw the knife. "Jehan! Drop the knife! Don't kill her, too!"

The light seemed to frighten Babylonia. She released Jehan and covered her eyes. Jehan turned on Solomon, anger overcoming his fear.

"Don't be an ass," he said. "I just found her here, like this. It's the madwoman that's killed him. Look for yourself."

Cautiously, Solomon came closer.

"You can't have him." Babylonia bent protectively over the body. "Go away!"

She pushed at Solomon, who recoiled from her gory hand. Laid across the woman's lap was Samuel. His face and chest were covered in blood; his eyes wide open, staring into infinity.

"My baby, my poor innocent child!" Babylonia crooned to the body. "But now you are with the angels. *Kiddush ha-Shem.* They won't take you from me again. You're safe in heaven."

The two men looked at each other, united in shock.

"What's she babbling?" Jehan said. "And how did she get loose?"

"I . . . I'm not sure." Solomon tried to tear his eyes from the sight as Babylonia kissed the bloody wounds on the boy's neck and face. "It doesn't make sense. I know she hates Jews, but I can't believe she'd do this."

"She's completely mad," Jehan said. "she could do anything."

"I know," Solomon said. "But look at her; she's mourning him."

"That doesn't mean she didn't kill him," Jehan said firmly.

"No, it doesn't," Solomon admitted.

"We have to get her tied up again," Jehan said when Solomon didn't move. "And find out if there's a place in town to bury a Jew."

"Yes," Solomon said, unable to look away. "I'll guard her. Go get help."

Jehan nodded and left. Solomon lowered the lantern. He didn't need to see Babylonia to know she was there. Her keening was constant and shrill, piercing even the storm.

Someone else had heard it.

"Babylonia!" Yusef called out from the darkness. "Solomon, did you find her?"

He stumbled toward the scene.

Solomon was suddenly filled with rage at this man. If Yusef hadn't taken Babylonia into his home, if he hadn't brought her with them, poor Samuel would still be alive. It took all his strength not to swing the lantern at Yusef's face as he approached.

"Come see what your misplaced charity has done!" His words came from between clenched teeth.

"What do you mean?" Yusef stumbled in the dark and fell, scraping his hand. Solomon made no move to help him.

"Solomon, what is it?"

Rubbing his muddy hand on his cloak, Yusef reached Solomon. When he saw Babylonia, he gave a great wail.

"Oh, woman! How could you?" he wept. "He had done nothing to you! The boy was innocent."

She looked up at him. "Yes, my poor baby," she said. "My innocent child."

She caressed Samuel's face, leaving streaks of blood. Then the keening started again.

"I don't understand," Yusef turned to Solomon. "She never minded Samuel. I don't think she even noticed him. And she's been calmer since we left Toulouse. I thought she was improving. What could have made her do this?"

"How can anyone guess the reasons of the insane?" Solomon said. "That's why they should be kept under guard. In her ranting, she said something about *kiddush ha-Shem*. Why? Who told her about that?"

Yusef dropped his head and covered his face.

"Oh, Babylonia!" he cried. "Solomon, I had no idea she had relapsed so far. You must believe me. She was doing so well, despite her attack on Josta. It's too long a story. One I hoped never to tell. Later. Now we have to get her out of here."

"And what do we do with Samuel?" Solomon said coldly. "Leave him for the ravens?"

"No, no," Yusef said. "Of course not. His poor father!"

"And poor Belide," Solomon said. "She was to marry him."

They heard shouts from the road. "This way! Mind your step!"

"That's Jehan," Solomon said. He signaled to him with the lantern.

Yusef tried to see who was there. The light fell on three men, first Jehan, then Aaron then . . . Solomon's heart sank. Brother James.

"Jehan, what's he doing here?" Solomon shouted.

At the same time Yusef called, "Aaron, don't come any closer!"

Aaron stopped. The other two continued.

"I thought Brother James should be informed," Jehan said. "And why don't you want Aaron? He's young and strong and he was already out in the wet. We need him."

"He can't help." Brother James knelt to examine the body. "Aaron is a Cohen. He can't be contaminated by contact with a body."

"*Hein?*" Jehan looked at Solomon who nodded.

"Jacob, I swear I don't know how she got loose," Yusef was saying. "Nor why she would have killed Samuel."

The monk took in the scene, his eyes passing over Solomon without a flicker.

"She didn't kill him," Brother James said.

"What?" the other three spoke at once.

"Are you all blind as well as stupid?" James asked. "For one thing, he was stabbed in the stomach and then his throat cut for good measure. Do you see a knife anywhere near her? For another, look at the blood. It's on her face and hands and where she's held him, across her breast and shoulder. If she faced him and made those cuts she'd be covered from head to feet. Now, is there a great pool of blood on the ground here?"

"Well, the rain," Jehan began.

"This alcove is sheltered both by the vines and by the stone arch of the wall." James pointed up without looking. "If he'd been killed here, there'd be splatters all over and your boots would be sticky with blood."

Behind him, Solomon examined his boots and had to admit that the bastard was right.

"She could have killed him out in the rain and dragged him here," Jehan suggested. "And it's easy to dispose of a knife."

"Possibly." Brother James bent further down to examine the hem of Babylonia's robe. "And, even though it would be a great task for a woman of her size, madness often confers unusual strength. But the stains on her clothes still aren't right. Nor are these cuts the sort made in a frenzy. I think that she either saw the murderer dump the body here or simply stumbled on it while hunting for a refuge. I'd guess the former, by the freshness of the blood on her hands."

"She didn't kill him?" Jehan was still having trouble with the idea.

"Then why is she talking about *kiddush ha-Shem?*" Solomon asked.

"That is something I'm sure Yusef knows much better than I." Brother James stood. He could feel his back creak as he did. A midnight walk in a cold spring storm was just what he had needed for it to give out completely. If only he could get back to his bed at the monastery before that happened.

He carefully avoided looking at the man with the lantern. It was hard not to. He could feel the fury of Solomon's hate burning through the chill, the damp, and his woolen cloak. A time would come, he knew, when he would have to face it, but not now.

"What should we do with them?" Jehan asked. "We can't stay out here all night. I'm freezing and drenched to the core."

"Someone take this woman away, wash her, and see that she's restrained," James ordered. "As for the body, that's up to his people."

Solomon growled deep in his throat. The old monk must have heard, they were less than an arm's length apart, but he gave no sign of it. James turned to Yusef.

"He may have been set upon by thieves," he said. "Just as they tell me Brother Victor was. No one is safe out alone after dark. You can go to the local lord or his provost for justice if you like, but I doubt anyone will do anything."

"I know," Yusef said. "You're sure Babylonia didn't kill him?"

"Moderately," James told him. "That doesn't excuse you from being lax in your custody of her."

"I know that, too."

Yusef leaned down and gently pried Babylonia's hands from Samuel's body.

"Come with me," he said. "Come, Babylonia. I'll see that no one hurts you."

"Better see that she can't hurt anyone else," Jehan said. He wasn't convinced by Brother James's interpretation of the scene.

"There's nothing I can do here," James announced. "Jehan, please escort me back to the monastery. I presume we won't be able to resume our journey in the morning. It's just as well, since Brother Martin needs rest. But I can't let this delay us more than a day."

"What's going on?" Aaron yelled from the path. "Is Babylonia all right?"

"I'll tell him," Yusef offered as he pulled the woman to her feet and forced her to move away from the body.

"I suppose that leaves me with guard duty," Solomon grumbled. "We'll have to bring Samuel back to the inn. Tell Berengar, Guy, and Arnald to bring blankets and poles to make a stretcher."

This was all that was needed, he reflected, to guarantee Caudiza's refusal to share her bed with him. He'd brought violence into her house, the one thing worse than not paying one's bill. She would see that he received no more special care. He was ashamed of the thought but couldn't deny it. He had been anticipating this night since he left Paris. Even the shock of Samuel's violent death couldn't erase his yearning.

And, instead of going immediately back to the inn where he might have a chance of convincing her to open her door to him, Solomon found himself alone in the middle of a dark and stormy night, with a rapidly stiffening corpse.

By the time that Yusef and Aaron had reached the inn, the rain had washed the worst of the blood off Babylonia. Nevertheless, she still looked wild enough that, when they had heard the news, Arnald, Guy, and Berengar had to be prevented from hanging her from the rafter at once.

"And you should be next to her," Berengar told Yusef. "You knew she was violent."

"Your monk friend thinks she's innocent of the boy's death," Yusef told them. "He says it was likely thieves, lying in wait for travelers."

"I don't understand. I thought Samuel was going to stay here," Guy said. "How did he get all the way over to the priory?"

They all thought about that.

"Maybe the woman who runs the inn is in league with the cutthroats," Berengar suggested. "She could have lured him outside for them to attack. That is, if this madwoman didn't kill him."

This sounded plausible. Everyone knew stories of hostellers who murdered incautious travelers, stole everything they owned, and threw their bodies in a midden or handy river.

Guy sighed and pulled on his wet boots.

"Whatever happened, he was a good man for a Jew and doesn't deserve to be left out in the rain. Berengar? Arnald? Do we have anything to carry him in?"

When the Christians had left, Aaron and Yusef tried to plan what to do next.

"There's not likely to be a Jewish cemetery here," Aaron worried. "And Narbonne is too far to take him, especially if the weather turns warm again."

Yusef was trying to get the remaining stains off Babylonia's face. She was docile now. The only sounds she made were random whimpers. They'd get no sense out of her tonight. Yusef feared that she had lost the small amount of reason she had left.

"There, there," he repeated. "It will be all right. I won't let them hurt you. It will be all right."

Even as he spoke, he knew how stupid it was. Of course it wouldn't be all right and how could he prevent her being hurt? He hadn't done very well so far.

"The burial, yes." He made himself concentrate. "If we could get the body over the mountains, there are communities in Navarre. We could pay to have them bury him, if they have room. But I don't like throwing him over a mule like a sack of beans. Could you get me another clean cloth?"

"Of course." Aaron went to rummage in the pack for something that could be torn.

"What's going on out here?"

The innkeeper, Caudiza, was standing in the doorway to her chamber. She had thrown a rumpled *bliaut* over her *chainse* but she was still wearing her sleeping cap. She carried her daughter on her hip, the child half-asleep.

"I'm sorry, *Na* Caudiza," Aaron said. "We've had some problems. Yusef's servant . . . that is, our friend Samuel. There was an accident."

"Where's Solomon?" Caudiza asked. She held the child more closely.

"He'll be back soon," Aaron said. "But Samuel is dead. A

terrible tragedy. May we put his body in your stable for the night? Yusef and Solomon will keep watch."

"And you?" she asked. "You won't sit with your friend?"

"I can't," Aaron said angrily. "I can't do a blasted thing."

"It's our Law," Yusef explained. "It's my responsibility, in any case."

"How did he die?" Caudiza wanted to know.

"We think he met up with thieves." Yusef was now concentrating on Babylonia's hands.

"Did they attack her, too?" Caudiza looked curiously at Babylonia.

"I don't know," Yusef said. "She can't tell us yet."

Caudiza shifted her daughter to her other hip. "You're lucky that you're the only ones here tonight. Otherwise I'd throw you all out. People in and out long after Compline. Leaving doors unbarred. And now one of you gets himself murdered."

She paused, watching Babylonia.

"Here, let me," she said, putting Anna down next to Yusef. "She's all over blood. She shouldn't stay in these clothes. Does she have any others?"

Babylonia ignored the woman. With a look of awe, she held out her hand to the child.

"Innocent baby," she breathed, her face alight.

"No!" Yusef quickly lifted Anna out of her reach. "This is not your baby!"

Caudiza looked up in alarm. Then, seeing that the child was safe, she turned back to Babylonia.

"Did you have an innocent?" she asked.

Babylonia smiled wistfully. "One girl. My husband was angry. But he was always angry with me. Then we had a son. But soon after that the ones who worship the hanged man, they caught me and took me away."

Caudiza was about to ask more but Yusef stopped her. "Not now, please."

She patted Babylonia's arm. "There, that's as clean as I can get you without a tub. If *Senhor* Yusef will find you something better to wear, you can come to my room and change."

Babylonia stood up and tried to smooth her skirts. "Thank you," she said, trying to appear sane. "You're very kind."

Caudiza took Anna back and the women went into her chamber.

"Is she safe?" Aaron asked.

"I think so," Yusef said. "There's something about the child that seemed to calm her."

"Of course. Little Anna has a stainless soul," Aaron said.

"What?"

"I've seen children like her before, not many," Aaron told him. "Most people think they're good luck."

"Hmm." Yusef wasn't interested in superstitions. "Perhaps, but it seems strange. Other children only annoy her. Those twins of Bonysach's make her wild."

"Along with the rest of Toulouse," Aaron commented. "Yusef, if Solomon won't, I'll take a turn at sitting with Samuel's body."

"No. I won't have you contaminate yourself," Yusef said. "Solomon will help. In his heart he's a good Jew. I only wish the rest of his body would pay attention."

A few moments later Caudiza returned with Babylonia, now dressed in clean, if worn robes. She gave the stained clothing to Yusef.

"Did she tell you anything more?" he asked.

"Not about the death of your friend," she said. "We talked about childbirth."

Neither man had any response to that.

The wind had died down outside enough for them to hear the thump as something heavy was dropped outside the door. Caudiza went over and lifted the latch.

Solomon stood in front of her, one hand raised to knock.

"You look like hell," she said.

"Good," he answered. "I'd hate to feel this awful and not show it. Did Yusef explain?"

"Yes, you can put your friend's body in the shed where I store the hay. Put something under him to keep from staining the floor."

"Don't worry." Solomon was swaying with exhaustion. "We'd do that anyway. But I don't think he's got much blood left."

"Doesn't look like you do, either," she said.

Solomon turned to the guards. "Put him out back in the shed," he called to them. He leaned against the lintel.

"Will you let me in?" he asked.

She looked at him a moment. "Yes, I think I will," she answered.

A sudden hope rose in him like the morning star. Solomon entered the inn.

Aaron and Yusef already had put on their tallit and were looking at him expectantly.

"Oh, no," Solomon said. "I know what you want. I don't know the prayers to say. Yes, he mustn't be left alone and I'll sit watch but can't my turn wait until morning? *Avoi*, it almost is morning. I'm frozen, wet, hungry, and . . ."

"We can see," Aaron said. "You're in no shape for lamentation. I'll pray while Yusef watches."

Yusef was about to protest, but then looked at Solomon, who was looking at Caudiza. It was wrong, of course. They should keep him from her. Sleeping with a Christian woman was not only a sin but dangerous. Then he remembered how Brother James had treated them all as if they were vermin infesting his life. Not once had he glanced at his son. And Solomon had held the lantern steady for him even so.

"Yes, I'll take the first watch," he said. "Come, Babylonia. You need to sleep, but you must be bound for your own safety."

Guy, Berengar, and Arnald were only in the shed long enough to see that Samuel's body was decently covered and the door barred to scavengers. But they returned to find the hall of the inn empty, a pot of broth left on the coals of the brazier, and a pitcher of wine on the table. When Jehan finally arrived, not even that was left.

Caudiza helped Solomon off with his clothes. It would have been more sensual if he could have stopped shivering.

"Get under the covers," she told him. "You're almost blue."

"Not my usual form, I'm afraid," he said through chattering teeth. "I'm sorry."

Caudiza smiled. "You'll warm up."

"I mean about the trouble I've caused," he said.

"You'll have to pay extra for that," she warned.

Solomon glanced at the trundle bed next to him. "What about her?" he asked.

"She was back to sleep as soon as I laid her down," Caudiza said. "She won't wake until morning."

"Ahhhh!" Solomon gave a sigh that was half pain, half comfort as he felt the feather bed envelope him. His feet were icy, his hands clammy, his dark curls dripping. Caudiza pulled her *bliaut* over her head and let her *chainse* fall to the floor. She blew out the light and joined him in the bed.

Her skin against his was so warm that it burned, sending soft solace deep into his body. He could feel his bones, even his heart, thawing. That must have been why he felt tears on his face. It was like a river smashing through the ice. Once the first crack had been made, he couldn't stop.

Caudiza held and rocked him as if he'd been a child, until the sobbing ebbed. She knew this wasn't only grief for his murdered friend but the pent up sorrow of years. She didn't ask him to explain but hummed an old lullabye. As he grew quieter she began moving slowly against him in rhythm with the tune.

Solomon had been sure he was completely drained of energy and feeling. He was mistaken.

In the shed, Yusef found that the men had left Samuel's body on a blanket on the floor. They had arranged him as well as possible. Yusef lit the candle he had brought and sat to watch over him. The shock of the evening was fading. It made it hard for him to keep his eyes open. If only Aaron weren't a Cohen. Yusef knew the Law had been given to them for a reason, but it was hard sometimes to accept this. Yet he never dreamed of questioning. There were Jews like Solomon, who ignored the Law most of the time as too inconvenient for modern life. They filled Yusef with concern. He knew how easy it would be for them to drift away. Perhaps not convert but be lost all the same.

The ferryman had joked that the Millennium wouldn't arrive until there were no more Jews in the world. That idea frightened Yusef even more. He knew that unless the Jews held firmly to their faith, there would be no one for the Messiah to lead and no chance of a Millennium at all.

So he sat and struggled to stay awake. He listed to the scurry of rats in the thatch and the snuffling of a larger animal against the outside wall.

The power was in the words. But here Yusef couldn't pray, or eat or drink. Not here. Samuel was now denied all those things and it would be cruel to do them in his presence.

He tried not to look at the body. It seemed a stranger, so pale, with lips almost purple and that horrid gash across its throat. Instead he addressed the ceiling, as if speaking directly to Heaven.

"I don't know what we'll tell your parents." He sighed. "I don't even know if they have other children to comfort them. Even though Jacob is a wicked apostate, I hope he's right that Babylonia didn't do this to you. She's mad but not wicked, not like this. She's suffered so. And why were you out at all? You were supposed to stay at the inn. Did you see something? Did you suddenly decide that you knew where Babylonia might have gone?"

"No." He stopped himself. "I hope that's not it. Then it might mean that you were the one who found her."

He was quiet awhile. The animal outside grew more persistent, scratching at the door now. Yusef didn't blame it. No one should be out on a night like this. The rain was so sharp that he could no longer make out the squeaks of the rats above.

"It's odd," he mused. "That monk in Toulouse was out when he shouldn't be, as well. Of course, they say that any man who walks alone after dark, walks with the devil. But it is strange that there should be two such deaths so close together."

The scratching at the door grew louder. Yusef hoped that Solomon would finish wallowing in his bed of lust soon and come take his place. He remembered a story his old aunt had told him about a man who fell asleep when he should have been guarding a body. When he woke up, demons had broken in and taken both the dead man and the sleeping one to a dark, frozen cave with no way out.

His teachers had told him that was nonsense. They taught him to read the true words of the Holy One. And later he had begun to study the meanings hidden in those words, the secrets of the Chariot, the messages the Lord meant only for the most learned and devout of His people. The scholars assured him that there were no ugly little demons with the ears and beards of goats.

Then what was so intent on gnawing its way into the shed?

Solomon woke to a tug on his hand, followed by something that felt like a puppy licking his fingers. He peered over the side of the bed and saw in the dim predawn light, Caudiza's daughter, Anna. She gave his hand a damp kiss, rubbing her runny nose against it. The child grinned at him, her oversized tongue back in her mouth for the moment. She pulled his fingers again.

"Nice man," she said.

Solomon grinned back. He couldn't help it. He tried to wipe his hand on the sheet but Anna held it tightly.

Caudiza stirred against his side. She lifted herself across his back to pick the little girl up.

"Mama," Anna said, and snuggled down between the two of them.

Solomon tried to remember when he had last seen Caudiza. It must have been more than five years ago. The girl couldn't be more than three or so.

"Did you marry again?" he asked.

"No," she answered.

"Your daughter, she seems . . . um . . . different," he said, as Anna made another grab for his fingers. "Was her father a foreigner?"

"Probably," she answered. "Just one of the travelers at the inn, no doubt."

"Ah." He started laughing. Anna was tickling him.

"Silly man!" She giggled.

He picked her up and lifted her out at arms length. Anna twisted and then went limp. The dead weight was so sudden that he nearly dropped her.

Caudiza got out of bed and took the girl from him. She set

her on a chamber pot and gave her a piece of cheese to keep her there.

"Is she all right?" Solomon asked finally. "I mean, one of my companions said she was an idiot child. Is that true?"

"She's an innocent," Caudiza told him. "Just like that woman said last night. She learns very slowly, but she does learn. The herbwoman says she probably won't last more than a few more winters, though. She's sensitive to the choking sickness."

"I'm sorry," he said. "I'm sure that it isn't because of anything you did."

Caudiza stared at him with an expression he couldn't comprehend.

"Do you think she was born like this as my punishment?" she asked in astonishment. "You *burugabeko!* Anna is a gift. A sinless being. She is nothing but love. I treasure every moment I'm allowed to keep her."

"Of course," Solomon said in bewilderment. "It's only that . . ."

He looked at the little girl, who was grunting on the pot. She finished and ran back to the bed, trying to climb in. To Solomon's relief, Caudiza caught her and tucked her under one arm as she set a pan of water next to the dying coals on the brazier. When the chill was off it, she poured the water into a shallow trough and set Anna into it, rinsing her off quickly before wrapping her in a thick cotton cloth. Then she brought the girl back to bed with her.

"I don't suppose she'll sleep anymore," Solomon said as Anna crawled up his chest.

"Not likely," Caudiza said. "Don't you have to relieve your friend at his watch?"

"*Enodu!*" Solomon exclaimed. "Poor Yusef! I forgot all about him and Samuel. How could I?"

"I can't imagine," Caudiza said. "Here, give me my baby and get your clothes on."

A sudden ray of morning sun illuminated the little girl's face as Solomon held her up. He stopped and stared. In that oddly-formed face with its small nose and chin and wide mouth were the most unusual eyes he had ever seen. They were a deep azure blue at the rim and around the pupil, like thin bands of lapis lazuli. But in the center they were the green of new leaves flecked with shafts of sunlight.

"What beautiful eyes!" he exclaimed. "Where did she get them?"

Caudiza gave him another strange glance.

"I have no idea," she said.

Solomon raced through the hall, not stopping to speak to Arnald and Guy, who were playing tric-trac for olive pits. He hurried out to the shed, full of apologies. When he got to the door, the first thing he noticed was that it was open. The second thing was that there were deep, fresh cuts in the wood, like those made by the claws of a lion.

"Yusef!" he called. "Yusef!"

"I thought you were going to be here before cockcrow," came a grumble from within. "Aaron and I have to say morning prayers, you know."

"I'm sorry, Yusef," Solomon said. "I overslept."

He was glad he couldn't see the other man's face at that moment.

Out of respect for the dead, Yusef made no comment.

"I'll be back later when we find out if we can bury him here or if we have to take him into Spain," he said.

"What made those marks?" Solomon pointed to the door.

Yusef shook his head. "I never went out to look. My mind

was on my duty to Samuel. Therefore, the Lord heard my cry and protected me from the terror that prowls by night."

Solomon left the door open after Yusef left. If there was also a terror that prowled by day, he wanted to see it coming.

The first rigidity had passed and Samuel's features were becoming more natural, even with the wound on his neck lying open like the gateway to hell.

"You would have been a good husband to Belide," Solomon told him. "You would never have noticed that she was running your life."

He tried to think what he could have done to prevent this. Samuel should have been the safest of all of them, sitting comfortably at the inn. Why hadn't he stayed there?

An abrupt thought hit him. In his desire for Caudiza's body and her bed, he had completely forgotten to ask if she had seen Samuel go out. A flush of shame rushed over him. The answer might explain everything. If he had asked it at once, there might even have been the chance of catching the one who had killed him.

He nearly got up to go find Caudiza before he remembered his obligation to see that Samuel was not left alone. He passed a few moments in cursing his own selfishness and stupidity, then he noticed something about the body.

Samuel lay wrapped in the cloak he had been wearing when he was found. The silver brooch at the neck was still pinned to the wool. Solomon checked the man's hands. The index finger on the right one wore a gold ring set with onyx. Had it been too tight for the robbers to remove? He grasped it and it slid off with ease. Quickly, he put it back.

That was puzzling. Even in pitch blackness an experienced thief could strip a body almost before it fell to the earth. Had Samuel been killed by apprentices? Or had "Brother James" been mistaken. Perhaps Samuel had gone out after Babylonia despite his orders and she had sprung at him, her disordered mind seeing him as an enemy.

Solomon wished he had stopped long enough to drink a cup of water or clabbered milk. His empty stomach was making too much noise for him to think.

It wasn't fair. It was his cousin, Catherine, Hubert's daughter, who seemed unable to move without tripping on a murder victim. True, he had been dragged into the consequences of her discoveries, but he had always felt it was some flaw in her that caused it.

Now he wondered if it could be a family curse.

A shadow blocked the sunlight coming in from the doorway.

"I brought you some bread and grape juice," Berengar said. "The monks are here. They want to know how soon we can leave."

"It's not up to me," Solomon told him. "I'm just the guard here, like you. And thank you for the food, but I can't take it while watching."

Berengar took a bite of the bread and washed it down with the juice.

"Suit yourself," he said.

Solomon waited. Berengar took another bite.

"Perhaps you could finish my breakfast somewhere else?" Solomon suggested.

"What? Oh, yes. Sorry." Berengar finished the juice. "I was just thinking, once he's in the ground, then what? I mean, you don't have Masses said for his soul. How do you help him get into Heaven?"

"We don't," Solomon said. "I think Samuel will get there well enough on his own merits. That's what the Last Judgment is for, to assess each man in himself, not to see how many saints his family was able to bribe to plead for him in heaven."

He shouldn't have said that. It just came out. More than

thirty years of sermons and earnest lectures had given him a deep aversion to any discussion of dogma.

But Berengar didn't seem inclined to debate. "Funny idea," was all he said.

Yusef returned soon afterward.

"Aaron thinks he has found someone who will let us bury Samuel safely on this side of the mountains," he told Solomon. "But he wants you to help convince your friend at the inn to sell us material for the shroud and find a seamstress. I'll stay here for now."

Solomon was glad to have a second chance at some nourishment but he didn't think he was really needed to bargain with Caudiza. If she had material to sell or knew a seamstress for hire, she would set the price with Aaron. He knew he didn't mean enough to her to make a difference.

He was hurrying, following his nose to the scent of fresh porridge burning and so didn't see the man coming out of the door to the inn as he was going in.

At the last moment, the man looked up and avoided the collision.

Solomon felt as though a battering ram had run him down.

He was looking directly into the face of his father, Brother James, and at eyes that were azure blue, the color of lapis, at the rim and near the pupil, with the rest of the iris a startling shade of green, flecked with gold.

Fifteen

Outside the inn. Santa Maria Cabo-la-Puente. Thursday, 24 Nissan 4908, ninth day of the Omer. 10 kalends May (April 22) 1148, Feast of St. Vital, who was buried alive.

Si quis fidellis cum judea vel gentili fuerit mecatus xv annos penita.

If any of the faithful have sex with Jews or unbelievers, fifteen years of penance.

—Penitential of Silense

"*W*ill you let me pass?" the monk said coldly.

Solomon backed away, still spellbound by the eyes that were exact mirrors of those of the innkeeper's child. Brother James pulled his cowl down over his forehead and stalked off.

Solomon realized that he was shaking. He took a deep breath and forced his body to appear calm.

"What did that man want?" he asked as he entered.

Jehan was twisting rope into a cradle for lowering Samuel's body into the earth. The younger guards had been sent out to dig the grave.

"To know if we would be ready to continue tomorrow," Jehan answered. "Aaron says that will be time enough."

"Heartless *mesel*," Solomon said.

Jehan shrugged. "The dead man was nothing to him. Nor me. We have a mission to complete. None of you knew him that well, either, did you?"

"No," Solomon admitted. "He was just a harmless scholar who thought he should have an adventure before he settled down."

"Well, he's settled now." Jehan tugged on the splice to make sure it would hold. "Shouldn't we make some sort of marker?"

Solomon grimaced. He should have thought of that.

"Where are we putting him?"

"There's a plot some peasant set aside for foreigners," Jehan said. "Saracens, Jews, excommunicants, that sort. Makes a good living with it, looks to me. Samuel won't be alone."

The last was said with a tremor that Jehan covered with a cough. Solomon pretended he hadn't noticed.

"We can make something, a cairn of stones," he suggested. "So his family will be able to find him if they want to take him back to Narbonne. What about a coffin?"

"That wasn't hard to find in a pilgrim town," Jehan said. "For every person healed by a miracle, there are a thousand God ignores."

"So all we need is the shroud," Solomon said.

"Right," Jehan said. "Then we can be on our way."

"I should speak to Caudiza about that." Solomon looked around. "Do you know where she is?"

"In the kitchen, I think," Jehan answered vaguely. "Or out at the oven."

Solomon found her at the hen house. She had put Anna on a barrel to keep her from getting pecked. The girl sat happily watching as her mother tossed grain to the scrabbling chickens. Solomon took the opportunity to check her eyes again. They were identical to his father's.

"Caudiza," he asked. "The monk traveling with us, does he pass this way often?"

"What?" she asked. "Here, toss some of this toward the geese, would you."

"Solomon took the dish of grain but didn't move. "Brother James," he repeated. "Is he a frequent visitor at the inn?"

"I don't know who you're talking about," Caudiza said. "I never get monks. They stay for free at the priory."

"Maybe he wasn't dressed as a monk," Solomon suggested. "An old man, almost completely gray, but with black eyebrows, no beard and eyes"—he paused—"eyes much like Anna's."

She took the dish from him. "Here, if you won't help, let me get on with the work. No, Solomon, he doesn't sound like anyone I know. Why? Do you think he had something to do with the death of your friend?"

"No, I . . ." Solomon stopped. That hadn't occurred to him. Could Brother James have somehow left the priory, found Samuel and killed him in the time Jehan had taken to explore the area? Possibly. But what could Samuel have done that could make the monk angry enough to kill? And why would James have then insisted that Babylonia wasn't the murderer? It would have been easy to place the blame on her.

Reluctantly, he gave up the idea. It would have been so satisfying to mark Brother James as a profligate who seduced women at inns and murdered inoffensive Jews. After all, a man who would abandon his wife and young son to poverty and starvation would commit any crime.

"Caudiza," he started again.

"That Yusef told me you needed linen for a shroud." She gave him the empty bowl and plucked Anna off the barrel. "I told him I didn't have any, but he seemed to think you could make me unlock a secret cache."

"He's distressed by all that's happened," Solomon said. "I know that if you had any linen, you'd sell it to us."

"If I had any, you *zozo*, I'd give it to you," she retorted. "However, I'll send Xabier to ask the neighbors. Someone will have enough."

"I'm surprised that, with a coffin maker and a plot for alien dead, there isn't someone who specializes in shrouds, as well," he commented.

"Perhaps I should," she said. "There's no shame in supplying the needs of the pilgrims, after all. And this is just another."

He followed her back inside, feeling well chastised but not sure why.

∞

That afternoon two girls from the town came in to help Caudiza. She sent them out to kill and dress two of the hens that hadn't resumed laying that spring. Then she started an enormous kettle of soup, throwing in spices recklessly.

"We'll consider it the funeral feast," she told Aaron, who had come in to thank her for her help. "If that doesn't offend your customs."

"It's kind of you," he said. "The smell of this soup alone would lure me back from the precipice of death."

It wasn't until after he had left that Caudiza remembered. No matter how good it might be, Aaron would eat her food only if it were that or starvation. Not all Jews were as careless as Solomon about their laws.

"Well," she comforted herself. "At least I didn't use the bacon. If I tell him that he might take a sip."

They buried Samuel that afternoon. Solomon was surprised to see Brother Martin at the gravesite.

"I thought you were ill," he said.

"It was nothing," Martin told him. "I felt that, since Samuel was one of our party, I should attend his burial. And, I thought you might need help in lowering the coffin."

"Thank you, but we've managed," Solomon said. "You can tell your partner that we shall be ready to continue tomorrow morning."

"My partner? Oh, Brother James!" Martin smiled. "Yes, he'll be glad to know that. We mustn't let this delay us. Those poor men have been languishing in Saracen prisons too long already."

Solomon felt no sympathy for the Christian knights. Poor Mayah was in a far worse place because of men just like those. Why should they be freed? He was glad that Belide had accepted the money from Brother Victor. It was only fair. With luck and good weather, they could be at Fitero within a week.

And then what? Solomon had tried not to imagine what they would find at the monastery. He couldn't bear to think of Mayah with a painted face and cheap bangles forced to offer herself to any man. He wondered how Aaron stayed sane, knowing what must be happening to her. Some part of him hoped she had already died.

The inn was full when they returned from the burial. It seemed that most of the villagers had smelled the soup and followed their noses there. There were also a few people carrying a pilgrim's staff and wearing the cockleshell on their hats denoting that they had achieved the shrine of Saint James at Compostella.

One of Caudiza's helpers gave Solomon a bowl of soup when he came in. Not having Aaron's or Yusef's scruples, he took it gratefully and looked around for a place where he could eat it without being elbowed by one of the other guests.

In a corner near the wine cask an old woman was sitting on a bench. She had a bowl of soup in her lap and was soaking bread in it. Next to her on the floor, sat Anna. She had her face turned up, mouth open, and every few moments the woman would feed her a piece of the softened bread.

Solomon noticed a space at the end of the bench and carefully wedged himself into it.

The woman moved to make room, giving him a smile that showed her five remaining teeth.

"*Agur yauna andrea,*" she greeted him.

"*Bai zuri ere,*" he answered, then continued quickly. "I have few words in your language. Do you speak French?"

"*Oc,*" she answered. "But your northern accent is hard to follow."

She took another bit of the bread, soft and dripping, and gave it to Anna. "Are you family?" Solomon asked.

"Caudiza is my sister's child," the woman answered. "I am Zurialdi. And you are Solomon. Caudiza told me."

Solomon wasn't sure this was good, but the woman showed no animosity.

"I was surprised to find she had a child," he said. "Of course, it's been some time since I was last here. Did Anna's father live here?"

"No, he was just a traveler." Zurialdi laughed. "I wish I had been widowed young, like Caudiza. She can choose anyone she fancies, any time. Ah well, come up here, *uso*, and sit on my lap."

"Excuse me?" Solomon said. Then he realized that Zurialdi was speaking to the child.

Anna clambered up, the last piece of bread hanging from her mouth. She wouldn't sit still, though, and kept trying to get back onto the floor.

"No, Anna." Zurialdi tried to hold her but the child seemed able to slide out of any grip.

"She'll be stepped on in this crowd," Zurialdi explained to Solomon. "Anna, please stay here."

"Anna," Solomon asked. "Will you come to me?"

"*Bai*," she answered and threw herself onto him.

He accepted her gingerly. There seemed a lot about her that was damp, from nose to feet. The soup-sodden bread was smeared around her mouth. He wiped at it with his sleeve, finishing up on her perpetually runny nose.

He couldn't pretend that she was a pretty child, or graceful or bright. But there was something about her. He didn't understand it but having her snuggled against him, planting puppy kisses on his hand, eased his heart. The grief and guilt over Samuel's death, the resentment against his father, even the deep hopelessness that was a part of his soul, all of those still existed. They simply weren't so important.

Next to him Zurialdi laughed.

"I can see it in your face," she said. "Our Anna-*uso* enchants all but the most unrepentant sinners. Our little dove could truly make the lion lay down with the lamb."

Anna had quieted now. She curled sideways on his lap, holding tightly to his hand. Her attention was on a pair of singers on the other side of the room. They didn't seem to be professionals; they had no instruments. The song was pretty, even though he couldn't understand the Basque words. Anna's head moved back and forth in time to the music.

"She likes it?" he asked Zurialdi.

"Oh yes," she answered. "She loves music. But she enjoys the poetry more. It should be good tonight. Three of the best *olerkari* are here."

Solomon was fairly sure the woman was joking. He had been to a Basque poetry contest before. It went on forever. Each poet was expected to improvise on the spot and they seemed to have no trouble finding the words. He suspected that even if he had understood the language, he would have found it tedious.

Jehan, Berengar, Guy, and Arnald were at a small square table across the room from him, deep in conversation. It looked more serious than the usual tavern banter. Solomon wished he could find out what they were plotting. With Jehan involved, it wouldn't be anything good. He wondered if they would use Samuel's death to insist on leaving the Jews behind. Arnald looked worried. Solomon hoped he wouldn't be convinced to abandon his friend Aaron.

Guy noticed Solomon watching them. He smirked and nudged Jehan. Berengar looked over and said something that made all but Arnald laugh.

"Would you take Anna in to her mother?" Zurialdi asked him. "She has to be washed before bed and I don't want to miss the poetry."

It was a natural favor to ask. A moment before, Solomon

would have been happy to oblige. But between him and the door
to Caudiza's room were the three Christian guards who seemed
to find his connection to this child very comical.

There was no way he could refuse.

"Anna, I'm taking you to Mama," he said.

"Mama." She nodded happily.

As they crossed the room, Anna twisted in his arms to keep
the singers in view. Solomon was hard put to keep from dropping
her.

Berengar stretched out his legs as they approached, blocking
the way.

"Solomon!" he said. "We were just wondering about your pet
monkey there. Is that what happens when a Christian woman
couples with a Jew? She'd have got a prettier child if she'd lain
with the sheep in the field."

"Ah, now I know why the lambs on your father's land are all
so ugly," Solomon answered. "Move your feet, Berengar. You don't
want to hurt the child."

"Looks like a monkey to me," Guy joined in. "Just the kind
of soulless creature you'd whelp. Heh, *ma douz*." He tried to tickle
Anna. "Are you a little jew monkey, just like your papa?"

"She's none of mine," Solomon said. "Some good Christian
pilgrim planted her on his way home to his devout wife, I've no
doubt. Perhaps your father?"

Guy was on his feet at once. "How dare you!"

"Give me my daughter!"

Anna was snatched from Solomon's arms. Caudiza spun
around to face Guy.

"Out," she said. "Now."

Guy's smirk fell. "*Na* Caudiza, I didn't know you were there.
I beg forgiveness. We didn't mean anything by it. Just trying to
prick Solomon's conceit a bit. You have a lovely child."

Berengar smothered a laugh. "Adorable," he agreed. "We know that her father was a much better man than this."

"Better than you," Caudiza said quietly. "I don't keep your kind under my roof. All four of you, go find a bed with your monk friends, or perhaps, *Senhor* Berengar, you would prefer the sheepfold?"

The room erupted with laughter. The men realized that they would get no support from the people of the town. Jehan stood.

"We are leaving at first light in any case," he said. "Arnald and I will find someplace else to sleep. You two"—he glared at Berengar and Guy—"you can pass the night guarding our animals and packs."

"You laughed, too," Berengar muttered.

Jehan raised his fist to strike, then reconsidered.

"A private joke and a public taunt are two different things," he said. "The latter can get a man killed, and his friends. Learn that before you bait someone and then rely on the swords of your companions to save you from his wrath."

No one said a word as the four men walked out of the inn. Jehan led with Berengar and Guy trailing after him like sullen schoolboys. Arnald went with them, looking both shamed and confused.

When the door shut behind them, the singing resumed. The empty table was immediately occupied.

Caudiza carried Anna into her chamber. Solomon went after her, hoping that he could fashion a decent apology before she threw him out, too. It would be tricky. First he had to figure out what part of his behavior had made her angry.

"I'm sorry," he said. That was usually a safe beginning.

Caudiza's stiff back didn't relax. She undressed Anna and poured warm water over her, washing the girl gently.

Solomon's realized he would have to make a blind leap.

"I wouldn't have let them hurt her," he started.

"Not a person in this town would let them live if they had," she answered, not turning around.

"I shouldn't have brought men like that to your inn," he tried again.

"There've been worse." She dried Anna off and put a clean tunic over her head. "Now the stockings, *maitagarri*."

He knew she was speaking to the child by the tenderness in her voice.

"Caudiza, you don't think I believe what they said, do you?"

Silence.

"I know you," he said. "I don't think you share your bed with just any one. You honor me. I'm sure Anna's father is a fine man."

"I'm not." She turned around and faced him with Anna in her arms. "Just what makes you so sure you had no part in the making of her? Are you too arrogant to think you could produce anything imperfect?"

"No!" he answered. "But I haven't been here for nearly six years and she can't be more than three."

"If that's all," Caudiza said. "I have good news for you. She's small for her age, that's all. Anna was five this winter past."

Solomon's fingers moved, counting months. If she was telling the truth, then there was no reason why he couldn't be Anna's father. He studied the child's face in the light of the candle on the table next to the washing bowl. The fear that had been slithering in and out since he had come face to face with Brother James now landed hard on his gut.

"She has my father's eyes," he whispered.

"So do you," Caudiza said. "It horrifies you, doesn't it? You're thinking that it was your sins that caused her to be like this. I can see it in your face. A bastard isn't so bad; most men have them. But one with a strange face and a simple mind, it makes you wonder what other monstrosities lurk inside you. You don't want your friends to wonder, too."

Solomon closed his eyes. He couldn't deny it. He had been thinking of how his friends would treat him if they knew Anna was his. And Yusef! His reaction would be the same as that of Berengar and Guy. This is what happened when a man flouted the Law God had established for his people.

Then he looked at Anna, who yawned and smiled at him.

"You needn't worry, Solomon," Caudiza said. "It's not as if I want you to claim her as your own. If anything, it would make her life worse. There are others who feel the same as your friends. I tried to tell you before. As things are now, she's well treated. God gave Anna to me as a treasure, a trust. The people here in town all know that. She was baptized but, unlike the rest of us, her soul is still without stain. Anna will never sin."

Caudiza smoothed her daughter's hair. Anna shook it back out of place with a laugh.

"She is the most miraculous thing in the world," Caudiza continued. "Have you ever known a person who is pure love? Who doesn't understand hatred or resentment? Who isn't afraid of tomorrow because she lives only in this moment? Does that sound like a punishment? Or is it just possible that she was given to me as a talisman, to give me joy and remind me of the heaven we all hope to attain?"

The words rolled over Solomon like the sermons forced on him in childhood. But that wasn't what convinced him. Anna was her own best advocate. The more he looked at her, the more beautiful she became.

Caudiza realized that he had stopped listening to her.

"Well?" she said.

He came closer.

"Do I really have eyes like that?" he asked.

"Identical." Caudiza chuckled. "And incredibly expressive. You don't think it was your wit that got you into my bed, do you?"

Solomon stretched out his arms.

"Anna." His voice was trembling. "Will you let your papa hold you?"

Brother James was more concerned about Samuel's death than he let anyone know. His abbot told him often that he saw connections where there were none and that he suspected everybody of something. This was not a proper attitude for a monk. The unspoken reproach was that it was a Jewish way of thinking that he needed to uproot and burn.

James had tried. He wanted to be a monk of pure and simple faith. But, after several years he had come to the conclusion that there were connections beneath the surface of things that the abbot couldn't see. About the same time he regretfully determined that almost everyone was guilty of something.

After much prayer and soul searching, it became clear to him that these conclusions had come from direct observation and not the Talmud.

So the idea that both Brother Victor and Samuel had been victims of coincidence didn't sit well in his mind. People said that a man out alone after dark was begging to be robbed and murdered. So when it happened no one thought to question further. But James saw nothing but questions. Why had both these men taken the risk and ventured into the night? Why had Victor taken part of the ransom money with him? What had he planned to do with it? And was it a coincidence that the first person to find him was Hubert? James couldn't believe that. He smelled a conspiracy to discredit him among his Christian brethren.

But then why should young Samuel also be killed? Samuel, by Yusef's account, was not supposed to have left the inn. Yet he was found nearly a mile from it, next to the monastery where James was staying. What had called him out? Had he seen something that incriminated one of the others? He might have been naive enough to confront his suspect. The young man had spent most of his life in study. One did not learn duplicity from the Responsa of the sages.

James knew there was a connection between the murders. He just had to find it and soon. If the deaths were related, the logical assumption would be that someone in their group was responsible for both of them.

Until he knew why, he wouldn't be able to find out who. He was determined to find the link before someone else was killed.

James's problem was that he could see any one of the group as a murderer. Even Brother Martin might be wilier than he appeared. He could have arranged to remove Victor in order to take his place on the journey and win accolades from the abbot. The night Samuel died Martin might have feigned illness and gone back out to the inn, instead.

At least that could be checked with the infirmarian. James resolved to do so at once.

He sighed. If he was to decipher this, he would have to talk with all his traveling companions. That meant being amiable to the guards, who were at best depraved barbarians. That was distasteful, but tolerable. The Jews would be worse. Yusef would cooperate to save that slattern servant of his and James knew how to discourage him from recalling their old familiarity. Aaron was a puzzle unto himself. James had never known a bridegroom so disinterested in discussing the upcoming wedding. Even if he dreaded it, one would expect him to say something. And where were the bride-gifts? Perhaps the marriage was a fabrication to hide Aaron's real purpose.

That in itself was a mystery worth pursuing, but carefully.

There was one more person who had information he needed.

James shrank from the thought of any contact with him. Solomon must never realize how much his hatred affected James. It horrified him that this was the child he had kissed good-bye so long ago.

The child he had named after his father was now a man capable of any crime, James believed. Solomon was only on the journey as Aaron's friend, he said. But what if instead he was the leader of a plot to keep the ransom from reaching the Saracens. That would explain a great deal, especially the presence of that Christian madwoman.

James felt a glow of satisfaction. If Babylonia had been brought to serve as a scapegoat for the crimes of the others, he had managed to thwart them, at least for the present.

James was forced to conclude that the only way he was going to solve this was to confront Solomon.

But in order to do that, James would have to face the rage his son had for him. And he would have to overcome his own loathing for a man who was the most glaring reminder of a life he wanted to forget.

James didn't know if he could endure that, even to find the truth.

Yusef had tied Babylonia's hands together and thrown the rope over a rafter to secure it. He brought her food and took away the waste bucket twice a day. At night he slept on a pallet across the door. Even though no one had said anything, he knew that it was only Brother James's command that was keeping her alive. If the monk changed his mind, Babylonia would be hanging from the town gibbet within moments.

That evening Aaron took him aside.

"Yusef," he said. "After all that's happened, don't you think it would be better to find a place nearby for Babylonia? We still have mountains to cross. The paths are treacherous enough without the fear that she'll have another fit and throw herself at one of us."

"She didn't kill Samuel and she won't attack you," Yusef answered. "If the rest of you refuse to let me go with you, we'll have to find another way."

"I won't abandon you among the Edomites," Aaron said. "But even if she didn't kill Samuel, that woman is a menace. Was there no place closer to Toulouse where you could leave her?"

"No." Yusef paused, aware that Babylonia was watching. "This is her only chance. On one of my journeys, I met a man who told me of a physician who had cured people far more insane than she. He's an Ishmaelite living near Tortosa."

"Tortosa? Yusef, there's an army on it's way to lay siege to Tortosa right now," Aaron exclaimed.

"Yes," Yusef snapped. "That's why I have to get her to him quickly, before the fighting makes it impossible."

Aaron rubbed his forehead wearily. Who was he to berate Yusef? Wasn't his own mission equally reckless?

"Very well," he told Yusef. "If there is a vote, I'll stand with you. And Solomon will stand with me."

The group that gathered at the monastery gate the next morning was too dispirited to object to Babylonia's presence. Jehan was furious with Guy and Berengar for depriving him of a warm bed the night before. Those two were sulking because they had been forced to endure Jehan's tongue lashing half the night. Arnald wasn't sure which side he was supposed to be on. He was thinking wistfully of his mother's porridge and the way she fussed over him.

Aaron arrived with Yusef and Babylonia, prepared to insist that they be allowed to continue the journey. He was vaguely disquieted to be ignored.

"Where's Solomon?" Arnald asked. "The bells for Lauds have rung already. The monks will be out soon."

"He was starting to load his gear when we left," Aaron said. "He should be right behind us."

"Probably went back for a last poke," Guy muttered.

The others let that pass.

Solomon appeared soon after. His expression was enough to stop even Berengar from a gibe.

"The sun is a handbreadth above the horizon," he growled. "Where are those damn monks?"

As if in reply, the bells of the chapel began ringing, signaling the end of the Office. Before the tolling had faded, the monastery gate creaked open and Brothers James and Martin came out.

Brother James gave a practice smile.

"Thank you all for being so prompt," he said. "The weather is with us, for a change, so we should have no trouble reaching Roncevalles by evening."

The rest of them gaped at him.

"Shall we get started?" James continued. "Brother Martin?"

"Certainly." Jehan recovered in time to take his place in the lead, Berengar next to him.

The others fell in line. Somewhere nearby a lark was singing in ecstasy. More than one person in the party felt the urge to wring its neck.

The day continued clear; the road smooth and well kept. The incline was gradual and the air filled with the perfume of lilacs. Somewhere ahead of them a group of pilgrims were singing hymns with remarkable skill.

Arnald was the first to recover his spirits. He began humming along with the hymn even after the voices died away. Solomon was riding just behind him and so became the object of Arnald's cheer.

"Can you really see the stone at Roncevalles where Roland and Olivier fought the Saracens?" he asked.

Solomon would have preferred to continue brooding but roused himself enough to answer.

"Yes," he said. "I've seen it many times. You can touch the rock that Roland split. It's not far from the hospice where we'll stay tonight."

Arnald's eyes shone. "I can't wait to tell Belide about it. She'll be so impressed. Oh!" His face fell. "I forgot. Do you think it was wrong to go on and leave Samuel behind like that, without even finding his killer?"

"It's one of the hazards of travel," Solomon explained gently. "We've all had to do it. That doesn't mean any of us will forget him. Aaron has his things, to give to his family. And they will perform the proper ceremonies of mourning."

Arnald seemed content with this answer. "My father never told me trade was so dangerous. But he just gets the salt from our marshes and sells it in the area. Oh, look! A hawk! Do you think there are hunters in the woods?"

He rose in the saddle, twisting to follow the flight of the bird. Solomon marveled at how easily his attention shifted.

"I don't see any jesses," Guy said from behind them. "It must be wild."

Each turn in the path brought something to excite Arnald. Solomon realized that he had lived only a few days journey from the mountains all his life and never known what they were like, much less what lay on the other side.

"Look! Down there!" Arnald leaned far over the edge of the path. "Tiny sheep! Or are they white rocks?"

Solomon glanced over. "Neither. Those are clouds."

Arnald laughed. "I'm not that naïve. What are they really?"

Guy decided to take over his education. "They're floating cows," he said. "The Basques use magic to make them glide above the earth so they can feed off the grasses on the precipices."

"Floating cows!" Arnald was impressed. "Amazing."

Solomon gave up. "Wait until you taste the cheese."

They stopped early in the afternoon to eat and water the horses at a mountain stream. Solomon contrived to sit with Aaron away from the others.

"When do we break off from the group?" he asked.

"At Pamplona," Aaron said. "I have directions to Fitero from there. It's about two days ride south, near Tudela."

"Are you sure you want Arnald to come with us? He's so eager to help that he might get us killed."

"He understands how important this is," Aaron said. "When the time comes, he'll do his part."

"If you say so." Solomon bit into the cheese and pickled turnip that Caudiza had given him that morning.

Aaron chewed on his lip in concentration. "What about you, Solomon? You've been distracted all day. I've never known you like this. Is it because of that woman, Caudiza? What did she do to you?"

Solomon shrugged. "I guess you could say that she tried to get me to convert."

Aaron snorted. "Most of the Edomite women you know try that."

"Yes." Solomon gazed down at the "floating cows" and the narrow valley beneath. "But for the first time in my life, I was tempted to do it."

He wrapped up the remainder of the cheese and put it in his pack.

Sixteen

The hospice at Roncevalles, Saturday morning. 26 Nissan 4809.
Sabbath. Eleventh day of the Omer. 8 kalends May (April 24)
1148, Feast of Saint Dismas, the patron saint of repentant
thieves.

ושכתב האי ישראל שפסק דמים לסום בשבת וקבלו והכניסו
לרשותו.

I have been asked about a Jew who made an agreement
regarding the price of a horse on the Sabbath and who
received the horse and brought it into his domain. [Is this
permitted?]

—*Responsa of Rabbenu Gershom (c. 960–1028)*

*D*on't tell me they're going to walk all day again," Guy said to Jehan. "Do they do this every Saturday?"

"The really devout ones do," Jehan said.

Guy shook his head. "Insane. It would be like going to Mass and taking communion every Sunday. Nobody has time for that. That's what monks are for. With all those laws to obey, how do Jews ever get any work done?"

James overheard this and would have given an impromptu sermon on the importance of lay attendance at Mass, but at the last minute he managed to restrain himself.

"Jews are wily; they find ways around the rules. Sometimes they hire Christians to do what the law forbids them," he told Guy instead.

"Really? Lazy bastards." Guy stretched before mounting his horse. "So the road is all downhill from here, right?"

Jehan gave him a humorless smile. "Right," he said. "Smooth roads, easy fords, and featherbeds every night from here to Valencia."

"Just watch out for the Navarrese," Berengar warned. "We'll be going through their land next. They'll steal your clothes and rape your horse."

"What?" Guy looked at him in alarm and then back at Jehan.

"Oh, yes, it's well known," Jehan told him. "The Navarrese

put a lock over the rumps of their animals at night, so no one else can get at them. Then they attack travelers passing through, steal their goods and violate the horses. You'll see."

"I hope not." Guy wondered if this story was like the one about the floating cows. Of course everyone knew that shepherds got lonely in the summer pastures, but horses! This was too much. Did they think he was as gullible as Arnald?

"Are we ready?" Brother Martin asked. "I might walk part of the road today myself. My poor mule is worn from climbing all that way yesterday with my weight on her back."

"That would not be wise," James told him. "It would appear that you were following their customs."

"But Placida, here"—Martin patted the mule's back—"she'd think it a blessing to have a day of rest."

"Then give it to her tomorrow," James said. "Do you want the others on the road to think you've been judaized?"

Brother Martin hung his head, abashed. "No, I would never want that. Of course I'll ride."

"Sorry, Placida," he whispered as he climbed on. "I'll see if I can find you some wild carrot for a treat tonight, instead."

Jehan rode over to Brother James. "Do you want me to make Arnald ride, as well?" he asked.

James pursed his lips. He did, but it would be better not to annoy the young man until he had been questioned about his friends.

"Arnald is not wearing the robes of a monk," he said. "Likely other pilgrims will assume he's one of the Jews. That might make him think twice about spending so much time with them."

"Very well," Jehan said. "Arnald can be the rear guard today. Then Aaron can't say we aren't keeping to our end of the bargain. The rest of us won't need to slow our pace for them. We might even make it to Pamplona by sundown."

Berengar and Guy approved the plan with enthusiasm.

"I know of a bathhouse in Pamplona," Berengar told them, "where you can get food, wine, and women without ever leaving the tub. My uncle told me about it."

"I wouldn't mind a bath," Guy agreed. "And a shave, and a pretty girl to wash my hair and back. Of course, I'd need some money in hand to get those things."

He looked at Brother James without much hope.

James cleared his throat. "It might be possible to advance you a sum for the purpose of cleanliness," he said.

Jehan turned around to make sure it was really Brother James who had said that. The monk looked at him and shrugged.

"Of course I would expect you to refrain from licentious be-havior," he added.

"Oh, most certainly!" Berengar grinned. "I intend to say a prayer of thanks as soon as my tired body enters the water and I know God won't be far from my thoughts throughout the eve-ning."

"I pray all the time," Guy assured him.

"I've noticed," Brother James said. *"Especially,"* he thought, *"Just before you turn over the dice cup."*

They set off down the mountain. Sometime later, Brother Martin looked back and noticed, with concern, that the men on foot had fallen so far behind that they were out of sight.

The other people at the hospice that morning gave Aaron's group some curious looks, but not because they were leading, rather than riding, the horses. It was Babylonia who attracted their at-tention

"What's she done?" a man asked Yusef as he put her onto his saddle and then tied her hands to the harness.

Yusef didn't answer. The man turned to Arnald.

"If she's a criminal, why does she get to ride?"

Arnald thought quickly. "She's not a criminal. She's taken a vow not to make rude gestures while on this journey and is afraid that, without having her hands bound, she might forget."

The man looked up at Babylonia, who wiggled her little finger at him.

"I see," he said, and backed away.

Solomon laughed. "Very good, Arnald. You're learning."

Arnald basked in the praise. He had been feeling unprepared to deal with the variety of people they were encountering and he was still unsure about the cows. But it did seem that most people preferred to create tales rather than give a stranger the truth.

"Aaron told me that we're only a couple of days from Fitero," he said to Solomon. "What are we going to do with Yusef? Aaron doesn't want him to come with us."

Solomon threw up his hands. "I have no idea how to get away without making it seem that we've forsaken him."

"That is a problem," Arnald agreed. "Maybe Aaron has a plan."

"He'd better," Solomon muttered.

As people passed them on the road, more than one stopped to stare at Babylonia. With her wild hair and rough stained clothing, she was out of place on horseback. Several greeted her, asking about her penitential pilgrimage. She ignored them all, leaving Arnald to invent various explanations.

"Do you mind his nonsense?" Solomon asked Yusef after listening to Arnald telling a family from Dijon that Babylonia was his aunt, afflicted by sudden fits of wanting to walk on her hands.

"No, it keeps people from making their own conclusions," he answered. "I didn't know the boy had such a good imagination. He was always just one of those drunken troublemakers in Toulouse."

"His father may have been right in sending him with us," Solomon said. "But you and I know Babylonia isn't on a pilgrimage. And I don't believe in some physician in Tortosa with miraculous cures. Where are you really taking her, Yusef, and why?"

Yusef set his jaw. "That is our business," he said.

"Very well." Solomon sighed. "Then where did she learn about the sanctification of the Name? I know that, when the Christian mobs came through Germany on their way to free the Holy Land, many Jews chose suicide instead of conversion. But most gentiles don't know that it's called *kiddush ha-Shem*. Babylonia does."

"She's worked in my house for several years." Yusef avoided looking at him. "I imagine she overheard it in a conversation."

"Of course," Solomon said. "And when she found poor Samuel's body, she immediately decided that was what he had done. Why would she leap to that conclusion?"

Yusef shrugged. "You know her mind is twisted. Her thoughts don't follow the usual paths."

"That's not good enough, Yusef," Solomon insisted. "Why would she treat him as a dead child? Did she lose a child? Did she commit infanticide?"

Yusef stopped in the middle of the road and looked Solomon straight in the eyes.

"No," he said. "Babylonia did nothing wrong. Nothing."

And that was all he could get from Yusef.

Solomon decided that it was time to tackle Aaron.

They were coming to the lower slopes of the mountains. The countryside was green with new shoots and the drone of bees could be heard from flowering bushes along the road. In Toulouse spring was settling in. Here in Navarre it already felt like summer. They shed their cloaks and rolled down their hose, savoring the touch of the sun on winter skin. Even Babylonia seemed affected by the gentle weather. She let her hood fall back, showing a less forbidding expression than Arnald had ever seen. He dared to ask if she needed a drink of water.

The question startled her. "Water. To drink. Yes, I am thirsty, thank you."

He poured a cup from the skin slung from his shoulder and handed it up to her. She took it between her bound hands and bent down to tip it toward her mouth.

She managed to get a few swallows before the cup slipped out of her fingers and to the ground.

Arnald ran after it in a crouch as it tumbled down the path.

"Arnald! Watch out!" Babylonia screamed.

He looked up to see an enormous horse bearing down on him. The rider was trying to pull up on the reins but he had been cantering on this open stretch, not paying attention and didn't see Arnald until the last moment.

"Roll, you idiot!" Solomon shouted, running toward him.

As the great sharp hooves descended, Arnald fell to the ground and rolled out of the way.

The cup was smashed to shards.

The next moment, Arnald felt the sting of a whip across his back.

"*Vilanet!*" the man shouted. "Why didn't you watch where you were going? You could have crippled my destrier!"

With another lash at Arnald he rode off.

"Arnald, are you hurt?" Aaron ran up to him.

Arnald rubbed his shoulder where he had landed on a rock. "No, I'm fine," he said. "Did anyone see his face?"

"I couldn't make out his features under the helm," Aaron said.

"Well, I won't forget his voice." Arnald was furious with himself for leaving his sword in its sheath hung around the neck of his horse. "And people ask me why I loathe noblemen."

Babylonia tried to reach down from the horse to pat him.

"Poor innocent," she murmured.

Solomon gave her a look of alarm. "Arnald is fine, Babylonia," he said. "And he's *not* an innocent."

"What are you talking about?" Arnald asked.

"Yusef knows." Solomon's voice carried a warning. "And he's going to tell us the whole story tonight if he wants to continue on with us tomorrow."

"But, Solomon!" Aaron protested.

"I'm not traveling with a woman who's liable to slit our throats or smash our skulls," Solomon declared. "No matter what that monk said, I'm not convinced that she's innocent in Samuel's death."

"You only say that because you can't stand the monk," Yusef responded. "Jacob based his opinion on the evidence, not his prejudices."

Arnald was beginning to think that the near accident had shaken his wits as well as his body.

"I don't understand anything you're saying," he whined. "Except that we'll never reach Pamplona today and I wanted to go to the bathhouse with the others."

He slapped at the seat of his *brais*, raising a layer of dust.

"It can't be helped," Solomon decided. "The sun is too low. We'll still be north of the town by the time it's full dark. You can have your bath tomorrow. I'll take you there, myself. For tonight we'll find a place to make camp and then Aaron is going to tell Yusef where we're really heading and Yusef will give us the complete story about Babylonia."

"And you, Solomon?" Yusef asked. "Will you also disclose your secrets?"

"Me? I have no secrets that have anything to do with the journey we're on now," Solomon said.

Yusef shook his head. "I think that you do. Before we rejoin the monks, you need to tell your friends about Brother James."

∞

The bathhouse in Pamplona was everything that Guy had dreamed of. The tubs were in private curtained chambers. Next to each was a table laden with cups, wine, fruit, and meat pies within easy reach. Every so often more hot water would be brought in by beautiful women barely covered in thin saffron-colored, sleeveless tunics.

"A Saracen captive told me once that this is their idea of heaven," Jehan commented as he leaned back to have one of the attendants pour soap over his hair.

Berengar frowned. "That's sacrilegious. I don't like it. Heaven is where you are free from the demands of the body, no longer tormented by temptation."

"I thought that was only because saints don't have bodies," Guy commented. "In heaven, I mean. They're all over the place down here."

Jehan ducked his head under the water to rinse. "Well, at the final judgement, we get our flesh back, they say and in perfect form. If so, I want a heaven where I can give it some fun."

"That reminds me," Berengar asked. "Did the old buzzard give you enough coin for a bit of *jeu d'amor?*"

"I'm astounded he released any coin at all," Guy said. "I thought he had it glued to his chest."

"I'll bet he keeps the ransom money stuffed up his ass," Berengar said. "He has the look of a man who's permanently constipated."

"Ahem," Jehan interrupted. "You are speaking of our patron. The man who unwittingly handed me three *rossol* instead of three *pogesi.* We have enough for a woman each, my lords. And another pitcher of wine."

"At last!" Guy sighed. "I never thought I'd see a *maille* from all those tithes I've paid over the years. About time the Church put my money to good use."

Vespers was ending. In the chapel James stood with the local monks feeling more at peace than he had in days. If only the journey could continue without the Jews. Those people brought discord wherever they went. Who would know it better than he? They couldn't even observe the Sabbath without disrupting the routine of those around them. By flaunting their heterodoxy, they were almost begging to be murdered.

Of course, it was sad to think that the young man, Samuel, would never have the chance for salvation. In that sense, it was worse than the death of Brother Victor, who was certainly in paradise now.

And what about the two bags of missing gold? Whoever had taken them had condemned valiant Christian knights. Even though Berengar's father had made up the loss, the theft itself was a deliberate effort to thwart the liberation of pious noblemen who had risked their lives for the Faith.

He wondered if Samuel had discovered who had taken the missing gold. Many an unwary man had died because he'd seen something he shouldn't. Or he might have been part of the plot and had second thoughts.

James would prefer the culprit to be one of the Jews but he wasn't going to exclude anyone, especially the men he had hired to guard the treasure. All of them had been in Toulouse the night Victor died. And none could be accounted for every minute on the night Samuel was killed.

Three *rossols* was a lot of money but James was confident that it would be well spent. A night of debauchery would make the guards much more pliant when he set about wringing information out of them.

Just after sunset, Aaron found a place not too close to the road that was safe for them to pitch their tents. Although they didn't need the campfire for warmth, they made one anyway. It was something comforting to sit by. Other travelers must have felt the same for there were bright splashes of light dotted across the plain. They made sure that the nearest one was well out of hearing range.

The men had washed, prayed, and eaten. Aaron brought out a skin of his sister's wine. Babylonia was curled up next to a tree, the rope extending from her feet and hands to a branch above.

"You first, Aaron," Yusef said when they had started on the wine. "Solomon says I can help you in your quest. Since when do you need me to get yourself married?"

"Are you sure he's safe to tell about this, Solomon?" Aaron asked.

Solomon poked at the fire with a long stick. "If he's kept Babylonia's story to himself all these years, it's likely you can trust him with yours."

"He's right about that, Aaron," Yusef said. "I keep my own counsel."

"Very well." Aaron took a deep breath. "I am going to fetch my bride, just as I said, but there's been a complication."

He told what had happened briefly, holding back all emotion, ending with, "She's being held at Fitero near the monastery. Solomon and Arnald are going to help me get her back."

Yusef was silent.

"Well?" Aaron asked. "When we return home, are you going to keep the secret of what happened to her or will you betray us?"

Yusef stared into the flames.

"I won't betray you, Aaron," he said finally. "You'll have enough without that fear. I don't know how much use I'll be in your rescue, but I'm willing to do what I can. It does seem to me that it was wrong of you not to tell the community at once so the ransom could be raised. She's had to endure her shame that much longer."

"We don't even know if she can be ransomed," Solomon spoke up quickly. He didn't want Aaron carrying any more guilt. "As far as we know, her owners think she's Saracen."

"Don't they ransom their women?" Yusef asked.

"I don't know," Solomon said. "If we can, we'll pay. If not, we'll kidnap her from them. Anything we must do to save Mayah. You don't know her, Yusef. She was . . . is, the gentlest, brightest child. The jewel of her father's heart. I'll cheerfully gut the men who have her now."

Arnald wasn't paying attention to the debate. His course was decided. He would do whatever Aaron asked. That was why he was the first to notice the odd noise. At first he thought it was from the creek or wind in the trees. Then he realized that someone nearby was weeping in a steady, low tone of perpetual despair.

"Babylonia?"

He started to get up, but Yusef stopped him.

"You can't comfort her," he said. "Let her be."

"Are you sure?" Arnald sat down reluctantly.

Yusef sighed. "Yes. Now that I've learnt what you plan, Aaron, I hate even more to reveal Babylonia's history. But before you attempt this deception, you should hear how one step outside the Law can destroy a whole community."

They all waited, but he didn't begin the story right away. First he went over to where Babylonia wept. He untied all the ropes, helped her to stand, and brought her back to the campfire.

"Look at her," he told the men. "Ten years ago she was a respected woman with servants of her own. She had a wealthy husband, children . . ."

"My innocents," Babylonia interrupted. "Beautiful babies."

Yusef put a hand on Babylonia's shoulder.

"I'm not sure I have the whole truth of the matter yet," he went on. "Her family lived in one of the smaller towns in Spain, not far from Tudela. The place was one that had recently been taken over by the Christians. One day Babylonia was walking in to the market when she was overtaken by a group of soldiers."

"And they abused her so vilely that she lost her senses?" Arnald said in horror, "Just as I always said. It's the chain mail. Makes them think they're gods."

"I think that was only part of what happened," Yusef said. "They carried her off with them. It was nearly a month later when a neighbor spotted her in the streets of Calaverra. It appeared that she had been raped, badly beaten, and thrown out when they were done with her. He brought her home."

Solomon thought of Edgar's sister, Margaret, who had been left for dead by a mob. She still had scars on her face and body. He wasn't sure if her spirit had ever healed.

"I'm sorry, Babylonia," he said to the trembling figure huddling next to Yusef. "It must have been an appalling torment. But, Yusef, I still don't understand how she came to your door."

"She came because mine was the only door open to her," Yusef said. "I haven't told the worst part yet. When she was brought back, her husband refused to let her return to him and his family and friends supported him."

"That's not right!" Arnald exclaimed. "How could that be?"

"Finding the answer took a long time and several trips to the area to learn," Yusef continued. "It seems that Babylonia's marriage was not a happy one. Her husband berated her often in public and some of the people I spoke to had seen him hit her. There were rumors that she hadn't been kidnapped, but had run away. She denied them, but he had the support of the community. He couldn't have taken her back in any case but the accusation that she was a willing adulteress meant that he owed her nothing. So she was thrown out of her home, without even a marriage portion. Her husband forbade her to come near her children. She had no family of her own in the town. There was nowhere for her to turn."

"That's terrible," Arnald said. "No wonder she went mad."

"There's a piece missing in your story," Solomon said. "What have you left out?"

"Just one thing." Yusef paused. "Babylonia's husband was able to do this because the Law said he should. He was a Cohen."

Aaron inhaled sharply, as if he'd been kicked in the gut.

"She's Jewish? But how? Why?"

"Solomon understands," Yusef said. "I can see it on his face."

"She went to the Christians, didn't she?" he guessed. "When her own people wouldn't have her. They baptized her, of course, and then what? Tried to find a man of the parish to marry her? Or did they send her to the nuns?"

"No nuns, nothing of nuns," Babylonia chanted.

Yusef stroked her arm softly. "I suspect that by then she was already unbalanced. From what I can find out, the local bishop made an example of her, bringing her up during sermons to tell everyone how she had been saved by Jesus."

"*Godesblod!*" Solomon exclaimed. It was one of Edgar's favorite invectives and seemed to fit at this time.

"Exactly. Eventually she became too erratic to show off, so she was dumped on some pilgrims heading for Rome. They mistreated her, as well. She tried to get help from the Jewish community. She even went to our courts in Narbonne but her husband's version of the story had already reached them. No one would help. Finally, she arrived in Toulouse. I found her at the Bazacle. She was about to throw herself under the millwheel."

Aaron could stand it no longer. He stood up and moved away from the fire. After a moment, he turned to face them.

"I understand what you're saying." He kicked up a clump of sweetgrass with the toe of his boot. "It's a horrible thing that happened to Babylonia, but I have no intention of turning Mayah out, no matter what has been done to her. I want to take care of her and protect her."

"So you'll live your whole life as a liar and lawbreaker?" Yusef asked.

"If it's with Mayah, yes!" Aaron said proudly.

Solomon got up on his knees to bank the fire. "I've tried to reason with him," he told Yusef. "It didn't work. There's nothing you can do unless you expose them to the community. It's something Aaron has to decide. He's the one who'll have to live with the consequences."

Babylonia had spent all her tears and was dozing with her head on Yusef's lap. He roused her and led her back to her pallet. He picked up the ropes.

"Yusef, do you have to keep her tied up?" Arnald said. "It seems cruel after all that's been done to her."

Yusef hesitated. Then Babylonia put out her hands, wrists together.

Solomon went to help him.

"It is cruel," he told Arnald. "But it would be worse if she went wandering alone in her state. Or if she decided that we were a threat to her and had to be stopped."

They made sure the knots were tight.

The next morning they awoke to a blend of raucous birdcalls and distant church bells.

"I don't think I was meant to sleep on hard earth," Arnald complained. "I never found a place to lie that didn't have rocks sticking into me."

The others were in no better mood. Aaron was sulking. The idea that he might treat Mayah as Babylonia's husband had, made him angry. Solomon and Yusef should know him better. And, as for the Law, well this one was stupid. So he was a Cohen. There was no more Temple, no priests. He didn't officiate at services; he was just a horse trader. What did it matter who he married?

Babylonia was also worn out. She slumped half-asleep behind Yusef as they rode.

To Solomon, the last miles to Pamplona felt like the walk to the gallows. Babylonia's story had rattled him. All his life he had held the firm conviction that his people were better than the Christians. He believed that the scholars and judges could find a way to soften the harshest of God's inexplicable commandments. If her husband didn't want her back, then Babylonia should have been given her marriage portion and been allowed to start again. Instead, she had been driven to the Christians. The fact that they had treated her no better was small consolation.

He finally thought he understood why Yusef had taken her in. 'Israel is still Israel' and Yusef believed in caring for his own. He might have told his friends about Babylonia and trusted them to show her some charity as well, but that was Yusef. He would consider it impious to disclose good deeds. Nor would he expect others to participate in them.

He wondered if Babylonia's children believed that she had run off and left them; that she didn't love them anymore. Or had they just been told that she was dead? It was easier to pretend that the missing parent no longer existed. That's what his family had done with him. If only he had never come face to face with the truth.

And now, in Pamplona, he knew he would have to face it again.

Brother Martin was sure that if he bowed one more time, his head was going to fall off. He had awakened with a pain across his eyes and an inability to breathe through his nose. He called it the spring sickness and there was never a year when he escaped it. The infirmarian at Moissac had made him try a dozen different compounds but nothing helped for more than a day or two.

Sometimes the symptoms lasted only a few hours, sometimes for days.

So far, he had always recovered. But he was miserable while the disease lasted. It was a weakness that he hated to admit to. If Brother James saw him in this condition, he might send Martin back. No one enjoyed traveling with a man who had a head full of mucus.

James had already noticed that Brother Martin's chanting was even less musical than usual. The man's eyes were red and he gasped through his mouth at the end of every phrase. It looked to James like a case of ague. That could pose a problem. He didn't want to be the only cleric in the party. Martin's bulk was a support in his dealings with the guards and others. Yet it would be unconscionable to drag a sick man on a journey like this.

It was a difficult decision. James brightened. And a perfect excuse for him to consult with the guards. Now he just needed to seek them out individually and then lead the conversation to what he really wanted to know.

First he had to see about Brother Martin.

Martin had hurried to the guest house as soon as released from Lauds. James found him sitting on his cot with a linen bag to his nose. He dropped it as soon as he saw his fellow monk.

"You haven't folded your pack yet," he said to James.

"We'll stay here today. If the Jews observe their Sabbath even while traveling," James said. "We should be no less mindful of ours. Also, we need supplies and the markets won't be open until after None. How are you feeling?"

"Me? Fine." Martin smiled. "Hale as a horse."

"Good," James answered. "I'll arrange for the supplies then."

As soon as he had gone, Martin picked up the bag from the cot, loosened the tie and tried again to smell the pungent mixture. Even though his eyes began to water, his nose refused to clear. The pain across his cheeks was so strong that he could barely see. He had to find a remedy for this or resign himself to being left behind.

The inn where the guards were staying wasn't far from the monastery. James strolled over, enjoying the mild air and the scent of flowers. As he'd hoped, all three were still abed when he arrived. He sat at the foot of the ladder and waited.

Berengar was the first to come stumbling down. When he saw Brother James, he missed the last rung and landed with a clatter.

"Good morning, My Lord Berengar," James said pleasantly. "Did you enjoy your bath last night?"

"Oh, yes," Berengar managed to croak through his hangover. "Just what I needed." He tried to focus his bloodshot eyes. "Is it time to leave? I didn't hear the bells."

"No, no." James offered him a hand. Berengar managed to stand up. "It's not yet Tierce. We may not leave until tomorrow. Our route will soon diverge from the pilgrim way. We'll pass through less populated areas. Brother Martin and I think we should get fresh provisions now."

Berengar tried to cover a deep yawn. "Good idea. Is there anything to drink around here?"

James raised a pitcher from the counter and sniffed the contents.

"Mint water," he said. "With a touch of wine. Shall I pour you a cup?"

Berengar sat down across from him and held out his cup. He drained it and held it out for more.

"Very dry throat this morning," he said. "Must be the weather."

James refilled the cup.

"Martin is in charge of replenishing our supplies," he said. "But he also seems to be affected by the weather. He gave me a list."

He fumbled with a knot in his sleeve and took out an irregular piece of parchment, scraped and written over many times. He squinted at the writing.

"Dried meat, raisins, oranges." He handed it to Berengar. "Can you take care of these?"

Berengar looked at the list, at Brother James, then back to the list. He studied it for a while.

"Perhaps you should ask Arnald to do this." He handed the parchment back to James. "He has more experience with buying and selling than I."

"Ah, yes, his father is a merchant of some sort, isn't that right?" James asked.

"Salt," Berengar said. "He's only with us because my father owed his father a favor. Not that he has no training at arms," he added hastily, remembering that he had been the one to recommend Arnald. "Those men train their sons far above their station."

James gave a thin smile. "He's raw, but willing, I've noticed. His only flaw seems to be in his choice of friends."

"You mean Aaron?" Berengar asked. "Well, that's natural, you know. They're really all the same, the burghers and Jews. And, in the Cité, people don't pay so much attention to the proper order. If a man can build a fortified house with a tower, he's seen as practically a nobleman, even if he doesn't know the name of his own grandfather."

Berengar's voice was sour with old resentment.

"But the other men you recommended, Guy and Jehan," James prodded. "They seem to be of a different sort."

"They're real knights!" Berengar said with enthusiasm. "Sons of noblemen who live on the skill of their arms. You wouldn't believe some of the deeds they've performed!"

"I understood that Jehan's recent deeds have been performed in expiation of a crime," James commented.

Berengar set his cup down with a clink.

"You've been talking to that Solomon, haven't you?" he challenged. "They knew each other in Paris, Jehan says. Solomon bears him old resentments and so spreads lies. Jehan killed a man in defense of a lady's honor. But Solomon and his Christian friends accused him of base murder. He was sent away in chains but his natural aristocracy of manner shone through and soon he was released to destroy the enemies of Christ."

Berengar poured another cup of water.

"Personally," he said. "I think he should start with Solomon."

Seventeen

Pamplona, Navarre, Spain. Sunday, 27 Nissan 4908, twelfth day of the Omer. 7 kalends May (April 25) 1148, Feast of Saint Mark, physician and author.

Et quidam miles Toleti, cum aliis militus Christianis captivus factus est in supradicto bello et ductus est in Codubam et miserunt eum in carcerem et aflixerunt eum fame et siti. Post multos autem dies dedit pro se aurum et argentum multi et mulos et equos et arma multa et redimens se venit in Toleto.

And a certain knight of Toledo, along with other Christian knights, was captured in the aforesaid war and led to Cordoba and they threw him in prison and afflicted him with hunger and thirst. After many days he gave them much gold and silver and also many mules, horses and weapons and, having been redeemed, he came home.

—Chronicle Aldefonsi, 1148

*J*ames controlled his expression to mild surprise.

"Really?" he asked. "Why kill Solomon, particularly?"

Berengar had finally quenched his thirst. Now he wanted something to eat. He knew his stomach would stop roiling if he gave it some bread.

"Even before Jehan told me about him, I was suspicious." As Berengar spoke, he wandered about the room, looking in jars and boxes for something edible.

"Just the thing," he said finally. He came back and sat down, holding a handful of small cakes made with anise and caraway. He stuffed them in his mouth one at a time as he continued telling James his opinions.

"He's too much at home with Christians," he said, spraying crumbs across the table. "But I know he sneers at us in private. He corrupts our women. Jehan says that the innkeeper the other night isn't his only conquest. I know he carries a knife and not just for cutting meat. That's forbidden both to Jews and merchants. What do they think we guards are hired for?"

"It's the custom for most travelers to arm themselves, even if they are guarded," James said. "Has he done anything else that worries you?"

Berengar shook his head. "But I've had my hands full seeing that no one robs you and Brother Martin," he said. "We all think it would be safer if you let one of us carry the ransom for you."

He was struck by a thought.

"I'll bet that's why Samuel died. He seemed a decent man. What if Solomon had decided to take advantage of the search for the madwoman to sneak into the monastery and steal your gold? Samuel could have tried to stop him and been killed for his trouble."

"That is an interesting theory," James said. "I'll certainly consider it. As for entrusting the money to you and your fellows, that's a burden laid on me and Brother Martin alone. It would be wrong to make you responsible for it."

Berengar wiped his face, brushing bits of cake and caraway to the floor. "Yes, I can see that," he admitted. "And, while I think Guy is a good warrior and an honorable man, he does have trouble resisting the rattle of the dice. Better not add the temptation of all that money."

He stood up and gave his clothes a shake.

"If Arnald doesn't show up soon, I'll take care of the supplies," he said. "But I'm sure he'd get you a better price."

He vanished back up the ladder. James could hear him rousing the other two. The monk left the inn. He didn't want to be late for the next Office. He also wanted to digest the information Berengar had given him.

First, it was obvious that Berengar didn't want to take the list because he couldn't read it. James wondered why he hadn't wanted to admit that. There was no shame attached. True, more of the nobility in the south took the time to have their children taught their letters and numbers, but only those intended for the Church had a serious education.

Second, Berengar very much admired Jehan. A murder or two in the man's past wasn't important. If anything, it made him more intriguing to the young lord. Berengar had been the one to arrange the hiring. At the time it hadn't seemed odd that a man of good family would take on the task. The knights of the Temple had set the example and the ransom of captives was one of the reasons they were founded. But now James wondered just what the young man's prospects were. His father had both wealth and power. How many other sons did he have? Was this sort of task all the future Berengar could expect?

It would be enlightening to know what the two older men thought of him.

Finally, James needed time to control the disquiet that rose in him at the thought of Solomon as the murderer. It was true that he had once accused Solomon of killing a monk, but that was before he found out that the man was his son. James tried to quell his feelings. He told himself that the relationship shouldn't matter. Berengar's suggestion deserved to be considered dispassionately. James could imagine Solomon capable of any crime. The man was a cauldron of resentment. A perfect example of all that was wrong with the Jews. The sight of him was like a constant reproach to Brother James.

All at once it hit him, like a sponge of cold water squeezed over his sleeping face. He covered his mouth to stop the cry of pain. "Good fruit comes from good seed." It wasn't residual affection for his son that made him hope Solomon wasn't a murderer. It was his own pride. He couldn't bear the thought of having produced something twisted and rotten. The abbot had often told him that the sin of arrogance would be his downfall. Without humility he could never find true *caritas*, and without charity, he would never have peace.

Brother James sighed. Believing in Christ had been so easy. Becoming a Christian seemed to be almost impossible.

Solomon barely noticed the town of Pamplona growing closer. He was lost in his own world of concerns. The mood of the rest of the group did nothing to dispel his worries. Aaron had still not provided them with a sensible plan for rescuing Mayah and from his brooding silence, Solomon suspected that he didn't have one. Babylonia hadn't spoken at all since the night before, nor had she stopped crying. Her tears welled and spilled over from some bottomless spring of silent grief. They seemed to drain her of anger and with it, the strength to live. She was slumped on her horse, held up only by the high front rim of the saddle.

And he still didn't know where Yusef was really taking her. The man had managed to tell them her story without revealing his plans at all.

Of course, Solomon admitted, he had avoided telling the younger men about his father.

This was not the kind of trust needed among friends on a mission.

"Solomon!" Arnald's voice called from behind. "Did you mean it when you said you would come to the baths with me?"

Solomon rubbed his eyes and tried to pinch back the headache that was forming just behind them. With a sigh, he reined in long enough for Arnald to catch up.

"You need to find the monks first," he told the young man. "If they have no objection, I'll take you tonight. Although it would make more sense if you stayed with the other guards."

Arnald scowled at the approaching town. "I don't feel at ease with them. Berengar looks down on me because my father sells salt. Guy's accent is so thick I can't understand most of his jokes and Jehan, well, to be honest, he frightens me."

"I see." Solomon nodded. "Guy does have a strong Norman flavor to his words but he's clear enough to me. Berengar is angry because he thinks your family is wealthier than his and resents it. But why does Jehan scare you? Has he done anything threatening?"

"No, not exactly," Arnald admitted. "It's more the way he

looks, the way he moves. I keep feeling that at any moment, he might spring at me."

"Then you have his measure," Solomon said. "He says he's changed and I have noticed a difference in his manner from the old days, but I'd no more turn my back on him than an enraged bear. Still, these men are supposed to be your comrades in arms."

"Only because my father is such a pig!" Arnald complained. "He forced me to do this. I only agreed so that I could get out of Toulouse with Aaron. I never meant to stay with them."

"I know that and we need to think of a good reason for you to go on with us to Fitero. There must be a Christian in the party. But first find out from the monks what they expect of you," Solomon told him. "Your father may be back in Toulouse, but Jehan is here and what he'll see is a man who took on a job and now wants to desert."

Solomon let him chew on that until they reached the town. It was time Arnald learned to consider consequences. His life so far seemed to be one rash act after another. It amazed Solomon that he was still among the living.

The Basques called Pamplona simply Iruñea, 'the city'. It was the first town of any size they had stayed in since leaving Toulouse. Solomon had been there many times before and always enjoyed it. There was a small Jewish community to stay with, if he wanted to. There were also a number of inns run for the benefit of French-speaking pilgrims. Once the kings of Navarre had retaken the town from the Saracens, they had encouraged settlers from the North. So even travelers from Paris had no problem finding someone who would fleece them in their own language.

For this stop Solomon agreed to stay with Aaron, Yusef and Babylonia in the house of a Jewish widow who welcomed the chance to give traders a properly prepared meal and a place to pray without being mocked. She was a good woman, still attractive in her fifties with a smile that offered a warm welcome to the right man, but Solomon had no interest. He was haunted by Caudiza and the child he had helped to create.

Except when his travels brought him to her door, Solomon had never really thought about Caudiza. She was refreshingly different from the women he usually passed time with. She wasn't interested in another husband and not eager to make public her relations with a Jew. When he appeared at the inn, her bed was usually open to him. She had made it clear from the start that she wanted nothing from him beyond the use of his body. He never thought that he might have given her something more. Anna had been a thunderclap that shattered his complacence.

His reaction to the child unsettled him acutely. He couldn't help but be drawn to her. Anna had a joyful radiance that shone on all. Caudiza had said that Anna was pure love. It was easy to believe that she was a special gift, something to be treasured, certainly. But it was also obvious that however long she lived, she would never reach the age of reason. If that meant she didn't know how to sin, did it also mean she would never know how to pray? What was she in the eyes of her Creator? And, Solomon cringed inwardly, there were also the eyes of men. There was no way he could convince himself that she was a pretty child. Her flat face and large protruding tongue could never be molded into conventional beauty.

Caudiza was adamant that he not acknowledge Anna as his daughter. Solomon was ashamed at his relief. What if Anna was God's message to him, a warning to stay away from gentile women? Would all his children be born defective? He wished he could see Anna as Caudiza did, a household saint who would smooth the path to heaven for those who loved her. Instead he only felt that he had done something terrible and the penalty for his sins had fallen on a fragile and innocent child.

The guilt ate into him, biting more deeply each day.

He found himself hoping that they would have to fight to free Mayah. Life was so much simpler when someone was trying to kill him.

"I'm completely well," Brother Martin assured Brother James. "I haven't sneezed in hours. The herbal bag worked again. My mother sent it to me. She had it blessed at the shrine of my name saint at Tours."

"I've heard that Saint Martin takes care of those who honor him," James said. "I shall say a prayer of thanksgiving for your recovery. It would have been a great sorrow to me to have to leave you behind."

"To me, as well," Martin said. "I have so wanted to be part of a true mission. I know how important our prayers are to the faithful, but lately it has seemed to me that I could serve Our Lord better in some other way."

"You cheerfully take on any task you are set and perform it as best you can," James told him. "That is the essence of true service."

The platitude seemed to comfort Martin.

"So we set out again in the morning?" he asked.

James nodded. "I have our guards out getting more provisions. The only one still missing is Arnald. The boy spends too much time with his friend, Aaron. I'm concerned that he isn't committed to our goal of ransoming the imprisoned knights."

"He's a boy on his first real journey," Martin said. "It's natural that he wants to stay close to the ones he knows best. The other guards haven't welcomed him as much as they might have, either."

"Really?" James was surprised at the accuracy of his fellow monk's observation. He hadn't noticed before. Perhaps he should talk with Arnald next. The boy might be a good source for the misdeeds of the others if he didn't feel any loyalty to them.

James adjusted his cowl to cover his head. "I need to make certain that the other three were able to get everything we need. If Arnald reports to the monastery, will you tell him to wait here for my return?"

"Of course." Martin grinned. "I'll stay here until you come back."

He liked having an assignment that required no knowledge of Latin or music.

Guy cursed and scratched at a flea that was eating its way across his leg.

"*Le malfé!* I don't think that laundress did more than dump my hose in a bucket with a hundred others and pour them out again," he grumbled. "There are more fleas in them now than before I gave them to her."

Jehan agreed. "You've got to watch out for that. I've a powder that you can put on your hose before you wear them. It kills the fleas but you need to rinse it out again right away or the stuff eats through the wool."

Berengar looked from one to the other of them in disgust.

"I thought you two were fighting men!" he said. "You sound like old women comparing cures for flatulence."

Guy and Jehan stared at Berengar and then both began laughing. Berengar smiled uncertainly.

"Were you doing that to tease me?" he asked.

"Not a bit," Jehan said. "You still think that a soldier's greatest enemy is the army ranged against him. What brings most men down is fleas, biting flies, ague-laden air, bad food, and worse water. You try to fend off an enemy while you're doubled over with cramps and diarrhea and you'll understand."

"Or try to ride when your hands are shaking with fever and you're coughing so hard that you can't keep your seat," Guy added. "Sometimes the only reason you survive is because the other poor bastard feels even worse."

"Then there's blazing sun," Jehan continued.

"Or cold rain and mud," Guy added.

Berengar was becoming angry. "You're only talking like that to make sport of me again. What about tournaments and great battles and winning the hearts of beautiful heiresses?"

"I haven't done a tournament in years," Jehan said. "It's good enough if you need to be noticed by some lord who'll take you on. There are knights who do them just for sport. But it's too easy to lose all you own, including your life."

"There are priests who won't give last rites to men who die tourneying," Guy added.

"But you've both been in battle," Berengar persisted. "Jehan, you were at the siege of Lisbon. Weren't you given part of the treasure of the city? And the women, soldiers can take anyone they want, right?"

Jehan snorted. "Oh yes, they let the men loose for a night or two, to loot what they like and rape anything they can catch. But then the lords put a stop to it so that they can divide the spoils among themselves. In Almeria, they say nothing changed except the names of the men who get the taxes. Yes, I got a few things from Lisbon. A couple of rings, a good cloak, a handful of coins. It was enough for me to stay drunk for a month or two. No more."

"But if it's so awful, why did you choose this life?" Berengar asked.

"Choose?" Guy said.

"Choose?" Jehan echoed. "Who gets to choose? The land my father controlled was barely enough for my oldest brother to survive on. I suppose I could have gone into the church but I've no head for Latin and no interest in being a parish priest. What else could I do?"

"My father chose," Guy said. "He picked Robert of Normandy over Henry of England. Henry defeated Robert, gave our land to one of his men and had my father hanged as a traitor. Left me with a cracked piss pot and two sisters to find husbands for."

"Did you?" Berengar asked.

"One died," Guy said shortly. "The other had a bastard by the count of Anjou. He married her to one of his castellans. So, unless your father has a mistress he wants disposed of, this is my only trade."

Berengar was silent. The three men were busy loading the mule packs with the dried fruit and meat, cheese, and bread they had bought.

"The knights who come to my father's hall never told me such things," he said at last. "Perhaps you have simply been unfortunate."

" 'Unfortunate'! Saint Sulpicia's unsucked tits! Dame Fortune had plenty of help in bringing me down. I've been cheated, tricked, slandered, and cursed!" Jehan exploded. "What makes you think it would be any better for you? At least I can defend myself."

"You think I can't?" Berengar reached for the knife at his belt.

"Avoi!" Guy nudged him.

Berengar quickly slid the knife back into its sheath. "Good afternoon, Brother James," he said. "As you can see, we managed to get the supplies without Arnald's help. Has he arrived yet?"

"I'm sure he'll be ready to leave with us in the morning," James answered.

He came over and examined the parcels.

"You did well," he said. "Although I think the figs weren't properly dried. There's mold on them. Where did you buy them? I may have a word with the vendor."

"They were on a table at the market," Guy said. "The price

was good. What's a little mold, anyway? The cheese is full of it."

James gave Guy a sharp look. He wondered how much of the money Guy had been given to buy food had been gambled away instead. It was too much to hope that the man had won.

"You'll find out," was all he said. "I'm also pleased to note that you are keeping your military skills honed. The road from here south is dangerous. Some of it is newly regained from the Saracens. Other parts are inhabited only by brigands and cut-throats."

"We won't be following the pilgrim road any longer?" Guy asked.

"No, we'll take the old trade route," James said. "In years past, when the Almoravids ruled in Andalusia, it was patrolled by both Christian and Moslem guards. But now outlaws roam freely, prey-ing on anyone too weak to resist them."

"Are we joining a merchant party then?" Berengar clearly expected a positive answer.

"There isn't one going that way," James answered.

He finished checking the provisions and stood, dusting his hands on the back of his robe. "We shall have to rely on Christ's mercy and your strong arms," he told them. "Until the morning, then."

He gave them a blessing and departed.

Without another word, Jehan and Guy went to work, check-ing for chinks in their mail shirts, testing the sharpness of their swords and making sure that their helmets were well padded. Ber-engar watched them for a moment.

"He isn't serious, is he?"

Jehan didn't look up.

"I need something thicker to keep the links of this coif from cutting into my head," he said. "Any ideas?"

"You could use the figs," Guy suggested. "Put them in the folds of the cloth."

"Not bad," Jehan said. "It will help the helmet stick to my head as well."

Berengar suddenly wished he hadn't laughed at his mother when she had begged him to stay home and marry Pelfort of Foix's daughter, who was nice enough but had a squint. He had planned to win himself a Castilian princess. Now that squint seemed positively alluring.

He set about sharpening his knife and sword.

"We may have to manage without Arnald," Solomon told Aaron. "If he backs out of his agreement with the monks, he'll be sent back to Toulouse in grain sacks."

"Where is he now?" Aaron asked.

"Gone to buy himself a decent hauberk," Solomon said. "Brother James told him he's to stay with the other knights and leave with them at dawn. Why did you ever bring him into this? He's going to get himself killed."

"I didn't make him come with us," Aaron answered. "I shared my problems with him; we've been friends for years. He offered to do anything he could. He was the one who went to Brother Victor for help."

"*Avoi*," Solomon said. "If you really need a Christian to buy Mayah back, I can play the part. I've done it before."

"I don't know." Aaron shook his head. "It would be a risk. What if someone recognizes you?"

"Who? I know no one in Fitero." Solomon wasn't interested in further discussion. "Now, I'm going to the kitchen to make sure that Babylonia hasn't had another fit and broken in to ruin our dinner. Then I told Arnald I would meet him at the tavern across from the cathedral to tell him what we've decided."

"Don't drink raw wine and start a fight, please," Aaron said.

Solomon was about to give a quip in answer but then realized that Aaron was serious.

"I promise," he said. "I shall have all my wits intact for the task before us."

Arnald was sitting uncomfortably on a bench outside the tavern when Solomon arrived. The cause of his discomfort was the parcel he was sitting on.

"I was afraid I'd forget it or someone would steal it," he explained. "Do you know how much a decent hauberk casts?"

"Yes," Solomon said. "I just hope you got one."

"Guy went with me," Arnald said. "He said this was the best we'd find already made. It's a little long, but that should be all right as long as I don't have to dismount. And the holes are not over vital areas."

"That sounds promising." Solomon sat opposite him and signaled for a pitcher of thin wine. "Well, it does look as though you'll have an adventure to keep that woman of yours enthralled with."

"If she hasn't found someone else by the time I get back," Arnald muttered.

"Then you'll impress someone else." Solomon spoke from experience.

"The one I really want isn't impressed by anything I do," Arnald grumbled. "And what about Aaron? He needs me."

The potboy brought the pitcher. Solomon sniffed it, grimaced and then poured a cup.

"Aaron will manage," he said. "Whether you meant to or not, you agreed to go to Valencia with the monks and, if they won't release you, you must go. There's nothing worse than an oath-breaker."

"I know." Arnald sighed. "Can I have some of that wine?"

They sat in silence as they emptied the pitcher. Solomon had no more advice to give and was about to return to the widow's home when Guy ran up to them.

"Have you seen Brother James?" he asked. "I have to find him."

"Why?" Solomon asked. "Are you in trouble?"

He looked around Guy, expecting a pack of irate dice players to be right behind him.

"I have important news," Guy answered. "Brother James needs to know at once."

"He may be back at the monastery," Arnald volunteered. "Do you want me to go with you? I was just about to add my new hauberk to my pack and put it with yours to be ready to load in the morning."

"Well, you may be spared that," Guy snorted. "While we were dawdling about, waiting for more funds and the end of Eastertide, it seems that a group of knights of the Temple rode in and rescued all the prisoners in Valencia."

"What?" Arnald was dumbfounded. "But . . . but . . . we were supposed to . . . what about the ransom?"

"That's the first thing I'm going to ask," Guy said. "Come on!"

They two men left in a hurry. Solomon stayed behind to consider this news.

It might not be true. Rumors about such things were always thick as flies on fresh meat. But if it were, how would Brother James take it? Would he rejoice that the men had been saved? Then he would be free to scurry back to the protection of his monastery walls. Or would he feel a fool; a man prepared for a dramatic martyrdom and then ignored. The image gave Solomon a moment of satisfaction.

Presumably this would free Arnald to go with them to Fitero. Certainly that would be a help to Aaron.

But first he had to find someone trustworthy who could give him the truth of the matter.

After that . . . Solomon stopped. His ticked off the list of tasks before him: avoid having to see his father again, rescue Mayah, send Yusef and his mad servant on their way. But then what?

He had been so involved with everyone else's problems that he had almost forgotten his own reason for being in the South. It was supposed to have been a simple trip to Almeria to get the spices his uncle had ordered from Cairo. He and Edgar had planned to see how the new regime in Andalusia felt about trade with Christians and Jews, maybe get some presents for the family. How had he been sucked into this maelstrom? And how was he to escape it?

Guy's information made Brother James also feel as if caught in a whirlwind.

"Who told you this nonsense?" he shouted at Guy. "Some vagabond with a gaming board and dice cup?"

"Well, yes . . . that is, no!" Guy looked to Jehan for help. "He said he had just come from Toledo. He learned the news from a man who had seen the knights on their way back."

"Are you sure it was the men imprisoned in Valencia?" James demanded. "They were French knights. Why would they be in Toledo?"

"I don't know!" Guy held up his hands to fend off more questions. "I'm only reporting what I heard."

Jehan decided it was time to rescue Guy.

"It would be easy to verify this," he said quietly. "Send someone to the nearest consistory of the Temple. There must be one nearby. I'll go myself. Certainly they'll know if their knights have rescued anyone."

"Excellent." James turned his attention to Jehan. Guy sagged in relief. "Brother Martin, ask the porter where we can find an official of the knights of the Temple of Solomon. We will make no decisions until we know the truth."

"But if the men have already been freed, that means we can go wherever we want, right?" Arnald asked. "I mean, you won't need me."

James fixed him with a glare. "Are you so eager to give up your duty? Do you think that these men were the only captives in Spain? We have been entrusted with funds to restore Christians taken by the Saracen. We will not return until that has been accomplished."

Arnald's heart fell. He had thought his own freedom was imminent. Now he imagined himself hunting through dark corners of Andalusian towns for enslaved Christians. It sounded like a never-ending quest. Arnald had no intention of giving the rest of his youth to good works. He had to think of a way out.

Solomon found Aaron pacing back and forth in the courtyard of the widow's house.

"We're so close," he said. "I can't stand waiting any longer. I should never have been so cautious. Once I knew where she was I should have stormed the place. Instead I made plans and sold horses to raise funds. Not exactly like the hero of a *cantos*."

"If you really listen to those tales, you'll note that heroes usually pay for their rashness," Solomon told him. "If you'd gone alone you'd have been killed and Mayah lost forever. A good story, a lousy reality. Now sit down; eat some dinner. If the weather holds fair we can be outside Fitero by tomorrow night. Then what do you intend? You said you had plans."

Aaron didn't slow his pacing. "I thought Arnald could pose as a rich young lord who had a fancy for exotic women. He could go to the brothel and make an offer for her. With the bag of gold that Victor gave to Belide, we have enough to meet any price they might name."

"It sounds simple enough," Solomon admitted. "I could do it, if necessary, as long as she has the sense to pretend she doesn't know me."

He didn't voice his fear that she might not know anyone. Mayah was strong, but could she survive such an ordeal and not lose her sanity? The example of Babylonia made him wonder.

Like Aaron he wouldn't consider that Mayah might be dead.

Aaron grunted something. He was now crisscrossing the small courtyard with an energy that was wearing a path in the soft earth. Solomon moved to one side and sat down on a stool next to a lemon tree. The flowers had fallen and tiny green fruit hid among the leaves. Solomon picked one and bit into it. He quickly spit it out. The bitterness stayed on his tongue.

Suddenly Aaron stopped and faced him.

"What if she's pregnant?" He forced the question out. "What do I do then?"

Solomon opened his mouth, then realized he had no answer. It did seem that this was something Aaron should have thought about sooner.

"I think that . . ." he began slowly, not sure what he would say next.

"Aaron! Aaron!" Arnald's voice became louder as he ran though the house and into the court.

Solomon thought a devout prayer of thanks. A moment later, he took it back.

"Aaron, you'll never guess!" Arnald grabbed his friend by the shoulders and shook him in delight. "The men were freed by the Temple knights, so we don't have to go to Valencia after all! But even better! Brother James wanted to find someone else to ransom so I told him about Mayah and he said he'd come with us and take care of everything. Isn't that wonderful?"

He stepped back, grinning with pride.

All the color drained from Aaron's face. He gave a long rattling breath. His eyes rolled up in his head as he fell over.

Arnald bent over him in alarm.

"Aaron?"

He looked at Solomon in confusion.

"Did I say something wrong?"

Eighteen

Pamplona, the widow's house, a moment later.

. . . Ego Sancho Lopez de Tarazona vendo vobis domno
Raimundo abbati de Nezeuis . . . unam pezam in Fitero que
est circa pezam de Petro Banz per iiii morabetinos marinos.

*I, Sancho Lopez of Tarazona sell to you, Lord Raimond, abbot
of Nezensis . . . one plot of land in Fitero, near that of Petro
Banz, for four gold morebetinos.*

—Charter of Fitero, 1147

*A*aron moaned and tried to open his eyes. Arnald bent over him, unsure of what to do.

Solomon knew what to do. He spun Arnald around, grabbed him by the upper arms, and shook him until his head snapped back and he gasped for air.

"You *mingre* idiot!" Solomon shouted. "What right did you have to tell anyone Aaron's business? Do you have any idea of what you've done?"

He didn't wait for Arnald to draw breath for an answer but threw him on the ground. A moment later, he was through the house and out into the roadway without stopping to change his soft shoes for boots. He was so angry that he didn't notice the sharp pebbles bruising his feet as he strode to the monastery. He gave the bell cord a vicious tug. The clanging was loud enough to call down the carved saints from the portico.

"I want to see Brother James," he announced when the irate porter opened the viewing slot. "He arrived the other day from Moissac."

"All the monks are at Vespers now." The porter tried to shut the slot, but Solomon's arm was in the way.

"Get him out," he said. "Now. Or I'll come in and get him."

"I'll call the guard!" the porter squealed, daunted more by Solomon's fury than the knife he had just drawn.

"This is an emergency!" Solomon hissed. "A man may die if James doesn't come at once."

"Oh, why didn't you say so?" The porter tried again to shut the slot. "I'll send word to him at once. No! You can't come in. Give me your name and I'll see that he's informed."

"Jehan of Blois," Solomon answered. "Remember, it's life and death! If Brother James gets there too late, it will be on your soul!"

He could hear a muffled conversation on the other side of the door and the sound of running steps. Then nothing.

Solomon leaned against the solid wooden door, breathing heavily. As the minutes passed, so did the white rage that had brought him there. He tried to remember what his purpose had been in deciding to confront James.

Then he heard the flap of someone running in sandals and the lifting of the bar across the door. He moved away just in time to avoid falling as it was flung open and Brother James faced him.

The monk showed no surprise.

"I doubted that Jehan could have been the one asking for me," he said. "I sent him and Berengar on an errand to the monastery of Leire not an hour ago. What do you want?"

"I want to know what Arnald told you," Solomon said. "But not out here in the street."

"I don't suppose you'll come to the monastery entry," James said, surprising Solomon with his acquiescence. "Across the road, then, in the olive grove. No one will hear us there."

Solomon followed him into the grove. The earth around each tree was bare from the feet of the gardeners and olive pickers but there was an open patch of grass scattered with wildflowers in bloom. James headed for this.

"Now," Solomon continued. "Arnald came to you this afternoon with a proposition. What was it?"

James raised his eyebrows. "I presume you know. He wanted

me to come with him to negotiate the release of a Jewish woman being held, he seems to think, by some Cistercian monks. Is there any truth to this?"

"It isn't your affair in any case," Solomon said. "But yes, it's true. All I want to know is what you intend to do with this information."

"I told Arnald that I would help in any way I could," James said mildly. "Didn't he report that?"

Solomon felt his jaw and fists clench. Did the man have no emotion left in him?

"And just what help did you plan?" He forced himself not to shout. "To warn your fellow monks? Perhaps have Aaron and the rest of us arrested and hanged?"

James gave a half smile, a mocking expression calculated to infuriate.

"You are probably not aware that the relations between Cluny and Citeaux are not always of the warmest," he said. "The monastery at Fitero is the first the Cistercians have built in Navarre. The abbot here in Pamplona is worried that they will draw donations from our houses."

Solomon snorted. "I see. So the news that the monks were supporting a brothel for their Muslim workers would be . . . ?"

"A shocking revelation," James finished. "It would be our duty to visit our erring brothers in order to persuade them of the immorality of their actions."

"And if you can't?" Solomon asked.

James shrugged. "It might still be possible to arrange for the purchase of one of the women."

Solomon started to relax.

"Of course," James added. "It would be better if she accepted baptism first."

"You bastard." Solomon took a step away from him. His right hand longed to draw his knife. "If you do anything that keeps

Mayah from returning to us, I swear I'll kill you."

James didn't move but looked Solomon up and down.

"I wasn't aware that you needed an excuse for that," he said. "I've been expecting a knife in my back since we left Toulouse."

Deliberately, he turned and slowly walked away.

Solomon felt angry tears at the edge of his eyes. He swallowed hard, trying to keep his voice steady.

"What makes you think," he told the retreating monk, "that you're worth the trouble of staining my knife?"

James's step faltered. He shook one foot to release a twig caught in his sandal. Then he walked on.

Solomon stood motionless until the monastery door opened and closed behind his father.

When Solomon returned to the house he found the uproar worse than when he had left. Arnald met him at the door.

"Aaron says he must leave at once, before the monks try to stop him," he said. "He won't even wait until morning. And he won't let me come with him. You have to talk to him."

"No, I don't." Solomon brushed past him. "Aaron's right. You've put us all in jeopardy, including Mayah. I'll get my things. We can be well on the road by sundown."

He entered the living hall where he found Aaron's pack ready to load. A moment later, Yusef came in.

"You went to see Jacob, didn't you?" he said. "You should have sent me instead."

"I didn't think of it," Solomon answered. "Don't worry; he's unharmed. Are you coming with us?"

Yusef shook his head. "I have to see to Babylonia. But, if you need help or more funds, you can reach us in Tudela."

"Tudela? Why didn't you tell us that in the first place?" Solomon asked. There was a large Jewish community there. It was a natural place to find someone who would care for the woman. "What's in Tudela that should be such a secret?"

"Babylonia's son." Yusef lowered his voice. "After his father died, Juce broke with that side of the family and moved to Tudela. My informants think it was because of the way they treated his mother."

"You think he'll take her in?" Solomon was skeptical of sentimental family reunions.

"I don't know," Yusef admitted. "But at the least he might be persuaded to support her. He's become very wealthy dealing in property in the countryside."

"Well, I hope he will," Solomon said. "She deserves comfort, if nothing else, after what she's endured. If he doesn't, I suppose you'll continue letting her stay with you."

"It's not so bad," Yusef answered. "Perhaps time will dull her anger at the women who didn't defend her against her husband and she'll stop trying to profane their kitchens."

"Perhaps." Solomon was just glad that Babylonia was someone else's problem. "Where's Aaron?"

"Getting the horses," Yusef answered. "Do you really think Jacob will try to stop him from rescuing his bride?"

Solomon gave a deep sigh. He hadn't realized until now how exhausted he was. "I don't know what the man is planning," he told Yusef. "I only want to get as far away as we can before he acts."

Aaron and Solomon were almost finished loading their horses when Arnald rode up.

"Please let me come with you!" he begged. "I know you're both angry with me but, really, I thought telling Brother James would help all of us. He said he would talk to the abbot of Fitero. Mayah could be freed without us having to pay."

"You *sauvagin!*" Solomon looked at him in exasperation. "Everything has a price. Your monkish friend told me that he would only free Mayah if she submitted to baptism!"

"Well, why not?" Arnald asked. "It doesn't hurt."

Aaron mounted his horse. "Let's go."

Arnald followed them through the town and out the southern gate. "I'm coming with you. You can't stop me," he declared. "Please! I won't do anything without asking your permission. I swear! You said you needed me."

His litany continued unceasingly until the sun hung low in the sky. Finally Aaron gave in.

"Very well, Arnald," he called. "I accept your apology. But if your heedlessness has endangered Mayah, then our friendship is at an end."

Arnald gave a grin of satisfaction. "I knew you'd relent," he said. "Don't worry. You can rely on me!"

As they continued on the path, Solomon reflected that the only thing he could rely on Arnald for was more trouble. If the young man did anything to keep them from saving Mayah, he would lose more than friendship.

It was well past Compline and nowhere near Lauds when Brother James was unceremoniously shaken awake by the monastery porter.

"There's two men down at the gate," he said. "They roused me from a good solid dream to say they had one of your guards tied up over a rafter at the Squealing Pig and unless you pay the money he owes them, they're going to flay it off him."

By the end of this announcement the rest of the room was also awake. Curious faces peeked out from under the blankets. Brother Martin sat up and yawned.

"That will be Guy," he said. "Would you like me to take care of it, Brother James?"

"That would be a generous act, Brother Martin," James answered. "Thank you." He took a couple of coins from the bag at his neck. "But if he has lost more than five deniers, then the rest will have to come from his hide."

Martin left with the porter and James tried to return to sleep. But he was far too angry. When Arnald had come to him with his plans for the ransom money, James had told him to stay with Guy until Jehan and Berengar returned from Leire. He should have known when Solomon showed up that the boy had ignored his orders once again. Very well. If Arnald insisted on casting his lot with the Jews, he would be treated like one. When they returned to Toulouse, his father and the local clergy would be informed that Arnald was outside the benefit of the sacraments until he atoned for his desertion.

It was near dawn when Martin stumbled back to his bed. James found him there, snoring like an enraged boar, upon his return from the Night Office. Gentle nudging had no effect and James hadn't the heart for more violent methods, so he left the solid monk in his bed and went down to the porter to get information.

There he found a chastened Guy kneeling on the stone floor, praying and scrubbing.

The knight bent even lower when he saw Brother James.

"*Ave Maria*," he greeted James. "*Plein de grace.*"

"Try saying ten *Aves* for each *maille* Brother Martin had to give your creditors," James responded. "And another hundred *Nostre Peres* for robbing the poor man of his sleep."

"Those bastards cheated me; I know they did," Guy muttered from the floor.

James squatted until his face was on a level with the penitent knight's.

"Guy, when will you learn that they *all* cheat you?" he said. "You were born to be gulled. Your only hope is to run the other way the moment someone brings out a *tric-trac* board or asks you to guess which walnut shell hides the white stone."

Guy sighed. "I know. Every time I start to win a little and decide to bet more, my luck deserts me. But I keep thinking that one day it will decide to stay."

"Even if it did, Guy," James said sadly. "It would never give you enough to make up for all you've lost. You have no horse; your mail is in disrepair. It's only a matter of time before you wager your sword and then you'll have nothing left to earn your bread. What will you do then, beg in the streets? Or become one of those who preys on others?"

Guy didn't answer. James could read his thoughts, though. Guy's mind wasn't on contrition, but revenge.

"For now," he continued. "I still need your sword. Use the penance Brother Martin set you to beg God's help. There is a demon in your heart that can only be expelled through divine grace. Take my hand. I'll pray with you."

Guy attempted to pull away, but for a small elderly man, James was surprisingly strong. The monk began the Lord's Prayer, in French, not Latin. The words in his own tongue drew Guy back to childhood. His mother had led him and his sisters in prayer every morning and evening. He had been sent away at the age of eight to be fostered, but the sound of a *nostre pere* always reminded him of his mother's love. By the end, he was sobbing into the scrubbing brush.

Brother James felt a thrill of satisfaction at the success of his homily. He wished his abbot could see him at this moment.

"There, there," he said. "Once you've placed your fate in the hands of the Lord, you're certain to succeed. Now, if I can just use your shoulder to stand. See, your strength is needed. Thank you!"

He left Guy to finish the floor and his prayers.

∞

"How far is it now?" Arnald asked.

They had been riding since first light. The area was rocky and dry, with few trees. Solomon hoped they had brought enough water. Even if they found a pool or well, it might not be drinkable.

"As I recall, Fitero is in the foothills of those mountains." He pointed toward the south but it was unnecessary. The mountains filled the horizen.

"Do you remember the way?" Aaron asked. "It doesn't look like we'll come across any villagers to ask."

"I think so," Solomon said. "I can get us close. If the monks are in the middle of building their monastery there should be a road wide enough to bring in the stones from the quarry. We'll find it."

"Today?" Aaron asked plaintively.

Solomon bit his lip. "With luck and if we can find safe water for the horses. A stream would be good. Don't trust any still water. There's something in it that burns the insides of men and animals."

Conversation ebbed after that. Arnald kept a close watch on both sides of the track, half expecting bandits to leap out from behind the rocks brandishing deadly flasks.

Solomon concentrated on finding the way. He believed that he had conquered his fears of what they would find at the end of this quest. Then the reins slipped from his fingers. He looked down and realized that the leather was soaked with sweat. He wiped his damp palms on the front of his tunic, hoping the others hadn't noticed.

Yusef was preparing for the trip to Tudela. It had been easy to find a party of Jews heading that way. Pamplona was on the trade route only two days north of the town. His heart already felt lighter. No more having to observe the Law unobtrusively or under the mocking eyes of Christians. If it weren't for Babylonia, he would have looked forward to the rest of the journey.

But what was he to do with her?

She had finally ceased her weeping but was still lethargic, eating little and moving only when told to. Her skin was sallow and her hair worse than ever, greasy and badly braided. He couldn't present her to her son in such a state. Could he make her understand that she had to bathe and wash her hair before they left? And if so, could he trust her in the bath house alone?

She was sitting by a window that looked out on a stone wall. A ragged bit of ivy clung uncertainly along the top. Other than that, there was nothing to see.

"Babylonia?" Yusef said softly. "Can you understand me? Do you know who I am?"

"*Senhor* Yusef," she said without looking up.

"Yes," he said. "I know this journey has been hard for you. I'm sorry we had to keep you bound. It was to keep you safe, mostly."

No response. Yusef forged on.

"We need to leave here tomorrow. This will be your last opportunity to wash for a few days. Pamplona has a fine bath house for women, or so I'm told. I can pay for a tub for you and an attendant to do your hair and even your nails, if you like. Won't that be nice?"

Still no answer. Yusef bent down to see her face. To his dismay, he found that Babylonia was crying again.

"What is it?" he asked. "Did I do something to cause this pain?"

Babylonia turned her face to his.

"Aaron," she said.

Yusef was taken aback. "Aaron? What did he do to you?"

She sighed deeply. "Aaron wants to find his bride. He doesn't care that the gentiles have used her. Yusef, why did no one want to find me?"

Jehan and Berengar were surprised to find Guy at the monastery guest house instead of the inn.

"What happened?" Berengar asked. "Did you decide to throw lots with the monks for your soul?"

Jehan gave him a kick in the ankle.

"What?" Berengar said. "I was just making a jest."

Jehan glared at him. "This isn't a tavern. Show some respect."

Berengar scratched his head. "If you say so."

"Did you find out about the prisoners?" Guy asked.

"Yes." Jehan put up a hand to keep Berengar from relating every detail of the excursion. "We should report to Brother James. Has he been sent for?"

"He should be here soon," Guy said. "We can wait here."

The two men started to cross the room but Guy stopped them.

"Wipe off your boots," he said. "This floor's just been cleaned. No point in tracking dirt through it."

They had just sat down and were reaching for the pitcher when the monks entered. Jehan stood to give his report.

"I spoke with the prior at Leire," he stated. "He informed me that the French knights were indeed ransomed by the knights of the Temple. I asked if there were any more captives of the Saracens needing rescue. He informed me that with the help of God and the Emperor Alfonso, the armies of Christ have had much success recently. He had some suggestions for the charitable distribution of any extra funds we might have, however."

"I'm sure he did," James said. "They're building a new church, aren't they?"

"Yes," Jehan answered. "How did you know?"

"If there is an extra *maille* in the treasury, an abbot will decide to build something," James said. "I would rather not support the greater glory of Leire."

"So, what are we going to do?" Berengar asked. "Will we still get paid if we don't go all the way to Valencia?"

Brother James put his hands together and bent his head a moment, as if in prayer. The afternoon sunlight shone on the crown of his tonsure. There was still some black among the gray hair that curled around it. The monk pressed his hand against his lips.

Jehan suspected that the pause was more for effect than piety. He wished the man would get on with it. He had just spent the better part of two days in the saddle and wanted a hot bath and a soft pillow.

Brother James was in no hurry to reveal his intentions. He considered the three knights gravely.

"When you were at Leire," he began. "Did they happen to mention their recent part in redeeming some captives?"

"Oh, yes," Berengar said. "They were very proud of themselves. The captives were an important nobleman and a royal counselor. The families of the men were very generous in their thanks."

"That's what I understand," James said. "These nobles were prisoners of the Saracens, is that correct?"

"I guess so," Berengar said. "I didn't ask."

"I did," Jehan interrupted. "They had been captured by the king of Navarre, not infidels. Where are you taking us with this, Brother James?"

James smiled.

"Would the three of you be interested in rescuing a noble-woman, even if she had been captured by Christians?" he asked.

"Is she an heiress?" Berengar asked.

"Possibly, although her father's property may all have been lost in the wars."

"Does she have any family who will pay to have her back?" Jehan wanted to know.

"I think the price might be as much as your trip to Valencia would have been," James said.

"Well, then, of course," Jehan said. "She must be well guarded for that amount. How many walls do we have to breach?"

"I don't believe that a direct assault will be called for," James told them. "More a certain amount of stealth. You see, there are others who wish to rescue this woman. But they only want possession of her body. I want us to redeem her soul. She must be saved in the name of the Lord."

"I will go gladly!" Berengar exclaimed.

"And I." Guy stepped forward, ready to take the oath, as the pilgrims had before they left for the Holy Land.

Only Jehan was silent. He had seen such ardor multiplied a thousandfold at Vezeley, when Bernard of Clairvaux had preached. Since then Jehan had spent nearly three years in the army of Christ. He had seen hundreds die; many at the other end of his lance. He had seen other things, too. Acts of great bravery and goodness. Deeds of unspeakable depravity. He had come to believe that the soul was a much more slippery thing than he had been taught. And the price for its redemption much higher than most men were willing to pay.

But when Brother James asked, he agreed to go.

It hadn't been that difficult to find the road to Fitero after all. They had just followed the dust until they reached the town.

"This looks like the camp of a great army!" Arnald exclaimed. "What are all these people doing here?"

Solomon laughed. "Working, of course. You don't think even

the Cistercians dig their own foundations and mix mortar, do you?"

"All of this is for the monastery they're building here?"

"Most of it," Solomon said. "When the town belonged to the Saracens, I think it was a popular place to come for the mineral hot springs. They still attract people in search of a cure."

"For what?" Arnald looked about nervously for lepers.

"To tell the truth, I don't know," Solomon said. "Do you, Aaron?"

"What?" Aaron had been looking around, too. "Where do you think she is?"

The town had a rawness to it. Most of the huts were new, the reed thatch of the roofs still green. The walls were made of clay bricks, some whitewashed, others still the color of the earth. There were no tavern signs that they could see, but Solomon followed his nose to a place with a curtain for a door and the sound of a plaintive melody being tortured on a vieille. Cautiously, he lifted the curtain and stuck his head inside.

There was a brief conversation and then Solomon's head emerged.

"This is what we want," he told the other two. "Now, remember, Arnald, you are to say nothing. Nothing! And Aaron, you don't have to drink their beer but you do have to order some and pay for it. Is that understood?"

Both men nodded. Solomon pushed the curtain aside and they entered.

A short stocky man with a grizzled brown beard was wiping something white and sticky from the counter. Aaron looked at it in horrified fascination.

"I don't have to eat anything here, either, do I?" he whispered to Solomon.

The man gave them a bright smile.

"Good afternoon, *Senhors*," he said. "Come in! I have the

best beer in all Fitero! Or would you prefer wine? We also have a fish pie. Fresh caught this morning!"

"Beer and the pie," Solomon ordered for them all.

"When do we ask about Mayah?" Aaron asked, when the man had left to fetch the pie.

"I've been thinking about that," Solomon told him. "You're sure that the women taken in Almeria were sold to the monks here?"

"The message was that she had been sold to Catalonians along with many other women. All were supposed to have been Moslem. I went to Catalonia first and managed to find someone who had been at the auction. She and two others were sold to an agent of the monks. He said they were for the Saracen slaves who were building the new monastery here. That's as definite as anything."

"Good," Solomon said. "I just wanted to be sure. Ah, here's the pie!"

The innkeeper brought it in on a wooden board and placed it before them.

"There, just like in the great hall of the king," he said proudly. "My cook even made a braided fish to top the crust."

"It smells wonderful," Solomon told him. "Arnald, this is your feast day, would you like to break the crust?"

"What?" Arnald started. "Oh, yes. Thank you."

He dug into the pie, sniffing in delight as a spicy steam rose from it.

"My friend and I are giving our young lord a treat for the first feast day of his majority," Solomon confided to their host.

"You can't start it better than with one of my pies," the man answered.

"I can tell," Solomon went on. "It should give him the strength he'll need for the rest of the evening, if we can find the right place to celebrate."

The man grinned. "In Fitero you can find most anything. You'd be surprised. I know where you can meet a woman with hair like spun sunlight and skin so white you can see the blood running blue through her veins. Tall, too, with long, long legs. You won't believe the ways she can twist them."

"Interesting," Solomon said. "But we're from the North. We can get women like that anytime." *I only wish*, he thought. "What my friend here needs is a supple Saracen girl."

"Oh, that will be no problem," the man said. "I can give you a score of names."

"Not your usual *jael*," Solomon said. "We don't want to bring him home diseased. We have heard that there is a house set up just for the needs of the Saracen workers."

"What, the Saracen Hole? You don't want that place!" The man laughed. "Disease would be the least of your worries with that bunch!"

Aaron stiffened and drew breath to speak. Quickly Solomon knocked against his arm so that the beer spilled over his tunic.

"Sorry," he said, turning back to the tavern keeper. "Now, what were you saying?"

The man seemed eager to gossip. He sat down on the bench across from them.

"First of all, I hear they aren't the most willing whores, or very talented," he told them. "The monks picked them up cheap somewhere, because they didn't want complaints from the rest of the workers that the Saracens were polluting Christian women."

"But that doesn't mean we can't pay them a visit, does it?" Solomon asked. "It sounds like a real adventure for my friend, here."

"Not the kind for a feast day." The innkeeper got up. "We've got any number of good brothels in town. Look down by the baths. I go myself now and then. Nothing like hot water and a supple woman to get the knots out of your muscles."

"Thank you," Solomon told him. "We'll try that. But just out of curiosity, is the house we spoke of near there?"

"Nah, it's out of town, up by where the monastery church is going up," the man said. "And that's another problem with it. There's no place to get a decent drink. Saracens have some odd rule about anything fermented, they say. Although most of the ones I know don't seem to pay it much mind."

Solomon and Arnald shared the pie before they left.

"It really is good," Arnald told Aaron. "There's nothing in it you shouldn't have, you know."

"I'm not hungry," Aaron said. "Fill your stomachs quickly and let's go."

"Aaron," Solomon said carefully. "Don't you think it would be better if Arnald and I went out there first? We can see what the situation is, make certain Mayah is really there. Then we can find out who to approach about getting her out."

"You must be out of your mind, Solomon," Aaron answered. "I won't leave Mayah there another moment. She's coming back with us tonight."

"Of course she is," Arnald agreed. "What's wrong with you, Solomon? How could he come all this way and then wait here in town like a coward?"

Solomon closed his eyes. "Thank you, Arnald. Very well, just remember that I warned you."

They found plenty of people willing to direct them to the construction site. Half the inhabitants of the town were part of the building, from stonecutters to smiths, to copper molders and pipe makers.

The church was only partly built, the walls not much above man height. A wide paved road had been created for the last mile to make it easier to bring in the huge stones and the enormous logs to support the roof. Around the area were huts for the work-ers and piles of materials; huge vats for mixing mortar, saw horses, coils of rope and lengths of scaffolding.

One of the huts was set apart from the others. It was win-dowless and fenced. Just inside the barrier a woman wrapped in a long, hooded cloak was throwing grain for a few scrawny chick-ens.

"Let's ask her," Arnald said. "She may be the brothel keeper."

"Arnald, just in case she isn't, let us do the talking," Solomon told him.

As they approached, they noticed a chain reaching from a band on the woman's ankle to an iron ring in the wall.

"I think we've found the place," Aaron said tightly. "*Salaam,* good woman."

The woman started at his voice. She straightened up and moved as far as she could from the men.

Aaron smiled at her, speaking in passable Arabic. "We're looking for someone. She may be living here with you. She's from Córdoba. Her name is Mayah."

The woman looked at him strangely. Then she shook her head.

Aaron came closer to her. She shrank from him, turning her face away.

"Please," he said. "I won't hurt you. I just want to know what happened to Mayah. Do you understand me? Can you tell me where she is?"

The woman looked back at him. Her eyes were rimmed with dark kohl, smudged from the previous night and her lips and cheeks were bright with rouge. But from behind Aaron, Solomon could see that her face was gaunt. There was a bruise on her jaw that powder couldn't hide.

"I'm sorry, *Senhor,*" she said in clear Occitan. "The woman you are looking for is dead."

At that moment the door of the hut opened and a tall man reached for the chain. He yanked it so hard that the woman almost fell. Quickly, she hobbled back inside.

Aaron turned to Solomon, his face blank with shock.

"Dead?" he said. "No! Dear Lord, No! Oh, my poor Mayah! How could this be?"

Solomon didn't answer. He looked from Aaron to the hut and back again. He didn't know what to say.

Despite his obvious grief, Solomon thought Aaron's voice also held a tinge of relief. He wouldn't have to marry a whore after all.

It didn't seem the time to tell his friend that the woman he had just been talking to was his beloved Mayah.

Nineteen

Near the town of Fitero. Tuesday, 29 Nissan 4908, fourteenth day of the Omer. 5 kalends May (April 27) 1148.

Bona dona, vostres suy on que'm sia
Et on que m'en ades vos duy aclis
Et s'avia trastot lo mon conquid
En tot volgra aguessetz senhoria

Good lady, where ever I may be, I am yours
Where ever I may go, I give you my devotion.
And if I should conquer the whole world
I would want you to be the ruler of it all.

—Alegret,
Provence of jongleur

Solomon followed slowly behind Aaron and Arnald as they rode away from the monastery. He hardly noticed the path. All he could see was Mayah's face, painted like a crude image at a peasant shrine. But beneath the paint was still the beautiful, brilliant girl he had watched grow up. How could Aaron not have recognized her? Adversity hadn't changed her appearance that much. What it had done to her inside was something he wasn't ready to find out.

Ahead of him, Aaron was sobbing. Arnald was trying to ride close enough to catch him should his grief overwhelm his balance.

Despite his total consternation at the situation, there were two things Solomon was sure of. The first was that if Mayah had wanted Aaron to know who she was, she would have told him. The second was that somehow he had to get her out of that nightmare.

Upon their return to the inn, Aaron threw himself onto his straw pallet and buried his face in his blanket. The wool did little to muffle his moans of anguish.

Arnald sat in the room below with a pitcher and cup. Now and then he would pause in his drinking to wipe his eyes.

"Now we'll have to go home and tell everyone that there will be no wedding." He sighed. "Poor Aaron! Solomon, why aren't you weeping with him? I thought Mayah and her father were friends of yours, too."

"I'll weep when I know there's reason to," Solomon answered.

He climbed the ladder to the sleeping loft.

"Aaron." He pulled the blanket off his face. "Aaron, you're too quick to accept such terrible news. How do you know the woman was telling you the truth?"

"What?" Aaron brushed dust from the rafters off his face. "What do you mean? Why would she lie?"

"To get rid of you," Solomon said. "To hurt you. Perhaps to protect Mayah. You might have come to harm her."

"How could anything harm her worse than that place?" Aaron asked.

"Or she might have just been malicious." Solomon took his arm and tried to make him stand. "Mayah might not ever have been there at all. Or it might have been someone else with the same name. It's a common one, after all. Don't you owe it to her to be certain?"

Aaron's expression was a mixture of hope and confusion.

"But how?"

"We go back," Solomon told him. "We find out who else was inside that building. If she really has died, then we find her grave."

Aaron seemed unable to comprehend this sudden call to action.

"Solomon, it's good of you to help me like this, but . . ."

"It's not you I'm thinking of, Aaron," Solomon said. "It's Mayah. If there's even a possibility that she's still alive and in captivity, I must find a way to free her. I won't return home until I know."

Aaron gave a shudder. "Of course. You're right. It's just that the place . . . it was so much worse than I had expected."

Solomon put a hand on his shoulder.

"I know," he said. "It would be easier to believe that death has freed her, that she is safe in the Garden of Paradise. But that may not be true."

It took Aaron a moment to compose himself enough to stand. His head grazed the thick thatch and bits of it stuck in his hair. It gave him a comical look that contrasted starkly with his red eyes and tragic face.

"Tell me what to do, Solomon," he said.

"First, go down and eat," Solomon told him. "I know it's *treyf* but you'll need your strength. I'll go back to investigate the area better. There's no moon tonight. Maybe the darkness will allow us to get close enough to the hut to find out who's inside."

He guided his friend down the ladder and left Arnald with strict instructions to stay with him and make sure he ate whatever the innkeeper had on hand.

"Even pork?" Arnald asked.

"No," Aaron said. "Even for Mayah, I won't disobey that commandment."

"Then bread, cheese, soup, pickled turnips." Solomon didn't care. "Just be sure that you can follow my instructions without fainting from hunger or alerting the guards with a rumbling belly."

It was only after leaving the inn that he realized he had forgotten to feed his own stomach. Just as well. With the turmoil he felt at the moment, he doubted anything would stay down.

He took their horses to a stable built against a rocky hillside. The ostler seemed to know his business and they were soon rubbed down, watered and contentedly munching a barley mash. Solomon felt a pang of jealousy.

He had decided that it would be better to explore the area on foot. Before he made any attempt to liberate Mayah, he needed to know what she wanted him to do. The problem was to get to her. A windowless building, cleared land all around it and a eunuch watching the one door; that shouldn't be hard to breach. The heroes of all those *mesfaé* stories never had any problem.

As he left the stable another party was entering. Solomon's heart fell when he saw who it was. He tried to dodge behind a pile of hay bales but was too late.

Jehan's face lit. "I owe you three *pogesi*, Guy!" he said. "Brother James was right. *Harou!* Solomon, I hear none of your own women will have you so you're out hunting Saracen whores. Couldn't you find any closer to home?"

Solomon gave a sigh. This was all he needed. He came out from behind the bales.

"Did you follow me here to get my leavings?" he countered. "No, wait. I haven't time to tilt words with you. I suppose that damned monk is somewhere around."

"He's gone up to this monastery to find out who's in charge," Berengar volunteered. "He took Brother Martin but told us to stay here."

Jehan cuffed his ear.

"He doesn't need to know that," he told Berengar.

"Yes, I do," Solomon answered. "Thank you, Berengar."

Jehan stepped forward. "Look, I don't know why you loathe Brother James so particularly, but I'm not about to let you lie in wait for him on the road. You're not going anywhere until they return."

"Jehan!" Solomon tried to push past them although he knew he had no chance against three. "At the moment, I need to speak with the man, that's all. If you want, you can come with me; but it can't wait."

The old Jehan would have smashed his face in. Solomon prepared to dodge the first blow. Instead the knight gave him a curt nod.

"Berengar, Guy, you two see to the horses," he ordered. "I'll go with you, Solomon, if only to find out what's so damned important."

Berengar started to protest but was quelled with a look.

"Find us a place to stay, preferably without vermin," Jehan told him. I'll be back here by sunset."

Reluctantly, Berengar agreed. "Stay alert," he warned Jehan. "I've seen how he moves."

"So have I," Jehan said. "And I know his tricks. That's why I'm the one who's going."

Regretfully, Solomon reclaimed his horse. There would be no chance now to explore the place undiscovered, at least not before dark. Still, it was better to find out what Brother James was planning. He didn't believe for a moment that the man had been moved by the plight of Aaron's betrothed.

The two men rode in uncomfortable silence back to the site. As they neared it, they heard shouting and the clank of metal on stone.

Jehan and Solomon looked at each other and reined in.

"Could just be the sounds of the building crews," Solomon said.

"Possibly," Jehan agreed. "Or a celebration of some sort."

"Of course Brother James might have managed to antagonize the men overseeing construction. They're probably making it clear to him that they don't need his interference."

"If that is the case," Jehan said. "It's my duty to see that he comes to no harm. From them or from you."

"I told you, I'm not going to attack the man, however much I might want him dead," Solomon insisted.

"But will you help me save him?" Jehan's words were a challenge.

"Oh, yes." Solomon gave a thin smile. "If only to see him choke when he finds out he is in my debt."

∞

The scene that greeted them was far beyond anything they had expected. Workmen and monks were milling around the half-finished church. Most of them were yelling with such cacophony that it was impossible to make out the reason for the excitement. Some men were busy moving a ladder against a naked arch that curved high over the main portal.

Solomon blinked and then pointed at the apex of the stone arch.

"What the hell is that?"

Jehan squinted, trying to make it out. "It looks like some giant black vulture perched over the doorway," he said.

He crossed himself hurriedly. "What have they conjured up? Do you think it's one of those Saracen idols, come to free the slaves?"

"They don't have idols," Solomon said. "You Christians do. It does look demonic, though. And oddly familiar."

"Oh, *merdus!*" Jehan exclaimed. "I knew there was something I meant to tell you. We passed your friend, Yusef, on the road. It seems that woman of his has run away again. I'd have let her go and good riddance, but he was bent on finding her. He said she might have been coming this way. It seems he was right."

Solomon shaded his eyes with his hand. Slowly the form became a woman wrapped in a black hooded cloak. What had looked from a distance like a long beak resolved itself into a face. As he watched, she tossed her head and a braid swung loose.

"What new madness is this?" he breathed.

Jehan had been scanning the rest of the site. "Perhaps not madness as all," he said. "Look over there."

Solomon did. While everyone was focussed on Babylonia's performance as the harbinger of doom, the door of the brothel had opened. First the eunuch came out to see what was happening. After a moment, he ventured farther out.

At this point Bablyonia sent up a wail that caused all the dogs in the area to howl in response. She balanced precariously on the unfinished stone, waving her arms as if about to launch herself into the air. The eunuch moved away from the hut to get a better view.

Solomon and Jehan continued to watch the hut. As Babylonia's shrieks began, the door opened again and two women rushed out, heading for the cover of some storage sheds nearby.

"They'll never make it away safely without help," Solomon said.

"I know," Jehan said. He searched the crowd of onlookers for the monks. Finally, he spotted the hulking form of Brother Martin. He seemed in no danger.

"Jehan!" Solomon had dismounted and was making his way to the place where Mayah and the other woman were hiding. "Are you with me or not?"

"I'm coming." Jehan tied the reins to a stunted tree and followed. "I wonder what the penance is for stealing Saracen whores from monks."

"Just cheer yourself with the thought that whatever they set you won't be an option for me," Solomon told him. "My choice will be conversion or the gallows."

Jehan grinned. "What a glorious prospect! Thank you!"

Solomon stopped abruptly. "But the object is for all of us to escape capture. Don't forget that!"

"I'm not likely to." Jehan's grin faded. "I've been imprisoned, as you know well. No one is ever going to shackle me again."

The workmen were now climbing the ladders toward Babylonia's perch. She wasn't making it easy, flapping her cloak and kicking chips of masonry on their upturned faces. Anyone who had a hand free was using it, not to ward off the scree but to make signs of protection against evil.

"Stop that!" a voice shouted in Arabic. "She's not a demon, just a human woman."

The overseer turned to Brother James. "There's a demon inside her for certain. Can you deny that?"

At that moment Babylonia began to laugh, a cackle that was more horrifying than her screams.

James clapped his hands over his ears. "No," he admitted. "I can't."

He raised his arms and began to intone a prayer of exorcism. As he did so, a group of monks in gray robes hurried over, summoned by the master builder. They ignored Babylonia and went straight to Brothers James and Martin. The leader was a man in his late twenties with an aristocratic bearing no humble monastic robe could disguise.

"Who are you?" he demanded. "What are you doing here?"

He paused to catch his breath. "A blessing upon you, all the same."

James smiled and bowed. "And to you, my brother. I am James, a monk of Saint Pierre of Moissac. This is my companion, Martin. We are at this place only by chance. However, we are acquainted with the woman who has terrorized your workmen. We encountered her on our journey."

The monk wasted no time with formalities. "Can you get her down?"

"I can try." James sighed. "If someone will hold the ladder."

As they crept from the cover of one rock to another, Solomon gave Jehan a quick explanation of who Mayah was and how she had ended up in such a place. Jehan had no trouble believing the story; it was common enough. It was Aaron's behavior that mystified him.

"He finds out where she's been taken and he goes north to sell horses for her ransom?" Jehan was aghast. "Then he ambles into Spain with us and when he finally finds her he doesn't even know her face? That's nonsense. Like those stupid minstral tales when a man puts on a beggar's cloak and tries to seduce his own wife and even the servants, who dress him every day, don't know it's him. *Tost fantasial!*"

"I don't understand, either," Solomon said. "But I'll wager a *sestier* of good pepper that he wasn't faking."

"Did she know him?"

Solomon hadn't considered that.

"I think so," he said. "She kept looking from him to me, as if not sure what was happening."

"Quiet!" Jehan warned. "They're just down there. Now how do we get their attention?"

The women were crouched behind a shed, looking toward the commotion at the church.

"There's always the old standby." Solomon picked up a small rock and threw it at the shed wall.

One of the women turned and saw them. Solomon tried to crouch and wave at the same time. The other woman turned as well. Solomon gestured for them to come up.

There was a brief conversation between the women, then the taller took the other's arm and the two made a dash for the rocks.

"Mayah!" Solomon whispered. "Hurry! We've got to get away from here before they find out you're missing.

"Solomon!" Mayah climbed the last few feet and collapsed into his arms.

"It's all right." He held her tightly. "You're safe now. I promise."

"You knew me." She tried to control her tears. "I saw it in your eyes. But Aaron . . ."

"Could we talk later?" Jehan suggested.

"Of course." Mayah took the other woman's hand and said something in rapid Arabic. "Which way?" she asked.

They had reached the horses and were heading back to the town when the uproar behind them died abruptly and then became one collective cry of horror.

"I think someone's found out you're missing," Jehan said as he urged his horse to a trot on the uneven ground.

"Don't worry," Solomon answered with a smile of pure malice. "Brother James is there to explain."

"Guy! Look what I found!" Berengar came out of the inn dragging Arnald by one leg. "Sitting there with a platter of sausages and wine like an *autun* lord. Thought you'd escape us, did you?"

"OW! Let me go, Berengar!" Arnald yelled. "You didn't need me anymore. Stop that!"

Berengar dropped him on the ground in front of Guy.

"I nearly got flayed alive because of you!" Guy squatted beside him. "You were supposed to keep me from tricksters and thieves. Instead you ran off with your Jew friends."

"It's not my fault!" Arnald said. "I only said I'd join you so that I could get out of Toulouse and help Aaron get his betrothed bride."

"But you were happy to take the money from the monks," Berengar sneered.

"But he offered . . . Oh, you mean Brother James," Arnald said. "I don't want his money. You two can have my share."

Berengar had drawn his knife and was idly brushing it across Arnald's cheek.

"What's that? I thought you were desperate to get enough to buy a vineyard or some such," he said. "Of course, you wouldn't be paid anyway. You haven't done anything to earn a reward, trying to ape the nobility. Do you know what a fool you look, with your fancy clothes and your airs? All of Toulouse laughs at you."

"Good. Fine. Let them laugh." Arnald squirmed away from the knife. "Now let me get back to Aaron. All this trouble and the woman turns out to be dead. The news has destroyed him."

Guy had had enough. He gripped Berengar's arm until the nobleman relaxed his hold on Arnald's collar. Arnald fell into the dirt, rubbing his neck.

"Dead!" Guy laughed. "So there's another captive our Brother James won't be able to ransom. I'll bet if he said he was going to buy back the souls in hell the devil would have freed them the week before. Look, Arnald, you and Berengar may have gone on this expedition for glory but I need to fill my stomach and buy a new horse. And Jehan won't take well to any more phantom prisoners. This mission was cursed from the day Brother Victor was killed."

Berengar gave Arnald a kick to relieve his feelings. "Get up, you *malestruc om*. You're right, Guy, I've had enough, too. When those monks get back, I'm telling them I'll play guard only if they are going back toward Toulouse. There are easier ways to make my fortune than putting up with the likes of you."

Arnald scrambled out of the way. He made it to the door of the inn before retorting.

"You don't deserve to be knights! You're no different than anyone else. All you want is wealth and power!"

He ducked inside the curtain.

Guy looked at Berengar. "Wealth and power? What is he talking about? What else is there?"

"Babylonia!" James called from halfway up the ladder. "You remember me, don't you? Brother James? We know you escaped your master. Don't worry, I'll protect you from Yusef. A good Christian woman like you should never have been forced to serve him."

"Pig!" Babyonia shrieked. She tried to push the ladder over but the weight of the monk held it in place. "Don't you touch me! You're all the same."

For a moment, James thought she had recognized him as a Jew. Then he decided that she must have meant men.

"I won't hurt you, Babylonia." He went up another rung. "I'm trying to save you. This is a dangerous place. You don't want to fall."

"I said, stay back!" Babyonia wasn't looking at him, though, but at something in the distance.

Suddenly she arose once again, flapping her cloak and screaming. All eyes turned up to her.

"What's that she's saying?" Martin asked the monk next to him.

"Some demon tongue," he guessed. "Or maybe Greek."

But James recognized it at once. The shock of it almost made him lose his grip on the ladder. The language was Aramaic. Babylonia was saying *kaddish*, the prayer for the dead. Did she know what it was or had she picked up the words in Yusef's home?

"*Dayenu!* Babylonia, enough!" he cried. "Stop this and come down."

She stopped in mid-wail. James was almost close enough to reach her. Instead she reached down and grabbed his shoulders.

"I know you, Jacob ben Solomon," she said. "Yusef told me what you did. What happened to your wife, Jacob? The Holy One knows you, even with your beard shaved. I thought Aaron was better than the rest. I came to help him get her back. But she told me he rejected her, just like my husband did. All of you prideful monsters!"

Her grip was surprisingly strong. James could feel her nails digging into his flesh.

"Don't let the *Edomites* take her!" She spat the words in

James's face. "Do you know what she told me? That men may have betrayed us but not the Holy One, the Creator of All. After all that has been done to her, she still prays. In that place, worse than any I've ever seen, she has faith. She told me I was the angel sent to comfort her."

Bablyonia's face altered before James fearful gaze. The madness slid away, replaced by radiant joy.

"Babylonia," he said softly. "Please come down."

"Oh, no." She smiled. "Never again. I was weak before but now I know I can be a witness to the truth. Tell your pious Christian friends that I died for Israel."

She stood and spread her arms again, not flapping as before, but to dive like an eagle from the sky to the earth.

They were on the edge of Fitero before Mayah lifted her head from Solomon's back and spoke.

"Where are you taking us?" she asked.

"For now, to an inn," he answered. "After that, I don't know."

"You stole us," she said. "They'll make you give us back. They may even try to hang you for theft."

"That won't happen," Solomon said firmly. "We brought enough gold to buy your freedom a dozen times over."

"And Zaida's?" Mayah asked.

Solomon glanced at the other woman, riding behind Jehan, her brown legs bare. Both women had tied their skirts up between their legs as makeshift riding pants. This was no time for the delicacy of riding pillion.

"Of course we'll ransom her, as well," Solomon said. "Who is she?"

"Her father is a merchant in Almeria," Mayah said. "He and my father have been friends for years. I was visiting them when the Edomites attacked."

"Is she one of ours?" he asked.

"She's Moslem, if that's what you mean," she answered. "Does that matter to her freedom?"

"Of course not," Solomon answered. "If she's your friend. I thought there were three of you. Where's the third?"

"She died." Mayah's tone warned Solomon not to ask anything more.

They slowed their pace as they approached the town. Suddenly Mayah called out to Solomon to stop. She spoke rapidly to Zaida who nodded eagerly.

"Please, Solomon, can you loan us enough money for a bath?" she asked. "I need to wash and scrub and scrub and scrub and . . ."

The tension in her body told Solomon that she wasn't as composed as she had at first appeared.

"Don't you want to go to the inn first?" he asked.

"No," she said, dismounting. "And clothes. We must have new clothes. Can you find us something, anything clean and plain. Very plain. My father will pay you back for anything you spend. You know that."

Solomon gulped. Of course she hadn't heard that her father and all his possessions had been lost at Córdoba. Now wasn't the time to tell her.

"I'll get you the best in town," he promised.

The woman at the bath house wasn't eager to let them in, but Solomon's coins soon convinced her. Mayah and Zaida vanished behind a curtain of steam.

"I'll keep watch out here until they're done," Jehan offered. "In case the monks send men to find them. You go buy the *chainses* and *bliaux* and other female fripperies."

Solomon gave a short laugh. "You? A man who once kidnapped a woman from the streets of Paris. Not likely. I'll stay."

Jehan's eyes narrowed. "I was bewitched then, mad. However,

you might remember that even then, I did the girl no harm. I don't take women by force."

Solomon did remember that Clemence had not been violated. He had thought then that it was only because Jehan had not had the time.

"You never committed rape? Not even at Lisbon?" he asked. "When you took the city?"

"Look, I know this sounds strange," Jehan said in disgust. "But sticking it to a woman who's screaming her head off with terror is not my idea of fun."

Solomon was inclined to believe him, against his common sense.

"Very well," he said. "I'll be back as soon as I can. If I find that you've bothered them in any way, your life will be worthless."

Jehan gave a mirthless laugh. He seated himself on a boulder and began polishing his knife.

"Just go," he said. "Don't waste your breath with hollow threats."

Babylonia's leap took James by surprise. Arms flailing, he slid the last half of the way down the ladder. The men below caught him roughly and set him upright.

"Are you unharmed?" Brother Martin ran up to him. "I prayed for you every minute."

"Thank you." James tried to smile at him. "I shall live. Where is Babylonia?"

"Her body is over here," one of the white monks said. "Where she fell. We've sent for the prior to tell us what to do."

"You need instructions to attend to a dying woman!" James glared at the monk in outrage.

He went over to where the body lay and knelt next to Babylonia. He started to make the sign of the cross on her forehead, but couldn't bring himself to do it. The woman had said *kaddish* for herself! Why? James had heard that at the time of the massacres in the Rhineland, when he was a boy, whole Jewish communities had committed suicide rather than submit to the Christian mobs. The tale was that they had also said their own *kaddish*, since there would be no family left alive to perform the ritual.

But Babylonia! It made no sense. She had done nothing but revile Jews throughout their journey. Yet she wanted the world to know she died faithful to the God of Israel. And now it was too late to convince her otherwise.

James reached out and closed her empty eyes.

One of the local monks knelt next to him.

"Who was she?" he asked. "Why was she here, of all places?"

"Just a poor madwoman," James answered, "who escaped from her keeper. Why was she here? I don't think I can say."

"No one can follow the reasoning of one whom reason has deserted," the monk agreed.

"Brother Gerond!" a workmen called to the white monk. "The Saracen girls have escaped!"

"Saracen girls?" James looked at Brother Gerond in shock. "Why would you have Saracen girls here? Were they being instructed in the faith?"

"It's nothing." Gerond got up hurriedly, dusting off his robes. "Servants, that's all. What are you going to do with the body?"

James remembered something Yusef had said when they met him on the road.

"I'll have someone see to it," he said. "Do you have a cart we could borrow? She should be buried in Tudela."

Solomon went first to the inn. He found Aaron just as before, prone with anguish. Arnald sat next to him trying to get him to eat.

"Did you find Brother James?" Arnald asked.

"Yes." Solomon didn't elaborate.

As Arnald ate, Solomon took a good look at him. "What happened to your face?"

Arnald rubbed the red welt. "I was trying to scrape off my own beard, but I don't have the knack."

"Don't you want money for a barber?" Solomon fished in his purse again. "You can go now, if you like. I'll stay with Aaron for a while. Then I have some things to buy."

Arnald took the money with a smile. "I won't be long," he promised.

Solomon sat next to his friend. He had known Aaron since they had been boys together. But he had known Mayah almost since she had been in swaddling. It was amazing that the torture she had endured hadn't left her as mad as Babylonia; at least he hoped it hadn't. Mayah had a core of strength that she had always been careful to hide. After her mother died, she had ruled her father and the household with a will of iron and still found time to become a brilliant scholar, fluent in Hebrew, Arabic, and French.

If Aaron had really loved her, he would have known her at once. Mayah deserved more. Solomon gave a sigh. It wasn't his decision, but hers. And, if Aaron didn't marry her, what could she do then?

"Aaron," he said firmly. "Sit up. I have to tell you something and I can't do it if you're lying there whimpering like a wounded animal."

Aaron sat upright at once, stiff with indignation. "Solomon! How can you be so unfeeling?"

"That's what I'm going to tell you."

Without being invited, James followed the monk down to the hut.

"Not a very pleasant place to house potential converts." He sniffed at the crude building. "Marie Magdalene's broken jar! They did have a lot of perfume, didn't they?"

"It's nothing for you to be concerned with," Brother Gerond insisted. "I'll see that you have a cart for the woman's body. Now, if you'll excuse me."

He gestured for some of the workmen to lead James away.

Brother Martin had trailed after them, not sure what was happening now.

"Brother James," he asked loudly. "I thought Arnald said that the women were here as a *harim* for the Moslems so they wouldn't go to Christian whores. Why would they run away? Weren't they being paid well enough?"

He looked around at the stupefied white monks.

"Did I have it wrong?" he asked.

James put his hand on the big man's shoulder. "No, Martin. I think you had it exactly right. Now I'm very curious to know if the abbot of Cîteaux authorized a brothel on monastic property. If so, I'm sure Abbot Peter of Cluny would want to be informed. You Cistercians are so much more pious than we worldly Cluniacs. We wouldn't have thought of buying slaves to slake the lust of our workers. Perhaps we've missed a form of charity that we should consider practicing."

A few minutes later, they were on the road. Brother Martin walked in front, leading the mule cart containing the body of Babylonia. James walked at the rear, to be sure it didn't fall out.

"Brother James," Martin said after some time. "What did we just do?"

James bent over the edge of the cart to adjust the temporary shroud.

"We just interfered with the internal matters of another order," he said. "We also gave a large amount of gold to that same order to keep them from tracking down two infidel women and forcing them to be prostitutes."

"Oh." Martin thought awhile. "It this a good thing or a bad thing?"

"I don't know Martin," James said. "At the moment it seemed the only thing. But it's very likely that our reverend abbot may have another opinion."

Martin was silent for a longer time.

"Brother James," he said at last. "I think we did a good thing and I'll tell the abbot so."

"Brother Martin." James's voice was low. "I now understand why you were asked to accompany me. Thank you."

They were passing a place where the rocks seemed to have been pushed from the earth by giant armies. Ravens were collecting in one of the crevices.

"Must be some poor lost sheep," Martin commented. "I hate to see them ripped up by the birds."

He dropped the lead and went climbing over the rocks.

"Get on!" he shouted. "Steal a poor shepherd's lamb, would you? Oh. Oh! Oh, my God! Brother James, come quickly!"

Twenty

Just outside Fitero, a moment later.

<u>תלמוד בבלי: מסכת גיטין, דף פא, עמוד א</u>

שבוייה אוכלת בתרומה, דברי ר׳ דוסא, א״ר דוסא: "וכי מה
עשה לה ערבי זה, מפני שמיעך לה בין דדיה פסלה מן
הכהונה?!"

A kidnapped woman may still eat from tithed food reserved
for priests, according to the opinion of Rabbi Dosa. Rabbi
Dosa said, "What, indeed, has this Arab done to her?
Because he squeezed her breasts, has he disqualified her
from marrying into the priesthood?"

—*Babylonian Talmud,*
Gitten *81a*

*T*he man lay face down, wedged in between the rocks. His back was a mass of blood, his leather tunic sliced to ribands.

"Brother James, hurry!" Martin called. "I think he's still alive!"

James slid in a puddle of blood and nearly fell on the body. Martin caught him just in time.

"It looks as though he's been attacked by some ferocious beast," Martin said. "A bear or a lion, perhaps."

James was checking for signs of life. The man's arm was thrown over his face. Gently, James lifted it.

"Holy Mother!" he exclaimed. "It's Berengar! Yes, he's still breathing! Give me something to cover these wounds. Then we'll have to get him to the cart."

"Will he live?" Martin asked as he tore his cowl into swaths to lay on the knight's back.

"God alone knows," James answered. "Some of these cuts are deep. There seems to be more blood on the ground than in his body. I wonder why he wasn't in his mail shirt. I thought those men even slept in them."

"It's very warm today," Martin commented. "If you help, I think I can carry him over my shoulders. That way his back won't be touched."

Berengar didn't even moan when they lifted him. James

feared that they would soon be hauling two corpses in the cart.

"This is the most unfortunate group I've ever known," Martin worried as they set out again. "We must have started our journey on an Egyptian day."

"The stars didn't cause this," James said angrily. "There's a human agent at work here, though he is beyond doubt in league with Satan."

Martin plodded along beside the mule, trying to guide it toward the least bumpy ruts in the road.

"I don't understand, Brother James," he said. "How could one person have caused all this disaster? Do you think someone pushed Babylonia?"

"No, of course not," James said. "There was no one close to her but me. No, her death is something else altogether. But I'm sure that Brother Victor's murder is the key. At first I thought that he had been attacked by one of those heretics we see these days, preaching against the clergy. My theory seemed confirmed when the dortor at Saint Pierre des Cuisines was broken into."

"It did seem that the destruction there was done in anger," Martin said. "By someone who hated clerics and everything connected with us."

"Yes, but then that poor young man, Samuel, was slaughtered," James continued. "And I knew I had been mistaken."

"But that was miles away from Toulouse," Martin pointed out. "I can see no possible connection between his murder and Victor's."

"I can think of several," James told him. "But I don't know which is the right one. And now here's Berengar, attacked out in the wilderness. The answer leapt at once to my mind. We have brought something evil with us."

"I'm sorry, Brother James," Martin said humbly. "Nothing is leaping at me. I'm not clever. Facts don't arrange themselves in my brain like they do in yours."

"Be grateful," James said. "I'll explain. The thing that bothers me most is that when they were attacked, each of these men was some place he had no reason to be. Victor was out after Compline; Samuel out in the storm when he should have been in the warm dry inn. And now Berengar. Why would he have left the town and gone to that desolate spot? He had no hunting hawk, no bow, no armor. He never struck me as a man who would seek out the desert places in order to meditate."

Brother Martin stifled a laugh. "Forgive me," he said. "Yes, now that you lay it out, I see. But why would anyone want to lure those men to a remote place to kill them? And how could they have been so foolish as to go?"

"We do foolish things every day," James said. "It's your first question that perplexes me. Why would any one person desire the deaths of a monk, a Jew, and a knight?"

Martin laughed again. "Oh, I am sorry, Brother James! I know my thoughts are not grave enough for a religious man, and this is not the time. It's only that what you said sounded like one of my father's jests. 'A monk, a Jew, and a knight meet under a tree in the forest and decide to throw lots.' That sort of tale."

"Throw lots," James repeated, thinking of Guy. "Possibly."

"Usually there's an enchantress in the tree," Martin offered. "She makes each one see something different. Or sometimes she sets them to arguing among themselves. When my father told the stories, the ending usually had a lesson attached. Very fond of giving advice, my father was. Ah! I'm sorry!" he exclaimed as the cart shook. "There was no smooth way here. How is Berengar doing?"

James checked the knight. His breathing was shallow and less regular. They had cushioned him with Babylonia's remains. It seemed an impious thing to do but they had nothing else to use.

"I don't think he felt the jolting," James said. "But he's failing.

Here, I'll lead the mule. You go ahead and get a bed ready for him. Ask if there's a healer in the town."

Martin nodded and set off at an ungainly run. Watching him, James prayed that he would reach the town before his sandal straps snapped and sent him tumbling. The cart couldn't hold another casualty.

Jehan was lounging on the bench outside the bathhouse when Solomon returned.

"Took you long enough," he said. "But they're still in there. I can hear them talking. Sometimes they cry. Then they call for more soap. Did you tell Aaron?"

"Yes," Solomon said. "He says he's mortified that he didn't know Mayah at once. He's busy now trying to think of a way to atone."

"He still wants to marry her?" Jehan asked. "That would be enough for most women."

"He says he does, but I can sense the doubt," Solomon answered. "The *ignamine!* What did he think he would find, an heiress in a tower, clean and pristine, guarded by Saracen dragons?"

"He and Arnald are a pair," Jehan said. "They both seem to think the *jongleurs* in the streets have the truth about how the world works."

"Arnald I can understand," Solomon said. "He's young and hasn't been much out of Toulouse in his life. But Aaron is a man grown, experienced in trade."

Jehan shrugged. "Love blinds us in the cruelest way, by making us think we are seeing clearly."

Embarrassed at his introspection, Jehan got up quickly. He called to the bath attendant.

"Could you tell the women inside that their clothes are ready?"

Solomon gave the woman the parcel.

"Tell them it was the best I could do for now," he said.

"You might also remind them that it's well past the dining hour," Jehan added.

Some time later Mayah and Zaida appeared. The robes Solomon had found were too long so they had used cords as belts to fold the excess cloth. They had covered their heads and wound the ends of the veils around their necks. All traces of the kohl and powder were gone. They stood in the doorway holding hands tightly, clearly afraid to venture out.

Solomon smiled. They looked like novice nuns. His eyes went down.

"Shoes," he said. "I forgot to buy you sandals. I'm sorry."

His obvious consternation broke the tension. Mayah and Zaida stepped out into the afternoon sunshine.

"We can get them later," Mayah told him. "Where do we go now?"

Solomon had considered that. The inn was too crude and crowded. It was also the first place any pursuers would look. There was no Jewish family in the town who might take them in.

"I found you a house," he told them. "The owner is away but he left his Moslem servants to tend to things. I offered them a chance to earn an extra wage. They have agreed to serve the two of you as they would him."

Zaida had been listening intently. She frowned and asked Mayah a question. Mayah shook her head.

"Zaida can understand French, if you speak slowly. But it's hard for her to speak," she told Solomon. "She asked me if the servants know where we came from."

"No, I told them you were well-born ladies who had endured many hardships after the fall of Almeria," he said. "You are here on your way to seek refuge. I also cautioned them not to ask about your sufferings."

Mayah translated quickly. Zaida gave a sigh of relief.

"We'll take you there now," Solomon said. "Jehan?"

"Of course."

Solomon walked before them leading the way and Jehan behind to guard them. It wasn't far. The only stately homes in town
were near the baths. Most lay in ruins, victims of the struggle for
control of Castile. The owner of this one had used stones from
nearby buildings to patch holes in the walls. The roof was tiled
in a hundred different shapes and colors. But the rooms were
clean and private and there was a small courtyard with a fountain
for Mayah and Zaida to sit by while they ate.

"You can speak to the servants better than I," Solomon said
when they arrived. "Order anything you need. I'll return tomorrow."

"What about the overseer at the monastery?" Mayah asked.
"The monks will send him looking for us."

"Even if they find you here, no one will be permitted to
enter," Solomon assured her.

"We'll make certain of that," Jehan said.

"And Aaron?" Mayah asked.

"He is awash in self-reproach," Solomon said. "He wants you
to know that he still considers you his betrothed. I would have
brought him with me but I thought you might need some time
to rest before . . ."

". . . facing him again," Mayah finished. "Yes. I don't think I
quite believe I'm free. There were so many times it was only a
dream. Tomorrow, perhaps I'll be ready to consider the future.
The first thing I must do is send word to my father."

"In the morning," Solomon said quickly. "Now, this is the
woman in charge of the household. She'll take care of you."

The woman bowed to Zaida and Mayah, greeting them in
Arabic. She gestured for them to follow her into the house.

"Solomon?" Mayah stopped and looked back at him. Something in his manner worried her. "What aren't you telling me?"

"Nothing," he said. "Eat, sleep, then eat and sleep again. You're safe now."

"Are they?" Jehan asked as they left.

"I'm coming back at sundown to guard the house," Solomon said. "Anyone who tries to recapture them will have to face me first."

"Now you sound like one of Arnald's heroes," Jehan replied. "Of course you won't need anyone to watch with you. A real hero never sleeps."

"Are you offering to share the duty?" Solomon asked in astonishment.

"John the Baptist's sacred foreskin! Never." Jehan recoiled at the thought. "I'm planning on being there to take your place when you collapse."

Brother Martin's abrupt arrival in Fitero caused general alarm. The women gathered at the well for a good chat were momentarily dumbfounded when he lumbered up to them demanding to know which of them knew how to stop blood from flowing.

When, with some effort, they had managed to winkle the reason from him, the women scattered, one for bandages, another for moss to staunch the blood, another for herbs to counter the fever. Martin allowed himself a moment to drain one dipper of water and spill another over his head before setting off to look for the inn.

Arnald and Guy were sampling the day's soup when the curtain covering the door was pushed back and Brother Martin's head appeared.

"I thought I'd never find you!" he cried. "Berengar's been mauled by a lion! Brother James is bringing him back. We need to make a bed for him at once!"

"A lion!" Arnald's eyes opened wide in astonishment. "Is he badly hurt?"

"I don't know," Martin answered. "Yes, I think so. We put him on top of Babylonia's body and he didn't flinch."

Both men were on their feet at once.

"Babylonia?" Guy asked. "Is that what you said? Slow down. What happened to her?"

"I saw it but I still don't know," Martin said. "Where is the innkeeper? We'll need to put a mattress on one of these tables. Oh, and I need to find those women and tell them where to bring the ointments."

He raced out again.

"Has he gone mad?" Arnald asked Guy.

"It does look like it," Guy said. "But, just in case he hasn't, we should set up the long table and find a mattress."

Solomon and Jehan reached the inn just as Berengar's limp form was being lifted from the cart.

"What did this?" Jehan rounded on Guy. "Why weren't you with him?"

Guy nearly dropped Berengar's feet in confusion.

"I didn't know he was gone!" the knight defended himself. "You told us to stay here and wait for you!"

"And you, Arnald?" Jehan needed to blame someone. "Where were you when your comrade was attacked?"

"Sitting with Aaron," Arnald answered. "I was afraid he might do something rash if left alone."

The innkeeper chose this moment to return, burdened with pillows. When he saw the state Berengar was in, he dropped them on the floor.

"You said you needed a bed, not a bier," he said. "Those stains will never come out. Who's going to pay for all this?"

Jehan looked at Brother James, who sighed. "I can't. I gave

the remaining ransom money to the prior to pay for the slaves that escaped while everyone was watching Babylonia."

"You mean no one is hunting for them?" Solomon asked.

"That's right," James answered. "They're free."

His expression challenged Solomon.

"Very well." Solomon untied the leather cord at his neck and took out the leather bag containing the money Brother Victor had given them.

"Since this is no longer needed to redeem Mayah," he said. "I'll pay for the care of this man."

Brother James's jaw dropped when he saw the bag. He stared at it in disbelief. Then, with a bitter cry, he threw himself at Solomon.

"I knew it!" he screamed. "It was you all along! Jehan! Tie this man up at once and keep him under guard. He murdered Brother Victor!"

Jehan's face lit with unholy joy.

"Finally! It's time you had a taste of what you gave me!"

He advanced on Solomon, but his way was blocked by the irate innkeeper trying to collect his fee, three women loaded with jars, bottles, and bandages, and a stable boy who wanted to know what to do with the body in the cart.

"Stop!" Solomon shouted. "All of you. I can explain."

Everyone paused to stare at him.

"Yes, this is from Brother Victor," Solomon held up the bag. "But it wasn't stolen. He gave it freely to Arnald and Belide to help rescue Aaron's betrothed. I never saw the man, alive or dead. Tell him, Arnald."

There was no answer. Solomon scanned the faces in the room.

"Where did Arnald go?" he asked.

Aaron was coming down the ladder from the sleeping loft, drawn by the commotion.

"Aaron, is Arnald up there with you?"

"No, I haven't seen him," Aaron answered. "What's going on here? Is Mayah all right?"

Jehan made another attempt to reach Solomon.

"It seems there's no one to vouch for you this time," he said.

"Just a moment." James raised his hand for attention. "Aaron, when did you last see Arnald?"

"This afternoon, just after I spoke with Solomon," Aaron said. "I was very upset. He gave me a sleeping draught to help me rest. The noise woke me only a few moments ago. What's the hour?"

James didn't answer. He signaled Jehan to hold off restraining Solomon.

"*Damledux!*" Jehan said. "I was so close."

Guy had been trying to follow all the revelations of the past few minutes. He didn't understand what had happened to Berengar but he knew there was one point he could clear up.

"You think Arnald set a trap for Berengar because of the fight they had this afternoon?" he asked. He licked his lips nervously. "That's nonsense."

"They had a fight?" James asked.

"It was nothing," Guy said. "Just a jest, really."

"Then where is he?" Solomon asked.

"The man with the fuzzy brown hair?" the stable boy asked. "He went out the back door not long ago. Probably to the latrine."

"Go after him!" Solomon insisted. "At once!"

"Wait." James pushed through the crowded room to stand next to Solomon. "Guy, go look for Arnald. But don't think his word will free you from suspicion."

Solomon gave an exasperated sigh. "Look, Victor gave this bag to Arnald and Bonysach's daughter, Belide, for the purpose of freeing Mayah from the clutches of your righteous brethren. She and Bonysach's wife, Josta, will confirm this. Or are you so deep in your revulsion for us that you think they would lie?"

"They might well do so to protect you and themselves," James said absently.

Something was hammering in his mind, demanding him to attend. "Wait. You say that Victor gave Arnald one bag. Just one?"

He pointed to the leather sack in Solomon's hand.

"That's right," Solomon said. "Neither Aaron nor I wanted to take it but I brought it anyway, in case we needed to pay more than we thought for Mayah."

"Victor only gave them *one* bag," James repeated.

"Yes, I told you."

"But there were two bags missing," James said. "If you are so innocent, then where is the rest of the gold?"

"Gold?" The word arrested the attention of the room. Even the woman carefully applying a thick paste to Berengar's ravaged back paused at the sound of it.

"We know nothing of another bag. Perhaps someone saw Victor give it to Belide and attacked him afterwards," Aaron suggested.

Solomon liked the idea but the logic didn't work. Brother James saw the same problem.

"If he saw Arnald receive a bag of gold, then any sensible thief would follow Arnald, not the monk who gave it to him," he said. "But also, if Victor intended to give Arnald one of the bags of ransom money, then why did he take two with him?"

Solomon looked at Aaron. "The man is your friend. What do you think? Could he have killed the monk for the rest of the money?"

"Of course not!" Aaron was indignant. "Arnald's a bit thoughtless and inclined to pranks but, at base, he's a loyal good-hearted friend. Why would he steal from Victor? Victor was his friend, too. And everyone knows that Arnald's father is one of the richest men in the Cité."

"He's taking a long time in the privy," Solomon commented.

He was becoming worried. What if Arnald didn't return to vouch for him? Perhaps he and Guy had some scheme of their own. What would he do if they didn't return?

"*Senhor* Aaron." James had another thought. "Arnald told us he was sitting at your bedside all afternoon; was he?"

"I have no idea," Aaron said. "I slept like the dead. But, if he says so, then I believe him. Arnald is my friend."

"Thank you, Aaron." Arnald came in from the back of the inn, followed by Guy.

Solomon relaxed. He wouldn't have to fight his way out after all.

"There you are!" Aaron exclaimed in satisfaction. "I knew it. You didn't kill Brother Victor, did you?"

"Me?" Arnald stared at him. "Where would you get such a bizarre idea?"

"If you didn't," James said. "Then what did you do with the second bag of gold that Victor was carrying that night?"

"Didn't know he had one," Arnald answered, eyes wide with surprise.

"Would you mind if we looked through your pack and your purse," Brother James asked. "Just to be sure you didn't forget he gave it to you?"

"Anything for the Church." Arnald took the purse from around his neck and handed it to James. "My pack is up above with the others."

"Brother Martin, will you go up and search?" James asked.

Martin eyed the ladder nervously but started the climb. The rungs creaked with each step, but held.

James emptied out the purse. There were a few small coins, a medallion from a local shrine, a twist of dark hair wrapped in oilskin, nothing more.

"You see?"

"Brother James?" Martin's head appeared at the opening in the ceiling. "I'm sorry. I think I found the other bag." He held it out for them to see. "It's full of *marbottins*. I've never seen so many in one place. It was in this pack. Is that Arnald's?"

"Now wait up here!" Guy said. "That's my pack!"

"Oh, Guy! How could you?" Arnald turned on him. "Why? What did Brother Victor ever do to you?"

"Nothing! No!" Guy stepped back, his hands outstretched to ward off the accusations. "I didn't!"

"Where were you this afternoon?" Arnald continued. "I didn't see you here while I was with Aaron."

"I . . . I was out losing my hauberk at dice, if you must know." Guy looked away from Brother James. "And Berengar's. He's going to kill me when he wakes and finds I lost it to a Saracen."

"You needn't worry on that score." The woman who was tending to Berengar spoke up. "He isn't going to wake."

Most of the people in the room crossed themselves and muttered a prayer.

"Poor Berengar," Arnald said, shaking his head at Guy. "I'm sorry now I mocked him. So you took his armor and then attacked him? Guy, that's not how a knight behaves."

"No, I didn't!" Guy cried in panic.

Brother James put a hand on his arm. "It's all right, Guy. Let me take care of this."

Arnald stood with his arms crossed, his expression the picture of a friend betrayed. Brother James moved closer to him.

"Arnald," James said quietly. "I am so grieved. I had faith in you. But now, you just made your third mistake."

"What?" Arnald's expression changed to confusion.

"The first was when you decided to keep half the gold for yourself," James explained.

Aaron gasped and would have spoken, but Jehan hushed him with a gesture.

Even though the room was crowded, a circle was beginning to open around the young man. Arnald noticed the change in atmosphere. His eyes went back and forth, searching for the best way out.

"You had to make sure Victor didn't tell anyone that there were originally two bags, didn't you?" James moved closer.

"You're mad." Arnald smiled at Aaron. "Totally insane, isn't he? Must be all that chastity."

"I don't understand why Samuel had to die," James went on. "Did he discover what you had done?"

"Solomon!" Arnald appealed to him.

With a thrill of horror Solomon knew. Suddenly all the pieces tumbled into place.

"You killed that poor boy because he wanted to marry Belide!" he said. "She's the one you really want, isn't she? You have dreams of owning your own vineyard. Your father is rich, but you can't have the use of even your own funds until you turn twenty-five. You planned on convincing Belide to convert and marry you, didn't you? But you knew it would be impossible if she were already married to Samuel. Arnald, you're a fool. She never would have turned to you, no matter how much wealth you offered."

"That's nonsense," Arnald hissed. He was backing away from them now, but there was only a wall behind him.

"Your second mistake"—James acted as if Solomon hadn't spoken—"was to hide the bag in Guy's pack. You must have done it this afternoon, after Guy left. That was incredibly stupid. We all know that if Guy had been carrying a fortune with him since Toulouse, he would have been gambling at every stop. And he certainly wouldn't have been driven to wager his chain mail."

Arnald's mouth opened and closed as he tried to think of an answer to this.

"Which leads to your third and, I hope, final misjudgment." James was within arm's length of him now. "You knew that Guy had taken Berengar's hauberk. You left after he did. Was that how you got Berengar out of town? Did you tell him that he needed to get to the game before Guy had bet and lost?"

Suddenly, Arnald grinned.

"Stupid, *orgoillos* pig. He didn't even take his sword. Anyone that arrogant deserves what he gets."

Aaron gave a deep moan. "Arnald, you don't mean that! Listen to yourself! He thinks you're admitting that you attacked Berengar."

Arnald's grin grew wider. "And so I did. Didn't think I had it in me, did you? No one guessed. I was just foolish old Arnald, always getting into trouble, embarrassing my friends and family. No one suspected what wonderful plans I had. I am sorry about Victor. He was trying to help. But then, he was so good, he's probably already in heaven. So I really did him a favor, sending him to God, don't you see?"

"Arnald, stop!" Aaron pleaded.

"And Samuel was an infidel so that wasn't a sin." Arnald seemed unperturbed by the growing horror directed toward him. "He'd have made Belide a terrible husband. He didn't even have the sense to stay out of the rain. The idiot saw Babylonia pass by the inn and followed her. He ran right into me. It was too good a chance to ignore."

"My son, you must realize what you are confessing to." James tried to remember that his first duty was to save souls. He longed to run a knife into Arnald's heart for what he had done to Victor. How many times would God test his resolve? "These are all mortal sins of the deepest hue. You took the lives of three people."

"But that's what a brave knight does," Arnald insisted. His arms were still crossed over his chest. He now began rubbing his left wrist nervously. "He has to win the lady. All those who come between him and the fulfillment of his destiny must be crushed. No one can stand in the way. Belide will be proud of me."

His right hand vanished into his left sleeve.

Solomon saw it coming before James did.

"STOP!" he screamed as he threw himself toward the monk.

It was too late. The knife strapped to Arnald's arm slid out like warm butter. He lunged forward, thrusting the blade deep into James gut.

James looked down in astonishment. The hilt protruded from his robes. A wet stain was spreading across the dark cloth.

"Brother James!" Martin dropped from the hole in the ceiling with a thump and reached out to catch James as he slowly crumpled to the floor.

Arnald made a leap for the doorway. As he flew past, Solomon caught his right arm and bent it back, causing Arnald to drop the knife with a cry of pain.

The rest of the people in the room were on him at once. In a few moments Arnald emerged from the crush, battered and bound.

"Why did you stop me, Solomon?" he asked in a voice filled with betrayal. "You hate Brother James. You said so all the time. You should be helping me defeat him."

"My feelings toward him make no difference, you monster." Solomon lifted him by the cords wound around his arms and chest. "He was an unarmed man. And, no matter how much I loathe him, he is still my father."

He dropped Arnald like a sack of table leavings and went to see to Brother James.

"Your father?" Jehan scratched his head in amazement. His face lit with pleasure. "A monk! That's priceless."

Aaron shook his head and sank slowly to the floor.

"This is all a nightmare," he whispered. "I don't understand any of it. I'm going to sit here quietly in the corner until someone wakes me up."

Brother Martin was praying over James, but made room for Solomon.

"Did he tell you who I was?" Solomon asked.

"No, I knew Brother James was a convert and I saw how similar you were in appearance," Martin said. "You have the same eyes, you know. But I said nothing. It wasn't my place. Your anger against him is obvious and perhaps you have good reason. But can't you try to make peace? You won't have another chance."

Solomon looked down on the face of the man who had abandoned him. Years of struggle and self-deprivation had lined it deeply. Solomon could barely remember his father, but he had an image of someone tall and strong with a thick black beard. This man was a stranger.

James's eyes were closed and his lips moving in prayer. His skin was pale as life drained away. Solomon felt Brother Martin watching him. He wanted to protest that James didn't deserve absolution. He wanted to keep his hatred pure.

Just once, he wanted his father to say his name with love.

"Father." Solomon forced the words out. "I don't understand what you did. But I will try to forgive you."

James opened his amazing green eyes. They looked directly into Solomon's.

"The last test," he murmured. "He tempts me to the end. No forgiveness from you; I had to follow my Lord. I was right. Tell my brothers, no *kaddish*. I want only Masses for my soul."

Solomon jerked away as if slapped.

James eyes closed again and his head rolled back. Martin's prayers grew louder. Around the room, others joined him.

"Here." Jehan gave Solomon his hand and helped him to

stand. Solomon was surprised to find that his legs wouldn't hold him.

Jehan supported him as they wove their way across the small room. "We need to get out of here and get some wine into you," he said. "This place is as bad as the carnage at Lisbon."

Solomon believed him. Berengar's body lay draped on the table, Babylonia's under a bench against the wall. Arnald was tied up in a corner, his loud protestations about to be gagged by a couple of the women. James was the central figure in the room now, ringed by people praying for his soul along with Brother Martin bent over the body, weeping.

The two men stumbled out into the warm spring air. With a grunt of relief, Jehan released Solomon onto a stool under a chestnut tree. Then he found a seat for himself.

"Your father, was he?" Jehan said. "No wonder you hate us so. You'd think the old bastard could have died a Christian and still given you a word of kindness."

"Not him." Solomon took a deep breath. He blinked back tears and steadied his voice. "No matter. It would have been years too late, anyway."

He stood, taking time to dust himself off before facing Jehan.

"We should go tell Mayah that no one will try to take her back into slavery," he said.

"Yes, it's the one good thing that's come from this." Jehan stretched and got up, too. "You know, Brother James didn't have to pay for her freedom. You might give him credit for that."

"He only did it so he could convert her," Solomon said.

"Maybe," Jehan said. "But maybe it was the only way he had to tell you that he was sorry."

"What are you talking about?" Solomon asked in irritation.

"Well, I think that when your father decided to accept Christ, he knew that he had to renounce everything." Jehan fumbled for the words. "The greatest gift he could offer was the one God had given us. He had to give up his only begotten son. You were the price he paid to become a Christian."

"That's cod tripe," Solomon told him. But the thought gave him a spark of comfort.

There was no need to let Jehan know that, though.

Twenty-one

On the way back to Toulouse, Thursday, Iyyar 8 4908, pridie nones May (May 6) 1148. Feast of Saint John at the Lateran Gate.

Etsi christianus voluntarie homicidum fecerit, ominibus vite sue publicam agat penitentiam et in exitu vita sue communicet.

And if a Christian willingly commits homicide then he must perform public penance all the days of his life and at the end of his life let him take communion.

—Penitential Cordubense

$\mathcal{B}$rother Martin and Jehan insisted on bringing Arnald back to Toulouse to be sentenced for his crimes. Guy was for hanging him at once.

"We can't do that," Jehan insisted. "It's for the families of the victims to judge him."

"After God, of course," Martin added. "But his fate in this world has to be decided by those he wronged most."

"And what about Samuel?" Aaron asked.

"His family, too," Martin said. "If they wish to come from Narbonne. If not, then the Jews of Toulouse should have a say, as well. Don't you think so, Jehan."

The knight frowned. "In this instance, yes," he agreed reluctantly.

"This will cause a terrible disruption in the town." Aaron sighed. "Arnald's family will be destroyed. Poor Vidian! He told me this journey would make a man of Arnald. He made me promise to watch out for him. If I hadn't been so absorbed in my own problems, I might have seen what was happening."

"Nobody saw," Solomon told him firmly. "Arnald's demon is a master of deception. I never thought of him as more than a rather annoying overgrown puppy."

Solomon turned to regard the "puppy" who was tied hand and foot to a two-wheeled cart that was bumping along the road home. Arnald gave him a pathetic smile. Solomon shuddered. Why couldn't the boy understand the iniquity of his crimes? He seemed to believe that, when they reached Toulouse, his father would take care of everything and, even more unsettling, that Belide would be proud of him for all he had done in her name.

"It's all right," he told Solomon sadly. "I don't blame you. But I thought Aaron would be a better friend. I'm afraid he'll have to pay for that."

Solomon moved far back from the cart. He didn't want to be near anything that evil.

Mayah and Zaida were also in the party. Aaron had insisted that his betrothal to Mayah had not been broken and that the marriage would be celebrated as soon as it was permitted. Solomon had offered to pay for the women to stay in Fitero until they had recovered from their ordeal, but Mayah feared that with her rescuers gone, the slavers would return for them.

"Zaida will come with me for now," She explained. "She lost all her family in Almeria. There may be some friends left in Córdoba who will take her in, but she needs to send someone to contact them first. And I don't want to lose her, not yet. She's all I have. Will you take us both to Toulouse with you?"

"Of course. Do you intend to marry Aaron then?" Solomon asked.

"I can't, Solomon." Mayah sighed. "I've tried to talk to him, but he won't understand. First of all, as a Cohen, this marriage is forbidden to him. Even if we told no one that I had been taken by gentiles, we would know. Our children would be *mamzers* under the law. What if all this were discovered years from now? Think of their fate!

"Secondly." She paused. "I don't know how to say this to Aaron, but I don't want to marry him, or anyone. Not now, perhaps never. The thought of sharing my bed with a man is so repugnant I can barely speak of it. Even being touched makes me want to scream."

She wrapped her arms around her waist as if to forestall any movement Solomon might make toward her.

"I understand that you feel that way now," he told her. "But you're young, Mayah. Time will heal you."

"Perhaps." She dismissed his platitude. "But there is no reason for Aaron to wait while it does. He owes me nothing. The *ketubah* was never signed. We have no contract. And I don't love him. I barely know him. What he loves is the image of a woman who doesn't exist any more. Help me to make him understand that he should find another bride."

"But what will you do?" Solomon asked.

She shook her head. "I haven't been able to think of anything yet. I would like so much to resume my studies, but I have no money. My books are gone, stolen, or burnt. I would be a laundress or scrub stone floors at a *bet midrash* somewhere if I could only listen to the teaching and use their library."

A germ of an idea planted itself in Solomon's mind.

So, in the end, they all returned to Toulouse. Jehan seemed fascinated by Arnald's lack of repentance. It was like seeing his own past madness from the outside. He hoped that in the time they had he could bring Arnald to a realization of the enormity of his crimes.

"Where will you go after this?" Solomon asked him one day.

"Not back to Paris, if you were worried." Jehan laughed. "Perhaps return to Lisbon. The king offered land to those who fought for him. At the time, the plot didn't seem big enough. Now I'm thinking it's time for me to plant a fig tree, a few vines and settle. I'm not going to win an heiress and there's only one I wanted anyway."

"Good, I wish you well," Solomon answered, meaning it, to his surprise.

In Pamplona, Yusef joined them on his way back from Tudela, where he had taken Babylonia's body for burial.

"They wanted to bury her next to her husband." He grunted. "I convinced her son to find her a better place. She will be honored as a martyr to the Holy Name."

As they neared Toulouse, Solomon felt a growing dread. He saw it reflected in the faces of Aaron and Yusef. Arnald was a citizen, the son of a respected merchant and a Christian. His accusers were three Jews and two men from the North.

"Do you think he can convince the council that he's innocent?" Aaron worried.

Jehan shook his head. "No. He's proud of his crimes. He'll boast of them. Let him talk long enough and everyone will see he's mad."

"I wish we could spare Belide from the scandal this will cause," Aaron said. "She was trying to help me find Mayah. I know she had nothing to do with Victor's death. Now she'll not only have lost her betrothed, but her reputation."

"Poor Samuel was only a suitor for Belide," Solomon answered. "I'm sure she will grieve for him, but only as a friend. But I don't know how we can keep her from being slandered by Arnald's lies."

Yusef had been listening. "People will talk, of course," he said thoughtfully. "But if she were married soon, to someone respectable, the gossip might subside."

Aaron looked at the man in alarm. "You aren't thinking of offering for her, are you?"

"And why not?" Yusef said. "I'm a man of property and I have no one to share it with. Bonysach might welcome me as a son-in-law."

"But you're older than he is!" Aaron was shocked.

"Not quite," Yusef answered. "And Belide might like the thought of being a rich widow."

He smiled at Aaron, seemingly oblivious to the younger man's reaction.

Solomon had watched the exchange with interest. Aaron was more than upset by the idea of Belide marrying Yusef. He looked like a man watching his home burn to the ground.

This was something that Josta and Bonysach should know about.

For once, Jehan's prediction was correct. When Arnald was brought before the council of Toulouse, he condemned himself. Even his own father couldn't defend him.

"This is not my son!" he wept after Arnald had confessed with pride to tricking and then attacking Berengar. "This is a devil in his body. What did you do with my boy, you evil monster!?"

He would have run a sword through Arnald, himself, if his friends hadn't restrained him.

Arnald's fate was sealed. Out of sympathy for his family, the body was cut down from the gibbet after only a week of dangling.

Solomon had done his best to avoid Belide during this time. Mayah and Zaida had been given shelter at a home near the synagogue. While waiting for the messenger to return with word from her relatives, Zaida spent her days learning more about the people of Toulouse.

"It's interesting," she told Mayah. "I always heard that the *Farangi* were beasts who never washed and ate their food like pigs."

"Yes, I did too," Mayah said. "It is true that pigs are a large part of their diet."

"And they don't wash as often as we do," Zaida agreed. "But really, they don't seem that much different from us otherwise."

"Yes, it's a shame they're Christian." Mayah sighed. "If not for that, they'd be quite nice."

Finally Solomon could put it off no longer. He went to visit Belide. To his surprise, Aaron was just leaving as he arrived.

"How are your wedding plans going?" he asked.

Aaron mumbled something he couldn't catch and hurried off. Solomon went on into the courtyard.

"Belide?" he said softly.

She was sitting on a bench, her back to him. Her head and shoulders were bowed in an attitude of sorrow. When she heard his voice, she straightened at once and turned to him with a smile.

"I was wondering if you were angry with me," she started.

"Of course not!" he said. "I never thought of it. I didn't want to intrude on your grief."

She sighed. "Arnald always said he loved me, but I thought it was one of his jokes. After all, he had that nobleman's wife. I never guessed that there was such evil inside him. To have killed poor Victor! They had been friends since they were children."

"Whatever he did, it's not your fault," Solomon said.

"I know, everyone tells me that," she answered. "He fooled us all. But I'll always wonder if there was something I missed that could have prevented all of this. I should never have agreed to go with him to meet Brother Victor."

"To be honest, I don't know why you did," Solomon said. "Although I'm beginning to guess."

Belide looked away from him. He could see the blush rise from her neck to her cheeks.

"Yes, that was stupid," she whispered. "I was being valiant, I thought, helping Aaron to rescue his beloved."

"Very self-sacrificing of you," Solomon commented.

Belide winced. "Yes, and now it turns out that she refuses to marry him. How could she? The poor man is heart-broken. He's just been telling me all about it."

"Has he?" Solomon gave a smile of satisfaction. "Then you must understand how she feels."

"I suppose so," Belide said wistfully. "But if he had done that for me . . ."

"The next time he visits," Solomon suggested, "why don't you tell him that?"

He returned to the synagogue to see his uncle. He wasn't surprised to find Mayah with him, the two of them reading together. Hubert had a blanket over his shoulders and warm slippers on his feet. Solomon felt sure that this was Mayah's doing. She had cared for her father in much the same way. He decided not to interrupt them but his shadow fell across the page and they looked up.

Mayah gave him a rapturous smile. "Solomon, Rav Chaim is going to take me back to Lunel with him!"

Hubert nodded. "I owe it to my old friend Yishmael to see that his daughter is taken care of. And," he added with a smile, "she can teach me the new mathematics and read to me when my eyes grow too tired."

"I'm happy for both of you," Solomon said. "And I know Catherine will be comforted to know that someone is there to care for her father, since she can't be."

"That reminds me," Mayah said. "Someone was looking for you. He came to the house of study while Rav Chaim was napping."

"What did he look like?" Solomon asked.

"A tall man, very, very pale," Mayah started.

"Edgar!" both men said together. "Where did he go?" Solomon added.

"He said you'd find him at the best tavern in town," she answered, puzzled. "I'm sorry I didn't tell you at once. Will he wait?"

"Of course." Hubert stood up and shooed Solomon out. "Hurry! Bring him back with you. I want to hear all the news!"

Solomon spotted him at once, sitting at a table outside under the awning.

"Edgar!" he shouted. "What are you doing here? Is Catherine all right?"

The man looked up, revealing a pale face with a sunburnt nose.

"About time you got here!" he said. "Come, sit down, have some cool wine and tell me all that has happened. And yes, Catherine is fine, back in Paris and very great with child. She's at the point where looking at me just reminds her of how she got that way so she sent me back to get you and the goods from Almería but I'm under orders to be home by St. John's Eve. She insists that's when the child will be born. So, what have you been doing? How was the journey to Spain?"

"Order another pitcher, Edgar." Solomon sat down. "This will take awhile."

Solomon spent the afternoon telling Edgar all that had happened. There was only one thing that Edgar found impossible to believe.

"Jehan." Edgar shook his head. "*He* was the sane one?"

"Next to Arnald and Babylonia, he was amazingly reliable," Solomon said. "I might not have survived without him."

"It must have been hell," Edgar said. "I should have been with you. I might have been able to intercede for you with Brother James."

"Don't harrow yourself up about it," Solomon said. "There was never a time between us where intercession would have done any good."

"I'm sorry," Edgar said. "I know what it is to have a father you can never like."

Solomon had forgotten. Now he remembered Edgar's father. He put a hand on his friend's shoulder.

"Thank you," he said. "It's good not to be told that I should try to forgive."

Edgar and Solomon set out the next week to finish the journey they had started months before.

"Stop here on your way back," Bonysach told them. "We may have a betrothal to announce."

He gestured toward the garden, where Aaron and Belide were in deep discussion. "My daughter marrying a Cohen! Imagine!"

A few nights later they stopped at Cabo-la-Puente.

"You know a good inn here, don't you?" Edgar asked.

"I do," Solomon said. "Just over there."

Just then a small form came out the door and saw him. Her mouth open in a wide grin, she came running across the grass with a lopsided, floppy gait.

"What in the world is that?" Edgar asked.

Solomon stretched out his arms, overjoyed that she recognized him. She held up her hands for him to lift her. He wiped her nose, kissed her, and smoothed her hair. Then he held her out for his friend to admire.

"Edgar," he said. "I would like you to meet my daughter, Anna."

Afterword

Those of you who have followed this series from the beginning may be missing Catherine in this one. There are two reasons why she isn't in this book. The first is that I've been wanting for some time to give Solomon a turn of his own. The second is that Catherine, being an ardent wife, keeps getting pregnant and she really wanted some maternity leave. So I gave it to her. And, for those who can't wait to find out, the new baby, born on St. John's Eve, as she predicted, is a boy. They name him Peter, after their mentor Peter Abelard. Heloise is delighted to be the godmother.

Now, unlike earlier books, *The Outcast Dove* does not concern particular historical people or events. The germ of the story came from research in early Cistercian records made by my friend, Fr. Chrysogonus Waddell. I am grateful to him for not trying to cover up his discovery of a brothel for the Moslem workers that the monks in Spain permitted. I have slandered the monastery of Fitero. As far as I know, they did not have a brothel there. There was one at a Cistercian abbey in Aragon, though a bit later, so there is a precedent. Mayah's story is also my own invention, but it's not impossible that a Jewish woman might have been taken with Moslem ones. There would have been little difference between them in the minds of the Christian conquerors. The ruling concerning a Cohen's wife is in the Mishnah and various commentaries. The character of Babylonia is from a Responsum in which complaints were made about a Christian servant.

As always, I have about ten times more material than I could put in the book. I'm sure you're grateful that I exercised some restraint. I became fascinated by the life in Toulouse at this time.

Although I don't believe they ever formed a commune like the cities in the North, for about seventy years Toulouse was governed by an elected body of "Good Men" drawn from both the nobility and the burghers. This republican government was ended by the invasion of the French during the Albigensian Crusade. For a very readable and fascinating history of this, I recommend the books of John Hine Mundy.

One last piece of trivia that I couldn't find room for but am determined to share: at this time rice was considered Jewish food. Since it wasn't one of the grains forbidden at Passover, Jews in Spain, Italy, Sicily, and Provence ate it during that time. I haven't been able to find out how they cooked it for sure, but Rashi says it was boiled and therefore he was sure it wouldn't sprout.

Finally, thanks to all of you for your continuing interest in this series. You can find bibliographies, photos, and further information on my Web site http://www.hevanet.com/sharan/.